MW00963243

CLONING FREEDOM

STEPHEN B. PEARL

Milton, Ontario
http://www.brain-lag.com/

This is a work of fiction. All of the characters, events, and organizations portrayed in this novel are either products of the author's imagination or are used fictitiously.

Brain Lag Publishing
Ontario, Canada
http://www.brain-lag.com/

Copyright © 2020 Stephen B. Pearl. All rights reserved. This material may not be reproduced, displayed, modified or distributed without the express prior written permission of the copyright holder. For permission, contact publishing@brain-lag.com.

Cover artwork by Catherine Fitzsimmons

Library and Archives Canada Cataloguing in Publication

Title: Cloning freedom / Stephen B. Pearl.
Names: Pearl, Stephen B., 1961- author.
Identifiers: Canadiana (print) 20200317997 | Canadiana (ebook) 20200318020 | ISBN 9781928011439
   (softcover) | ISBN 9781928011446 (EPUB)
Classification: LCC PS8631.E255 C65 2020 | DDC C813/.6—dc23

Also by the author

Tinker's Plague (Brain Lag)

Tinker's Sea (Brain Lag)

"Tinker's Toxin"
(in *The Light Between Stars*, Brain Lag)

The Chronicles of Ray McAndrues
Book 1: *Nukekubi* (Dark Dragon)

Worlds Apart (Dark Dragon)

The Bastard Prince Saga (Pendelhaven Press)
Book 1: *Horn of the Kraken*
Book 2: *The Mistletoe Spear*
(scheduled to be released 2020)

Cats (Ankh Shen Publishing)

Havens in the Storm (Ankh Shen Publishing)

War of the Worlds 2030 (Damnation Press)

Dedication

I wish to dedicate this book first and foremost to my wife, Joy, without whom it never would have come to pass.

I also wish to dedicate it to all those who wore the double S brand, and all those who exemplified its spirit throughout the ages. For those who do not know, it was customary during the American slave period to brand people who assisted in a slave's escape with a double S, denoting slave stealer. Thus, the establishment mutilated men and women of conscience who respected the dignity of their fellow man.

I mention those who exemplified the spirit because slavery has been with us for a very long time and has crossed all boundaries of race and culture. Be it serfs, thralls, indentured servants, orphans sold to the mills and mines during the Industrial Revolution, owing one's soul to the company store, or having an addiction forced upon you so a pimp can rent you out to the highest bidder or sell you to a rich scumbag as a personal toy. It's all the same. It degrades the slave but degrades the slave owner even more. It is past time it ended, not simply by changing the name we call it, but by elevating all persons into a state of dignity and value as human beings.

One note I wish to add. There are species of ants that enslave other species of ants. Research has been done where the slaver ants were separated from their slaves. Uniformly the once enslaved ants survive and prosper. The slaver ants starve en masse and cannot maintain their colony. I think nature has a lesson for humanity in this.

Enjoy the read.

Dedication

THERE'S NO BUSINESS LIKE SHOW BUSINESS

"This is not a good plan." Carl crouched behind some bushes at the edge of the ruined laboratory's grounds. His skin and hair blended with the background. A gutted building stood in front of him.

"You should have said that before," said Rowan.

"He did say that before," remarked Fran.

Ryan pressed a button on his console. The big screen in the control room for the *Angel Black* entertainment series shifted to Carl's perspective. Through Carl's eyes, Ryan could see Rowan's lean, muscular body clad in black jeans and a sweater. She carried a red fire extinguisher. Carl's eyes fell to her medium-sized breasts.

"Carl, you're staring at my chest again." Rowan's voice issued from the speaker.

"Was not!" Carl's perspective shifted to Rowan's pretty, fair-skinned face.

"Carl, honestly!" The view shifted to Fran, who also carried a fire extinguisher and had plastic packets taped to her belt. "Even when you camouflage, some things stand out. My boyfriend could show some control."

The empathic monitors beside the secondary screen dedicated to Carl jumped.

"Good boy, always count on you to eye up the ladies.

This will go great for the PG version." Ryan stared into the screen, which showed Fran's generous cleavage then shifted to her perfect American First Peoples face.

The visual screen went blank. Ryan checked his other inputs. "Going into battle and still in heat."

⊂══◆

"Will you two focus?" hissed a well-proportioned, middle-aged man who knelt beside Rowan. He'd put his fire extinguisher on the ground and was fiddling with its valve.

Fran broke the kiss. "Sorry, Gunther."

"I wish Angel were here," whispered a muscular, Japanese-looking man of about twenty, who waited beside Gunther.

"Why is that, Farley? You want to cheat on me with her again?" Rowan sounded sarcastic.

⊂══◆

Ryan shifted to Gunther's perspective. Rowan looked hurt. Gunther's emotional readings showed a mix of anger toward the younger man and affection toward his daughter.

"Emotions are too conflicted to sort the empathic input. We'll have to dub them before going to market. Have to keep it simple for the featherbrains in the audience." Ryan placed an editing marker on the timeline.

"I meant we could use some aerial surveillance. How often do I have to say I'm sorry?" Farley's voice was strained.

Willa looked up from inspecting her own fire extinguisher. "You slept with her best friend, Farley. What do you expect?"

Ryan shifted to Carl's view. His eyes traced over a red-haired woman with a lean, small-breasted body and a pretty face.

"Willa is old enough to be your mother, and you still got it bad." Ryan smirked.

"Mom, it's all right. I should have stayed focused." Rowan brushed a strand of her short, dark hair away from her eyes.

"Your father and I hate to see you so—"

"Shhh," hissed Rowan. "Do you hear—?"

"Well, what have we here?" said a voice from behind the group. Everyone turned. A k-no-in, its canine features pulled into a snarl, stared down at them. "Snacks!" The alien bunched its pony-like body and extended the gutting claws on its six, muscular legs.

Fran's hands locked into a claw shape and her nails extended. She raked her claws against a plastic packet on her belt. A cream-coloured grease oozed out of the packet onto her claws. Snarling, she leapt, driving her fingers against the alien pirate's throat. The k-no-in howled as the lithium in the grease catalysed a reaction that turned its blood into a corrosive poison.

Ryan watched as the screen labelled "K-no-in 2" went blank. He pressed a button, and it lit up again. It now bore the caption "Otterzoid Female 1."

"Wow!" gasped Carl.

Fran pulled a handkerchief from her pocket and wiped her claws. "Felinezoid powers have their advantages."

A whistle sounded.

"Time to go," said Gunther. They all raced toward the building.

Ryan watched Rowan on his screen. "Better cut to the other team; see what they're up to." He pressed a button on his console. The main screen shifted to an overview of a large, scorched room. A coffin-like device stood in the corner. A portable methane heater flamed in the room's centre.

A chameleonzoid huddled beside the heater. The alien had an eight-limbed, cylindrical body, ending in a head like a crocodile's at one end and a long muscular tail at the other. Its hide had shifted colour to blend with the soot-blackened, concrete floor.

A felinezoid, which looked like a two-metre-tall, humanoid cat, with short, thick fur and grey-tabby markings, moved toward the heater.

Valaseau groomed the back of her hand, then used it to smooth the fur beside her pointed ears. "Are you comfortable, Captain Hussut?"

The chameleonzoid moved its head slowly. "This world is cold. How long until the time-lock on the rescue pod opens? The sooner we summon our ship, the sooner I can return to Death Valley."

"Not long. I'll be so happy when we kill the upstart humans. They'll pay for corrupting my Toronk. We'll make them pay, make them bleed, make them suffer. We'll rule this world and make them all pay!" Valaseau's voice rose to an insane fervour.

"Yes, felinezoid. We will rule this world. Turn up this heater. I am growing sluggish."

"Now let's see how the diversion's going." Ryan set the

terminal to record the other feeds as he shifted the big screen's perspective.

Toronk threw himself at three k-no-ins. Two-point-one metres of felinezoid fury, clawing and biting.

A petite, black girl launched herself from the branches of a nearby tree, bat-like wings folded out from her back. She hovered above the battle as she took aim with an air-rifle and fired into one of the k-no-ins. In moments, the pirate was convulsing. The others were too busy with Toronk to notice.

The girl scanned the grounds, seeing three k-no-ins, a felinezoid and an alien that resembled an oversized, green otter, with an elongated head, racing toward them. The otter-like creature looked up. Angel's gun jerked out of her hands. "Toronk, they're coming. They have an otterzoid with them. It's a female." Angel swooped away as the otterzoid aimed the air-rifle at her telekinetically.

Toronk snarled as he threw one of his attackers into the other.

"ANGEL, NOW!" he bellowed.

Angel swooped through the side door of a van on the lab's parking lot. Toronk dove into the driver's seat and burnt rubber toward the street. The alien guards chased them.

"Back to the A-team." Ryan reset the feeds on his console to an overview of the laboratory's main hall.

Gunther leapt back as the k-no-in rushed him. A hypodermic needle floated into the air behind it and drove down, injecting its payload of lithium grease. The k-no-in barely had time for the pain to register before it died.

"That is so cool," remarked Fran.

"I like it," agreed Rowan. "You okay, Dad?"

"None the worse for wear," said Gunther.

Carl passed Fran his fire extinguisher, then crept along the hall, blending with the walls. He paused at the doors to a ruined workroom and glanced through the window. Ducking down, he willed his body to flesh tones, then motioned his companions forward.

"Good, now a little pre-game banter. Unrealistic as that is for this stage of an engagement. Have to keep the audience happy." Ryan adjusted the level of endorphins to Rowan's group, calming them and inducing a light euphoria.

"You sure this will work?" asked Willa.

"Are we ever?" Gunther cupped his wife's cheek.

"We're all insane. You do realize this?" remarked Fran.

"Nothing's been sane since Amitose grafted alien DNA to us and told us we had to keep the space pirates a secret while we fought them," replied Farley.

Gunther closed his eyes. "I hear them. Valaseau is on some mental babble about getting Toronk back. The chameleonzoid has the activate codes. If they reach that pod's FTL telegraph, we're doomed."

"Right then, let's stop them," said Rowan.

"With ya. Wish we had an AK-47." Carl grinned as he shifted colour to match the walls.

"With the gun control laws in this country, we were lucky to get Angel's air rifle," said Gunther.

"I can dream. One, two, three, NOW!" Carl dove through

the charred door, hit the dirt and rolled. A beam of light blasted through the wall above him. He leapt up and ran.

"Particle weapons! You didn't say anything about particle weapons!" griped Farley.

"It wasn't thinking about them. Move anyway," snapped Gunther.

The chameleonzoid stood on four of its legs, holding a rifle-like weapon in one of its three-fingered hands. Its slit-pupiled, reptilian eyes tracked Carl, despite his camouflage, so it didn't notice Farley enter and run at its back. Gunther followed, then Willa and Fran.

Rowan stepped through the door and yelled. "HEY YOU, LIZARD BREATH."

The chameleonzoid jerked around to face her. Rowan threw the fire extinguisher she carried, adding a telekinetic push. It slammed into the heater, smashing it, then venting CO_2 over the sparks. A jet of methane rose from the tank.

"That's not nice, human tramp!" Valaseau lunged at Rowan, covering three metres in a single bound.

"Eep!" Rowan felt a furry hand close on her throat. Claw tips pricked her skin.

⟢⟶

"Stardust!" Ignoring the memo on the control room's wall, Ryan let his hands race over his console. Valaseau's endorphin levels increased as her estrogen equivalent jumped.

"That should make her hot and playful. I hope it's enough."

⟢⟶

"I'll do it slow. I love it when they suffer," said Valaseau. Something slammed into her side. Gunther landed on top of the felinezoid. His knee smashed into the floor. Biting down on his pain, he rolled clear.

Farley rushed the chameleonzoid. Firing his extinguisher at the alien, he coated the reptile with frozen CO_2.

"NOOOO!" Hussut fired its weapon, igniting the gas jetting from the methane tank before the cold could force him into inactivity.

The explosion threw Farley against the wall. He crumpled to the floor.

The chameleonzoid roared as fire singed its hide, then receded. A jet of flame rose from the methane cylinder, igniting the ceiling.

"Chill out, hothead." Fran directed her extinguisher's spray against Hussut.

"Chill out, hothead?" Carl sounded incredulous as he came at the beast from the other side, coating it with CO_2 snow.

"Everybody else does it," countered Fran as Willa added her extinguisher to the assault.

Gunther grappled with Valaseau; the felinezoid's mouth descended toward his throat.

"Leave him alone!" snapped Rowan. A scorched lab table slammed into Valaseau, sending her careening through one of the room's shattered windows.

"Rowan," breathed Gunther.

She smiled, then fell to her knees, clutching her head.

"Stardust! Keep overreaching like that, you won't get a chance to see if you can survive with a No Intervention Order on you." Ryan checked Rowan's readouts.

"GUYS, NEED HELP HERE!" Carl's fire extinguisher had petered out, and the chameleonzoid was bringing its weapon to bear on him.

Gunther leapt up and fell groaning.

Ryan shifted to Gunther's panel, increasing adrenalin levels and muting his pain.

Gunther fought to his feet, yelled, "CATCH," then threw his fire extinguisher at Carl.

Carl lunged for Gunther's extinguisher, catching it after it slammed into the floor. He rolled, bringing its nozzle to bear. A chunk of flaming ceiling fell on his back. He hissed in pain as he shook it off.

"Stardust, why are you always so careless?" Ryan blocked Carl's pain and dispatched the nano-bots to seal the artery a nail had punctured.

Rowan crawled to Gunther's side.

"I'm out." Fran stepped away from the alien. The ceiling creaked. Flaming pieces began to fall on all sides.

Ryan triggered an adrenaline surge in Farley. "Wake up, prince of fools; you can at least be laser fodder."

Farley slowly came to his feet and moved to take Fran's place. Captain Hussut was frosted with carbon dioxide snow. He moved sluggishly.

The time-lock on the escape pod buzzed.

"Fools. Your human technology is less than a child's toy

to me!" Hussut lunged at Willa. She stepped back, losing her target. The alien stumbled toward the escape pod as its hatch swung open.

"NO!" Rowan's brow wrinkled. Her mind clutched Hussut. The sheer mass of the creature defeated her. She felt a hand slip into hers. Her universe expanded. The minds that surrounded her were an open book. She felt her own power increase.

Gunther wanted to help, needed to comfort. He took Rowan's hand in his; the universe opened. He knew the ways of matter, sensed the flux and flows of subatomic particles, saw how the forces of time and space interplayed.

The chameleonzoid slammed into a cinder-block wall with bone-shattering force.

Farley, Carl and Willa directed their extinguishers against their foe, who trembled on the floor. Rowan and Gunther seemed entranced. The air grew smoky; each breath became a battle. Fran stumbled to the escape pod. Willa's extinguisher died.

"Willa, help me here." Fran activated the pod's transmitter.

Willa moved to help. Farley began smashing his empty fire extinguisher into the alien's head. Grey blood spilt onto the floor.

Willa flicked her hand open. An interface extended from her forefinger. She jacked into the pod's data port, sending a binary message. *'Orbital incursion not secured, maintain status. Standard contact protocols.'*

"That should do it for another three months." Willa grabbed Fran's hand. They rushed from the escape pod. Its hatch closed and the time-lock reset.

"I wonder what you'd do if you knew there wasn't any ship orbiting Jupiter to be afraid of? I wonder what you'd do if you knew you weren't even in the Sol system, let alone on Earth? Stardust, I wonder what you'd do if you knew it was the seventh century after contact? That's show biz." Ryan sounded bitter and tired.

Carl's extinguisher went dead.

"Let's make like a tree and leaf." Carl coughed as he heaved the empty cylinder at the alien.

"Come on," called Farley.

They all moved to Gunther and Rowan. The kinetic and the telepath seemed entranced.

"Come on, hurry it up before one of them strokes out," hissed Ryan as he watched father and daughter through Willa's eyes. He spared her empathic readouts a glance. They showed such pride in, and concern for, her family it was mind-boggling.

"Like mother, like daughter. Both of them, hearts big as a planet. Why does John have to wreck it?"

"How?" asked Willa.

Farley pulled Gunther into a fireman's carry.

"Right." Carl took Rowan.

"About nova blasted time! Better slow things down on the fire trucks. Give the team a chance to get clear." Ryan pressed several buttons. A screen labelled 'Series Cross Over' filled with a view of a fire truck's dashboard and the street beyond, under the caption of *'THE STATION HOUSE'* and 'Fire Officer Willow Hennessy.' An icon in the corner was green, indicating that Ryan could take action without overly affecting the other series. He hit a key. The speedometer dropped as the audio feed gave the sound of an engine stalling.

"Computer, reset primes to defaults with notification protocols."

Rowan's team piled into Gunther's SUV. Rowan felt herself sag. It was always the same after battle, utter exhaustion. She glanced at her parents in the back seat beside her. They were holding each other, so obviously in love despite their years together. Rowan's gaze shifted to Farley, who sat in the front seat. Tears welled in her blue eyes.

Ryan watched the Rowan monitors.

"Bad enough they made him cheat on you, now a No Intervention Order. Why do they always want to ruin the best characters?"

THE HOLLOWNESS OF REALITY

2

Ryan watched Rowan snuggle into her bed. Her breathing was slow and steady. He'd used an endorphin to ensure she'd sleep well. He turned his attention to the secondary screens.

"Angel and Toronk, at it again. It's good for the adult version." On the screen, the petite, winged girl rode the large feline, her hands sinking into his soft, warm fur, his rough tongue stroking over her nipples. Her satin-like wings caressed him. The monitors showed that they were both nearing orgasm.

"Joslin will love this; she's got a real taste for fur." Ryan's voice was weary. He checked the wall chronometer. Seven-thirty-five, Sun Valley time, fourteen-thirty-five in his habitat zone. He stretched and heard the vertebrae in his back pop. Adjusting Rowan's screen to the pickup in her bedroom, he watched her sleep. He grinned at his own foolishness, then jerked when the door behind him opened. Swivelling his chair, he watched a Caucasian man, with thinning, brown hair, enter the room.

"John, hi. Could I get you a coffee?" Ryan forced his voice to be pleasant, even as he clenched his fist behind his chair.

"Didn't you get my memo? There is a No Intervention Order regarding the Rowan character." John slapped one hand into the other, causing his blubber to giggle.

"I realize that."

"Last night's quick log showed you doing hormonal and

endorphin manipulations on her. We need to let her die to punch up the next dramatic cycle. Why did you disregard my directive?" John smoothed the line of his suit and posed in the doorway.

You wouldn't have lasted five minutes during the Murack offensive, you self-important twit! Ryan kept his thoughts to himself. "Well... Mr. Wilson, we had to eliminate the Captain Hussut character because of the genetic abnormalities in the clone. Keeping that character's cancers in check was becoming cost-prohibitive. Helping Rowan opened the door to killing the Hussut character."

"That's stardust! One of these days you're going to run out of excuses, then I'll have your ass out of here. Don't think I won't, fakey!"

"Why do you want to destroy Rowan? She's the most popular character in the entertainment."

"The show's title is *Angel Black*, not *Annoying Scrub Tree*. You've been told, Chandler. No more help for Rowan. She sinks or swims on the defaults."

"Yes, Mr. Wilson."

John turned and slammed the door.

"Prat!" Ryan returned his attention to the screen. Rowan smiled in her sleep. He felt his heart lurch. "If only."

Ryan opened the door to his domestic unit. The smells of unwashed bodies and stale food assailed him. The living room was devoid of furniture, except for a battered sofa and coffee table. A virtual entertainment unit occupied the corner. The recliner-like device contained a wasted, middle-aged woman. She writhed, as if in orgasm.

"Great, just great!" Ryan moved into the efficiency kitchen. Dishes were stacked on the countertop. Opening the refrigerator, he saw that it was empty. Returning to the living room, he stared at the woman before pressing a button on the entertainment unit's armrest. The interface cover lifted from around her head. She blinked.

Ryan forced a smile. "Hi, Joslin. I was thinking. Why don't you grab a shower? We can go out to dinner."

Joslin brushed greasy, blonde hair away from her face. Her track pants and T-shirt were grubby and stank. "Ryan, you finished work already?" She sounded annoyed.

"I just got off. How about it? Let's grab a bite, then maybe we can go to the park? The Philharmonic is doing a concert. I'm sure we can pay at the gate."

"I'd rather not. Barry has been building up to asking out Amanda. I don't want to miss it. She so wants him to. I can't miss the reaction because..."

Ryan closed his eyes, ignoring his wife's babble as he struggled to keep his temper in check. Finally, he interrupted her. "How about later? I'll grab a snack, we can go to the concert and get dinner after."

Ryan knew the answer before she opened her mouth.

"I couldn't. Willow just slept with James, the fire chief on *The Station House*. Now that awful Officer Folly is trying to hold it over their heads—"

"Why not record it?"

"The recordings dampen the empathic inputs. Why experience it if you can't fully feel the emotion?"

"Fine. I'll be on the *Star Hawk* if you change your mind."

"You could jack in with me," offered Joslin.

"I spend all day making this stuff. I don't want to experience it on my off hours."

"That's why we have a problem marriage! You never want to do anything with me! I should have stayed on Earth!" Joslin threw herself onto the entertainment unit and pressed a button on its armrest. The sensory interface covered her from the shoulders up.

"Yup, I never want to do anything. 'I'm the evil fakey that died on Murack Five,'" he sang the line of the song, feeling the half-truth it represented more acutely than usual. Moving into the bedroom, he noted the sheets were filthy. Laundry littered the floor. He lifted a display case that hung on the wall. It was full of medals on bits of ribbon. "She'll never miss it. It's in the real world."

Taking the case, he left his apartment.

"Hello, darling. It is so good to hear your voice. I can't get the video to come in." Michael Strongbow settled into his chair at the Sensory Entertainment/Terraforming Engineers Inc. building. His office was larger than many apartments, with all the amenities befitting his position. The desk in front of him was antique oak, imported from Earth, with a large monitor screen on top of it.

He was a fit, older man, with a mane of silver hair. The laugh lines at the corners of his brown eyes gave him a grandfatherly warmth, but the solid line of his jaw and lean, muscular body spoke to a man it wasn't safe to cross.

"I know. My hand-held's pick-up is broken. It's audio-only." The woman's voice was soft, slightly nasal, very unique and full of character and warmth.

"How are the concerts going? Is the attendance good?"

"The orchestra should break even. With luck, we may even make a profit."

"That's great."

"So how are things with you? Did you speak to John?"

Michael tensed in his chair. "I tried. The man is a prat, but it's his show. He's gone ahead with the N.I.O. Sam Westleigh wants to start a new program using an AS-F class clone. You know it's too risky to have look-a-likes on set. They both want Rowan dead, and I can't stop them."

"It's so unfair!"

Michael smiled at the outrage in his wife's voice. She had more reason than any to hate the state of clone rights.

"I haven't given up yet, love. Do you remember Ryan Chandler?"

"Hmm... Body looks about twenty-five, copper skin, brown hair, average height, medium build, green eyes you could lose yourself in. A real hottie, if you aren't addicted to the classic type?"

Michael smiled. He'd never had a moment's doubt that her love was his, but she was also an incurable man watcher. It was how she was made. "That's him."

"Poor man, is his wife still an e-addict?"

"Sadly, yes. I had a doctor look into her case. He was of the opinion she's hopeless."

"Too bad, he seemed nice. A little sad, like you used to be."

"Very similar pasts, my love. No one survives the front lines without it changing them. In any case, he seems to be what I'm looking for."

"You're so sneaky. I think that's why I love you. So whatcha got planned?"

"Well..."

⌖

Ryan pulled his power-bike onto the levelled bedrock that formed the landing site and stopped. The mild hum of the bike's electric motor stilled. The safety field it projected around its rider cut off. Ryan could remember a time when Joslin had loved to ride with him, arms clenched around his waist, the wind whipping her hair out behind her. He muttered. "Now she watches *Bike Cop*. Why not, the vehicles look a lot alike?"

He focused on the present. The landing strip was hardly used since the terraforming of Gaea had moved into stage three. A rocky desert stretched out on all sides. To the west, Duchovny Tower, the "real" city, rose into the clouds. In front of him were two craft, each the size of an oceanic cargo vessel. They were of the same class, made up of oval domes of jet black, supported on a multitude of three-clawed legs with a long ramp opening towards what could be generously called their fronts.

The one farther from him looked complete. Its hull a

shiny black, its support legs all in place. The near one had a gaping hole in its side. Its hull plating had been cannibalised, leaving patches of cracked and broken material on its surface. Piles of rock took the place of most of its support legs. In places, he could see into its gutted interior.

Ryan checked the charge metre on his bike, then pulled closer to the far ship. The air was dry. Dust stung his cheeks before the safety field activated. He paused only to look at where the hull had been polarized to show letters spelling out 'STAR HAWK we will never forget' before he pulled up the ramp.

"Did you miss me, my lady?" he asked as he parked his bike. He was in a hangar the size of a large gymnasium. A single battered ATV troop-carrier was parked in the corner. The ATV's top-mounted turret was nothing but a jagged hole in the boxy vehicle.

"Oh, yes, darling. I missed you ever so much. Come up and give us a snog." A male voice pitched to take on effeminate tones blasted out of the speaker.

"Hello, Henry. What happened? You finally achieve your goal of watching every porno ever made?" Ryan moved to a door at the back of the chamber and pressed the button beside it. The door slid into the wall. He stepped into a nine-metre-square elevator and hit a button labelled Ops.

"What do you expect when you leave me alone with nothing to do and no one to talk to? It's her, isn't it? That hussy of a wife of yours. You love her more than me."

"Henry, hate to break it to you. I'm not in love with you. Leave Joslin out of it, or I might let the authorities know you aren't deactivated."

"Yeah, right. Who else could you get to run this antiquated tub?"

Ryan rolled his eyes. The elevator stopped. He stepped into a hallway a metre across by two high, which ended in a hatch twenty-five metres ahead of him. Doors opened off both sides of the passage, and its walls were covered with padding. The hall was spotless. "Did you run those tests on the grav-units I installed?"

Henry's voice lost its effeminate and teasing qualities. "Aye. We have Earth-normal throughout the space-crew section and officer territory. Half G in the landing force section. You gutted that for cargo anyway. Quarter G in the hangar, and one-tenth G in the bomb-bays. Inertial stabilization is full in Ops; three-quarters in the rest. It's better than most freighters. I'm sorry if I crossed a line about Joslin."

"Don't sweat it." Reaching the end of the corridor, Ryan pressed a button. The door pulled into the wall, revealing the bridge. Six workstations, each in front of a swivel chair anchored into the floor, made a horseshoe shape around the room's perimeter. A single chair sat in the room's middle, facing a screen that filled the top part of the horseshoe's closed end.

"I don't sweat. Nasty, biological thing to do," said Henry.

Ryan looked at the computer station on his right. The head, torso and one arm of a humanoid android were strapped into the chair and connected into the console with a mass of wires.

If the android had been human, he would have looked like a muscular man of African genetic extraction. The artificial skin on one side of its face was burnt away, and half its short hair formed a frizzled mass against its metal skull.

"If humans have so many disadvantages, why don't you let me build you into the ship?"

"Sex. Spaceships can't have it. I want my hips back, among other things. Oh yeah, baby." Henry pumped his remaining arm. "Caught an entertainment of Farley and Rowan. I can see why you like that Rowan. She is one sweet—"

"Shut up! Or deal or no, I'll turn you in. You want a humanoid body back? You serve as my operating system until I can get a proper unit. That means I'm captain. I don't want you to access anything to do with Rowan. That's an order!" Ryan moved to the engineering chair and threw himself down on it.

"Stardust, if I didn't know better, I'd say you were in love with the fakey."

"Shut up!"

"She's not real. Pull your head out of your ass. Joslin is an e-addict. You aren't half bad. Find some other fleshy to play with. Stardust, build me up as your dream girl; I'll play with you. I'm not picky that way."

"Rowan is real. She's just a clone."

"Yeah, like I said, she's a fakey. She ain't real."

"Then I'm not either." Ryan began running a systems check.

"Stardust, that's different."

"How?" Ryan swivelled his chair to look at the AI.

"That was medical. After that rad dose you caught, they had to grow you a new body. You still got all your memories and stuff."

"I'm still a clone. The law gave me rights because it was the result of a combat injury."

"But ain't no one's tinkered with your DNA, and your memories are real, not loaded in like some music cube."

"Rowan is real! More real than Joslin has been in years." Ryan turned to examine his engineering board. As a result, he missed the smirk that came to Henry's face.

"So, she's real. She's real, you're real, I'm real, and we're all nova blasted in a real world. You know she doesn't stand a chance with an N.I.O. on her. And you, sure you got rights, but you know you're a second-class citizen. You're engineering level, and the best you can do is a monitor on e-compilations? If they get hold of me, it's back to the scrap heap."

Ryan stopped working. "Run a space worthiness analysis."

"Did it this afternoon. Every system is above spec."

"How much time from the Equestezoid stargate to Surya

One?"

"They settled on Geb for the planet's name. It was on the news. It'll take about one hundred and seventy days, give or take a few. Trip total should be less than a year."

Ryan leaned back in his chair. "Joslin—"

"Won't even notice, if you do it right. She'll be happier."

Ryan bit his lip. "It's a one-way trip."

"You got something in this star-dusted galaxy you wanna see?"

Shifting to the middle chair, Ryan sat. "The colony does need ships, and the *Star Hawk* is better than most of the junkers they're getting."

"This ship has always kicked butt. Stardust, if you can get a control circuit, we even have weapons." Henry gestured to a dead control panel with his arm.

"This is ridiculous! Even if I smuggled her out, it would give her what? Sixteen years with the way they re-engineered her."

"Sixteen years more than she'll have, and maybe something will come up."

Ryan stood. "I'm going to the junker. There are still some parts I can scrounge, and I need to think, alone!"

"Think fast, man. Think fast."

Henry watched Ryan descend the ramp with an internal monitor. A smile creased his mutilated face. He closed his eyes, accessing the ship's link to the global communications net. A minute passed before the line picked up.

"Hello, S.E.T.E. Inc., Mr. Strongbow's office," said a female voice. Henry's visual field filled with the image of a large-breasted blonde with classic features, sitting at a desk.

"Hello, sweetie. I gotta talk to your boss. Tell him it's Ryan's polymer pal. He'll know what's up. Are those tits real?"

The secretary looked exasperated as she hit a button on her desk and spoke into the intercom.

A moment later, the visual field shifted to show Michael Strongbow sitting at his desk. "Henry, I'm assuming this is regarding our previous discussion."

"Got it in one. Not that the view is all that bad." The android managed to make his voice suggest a leer.

"Down, plastic man. You are not my preferred type, on many levels. Let us stick to business. What do you have to report?"

"He's on the edge. I think a little push from you will put him over."

"Excellent. What would you suggest?"

"Well, silver fox, this is what has a bug up his butt. First..."

HIDDEN ALLIES

Ryan pulled the filthy sheets off the bed and fed them into a boxy, clothes-hamper sized device.

"Fabric maintenance unit needs cotton fibres to do auto repair function," spoke a mechanical voice.

Ryan pulled open the dresser drawer, extracting an empty box labelled, 'Repair cotton.'

"Stardust!" Glancing around the room, he spotted a pair of Joslin's panties. He picked them up, shuddering with revulsion when he found out they were crusty with dried urine. "Couldn't tear yourself away even for that?" He dropped them into a chute on the side of the maintenance unit.

"Fibres acceptable. Commencing with clean and repair sequence, approximate time, five minutes," said the machine.

Ryan sat on the edge of the bed. *It's insane. It's grand theft. Could she even stand learning that her whole life was an entertainment?* He thought. The image of Rowan drifted unbidden in his mind.

It wouldn't be that hard to get her out. How to get away, and keep the rest of the cast in the dark? That's the challenge.

Rowan walked across the college's spacious, tree-covered grounds toward the concrete administration building.

"Hey Row, wait up." Fran raced to her side.

"Hi, Fran. I thought you and Carl would be off… studying."

Fran blushed. "I thought you might like to talk."

Rowan stopped walking. "'Bout what?"

"Come on. You and Angel being on the outs, it's not right."

"Neither is her sleeping with my boyfriend. Stardust! With friends like her, who needs enemies?"

"It hurts a lot, doesn't it?"

Rowan moved to a bench and sat. Fran followed her example.

"Farley… well… Don't tell my mom and dad."

"Promise." Fran made a crossing motion over her heart.

Rowan blushed. Her voice was little more than a whisper. "He was my… well… you know… my first and only."

"Figured that one. You weren't exactly the slut queen in high school. Truth to tell, I wasn't sure till now that Farley got past third."

"He did. Mom and Dad kinda suspect, I think, but they like to think I'm a 'good girl'. How can I forgive him and Angel, who I thought was my best friend?"

"They were being affected by that otterzoid male."

"My dad says it could only encourage them, break down barriers, like being drunk, not make them do something they really didn't want to."

"I can't tell you what to do, but for your own good, forgive them, or move on. I hate seeing you tearing yourself up like this."

"I'm scared, Franny."

"Scared?"

"Guys weren't exactly lining up before Farley. I don't want to be alone, and I think I'm going to be."

Fran took Rowan's hands. "Row, you won't be alone. You're great. Some guy is going to see it and sweep you off your feet."

"A white knight to take me away from all this? Every little girl's fantasy. I think after all the fighting and killing and heartbreak, I'm all little girled out."

Ryan sat in the forward pilot's seat on the *Star Hawk*'s bridge. Tapering off the grav-nullifiers, he let the massive ship drift to the ground. The landing place was by the largest of Gaea's oceans. Its levelled bedrock was littered with antiquated ships and vehicles. The sun was cresting the horizon in a sky that was a beautiful, Earth-like blue.

"These things are boring," complained Henry.

"I like the club meets. These people understand. Keep the bridge locked, and no outward communications."

"Yeah, right. What am I supposed to do while...?"

Ryan held up a data disk. "Episode seventeen of *Orgy Girls*. It's not even available on transmit yet. I swapped a shift with Malcolm for it."

"Boss, you're too good to me."

Ryan stepped down the ramp from his hangar onto the airstrip. The service coveralls he'd pulled on bore the crest of the Space Combat Corps, crossed by the silver braid that showed he was retired. They were warm enough to break the morning chill.

"You've done very impressive work on her," remarked a deep voice from Ryan's left.

Ryan turned and smiled at the studio head. "Thank you, Mr. Strongbow. I couldn't leave her to scrap after all we saw together."

"I know exactly what you mean, and it's Mike. We're all old soldiers out to pasture here." Mike wore a uniform similar to Ryan's but with a ground-forces crest on each shoulder.

Ryan smiled. "How's the *Lucky Seven*?" He gestured to the seven-metre-long by three wide, oval shape of a grav-tank. Its top-mounted, twin, laser turrets gave an impression of its once impressive destructive power.

Mike sighed. "Still operational, parts are a problem. If I don't find a source for grav-nullifiers soon, I'll lose her flight capacity."

"Bummer. I don't know if it would work for your tank, but I've worked up an adapter for mark-twelve nullifiers, so they can integrate with mark-five ports. I'll get you a copy of the schematics."

"Thank you. That's very generous, but my ports are mark-twos."

"You know, I inherited an old ATV when I bought my junker. Not much of any use on it, but its nullifiers are mark-fours. It shouldn't be difficult to get an adapter kit to make them match up with mark-two ports."

"What would you want for the beast?" Mike held his head to one side.

"I'd trade for control circuits, if they'd integrate with my tech, or maybe a gram of antiproton."

"Are you low on power?" Concern crossed Mike's face.

"I have enough to get around the system. You know how much they overcharge at the orbital station."

"Yes. Perhaps we can work something out. I'll arrange to have your tank transported to my estate so that I can have a look at it. I think you should retain ownership."

"Why?"

"Because my estate is closer to the studio than your landing field. Ryan, I'm glad you're here for reasons beyond your company and engineering expertise. I have a proposal for you."

Ryan shifted uncomfortably. "Oh?"

"Come aboard the *Seven*. We need a private chat." Mike led the way to his grav-tank.

Rowan walked along the dusk-shrouded streets. A truck

rumbled past, carrying a load of saplings to be planted by the foresters. A shadow flickered overhead. She dove for the cover of a nearby doorstep.

"Row."

Angel's voice caught her off guard. A moment later, the diminutive, black girl appeared on the street, buttoning up her shirt.

"Is there some problem?" asked Rowan.

"Between us. Look, I'm sorry for the hundredth time. I was scared, I mean... I'm dating an alien, and like, I'm stuck looking like a freak because of my power. I needed to feel human."

"Can't you just leave it at, 'I'm sorry'? I trusted you, Angel. I trusted you more than anyone in this world."

"I know. I—"

The sound of squealing tires split the evening's stillness. A car careened toward them.

"No!" Angel threw her wings out, tearing her blouse to shreds, and grabbed Rowan under the arms.

Rowan's brow wrinkled as she strained, mentally pulling up her own weight.

Angel flapped, and they lifted from the ground. The car skidded to one side. An injector dart slammed into the wall where Rowan had been.

Rowan focused all her concentration, taking more of her weight. The car's engine roared as it sped off. A minute later, Angel dropped Rowan on a roof.

"You gain weight or what?" asked Angel.

Rowan clutched her throbbing head. "I... I was lifting as hard as I could. I just couldn't..."

Angel launched herself into the air in time to see the car jerk to a halt two blocks over. A felinezoid leapt out and ran into a park.

Angel descended to the rooftop. "They're gone. It looks like we're in for another round of fun and games. God, I wish we could be normal, go to school, worry about STDs, not have 'save the world' on our weekly to-do list."

Rowan sat up. The pain in her head was subsiding. "At least we don't have to worry about finding a way to contribute."

"I'd like to have a normal boyfriend, get normal grades, have one-point-eight, normal children, a normal life."

"I kinda like making a difference, despite everything."

"Hey, Row, are we… well… are we friends again?"

Rowan looked at Angel. "Yeah, like, hey… best friends are too hard to come by. Especially ones that can get takeout at rush hour and have it back while it's still hot."

"What you figure the furry wanted, besides us as street pizza?"

"Who knows? It's too soon for another attempt at getting to the escape pod. We better talk to my dad."

Ryan walked across the airstrip. The setting sun painted the antiquated, war-machines red-gold.

If I do this, I do it all the way. Do I want this life? Of course, what kind of life do I have now?

He paused beside a battered, orbital-defence launch vehicle. The craft was saucer-shaped, about ten metres across by three thick, supported on three legs.

Resolve hardened within him. "Yancy, you here?"

"Hello, old boy. I was hoping you'd drop by. I saw you got your lander up in the air." Yancy appeared in the open hatch on the side of his ship. He was a balding, wiry man with a strong Silvanus accent and a black, handlebar moustache. Despite the apparent difference in their ages, Ryan knew he was born a year before the other man.

"Yes, she's space ready."

"Fantastic. Always glad to see one of the old girls returned to their glory. You going to take her out for a test cruise? Once around Zod?"

"I'm thinking of visiting my son. I can get a pass to visit Earth's moon because Joslin is original biology."

"Envy you, old man. Wish I had the scratch to cover a trip like that."

"When I leave, I'm going to let my landing lease go…"

"Makes sense. No use renting strip space you're not using."

"Right, well, you know I have a junker. Our ships are the same tech series."

"Ah. I won't lie. I could use some hull plating and circuits."

"They're yours. I need a favour in return." Ryan's face was grave.

Yancy smiled. "Planning something a bit dodgy?"

"A quick transport. Your home strip is still on the central continent, isn't it?"

"That it is, me boy. On the western coast. I've a lovely view of the ocean."

"I'll need a quick lift. Two passengers, no questions, your strip to mine."

A sparkle came to Yancy's eyes. "A quick hop now, is it? Let me know when."

"Thanks, Yancy. I appreciate this. I'll call you with the details."

"Not a problem. When can I pick up your junker?"

"Any time, just get it off my strip, so I don't have to rent space for it. Spread the word if you want to."

"Jolly good! Sangunis abl planeta." Yancy snapped off a salute.

"Sangunis abl planeta." Ryan returned the salute before starting back for his ship.

Ryan stepped into his apartment. The room was as filthy as ever. Joslin lay in the e-rig, occasionally making little sounds. He paused to stare at her. He looked up to the imager hanging on his wall. It displayed a picture of them from years before. He was in his dress blues. She in her wedding dress. She was lovely and looked so alive. He shifted his gaze back to where she lay. Moving to her side, he pressed a button on the armrest. The interface unit lifted from her head.

"I thought you were going to your Tech Restorer's event?" she said.

"I went already." Ryan cupped her cheek, affectionately.

"I was in the middle of your show. Gunther and Willa were about to call Angel to tell her how much she hurt Rowan. I was in Gunther's perspective. He is such a good father, he cares so much. I don't want to miss—"

Ryan kissed her. "It's late, why don't you come to bed? I'll give you a massage."

"I want to finish my show. If you like, you can jack in. I'm sure Gunther and Willa will make love soon. I don't know how they can be so passionate after all their years together."

"I, or one of the other techs, manipulates their biology then edits out everything that's less than perfect."

"Well, if you want to take the romance out of it! I'm going back to my show."

Ryan watched as the e-interface descended over his wife's head.

"This isn't living. Mike, it looks like you have your man."

The man was short with a wiry build. His sandy-coloured hair sat on his head in a trendy mat style that didn't suit his oval face. "I can assure you, sir, your loved one will receive the best of care here for the rest of his or her days."

"It's my wife. Will financing be a problem?" Ryan stared down the twin rows of interface tanks. Each held a person suspended in a brine solution, with their head hidden by an e-interface. Tubes for feeding and waste removal were connected to the bodies.

"Does your military pension have survivor benefits?"

"Yes, she's listed as sole recipient."

"Money will not be any problem. Just sign your pension over to us."

"Suppose she ever wanted to come out?"

The short man's face filled with professional compassion. "Sir. They never do."

Ryan looked along the tomb-like room and shook his head. "Let's sign the contracts."

Joslin was vaguely aware of a bump. The fleeting thought that Ryan might be coming to bother her again crossed her mind, but she was fully submerged in Willa's perspective as she planned to confront Angel. A tingle came from her cheek, but it passed. She enjoyed her show.

Ryan watched as the workmen slipped grav-lifts under the e-rig. He kissed his wife's cheek. "I love you, darling. Enjoy your shows." Tears brimmed in his eyes as the workmen pulled her from the apartment, e-rig and all.

Ryan collapsed on the couch. He'd done the laundry and cleared the floor enough for the cleaning robot to function. Turning on the wall screen, he scanned the responses to his ad. Three people willing to sublet. He selected one, setting the date for the end of the week before going to the bedroom to let his regrets assail him.

Henry monitored the workmen as they delivered the cargo. The old ground-forces barracks and bomb bays were filled, and the hangar deck was filling up.

"Watch it. You break it you replace it, no matter how nice your ass is, sweet thing," he commented through the ship's intercom to a shapely brunette who had roughly deposited her load.

"I don't have to take that kind of stardust, jerk!"

"Wow, you're a feisty one. I like a bit of fire."

"Idiot!" the woman stalked from the ship.

Ryan looked with distaste at the robust, Caucasian man that sat in his living-room.

"This really is first draft." The man had slipped a disk into a portable player and put the interface over his head.

"First draft is right. Every twinge, moan and ache. You want it?"

"Depending on your price."

"Two-hundred-thousand for the lot."

"One-hundred-thousand. If you have the deflowering of Rowan, I'd be willing to go up to three." The man gave Ryan a too-perfect smile.

Ryan fidgeted, then shook his head. "No, just what I've shown you. One-fifty?"

"One-twenty-five. I have shipping costs to absorb. The corporations are quite aggressive in their pursuit of people selling raw e-data."

"One-twenty-five. Deposit the money to my account."

"That will be rather obvious."

"I have it covered."

Mike stood beside the operating table staring down at Ryan, who probed his abdomen where the incision had been glued closed and covered with temporary skin.

"Are they done?" asked the younger man.

"Yes. I also had a signal relay chip installed in your handheld. It will send the telemetry through the planetary communications net if you get out of range of the units in the ATV and our satellites. I'd avoid using it, the signal might get picked up, but it's best to prepare for all eventualities. I now have everything I need from you." Mike paced across the room.

"Just keep your part of the bargain."

"I will. Right now if you like."

Henry watched on the internal monitors as Ryan and Mike dragged equipment, supported by grav-lifts, into the ship. They hauled their cargo to a cabin at the back of the Ops crew section. Henry tried to shift his monitor to the cabin, finding that the feed had been mechanically severed.

"Want to be like that, do you? Well!" The android increased the reception of the speaker in the hall.

"Everything up to last month's backup is in the feed unit. You'll need to add anything that comes after," said Mike.

"The time?"

"The rate is set. It should take fifteen years. The systems will be fully normalized. There should be enough time so long as Rowan doesn't burst a blood vessel using her power."

"Good. Here. I filled it out. After I… well… you know. The ATV and anything else I leave on Gaea is yours, as long as you pay off my credit balance."

"More than happy to."

"Thanks, Mike. Why do all this?"

There was a long pause. "I have several reasons, none of which you need to know. If you're still curious when this is over, look up a picture of my wife."

ON DEATH AND DYING

"**F**ool!" bellowed Hunoin, her otter-like body trembling with rage.

The felinezoid on the pool deck tried to leap clear. The patio chair altered course mid-flight and slammed into his head.

'Relax, my sweet Hunoin. Calm, quiet, ease your thoughts,' soothed a mental voice as smooth as satin.

Commander Hunoin rested against the entry steps of a large swimming pool. A glass greenhouse surrounded the pool area. Potted plants sat on the tile deck.

'Rest, preserve your strength, breathe deeply,' the voice continued.

Hunoin opened her mind, letting the owner of the voice have free rein. "My dear husband, my love, my mate, my Stransy, what would I do without you?" Hunoin felt a warm, wet, otterzoid body slide up beside her. She stared at her husband. He was slightly smaller than her, and his colour was a light mahogany, unlike her alga green.

"What would we do without each other?" Stransy lay his head over his wife's back and made a purring sound.

"You were worth every credit I paid for you, my love," remarked the female.

A bell chimed. The felinezoid moved to the greenhouse's door and peered out. "The specialist has arrived, Commander."

Hunoin snorted. "Which specialist, fool, is it a medic or something of use?"

Stransy wrinkled his brow and slipped away from his spouse. "It's the assassin. The medic is stuck in traffic with its human slave. Why can't the primitives build an effective transport grid?"

Hunoin splashed her paws at her husband's perpetual gripe. "Show him in."

The felinezoid pulled the door open. A man-sized creature with a bat-like body and wings, as well as a black head and neck like a snake's, entered. It walked on four legs, keeping the black wings folded tight against its back. When it reached Hunoin, it sat on its haunches, revealing that each forelimb ended in a seven-fingered hand, with an opposable thumb. The forefingers were tipped with claws.

"You requested my presence, Commander Hunoin." The winged alien spoke with a cultured voice and made supple sweeping gestures with its hands. It turned to look at Stransy. "And such a pleasure to see you again, Stransy. I swear, you grow more attractive with each passing moon. May the Great Flyer of the Skies bless your house and the hatchlings within it."

"Thank you, Croell, hatched of Creen, flown by Brock, may the shells of your eggs be strong."

Croell made a sound like sandpaper, and its chest shook. "I should know better than to trade niceties with a telepath."

"Actually, I've studied batzoid culture. Your species is truly fascinating. A culture of worth and greatness."

"Once we have subdued this world, I will have to take you to my aerie. It is humble but worthy of the Great Flyer of the Skies' favour in its keeping of tradition."

"Croell, as pleasant as this may be, I asked you here for a reason," interrupted Hunoin.

"Yes?" The winged alien focused its beady black eyes on the female otterzoid.

"I have a problem. My immune system is proving inadequate to the task of surviving on this planet."

"May the Great Flyer of the Skies bless you and keep you

at her right hand until you may be laid anew."

"I have not given up!"

"As you wish. What do you need from me?"

"The medics believe that they can adapt my immune system to deal with this world by grafting in DNA from a native creature."

"If that is the way of your species, the Great Flyer of the Skies flies many winds. What do you need of me?"

Hunoin swished lazily in the water. "For the DNA graft to be effective, it must be adapted to otterzoid biology. When we crashed, the medical bay of our ship was damaged. We do not have the means to make the adaptation."

Croell blinked and tapped his hands together. "The human defenders, Rowan and Gunther, I believe, have already had their DNA adjusted to be compatible with otterzoid traits."

"Exactly. You must bring me Rowan, the female. She will be the most compatible."

"I will bring you her corpse, Commander."

"No!" said Stransy.

"My mate is correct. For best results, the DNA should be drawn from a living host. The medicals can then make a perpetual cell culture. Once the cell culture is started, we can dispose of the human." Hunoin pulled herself up on her forelegs and stared at Croell.

"Why call for my services?" The batzoid seemed unimpressed with his host's show of strength.

"Because this is important. You are the best assassin in known space," explained Stransy.

"Flattery, my good Stransy, though, as the humans say, it does 'damn me with faint praise.' I will take the contract."

"Good. Speak to my aide, he has been instructed to provide you with anything you may need."

"I brought my own equipment." Croell placed his two hands together and made a bowing motion toward the otterzoids. "Always a pleasure. I do so hope we have time for a game of Gunlok before I leave, Hunoin. Worthy opponents are so hard to find." Dropping to all fours, the winged alien left the pool area.

Rowan watched as the liquid residue from the dart ran through the gas-chromatograph in the university's chemistry lab.

"Anything?" asked Carl.

Rowan jumped, then glanced around the room. A pair of Bermuda shorts and running shoes stepped out from behind a lab desk.

"Carl, you're blending, suppose someone walks in?" Rowan took the results of her analysis off the printer.

"Sorry. I forget sometimes." Carl's colour changed until he appeared as a Hispanic man.

"It's for your own good. I don't want to see you in some lab. Like, we've been friends forever."

"So, what you got?"

"A tranquillizer. It wasn't meant to kill." Rowan closed her eyes and thought of her father. *'Dad.'*

'I'm here, so's your mother,' came Gunther's mental voice.

'Did you catch the analysis results?'

'Yes. I think you should come home. Make sure Carl comes with you. There is safety in numbers.'

Ryan sat at the console, sipping his first coffee of the shift. "I'll save you, my Rowan. I swear." Shifting the screen to Croell, he upped the batzoid's adrenaline equivalent, sharpening his senses. "I want you at the top of your form, batty."

Shifting to Carl, Ryan spiked the younger man's insulin levels. "Give him twenty minutes, then let nature take its course."

Croell stood behind the open door of a van. His human slave, an emaciated man with dark hair, sat behind the wheel.

"Virtion leech venom should do the job, given human biochemistry." Opening a suitcase, Croell extracted a glass jar of yellow liquid. Removing its lid, he dipped his claws, then sealed and replaced the jar.

"Master?" asked the human driver.

"Yes, Irwin?"

"Can I please have my fix now? I promise I won't take it before I'm supposed to."

Croell released the short blast of breath that served his species as a sigh. "Pathetic. Addicts of any species leave the path of the Great Flyer of the Skies. You will wait. Do not displease me, Irwin, or I will cut your ration of vilicsa in half."

"Yes, master."

"It is almost night. We will wait for the cover of darkness." Croell moved to a rosebush and sniffed the flowers. "Lovely. All worlds have something to offer."

Returning to the van, he climbed into the back. "Very well, Irwin. Hunoin's pet human said Rowan was at the college. That will be where our hunt begins."

"I'm starving," complained Carl as they walked down the dark street.

"You're always hungry." Rowan sounded exasperated.

"Hey, I'm a growing boy."

"Sideways, if you keep it up." Rowan checked to be sure they were alone, then mentally picked up a pebble and tapped it against her friend's ribs.

"Quit it!" Carl grabbed at the stone. "Hey, the Garlic Palace is only a block away. Let's grab a slice."

"I want to get home."

⟨═══✦

Ryan adjusted the endorphin levels in Rowan and Carl, lowering their inhibitions, making them reckless.

⟨═══✦

"There won't be any of me left by the time we reach your place." Carl pinched the skin over his stomach.

"Why don't you go to the Garlic Palace? I'll be all right; it's only a few blocks."

"You sure?"

"Get! Fran would never forgive me if I let your strength fail you. Besides, I kinda want to be alone to think." Rowan made shooing motions with her hands.

"I'll grab a slab and catch you up at your place."

"NO ANCHOVIES!" Rowan yelled as Carl ran down a side street.

⟨═══✦

"Excellent." Ryan watched from Rowan's eyes as she was left alone. He checked the other monitors and used an alarm call to divert the patrol car that was about to turn onto the street. "I'm sorry, Row, it's the only way."

Pressing a button, he shifted perspective to an aerial view. The screen caption read "Croell-Batzoid-Assassin." He checked the monitors. The alien clone's emotional level was hyped.

"You love the hunt. You amoral prick. Well, hunt away."

⟨═══✦

Rowan heard the whoosh in time to throw herself to the ground. The batzoid swept over her. Focusing her thoughts, she threw a rock at her attacker. The batzoid back-winged. The rock sped past, then cut back and slammed into Croell's side.

"Very good, human. It is rare that even an otterzoid born could land a blow on me. I salute you." Croell swept up and away. Catching a tailwind, he turned and dove towards his prey.

Rowan scrambled to her feet and bolted toward a distant lit shop window. She heard Croell getting closer. Focusing with all her might, she pushed with her mind.

Ryan clasped his hands in front of him. A month ago, he would have increased her powers in this situation; now, he let the defaults hold.

"I hate this," he muttered.

Croell felt something like a punch in the gut when he grabbed at the girl.

"Arrrr!" Rowan screamed as a fore-claw scraped her shoulder, tearing her sweater and slicing the skin beneath. Adrenaline gave her an added push. She drove her power against the snout of her attacker.

The telekinetic blow left Croell dazed. Blearily, he flapped into the sky. He watched as his prey staggered toward the lit window. Flicking his tongue, he tasted blood on the wind. On his claw, he saw bits of Rowan's skin. "Good, I will let the poison do its work. I have time."

Ryan adjusted Rowan's adrenaline level to keep her active as she staggered down the street. "They'll be there to get you in a minute, I promise."

'Daddy, help! It hurts. Stardust, it hurts!' Rowan's mental cry blasted through Gunther's brain.

"NO! ROWAN!" Gunther focused his mind. He saw through his daughter's eyes.

"Willa, Rowan's hurt. She's at the corner of West and Main. Get the car!" Gunther projected his thoughts outward. *'Carl! Where in the divine's myriad names are you? You were supposed to be with her. West and Main, NOW!'*

Carl waited at a table in the Garlic Palace. The place was done up roadhouse style. The smell of Italian cooking permeated the air. He'd finished his second slice and was debating on having a third as he waited for the slab to cook.

'Carl! Where in the divine's myriad names are you? You were supposed to be with her. West and Main, NOW!'

Rowan felt her mind fogging. Her body ached, and she was so tired. The sound of wings approached. She was too blurry to focus. She trembled as sweat poured off her.

Croell sped toward his prey. Ten metres to go, nine, eight, seven, six, five, four, three...

Something slammed into his side, grappling his wing.

"What?" Croell looked down. The vague outline of a human could be seen, his colours blending into the background.

"LEAVE HER ALONE!" Carl clutched Croell's wing with one arm while driving his free fist into the alien's ribs.

Croell heard a cracking sound and felt pain. Flapping hard, he pulled his unwanted passenger higher into the air.

"Stardust! Can't let Carl get killed, that would be too much for one season." Ryan accessed Angel's controls, increasing her adrenaline levels while triggering an infusion of oxygen-charged artificial blood from her built-in drug pack.

Angel soared over the city, speeding to where Gunther had told her Rowan was. She drove her wings against the air, moving faster than she ever had before.

The shadowy image of the batzoid came into view. It seemed to be wrestling with something that was hard to see.

"Carl," hissed Angel. She dove towards the winged alien and its unwelcome passenger.

Gunther brought the black SUV to a halt and slammed the gearshift into park.

Willa had her door open before the vehicle stopped rocking. She threw herself at her daughter, who slumped against a brick wall.

"ROWAN!" Gunther's bellow split the night. He reached his daughter seconds after his wife.

"Mom, Dad, it hurts. It hurts. I…" Rowan started to sob.

"It's okay, honey. We're here," breathed Willa.

Gunther reached into Rowan's mind, blocking the worst of the pain. "Get her into the SUV; we have to get her home."

"Carl and Angel?" asked Willa.

"Can look after themselves. We need to find out what's causing this."

Croell hissed with pain, then did an aerial spin. Carl tried to cling to the alien, but the centrifugal force was too much.

"STARDUST!" Carl bellowed as he dropped.

Angel heard the cry, then saw the bright yellow form of Carl falling. Tucking her wings, she dove. The wind tore at her face, and water streamed from her eyes. She caught him under the armpits then spread her wings. The strain pulled muscles and wrenched tendons. She held on, using her momentum to stall his and bring a balance. Two metres off the ground, she felt the forces reach equilibrium, and she let him go.

Carl landed, crumpling into a heap.

Croell gasped with pain. The delicate ribs of his chest were shattered. Gritting his teeth, he flew towards his van, leaving his doomed prey.

Ryan added a clotting agent to Croell's blood to stop the bleeding into his lung cavity but did nothing to lessen the batzoid's pain. "Poor baby bat, did you forget that to fly you need light bones? Boohoo."

Ryan shifted his screen to Rowan. She lay in the back of the SUV. He watched through Willa's eyes as she tore off Rowan's sweater and inspected the scratch on her shoulder. The readout showed that Rowan was drifting in and out of consciousness.

"Poor Row, it's only for a little while." Ryan suppressed a shudder of sympathy.

DENIAL

"It's poison. I went through the alien database and cross-referenced it with human medicine. I think it's Virtion leech venom." Willa stepped into Rowan's room. The furnishings were simple, elegant and functional, made of simulated wood. Potted plants grew on the top of a dresser in front of her bay window. Rowan lay in her bed, blankets pulled up under her chin. Sweat poured off her, and she was shivering; at best, semi-conscious. Gunther sat in a vanity chair beside her. He didn't seem to hear his wife.

"What can we do?" Angel sat in a kitchen chair on the other side of Rowan. Her wings were folded against her back, and she wore a black, lace bra.

Willa hung her head. "The only cure is a nano-bot extraction. We don't have the tech."

"Could we steal it?" Carl stepped into the doorway.

"If we knew where to look. Why did you leave her? You were supposed to protect her." Willa turned on the young man.

"I know." Carl hung his head.

Fran sat on the couch in Gunther's living-room. A TV and stereo stood in the corner. Two loungers, a coffee table and a matching love seat made up the rest of the furnishings. The phone rang. She picked it up.

"Hello."

Ryan rubbed his eyes and took another hit off his coffee. He recorded Fran's reaction to the phone call that offered Rowan's cure in exchange for her living DNA. Then he shifted to the otterzoids.

Hunoin mentally returned the phone to its hook. "Primitive and cumbersome device."

"Will you really give them the cure?" Stransy swam to the edge of their pool.

"Of course not, my love. This is working out well. We are rid of a beetle in our hutch, and I will be cured. What is it the humans say? 'Two birds with one stone'."

Stransy splashed his forepaws at his spouse's quip. Hunoin slipped into the pool.

"Beloved, none of those who go to meet the humans can know of your deception. The human, Gunther, would sense any trickery."

"You are the better part of me. All those I send will believe they are bringing a real cure. In fact, they will be. The nanobots have been programmed to link to the venom."

"But my love..."

Hunion splashed her paws at her own cleverness. "The nano-bots will link with the venom and neutralize it, but they will resist being purged. After the cell culture is taken, all we need do is transmit a deactivate command. The nano-bots will release the toxin, then Rowan will die."

Stransy splashed his paws and swam in tight circles around his mate.

"You look nova blasted," said the twenty-something,

copper-skinned woman who entered the control room. Her hair was jet-black and fell to the middle of her back while her face was pleasant and open, with large, brown eyes and full lips.

"Hello to you too, Arlene." Ryan turned his chair to face the newcomer.

Arlene smiled. "Sorry. It's just you really do look beat."

"Rough couple of days." Ryan surrendered his chair. Arlene took a seat.

"I heard about Joslin. It's not your fault."

"How'd you find out about that?"

"Studio gossip. She chose to be an e-addict, no one made her."

"Maybe. You ever wonder about what we do here?"

"No, it would only upset me. Look, this is probably too early and all, but... well..."

"What?"

Arlene blushed and bit her lip. "When you feel ready, if you'd like, my group would be interested in dating you. I know Dee and Stella both think you're nice. Don likes you. Jack is a bit of a question mark. He always takes a while to warm up to new people. It would be nice to balance the numbers, male and female."

"Thanks, Arlene, but—"

"I know it's too soon, and you've never been in a group before, but don't knock it. We aren't into really kinky stuff, and everyone has their own study for when you need to be alone. Think about it."

Ryan smiled at the earnest young woman. "It will be a while. I think I need to do some things before I consider anything else. I'll think about it."

"That's all I ask. I really am sorry about Joslin."

"Can you do me a favour?"

"Sure."

Ryan fidgeted. "After shift tomorrow, I want to drop into the Garlic Palace. Can you cover for me?"

"If you get caught going into the set region, they'll can us both."

"Come on, we all do it. It's the best pizza on the planet! I'll dress the part. Just another extra back from planting trees." Ryan shrugged.

"Only because it's you. Get some sleep. You really do look nova blasted."

"Feel worse. Arlene... thanks, I appreciate the invite."

Ryan parked his bike on the landing strip by the *Star Hawk*. He scanned the empty space where his junker had been. "Club members and vultures, no difference." He smiled at his own quip, then climbed the ramp into his craft. A small forest greeted him. Saplings connected to automatic watering and maintenance systems filled the chamber, except for the one full vehicle bay by the ramp.

"You finally came home. Spent the entire night carousing I presume." Henry's voice issued from the speaker.

"I was at work. Any calls?"

"No. The delivery people left everything in the mate's quarters. Guess that's gonna be appropriate, stud."

Ryan shook his head and spent the rest of the journey to the Ops deck in silence. Opening the door to the mate's quarters, he smiled. The three-metre-square chamber was full of crates. A simulated wood floor covered the rubberised flooring that had come with the room.

Ryan opened a crate, revealing a simulation wood dresser. "Henry."

"Yes, cutie."

"Cut that out! Do up the walls with program Rowan One."

The walls shifted to match the wallpaper of Rowan's bedroom. A bay window, looking onto the branches of a chestnut tree, seemed to occupy one wall. Little birds flitted about the branches.

"That should make her feel at home." Ryan smiled as he

located the dresser and bolted it to the floor.

"Bet she'll pay you right and proper for all this. Aye lover, grrrr," Henry teased through the intercom.

"You are a pig!" Ryan opened another box and began putting clothing into the drawers.

"Come on, you gonna get some."

Ryan paused in the unpacking. "If it happens, it happens. I hope she learns to love me, but I don't know."

"Come on, give her a little endorphin tweak. It's so nova blasted simple."

"And spend my life wondering if it could have been real? No. I'm saving her. After that, she decides."

"Man, she's a fakey. She's built to entertain."

"She's a person! I don't like that word, 'fakey'. How you came into this universe has a lot less to do with who you are than what you do while you're here."

"Stardust, I thought I'd get to watch."

"You are such a pig!" Ryan threw the mattress on the bed, secured its Velcro retaining tabs and began bolting the unit into place. The drawers under the bed matched the ones from the series, except each was sealed by a clip latch, so they couldn't accidentally open.

Henry stared through the vid monitor into the mate's quarters. As much as the space allowed, the room was identical to Rowan's. He shifted his view to the pickup on the computer terminal sitting on her desk. It was working perfectly. *Make her feel right at home. 'Least I can watch her undress*, thought the android. Ryan had disappeared into the engineer's workshop and invoked privacy. Henry shifted his view to the captain's quarters. These were the same size and basic design as the mate's had been. A roll-down couch/bed occupied one wall. A closet filled the space beside the en-suite at the back of the room. The walls displayed a mountain valley, and the bed was rolled down. End table dresser units flanked the couch bed. A desk, with a built-in computer terminal, stood against the wall beside the entrance door.

"Give her all the homey touches, and you live like you were still serving. Gotta get over it, man!" Henry spoke into the chamber.

Ryan exited the workshop carrying a circuit board. "Henry, run a power-up check on all stealth systems."

"Aye, sir."

⌦⟶

Ryan held the circuit board he'd cobbled together. In a little over a minute, he would commit his first felony. Opening the bridge door, he moved to the disabled weapons console.

"Stealth units are looking good. What you..." Henry fell silent as Ryan connected a series of jacks to the circuit board.

"STARDUST... STARDUST... STARDUST! The nova blasted weapons systems are online! Where in the divine's myriad names did you get an activation circuit?" screamed the android.

"I didn't. Little known fact, the control circuit from an automated asteroid tracking station, coupled with the targeting circuit from the Space Patrol video game, wired into a stock A-347 jack mount, with three of the prongs removed, can mimic one mark-seven weapons activation and control circuit. If you know what you're doing."

"If they catch us in Gaea territory with that, we're both rogered with a cattle prod. Are you crazy?"

"Maybe I am. I don't trust the studio to let this go. Use the maintenance bots to cobble together some missiles out of the scrap I pulled off the junker. I'm going to get some sleep. Wake me at least four hours before my shift. Run a weapons system check. It's been a long time since those babies have been active. Also, check the prices for antiproton. I need to recharge before we reach Geb."

"On it. Stardust. I never knew my boss had such a big gun and it works too!" Henry made a lewd action with his lips.

"Do you even have a sliver of preference one way or the other?"

"Nah… Man, woman or furry, I'll play with it. Hey, it's your fault. In a way, you're my dear, dear daddy."

Ryan rubbed his hand over his face. "That's all I need."

Angel hovered over the deserted road. Her wings ached. A van parked at the exchange site. A moment later, Gunther's SUV appeared.

"It is a lovely day for flying," observed a grating voice from above her.

Angel back-winged, dove, twisted, and came up facing Croell. The batzoid had a bandage wrapped around its chest and hovered on an updraft. Angel brought her pellet-gun to bear.

"There is no need of that, human flyer," remarked Croell.

"What do you want?" demanded Angel.

"Presumably, the same thing that you do. To survey the ground for enemy forces. We are on the periphery of this conflict. There is no reason we cannot be civil."

"You tried to kill my best friend!"

"It was a job. Has anyone ever told you that you have beautiful wings?"

"What?" Angel was nonplussed by the comment.

"I do apologize. To phrase it as you humans do. I have always been a wingman. The delicate curve of your lifting membrane, the strong line of the supporting cartilage, not to mention the black sheen of their surface. They are all quite lovely. Frankly, for the most part, I find little that I consider attractive about homo-sapiens, but you are an exception."

"I can't believe this. You tried to kill my best friend. Now you're trying to pick me up?"

"I draw a strict line between business and pleasure. Besides, my wife has been asking me to take another mate. She's lonely for female company."

Arlene smiled as she increased Croell's arousal hormones, then glanced at Angel's readings.

"No need to do Angel. That girl has a real taste for fur. Wonder what that felinezoid hunk Toronk would say if he knew? Hmm... A little fur might be fun for the group to play with. Down girl, concentrate on getting Ryan. Speaking of sexy fur."

Toronk crept through the underbrush. His markings made him blend with the foliage almost as well as Carl, who he could smell from the other side of the road. He sniffed again. Fran was behind him. He listened, then froze. His claws extended.

Arlene watched Toronk's levels jump. He was honed for the hunt, a killing machine and loving every minute of it.

"Merrow, pussycat. Add some sex, this is going to be one hot episode for you."

With a press of a button, she brought up a screen with the caption 'k-no-in-guard-1'.

Toronk felt the hunt tension take him. The primal beast he held in check came to the fore as he stalked closer. The k-no-in huddled behind an outcrop of rocks with a particle beam rifle aimed at the road below.

The big felinezoid sprang. The k-no-in tried to turn. Toronk landed on the pony-like back and slashed with his claws. The k-no-in bucked but only succeeded in sinking Toronk's claws deeper into its body. Toronk shifted position, driving his teeth into the k-no-in's throat.

The k-no-in stiffened, shuddered and died as blood gushed from its throat.

Toronk bit down on a bellow of joy and savoured his kill in silence.

Willa drove up the dirt road and parked her SUV. Rowan was in the back seat, wrapped in blankets, her head cradled on Gunther's lap. Farley sat in the front passenger seat.

"Be careful, love. I don't sense deception, but it could still be a blind," cautioned Gunther.

"Let's go." Willa opened her door and stepped out. Farley followed her example.

A k-no-in approached them from the van. It walked on its four back legs, bending up so it could carry a syringe and DNA harvester in its front three-fingered hands. The claws on its back legs made little ruts in the dirt.

"Are you the medic?" demanded Willa.

"I am he, human."

"Is that the cure?" asked Farley.

"The nano-bots are pre-programmed. Where is the subject?"

Willa's eyes clouded as she listened to Gunther's mental voice.

'He's telling the truth. Fran, Toronk and Carl have all killed alien snipers. They can't be sure there aren't others. Angel is trying to keep a batzoid occupied. We have to have a talk with that girl about her sexual morals. The medic didn't know anything about the ambush. Bring him forward,

Rowan is getting worse.'

"This way." Willa led the k-no-in to the SUV and opened the back door.

"The cure first." Gunther looked into the medic's dog-like face.

"As you wish. It will take time to be effective."

"Honey?" asked Willa.

"He's telling the truth."

The k-no-in located a vein and pushed the hypodermic home.

"Now I need the cell sample we agreed upon," demanded the medic.

As gently as they could, Gunther and Farley turned Rowan, exposing her buttock.

"Yes, intestinal walls are best." With strict professionalism, the k-no-in inserted its collection unit. Rowan let out a little gasp in response to the intrusion. A minute later, the k-no-in strode to the van and sped off.

"I hope this works," said Willa.

"Dad, Mom. What happened?" murmured Rowan from where she was struggling to sit up.

Gunther and Willa fell into each other's arms, while Farley whooped for joy.

ANGER

Ryan kept the ATV on its tires as he drove over the rock plain. The stealth units in the hull were blending colour with the ground, and his heat signature was being neutralized by a feed of stored liquid nitrogen. The batteries were reading just over half full. Collecting the ATV from Mike's had been as easy as stepping up to the ground's gate and telling the computer his name. He topped a hill. A broad, slow river spread before him.

Checking the GPS on his console, he confirmed his location.

"That must be the Wolf River." He scanned the control board until he found what he needed, then focused his optics forward. On his screen, a distant smudge turned into a line of newly planted trees.

"There's the studio's forestation project." Ryan scanned the cockpit. It was compact, with two seats surrounded on three sides with controls. Over half the consoles had been stripped, leaving a jumble of exposed wires. A red light blinked on the control board to Ryan's left, indicating that the motor that drove the front right tire was disabled. He patted the console. "Hold together, you battered hunk of stardust. I must be crazy."

Climbing from his command chair, he moved into the troop section. This was a chamber two metres across by two high and five long. Fold-down billets occupied the long walls, stacked three high. The remains of a gutted gunnery station filled half the back wall. Beside the gunnery station gaped the hole where the antiproton power source had once rested.

Opening a side door, Ryan clipped two grav-lifts to his power-bike and walked it out of the ATV. He glanced skyward. If he was going to be caught by a satellite, this was when it would happen. He turned back to the ATV. A camouflage tarp was pulled over the hole where the turret used to be. The tarp was matching colour with the surroundings.

Ryan towed his bike to the road and tapered off the grav-lifts, letting it drift to the rock surface.

"One last ride, old girl. You've been fun." Carrying the grav-lifts, he checked to be sure the ATV hadn't left tracks before he returned to its cockpit.

"Hold up a little longer." Ryan crossed his fingers and activated the grav-nullifiers. A distorted hum went through the ATV as the boxy, seven-metre long craft rose off the ground.

"Just a few metres." Ryan grimaced as the sound of the malfunctioning anti-gravity system became worse. He eased the aging, war machine over the river. The hull automatically adjusted to match the colour of the water. He took a sounding on the far side.

"Perfect." He eased off the AG. The craft settled until its top was only a decimetre above the flow. Ryan shut down everything except the stealth system.

Shucking his clothes, he moved to the crew section. A ladder ascended the wall by the cockpit door. Pressing a button opened a hatch in the roof. Ryan climbed onto the ATV and closed the hatch.

"Here goes." He dove into the river and was shivering by the time he clambered up the far bank. Looking back, all he could see was a ripple where the ATV interrupted the current. Running to his bike, he pulled clothes and a towel from the saddlebags. Minutes later, he rode toward the studio support town on his power-bike.

Rowan bit into her pizza. The taste exploded on her tongue. It was as if she'd never been ill.

"It pleases me that you are recovered." Toronk sat in one of Gunther's loungers with Angel tucked into his lap. He began grooming her behind the ear.

"Toronk, cut that out. Everyone can see!" objected Angel.

"I am sorry. I forgot the oddity of human social imperatives."

"Don't lie to a telepath. You were showing off." Gunther settled on the couch beside Willa and grinned at the felinezoid.

"I will not deny it. I have the most beautiful of humankind to call my own. It would be foolish not to show off the fact."

"You." Angel nestled into the fur of her lover's chest.

Rowan watched them together. Sadness clouded her eyes. Her gaze shifted to Carl and Fran, who were snuggled together on the couch beside her parents. She glanced at her father, whose arm encircled his wife's shoulder. His eyes met Rowan's with a look of complete understanding and compassion.

"Rowan?" Farley stepped out of the kitchen.

"Yupper, that's my name."

"Can we... I'd like to talk to you, in the kitchen, maybe?" Farley offered his hand to help her stand.

"All right."

Rowan took Farley's hand. He helped her from her seat.

"Dad, no eavesdropping. I'll know if you do, I always know."

"Wouldn't think of it, dear." Gunther focused all his attention on Willa as Rowan and Farley left the room.

Willa blushed and gave Gunther a playful swat. "I swear, spending so much time with all these young people is affecting you!"

"What was he thinking?" asked Carl.

"Never you mind." Willa's blush deepened. She turned to face her husband. "We'll have to use the low-cal chocolate sauce, I'm watching."

"EW... Things I don't want to picture forty-somethings doing. Yuck!" said Angel.

Carl looked at Willa, a smile playing at the corners of his lips. "Ouch!"

"It's one thing to not be like Angel and think life stops at thirty, it's quite another to draw mental pictures." Fran retracted her claws as Carl rubbed his side.

⌖⊷◇

Rowan sat on a chair in the small, eat-in kitchen. "So, you wanted to talk."

Farley fidgeted. "Row, today when I thought we were going to lose you. I... I'm sorry for the thing with Angel. I was wrong."

"You're forgiven. We all make mistakes."

"Thank you." Farley dropped to one knee and pulled a small box from his pants' pocket. "Rowan, I love you. I—"

"Farley, don't! I... I can't. I realized some things. What I want, you can't give me. I'm sorry."

"I can try. Tell me what you want. I can change. I can, I swear I—"

"Farley." Rowan took the young man's hands. "What I want is what my mom and dad have. I want someone who's going to laugh with me and flirt with me, and fight with me, twenty years from now. A little bit of me will always love you, but you aren't that person."

"I could be."

Rowan released his hands and stood up. "No, you couldn't. We're too different."

"We aren't, we—"

"What's the equation for calculating acceleration over time?"

"I don't—"

"How about the significance of redshift in calculating interstellar distances?"

"That stuff isn't important."

"How about me then? I can barely play a couple of songs on the recorder. When I sing in the shower, it violates noise pollution regulations. I dance like a geek."

"You don't, you—"

"Yes, I do. When you perform, all I can do is sit there. We don't fit. I'm sorry—"

Rowan gasped and buckled.

"GUNTHER, EVERYONE, HELP!" screamed Farley.

Stransy lounged in the back of a van driven by a scrawny, female human. The screen on the transmitter he held in his front paw spelt out 'deactivated' in his species' phonetic characters.

"You may take me home now, Selma." The otterzoid thought for a moment. "Stop at the Garlic Palace on the way. You will go in and purchase a twelve slice with extra anchovies."

Ryan stepped into his boss's office. It was richly furnished with uncomfortable, chrome and vinyl chairs. John sat in a huge, leather swivel chair behind an oversized, sim-wood desk. The desk was topped by a brand-new computer and was situated in front of a large, west-facing window that the afternoon sun blazed through.

Ryan squinted into the light. "John?" he asked the shadowy figure in the swivel chair.

"What is it?" demanded the producer.

Ryan placed a sheet of paper on the desk. "I'm tendering my resignation. I'll work this shift, so you aren't left in the lurch, but I won't be coming back."

"That's gratitude for you. I always said you can't trust a fakey. Clones are all alike, unre... where do you think you're going?"

Ryan moved toward the door. "I quit, you mindless collection of stardust! I don't have to put up with you anymore, you cowardly, bigoted, spoiled jackass!" Ryan left the room to the sound of John's sputtered objections.

⌖

Rowan lay in her bed, sweating and shivering.

"They double-crossed us!" Gunther slammed his fist into his palm.

"We'll find them and get the cure. We have to," said Angel.

⌖

Ryan entered the control booth for what he knew would be the last time. He hated it as much as he ever had.

Greg's hulking, bald-headed form rose from the chair and turned to face him. The human's skin was emerald green, and his eyes were yellow, slit-pupiled orbs. A slender, forked tongue flicked out of his mouth. "Hi, Ryan. Ssorry about Josslin."

"Thanks, Greg."

"I have a meet of the reptile club today. If you need to talk, I'm free after that."

"I'll keep it in mind. Thanks." Ryan settled in the chair.

"Rowan'ss for it. Probably happen on Arlene'ss sshift."

"I'll keep it in mind. Hey, maybe the others will find a cure."

"Right, and I might jusst sstart dating a girl from Humanss Asscendant, the pure gene people." Greg left the room.

⌖

Ryan checked Rowan's monitors for what seemed the millionth time. She was slipping fast, too fast. He adjusted his big screen and stared at her through Gunther's eyes. Sweat soaked her face, and she was horribly pale.

"She won't last at this rate." Pressing a button, Ryan brought up the controls for the nano-bots in Rowan's system and activated a sequence.

"I have to drop the toxin's concentration. Can't let anyone suspect."

Mike pulled the rental truck to a stop in front of the *Star Hawk*'s entry ramp. Exiting, he surveyed the ship and smiled.

"Ryan does nice work." Moving behind the truck, he activated the grav-lifts on a box and propelled it up the ramp.

"Halt, who goes there, and are you willing to shag?" demanded Henry's voice as Mike topped the ramp.

"You really do have a one-track mind," observed the studio executive.

"Choo choo."

"What?" Michael guided the crate to the elevator at the back of the hangar. The doors opened. He pushed it in.

"Archaic reference. You ever make love on a train? It was a common fantasy in the old days."

"My wife and I spent our honeymoon doing a rail tour of Silvanus. Fascinating!"

"I bet. Your missus is a hottie."

The elevator doors opened on the engineering level. Mike pushed the crate out. "I always felt so. Are you sure you can keep this equipment hidden from Ryan?"

"You bet. The new grav-control unit he patched in takes up only half the space of this tub's original one. Slip your unit in beside it and hook it up to the auxiliary computer interface. I'll do the rest."

"Good, then I best get on with it. I need to be at the studio soon." Mike began removing the retaining bolts on a cover panel.

"Just keep your part of the bargain."

"I will."

⊂══➤

Carl hid in the corner of the Garlic Palace, eavesdropping on the conversations around him. Hoping that one of the alien's enslaved humans might come in and drop some useful information. None of the conversations he overheard were any help. A couple of pretty women, whom he assumed must be role-playing gamers, discussed how to defeat some kind of superhuman. They sounded so serious and, from his perspective, it seemed foolish.

A paramedic squad came in. They were talking about how Trixy had said the child would make it.

⊂══➤

"Hey, Ryan. How you holding up?" Arlene stepped into the control room.

"Fine. Rowan's in a bad way."

"You are having one nova-blasted week. I know Rowan was your favourite. Well... don't worry. They're activating another AS-F class clone for Sam's new show, the one about two girls rooming with one guy."

"There's an idea to last half a season. Who do you think he stole it from?"

"No idea. I don't watch pre-contact vids."

"You gotta wonder what admin uses for brains. You still good for covering me for my pizza run?"

"Sure, you need a break. Only be careful."

"Hey, I survived Murack Five. Well... in a way."

"That wasn't Mr. Wilson."

"It is a problem when you can't shoot the bastards!"

Ryan surrendered his chair.

Arlene sat.

"Thanks for everything, Arlene. You're a good friend." Ryan squeezed the woman's shoulder.

"Anytime."

"She won't last the day." Gunther sat by Rowan's bed, staring into her face. His body trembled. In his heart, he swore he was going to kill the aliens that did this.

"The others may find something. If we only had the activation codes for those nova blasted nano-bots." Willa sat beside her husband.

"Our little girl." Gunther grasped his wife's hand.

Arlene snuffled as she activated an endorphin to soothe the distraught parents' minds. "No reason for this. No reason at all. John is a jerk!"

BARGAINING

Ryan changed into the shirt and pants of a tree-planter extra and slipped into the set-region's access passage. An electric rail ran along a semi-circular tunnel. Vehicles, resembling roller-coaster cars, sat on the track.

"Felony heavy arms possession, misdemeanour trespassing, destruction of private property," Ryan muttered as he opened a panel and pulled the wires that would warn the studio that the system was in use. Boarding one of the cars, he hit its activate button, and it sped along the dimly lit tunnel.

Arlene rubbed her temples. Three hours into her shift, and already her head throbbed. She checked Carl's monitor in the Garlic Palace. The lunch crowd was starting to trickle in. Ryan entered Carl's field of vision.

"Enjoy your slice, cutie. You deserve it. Nova blast, what's he doing?"

Ryan moved to Carl's table and sat down. "I know you're there, Carl. You have to trust me if you want Rowan to live."

"Oh stardust, oh stardust, oh stardust!" Arlene muttered and shifted the feed to Fran as she beat information out of a chameleonzoid.

"Divine! Who are you?" whispered Carl.

"A friend. I can't waste time getting to Rowan. I need you to pave the way with Gunther and Willa." Ryan kept his voice low. A few of the other patrons shot him an odd look. They had long since learned to ignore most things.

"Why should I trust you?"

"Because I want her to live as much as you do. There will be at least three of you there, what harm could I do?"

"You know a lot."

"More than you can guess. If you aren't going to help me right now, I'll go it alone. Rowan doesn't have time to waste."

Mike Strongbow observed the monitor in a control room. Carl's confusion was mirrored in his readings. With an endorphin push, he put the clone over the top.

"This is shaping up nicely. I get to screw John over, and his own clones help me." Mike leaned back in his chair.

"Come on," hissed Carl.

The younger man led Ryan into the men's room where Carl's clothes were bundled up in a heating vent. A moment later, they were running along the street to Gunther's house.

Arlene shook her head. So far, she'd kept the system from focusing on Ryan, but she wasn't sure how much longer she could keep it up. "I need this job, you crazy pile of stardust! All this to save a fakey! Nova blast!"

Ryan followed Carl into Gunther's living room. He knew

every stick of furniture, every stain in the carpet, every nuance of smell, but this was the first time he'd experienced them with his own senses.

"Come on!" Carl's voice broke Ryan's reverie. He followed the younger man up the stairs to Rowan's bedroom.

"Who in the divine's myriad names are you?" Gunther came to his feet.

Rowan's breathing was ragged, and her face ashen.

"No time!" Pushing to Rowan's side, Ryan pulled an electronic tablet-like device from his pocket, folded it open and activated it. Numbers scrolled on its screen.

"What do you think you're doing?" Gunther lunged at Ryan.

Carl held his mentor back. "He's trying to help. Gunther, he may be her only hope."

"Honey?" asked Willa.

Gunther closed his eyes and reached for the stranger's mind. A shudder ran through him. He'd only once before known what he sensed in this stranger's thoughts. He looked at his wife, remembering the day, years before, they told him of her cancer. "It's all right. I don't know much, but on the matter of Rowan, we can trust him."

Ryan's hand-held's screen displayed the activate code. He hit the transmit button. The nano-bots the k-no-in had injected once more locked onto the venom, neutralizing it. Rowan shuddered, then took a deep breath.

"That was too close," said Ryan.

"Is she all right?" demanded Willa.

"It will take a while for her to regain her strength. A lot of her red blood cells were destroyed. We need to talk."

"Bloody right we need to talk. Who are you?" demanded Gunther.

Ryan stepped back. "Let's go to your living room. Rowan needs to rest."

Arlene kept the recorder focused on Toronk and Fran as they tore through a group of aliens. She'd stopped recording the clones around Ryan by shifting the protocols into sleep mode. Then she'd blanked the few seconds that had recorded before she thought of it. She focused her attention on the side screen that showed Gunther's perspective. Ryan was sitting in a lounger, his hands clasped in front of him. Willa sat beside Gunther on their couch. Carl had remained at Rowan's side.

Ryan employed the mental discipline the Spacing Corps had taught him to keep Gunther from probing past his surface thoughts. He had to believe the lie as he spoke it, make it his reality so the telepath would believe it.

"So, ten thousand years ago, these Equestezoids kidnapped a breeding population of humans to serve as slaves?" Willa echoed what she'd been told.

"My ancestors rebelled. Since then we've eked out a living working ships with no world to call our own."

"Why didn't you come back to Earth?" demanded Gunther.

"We looked at how violent and warlike you planetary humans are. I grew up in a society that is so different from yours; there are no grounds for comparison."

"Why come here now?" Willa stared at Ryan.

"Because the passing stargate allows for a two-way real-time trip. We suspected that the pirates might try to dominate you. No matter what else, we are all still human. My people want to help."

"How?" Gunther's brow creased.

Arlene stared at Gunther's levels. "Gotta help Ryan, or we'll both lose our jobs. Why on Gaea did he think they'd buy such a ridiculous story?" She ramped up the endorphins for euphoria. "Just be grateful that he saved your daughter. I have to get him out of there, but how? Hmm." Arlene paused in thought. "It might tip the scale. I hope you have some way to explain a missing body, boy-o."

Arlene released artificial blood into Rowan's system, then erased the record of the action.

Ryan fidgeted. "We space-born humans have been lobbying the Republic to send an enforcer squadron to this solar system. If a human deputized as a junior enforcer was to speak of the necessity of doing so before the council, it could win them over."

"What?" asked Willa.

"Stardust!" swore Gunther.

"Rowan would be an ambassador to the galaxy for the Earth-based humans," explained Ryan.

"Absolutely not!" Willa came to her feet.

"She belongs here!" agreed Gunther. "We appreciate your saving her—"

"I haven't saved her." Ryan looked into Gunther's eyes.

"What?" Willa and Gunther spoke in unison.

"I only reactivated the nano-bots. I don't have the equipment here to extract the poison. If the pirates deactivate the nano-bots, she will die!"

"That's blackmail." Gunther's face turned red.

Ryan relaxed, allowing the regret he felt at separating Rowan from her family to fill his surface thoughts. "If I could save her and leave her with you, I would. I need advanced equipment to cleanse the poison from her system. It's going to be dangerous enough getting her back to my ship."

Arlene watched Rowan's screen. Rowan was leaning heavily on Carl as she shuffled down the stairs. She reached the living room. Arlene's fingers flew over the console, releasing a chemical soup of hormones and endorphins into Rowan.

Rowan stepped into the living room and saw Ryan. Her heart lurched, and her blood pressure increased. Despite how awful she felt, she knew she wanted him.

"You can't take her away!" Willa wrung her hands.

"Mom, I'm twenty-one years old. I think I can make my own choices." Rowan's voice was strained.

All eyes turned to where she leaned on Carl at the bottom of the stairs.

"Honey." Gunther leapt up and reached her the same moment as Ryan. Both men helped her to the couch.

"Rowan, he wants to—" began Willa.

"I heard. I also heard that if I don't go with him, all it will take is the press of a button and I die."

"There has to be another way," said Gunther.

"Maybe there is, maybe there isn't. Can I afford to take that risk? Besides, from the sound of things, I can do some real good out there."

"Honey, you can't be serious." Willa took Rowan's hands.

"Why? Ambassador for Earth, it sounds impressive. If they do send an enforcer squadron, maybe I can hitch a ride back. How long will it take, two, three years? I'd be away that long if I did my doctorate out of town."

Ryan hung his head. He hated lying to these people who, one-sided as it was, he knew and considered friends. He hated the pain it would cause when Rowan never returned.

"What I don't understand is how you knew what was going on." Gunther stared at Ryan like he was trying to bore holes in his head with his gaze. The telepath gasped. "YOU!"

Ryan pulled his concentration back to the present. "Oh, boy! I..." His thoughts raced as Gunther's face grew red with rage. Ryan did the only thing he could. He dropped his defences, focusing his thoughts on the truth and the danger they were in.

Gunther recoiled as his mind was flooded with information. His world was turned upside down in an instant.

"Do you understand?" asked Ryan.

Gunther blinked. Ryan heard words form in his mind. *'The studio will murder us all if I let on. We have to get you and Rowan out of here.'*

Arlene watched Gunther's levels spike. "Get out of there, Ryan. John is going to have kittens."

Mike increased the interference. His face was grave, but he hadn't gotten where he was by not taking risks. "Careless, Ryan, careless. Of course, dealing with a telepath that powerful and determined was a bit much to ask. Now get a move on. I can't keep covering for you."

DEPRESSION

Ryan carried Rowan to Gunther's SUV. It was full light, but the street was deserted. Gunther came up beside Ryan, who whispered into the other man's ear. "Thank you, Arlene. I'm sorry to put you through this."

"You come from a sick and degenerate society!" Gunther opened the vehicle's door. Ryan lay Rowan across the back seat.

"I love you, Rowan." Willa leaned into the SUV.

"I love you, Mom." Rowan pulled herself up. Her mother hugged her.

"We have to go," said Ryan.

"Will I ever see her again?" Tears rolled down Willa's cheeks.

Ryan looked at Gunther, who shook his head.

"Who knows? You mustn't let anyone know she's alive. The pirates would hunt us down to keep her from testifying."

"Carl?" Rowan reached towards her oldest friend.

"Have fun out there." Carl leaned into the back seat and dropped a bulging gym bag on the floor. He then kissed Rowan's hand. "I'll tell the others you woke up before the end and said goodbye."

"Thank you." Rowan hugged her mother. Willa clung to Rowan. Carl had to pull the older woman from the back seat.

"I love you, Rowan, I love you! Be safe." Willa sobbed as the SUV pulled onto the street.

"Head to the western planting," said Ryan.

"Aren't you going to tell her the truth?" demanded Gunther.

"Tell me what?" Rowan tried to sit up.

Ryan pulled his hand-held from his pocket and keyed a sequence before pointing it at Rowan.

"What were you going to tell—" Rowan slumped unconscious.

"What did you do?" demanded Gunther.

"I used my hand-held to trigger a sedative they built into her. She needs to sleep and heal. Arlene must have used the oxygen boost to get her up. It won't last. That venom almost killed her. I'll tell her everything. She's not strong enough to take it right now. Besides, until I reach my ship, it would only put her at higher risk."

"You treat us like puppets. How can you justify what you've done?" Gunther turned the SUV onto a road that led to a gap in a set of middle-aged trees.

"How does a general justify sending men into battle? Don't get moral with me, Gunther. I've seen too much to care. I have a doctorate in engineering. After I was cloned, that didn't mean squat. All people saw was a fakey! I had to take a job at the studio. I couldn't live on my military pension, and I had a wife to support. I thank the stars that my son finished university before I was discharged."

"Am I helping you so that Rowan can be some sort of toy for you?"

Ryan stared at a man whom he'd come to respect. It saddened him that he would never have the chance to earn Gunther's respect. "No. When I can, I'm going to get a medic to remove most of her control pack. She'll be free to choose. That I swear."

"Why not take it all out?"

"Because that would kill her. The accelerated growth results in a lot of cancers. Add to that the genetic manipulations… If I deactivate the nano-bots that help maintain her metabolism, she'd be dead in three months."

"Take good care of her."

"I will, I promise."

Gunther glanced at Ryan. "In that, I believe you."

Arlene felt sweat trickle down her brow. "How am I going to explain this? I'm canned, at the least! Maybe if I call security I can…"

The vid-phone behind her buzzed. She rolled her chair back so that she was in front of it. "*Angel Black* control booth, may I help you?"

"Hello, Arlene. This is Michael Strongbow."

"Sir. I… I—"

"I'm calling because I need an editing tech for my new series. Ryan recommended you."

"Sir, I—"

"Don't worry. I'll take full responsibility for *stealing* you away from John. *You won't face any negative consequences.* There are advantages to being the senior studio producer, after all."

"I… I… What do you need me to do, sir?" Arlene looked at the secondary screen that displayed Ryan's face.

"I prefer to let my people's creativity flow. You'd be head monitor, so it is a promotion, with commensurate benefits. I do like Ryan's style, so: when in doubt, ask yourself, *what he would like you to do with the scene.* If you get my drift?"

"Yes, sir. I believe I do, sir. Thank you. I'd love to take the position."

"I thought that might be the case. Come to my office after your shift. We'll dot the t's and cross the i's."

Gunther climbed out of the SUV onto the rock barren

beyond the forestation project's edge. His gut was churning, and it felt like he had an ice pick sticking into his brain. Ryan looked over and held up his hand-held.

"I could help," he offered.

"What is this?" demanded Gunther.

"A programmed response. Any studio clone nearing the set's perimeter feels ill. It's part of why I wanted Rowan asleep for this."

"They have us coming and going. How am I supposed to live my life knowing it's a lie?"

"The people you save aren't a lie. The alien clones really kill the human clones. You protect people, that's real."

"I... Oh, stardust! I'm useless like this, do what you have to." Gunther collapsed.

Ryan held his hand-held up. Before he could press a button, Gunther relaxed and came to his feet.

"Thanks, Arlene," said Ryan.

"I hate that! Where's your vehicle?" Gunther looked pale.

Ryan moved to the river's edge and looked for the tell-tale ripples that marked the location of his ATV.

"I thought you knew where it was?" said Gunther.

"I have it located on the GPS. Spotting it is harder than I thought it would be."

"GPS?"

"Global positioning system."

"Right, they mentioned it in a film I watched once. What exactly are we looking for?" Gunther scanned the river.

"Ah." Ryan stripped off his jacket and pants before diving in. Gunther watched as Ryan swam to a point, then climbed up and apparently stood on the water.

"Stardust! He isn't a madman. It's true." Gunther went back to his SUV. He gazed at his daughter. "No wonder you don't look anything like your mother or me. I still love you, my little girl." He hugged Rowan's sleeping form. "Arlene, if you have any compassion or humanity, let me say goodbye."

A moment passed, then Rowan's eyes flickered open.

"Daddy."

"My little girl. I need you to know. I love you. I'm proud of you. This Ryan, he's a decent man. Follow your heart. I'll miss you. Always believe in yourself."

"I love you, Daddy. I love you." Rowan hugged her father. They held each other for a long time. Tears poured out of Gunther's eyes, then an unhealthy humming sound reverberated through the SUV.

"I love you, baby," Gunther said one last time.

"I love you, Daddy." Rowan closed her tear-filled eyes and drifted back to sleep.

"Thank you." Gunther croaked through a tight throat. He turned and did a double-take as a large boxy machine, coloured to match the terrain, hovered beside him. A hatch opened in the machine's side. Water poured out, soaking Gunther's shoes.

"Nova blasted thing leaked!" Ryan appeared in the doorway. The blending was so complete he seemed to be standing in a rock.

"Come on, I have to move. Satellites scan this area. If they spot your vehicle, we're done for." Ryan stepped to the ground.

"I'll take her. You get the bag." Gunther carried Rowan into the ATV. One of the billets near the front of the troop's section was folded down. He lay her on it.

"I'll look after her." Ryan hung the bag in the empty weapons cabinet.

"I know, advantage of being a telepath."

"Gunther."

"I'm going." Gunther kissed Rowan's brow, then stepped from the ATV.

Ryan pressed a button on Rowan's billet, activating a restraint field, then closed the entrance door.

Gunther watched the ATV lift into the air. The unhealthy

hum made his teeth stand on edge. Knowing where to look, he could barely make out its silhouette as it wobbled, then accelerated across the river. He waved, knowing that no one would see. Tears streamed down his cheeks as he entered his SUV.

⊂━━◆━

Ryan could smell the hot circuits of the grav-nullifiers as he sped over the river. He spared the power gauge a glance. It showed 15 per cent battery charge.

"Nova blasted thing shorted out. Stardust, what I wouldn't give for an antiproton power pack."

Reaching a patch of bedrock, he set down and killed the AG field. The ATV settled on its suspension.

"Come on." He threw switches and watched as the other front motor blinked red. He killed the power to it. "Nova blast, maybe once it dries out." Directing power to the back motors, he drove towards Yancy's space field.

⊂━━◆━

Michael Strongbow leaned back in the control booth's chair. The vid-phone behind him beeped. He activated it.

"Hello, darling," he spoke when his wife's face appeared.

"Hi, honey. I was wondering how things were going."

"Not bad. How about with you?"

"I have a minor crisis. The caterer called. The shipment of salmon that they had coming in from Earth was contaminated in a loading accident. They can't get more until next fall's harvest. Would you rather have beef, chicken or processed fish protein at the launch party?"

"I ordered Earth salmon. It's not as if it was a last-minute arrangement, or they don't have time to find an alternate supply. This is supposed to be a top-drawer affair."

"I know, dear. You want to impress the potential backers for your new show. What can we do? The caterer says there isn't any Earth salmon to be had for love or money. You know what a delicacy anything Earth raised is."

"Tell the caterer that we'll take lobster for the same price. It's their foul-up. If they don't like it, tell them that I could arrange for a couple hundred boxes of takeout from the Garlic Palace. That should scare them."

"You are something, love. How's Ryan doing?"

"Not bad. I don't think I can keep his activities quiet any longer."

"Too bad. Nothing can ever be easy."

"Easy makes for boring e-entertainments."

"You know, Mike. I love you, and you're a good man, but sometimes it's like you're a heartless bastard."

Mike looked sadly at his desk. "Sorry, love. This job would drive me nuts if I didn't objectify."

Her eyes shifted to look at the base of the screen. "I know. I'll call the caterers."

"I love you, honey," said Mike.

Mrs. Strongbow smiled. It was like the sun coming out from behind a cloud. "I know. I love you too. I'd better sign off."

The screen went blank. Michael set the system to auto-record before leaving the room.

People raced through the control station's corridors. John stood in the control-room, screaming at Arlene, who was splitting her attention between recording the clones' grief and her boss.

"Is there a problem?" Mike stood in the control room's doorway.

GO NOT GENTLY INTO THAT DARK NIGHT

Ryan stared at the digital readout regarding his one functional tank of liquid nitrogen. It was nearly empty. "When that bottoms out, we'll look like a nova on infra-red." He glanced to where his battery monitor was reading 5 per cent. The press of a button brought a map up on the screen to his left. The screen flickered dark then bright, making it hard to read.

"Something, anything?" He examined the map, then smiled. "Only four kilometres." Turning the wheel, he sped toward his goal.

Henry spoke in Ryan's voice while projecting a graphic of his human friend into the communications web. "It's not my problem! You wanted her dead. I think it looks good on you."

On the vid, John's face reddened. "If I find out you're behind this, you fakey, I'll—"

"Roger yourself with a cattle prod! I quit, I don't need to take this!" Henry disconnected the communications link and dropped the graphic of Ryan's face. The ruined android body drummed its fingers against the control console. "Get here quick, Ryan. If they come asking for a face to face, we're nova blasted."

Arlene stepped into Michael Strongbow's office. Mr. Strongbow sat at his desk, speaking into a vid-phone. He smiled at his new employee and waved her to a comfortable seat in the small lounge area in the corner of the room. Arlene looked around. Everything was good quality, expensive but arranged to give a homey atmosphere. A large oil painting depicting a slender, small-busted, teenaged girl with long, chestnut hair hung on the wall. She was admiring the painting when Mike's voice disturbed her. "*'Kids in the Band'* was my first big hit."

Arlene jumped then turned to face her boss. He was smiling.

"It's a lovely likeness of the Marcy character."

"Isn't it." Mike motioned her to one of the loungers before taking one for himself. "Coffee?"

"No thank you, it keeps me awake if I drink it in my evening."

"I understand, my wife can't touch the stuff. Caffeine makes her hyper. I take it that John released you from his employ?" Mike settled in his chair.

"He said I'd never work on this planet again." Arlene shifted uncomfortably.

"His power is far less vast than his mouth. If it weren't for the popularity of *Angel Black*, I'd have canned him years ago. Unfortunately, I have to keep the shareholders happy."

"Too bad. Everyone hates him."

"Yes. It is a pity, but it happens."

"Mr. Strongbow…"

"Michael."

Arlene smiled warily. "Michael, what's going on?"

Michael stood up and paced as he spoke. "Did you know that I was instrumental in getting the *Right to Life Act* regarding clones passed?"

"No. I'm afraid I was a baby when it went through."

"It was terrible back then. When a series wrapped, they'd

kill all the principals. My wife and I lobbied to change the law so that the principals would be permitted to live out whatever time their biology allowed."

"It made shooting harder, but it only seems fair."

Michael stopped pacing and stared at his guest. "Nothing about our industry is fair. There are, however, varying degrees of injustice."

"The N.I.O.s?" Arlene looked at her feet.

"Exactly. When they drafted the *Right to Life* Legislation, they left the loophole of death occurring as a 'natural' consequence of show activity. If the law is followed in good faith, it works, but it's too easily circumvented."

"What does this have to do with Ryan stealing Rowan?"

"I care about Ryan, and Rowan for that matter. He might not agree, but I feel a bond of friendship with Ryan. We have a great deal in common. He loved Joslin. Losing her was a shattering blow. I wanted to help him try to build a life he would consider worth living. I also wanted to prevent Rowan's unnecessary death. I don't approve of N.I.O.s. Sadly, I couldn't infringe on John's show autonomy."

"So, you helped Ryan steal Rowan."

"It is a little-known fact that this is not the first time this sort of thing has occurred." Mike's eyes seemed to twinkle. "Now, about your new position."

"You said it was a brand-new series." Arlene leaned forward and looked eager.

"Yes, it's a thing that has never been done in the history of e-entertainment, a ground-breaking concept, and I want you to be head tech."

"Great, so what's it about?"

Michael grinned. "You must give me your word that you'll keep this top-secret until the premiere."

"You've got it."

Mike drummed his fingers. "The concept is an escape scenario..."

Ryan pulled up to the entrance doors of a low building made of stone and stopped the ATV. Two large, squat tracks of rock cut across the barren ground out of sight.

Moving to the troop compartment, he shut down the retaining field on Rowan's billet and looked at her. She still slept, but her skin was losing its unhealthy pallor.

"Rest gently, my princess." Ryan kissed his finger and touched it to her lips. She murmured and shifted position. Reactivating the field, he moved to the hatch and opened it. The heat hit him like a sledgehammer. For a second, he couldn't breathe.

"Stardust! It should at least dry everything out." Climbing out of the ATV, he moved to the building's door and read the sign mounted beside it.

'*DANGER NO TRESPASSING* - Geothermal Generating Station 62 - *high tension electricity, live steam, geothermic disturbances - Authorized personnel only* - All others will be prosecuted by order of Planetary Governing Council, planetary edict 872-7. Any unauthorized intrusion into this site carries a minimum sentence of fifteen standard Earth sphere months incarceration and a maximum sentence of three standard Earth sphere years incarceration. *Keep out!*'

"Talk about making your point!" Ryan inspected the door. Sweat dripped off him, and he felt faint. The security was keyed to trigger with any tampering, and all the releases routed through the central office.

"Public works, bless 'em, still trust a human operator over a machine. Just as well I don't need to get inside."

Ryan shuffled to the waste steam transfer track. Huge slabs had been set upon boulders flattened at the top and bottom to create a massive structure with uneven walls. The heat was nearly unbearable. Ryan nodded, then returned to the ATV. Stepping into the troop compartment was like diving into a cold lake, and a shiver ran up his spine. Moving to the bridge, he pulled the ATV in tight against the waste steam track.

"That should do nicely for heat, now for the rest." Ryan climbed to the ATV's roof and arranged the camouflage tarp to cover the gap between the ATV and the rock track. The tarp's colour shifted to match the trackway.

"Excellent." Sweat was dripping off him, and he could hardly breathe.

Returning to the ATV, he downed a litre of water before venturing back into the heat. Opening a hatch on the vehicle's side, he spooled out a cable ending in two alligator clips and left it looped by the water supply trackway. Wedging the grav-lifts, which he'd used to carry his bike, against one of the rock slabs that formed the structure's roof, he turned them on. The overstressed devices whined. Slowly, the edge of the slab lifted. Scrambling through the gap, Ryan dragged the electrical cable into the trackway. Most of the space was taken up by the pipe that supplied water to the generating station. A narrow walkway ran beside the pipe with high-tension power lines against the far wall.

Scrambling over the cold-water pipe, Ryan stood on the walkway, enjoying the cooler air inside. After steadying himself, he inspected the wiring. A minute later, he held the insulated alligator clips open over a power feed. "Here goes. Trust in insulation. I have faith in insulation. If this doesn't work, I'm barbeque." Ryan thrust forward, released the clips, and then leapt back.

Taking a deep breath, he scrambled back over the pipe and shut down the grav-lifts before returning to the ATV.

"Felony power distribution tampering. Felony power theft. Another trespassing count. Who says my life isn't working out?" he muttered as he moved to the cockpit.

Throwing a series of switches, he set the ATV to run off the outside power source and started recharging the tank of liquid nitrogen and batteries. "Let them try to see my heat signature with all the interference out there. Ryan, you are a clever boy."

John stared into the blank vid screen and seethed. The intercom buzzed. He slammed his hand down on it. The image of his secretary, a Middle-Eastern-looking woman with perfect features and a tight body, appeared on his screen.

"WHAT?" he snapped.

"Mrs. Tallman is here," replied the secretary.

"Send her in."

The office door opened. A diminutive woman, with greying, dark brown hair and angular features, stepped in. She was dressed in a pantsuit that androgenized her figure.

"Good afternoon, John." Her voice was crisp, each syllable clearly enunciated.

"Mildred, what happened to my nova blasted fakey?"

The small woman pulled one of the chairs around, so she could sit and look at John without having the sun in her eyes. "It would appear that someone kidnapped her."

"WHAT?!" John went red in the face and leapt to his feet.

"After you informed security, we did a satellite sweep. There were tire tracks near the banks of the Wolf River. When we investigated further, we found they were from a Sun Valley vehicle, one of the mid-sized ones. We found intermittent tracks from a power-bike on the road paralleling the opposite bank. They seemed to be heading toward the studio support town."

"Who?" John was almost apoplectic with rage.

"We don't know. It might be an obsessed fan. I've said for years we need tighter security against this sort of thing. We're reviewing Rowan's fan mail. There is so much of it it's likely to be a while before that offers up a viable suspect. We've also been checking the studio support town. There are always tourists coming in and out of the place." Mildred steepled her fingers and stared calmly at John.

"What about the satellite recordings?" John leaned against his desk, his fat belly hanging out over the top of his pants.

"We're reviewing them, but the surveillance is intermittent. Unless the satellite noticed something out of the ordinary, it wouldn't focus on it. At best we might get some indication of the vehicles that were used."

"WHY CAN'T YOU DO YOUR NOVA BLASTED JOB? YOU'RE THE SECURITY CHIEF FOR DIVINE'S SAKE!"

Mildred's eyes went cold, and her body tensed, her voice was icy. "Mr. Wilson! I was a security officer when you were still fouling your nappies; don't raise your voice to me! I have made it quite clear that our security system is antiquated. You, among others, have refused to allocate the funds to upgrade it. The theft of one of our characters was only a matter of time."

John looked at the small woman. Her gaze froze his blood. He cleared his throat before speaking. "I'm..." His voice cracked, and he tried again. "I apologize, I'm very upset by this. What is our next step?"

Mildred eyed the man in front of her with distaste. "My people are following up every lead, but without interviewing Rowan's associates, our investigation is hampered."

"You could review the raw data."

"I have one of my people doing that. There are quite a number of gaps where Rowan is concerned. Do all your techs check out for security?"

"Of course they do. It would reflect badly on me if I were to hire an unreliable tech."

"Very well, we'll keep looking for an outsider... for the moment." Mildred stood and, without waiting to be dismissed, strode from the room.

Gunther held Willa as they stood in their backyard and stared at the stars.

"Do you think maybe, someday?" began Willa.

Gunther held her tight. "No, and you mustn't either. We were blessed for the time we had her."

Willa rested her head on his shoulder. "We were, and I know somewhere out there she still loves us."

"I'm sure of it."

Willa released a sob. Gunther held her as his own tears came. "We love you, Rowan, our little girl. We will always love you," he whispered into the night. Under the cover of his grief, in the deepest, most private recesses of his mind, he began to plan.

A BRAVE NEW WORLD, YIKES!

"Help! Help! I can't get out. I'm trapped! HELP!"

Ryan awoke to Rowan's screams. Hitting the field deactivate button, he leapt from his billet and raced to her side.

"It's okay. It's okay, just press this button." Slipping his hand through a gap in the field over the control console, he deactivated the restraints.

"Stardust! I…" Rowan sat up, taking in huge gulps of air.

"Relax." Ryan sat on the billet beside her and took her hand.

"I…" Rowan swallowed. "I've had a thing about enclosed spaces ever since I was eight, and a bouncy castle deflated on top of me. I'm fine as long as I know I can get out."

"I'm sorry. I should have warned you. It's just you needed to sleep."

Rowan nodded, then glanced around the troop compartment. "This is your spaceship?" She sounded incredulous.

Ryan smiled. "No, this bucket of bolts is an ATV. A rather nova blasted one."

Rowan let out a sigh, tried to rise and collapsed. Ryan caught her arm and helped her to sit.

"Sorry, I was dizzy for a second." Rowan smiled. It was all Ryan could do to keep himself from kissing her. She was everything he knew she would be.

"Um…" Rowan looked shyly about the troop compartment.

"What?"

"Well... um... could you tell me where the bathroom is?"

Ryan moved to a panel on the wall and opened it. A toilet and a canvas bottomed sink, connected to the wall by flexible hoses, folded down. "I'm afraid this was a troop carrier, there isn't much in the way of luxury. I'll sit in the cockpit until you're done."

"I always thought the alien technology would be so impressive and this is it?" Rowan heard her own words and blushed. "I mean, I'm grateful for you saving me and all. It's just, well..." She hung her head.

"This is human tech. I wouldn't want to see a chameleonzoid try and use this rig." Ryan gestured towards the toilet and grinned.

Rowan began to chuckle, then took a deep breath and forced herself to still. "Don't make me laugh unless you packed me a change of clothes."

"I'll go forward." Ryan moved into the cockpit and closed the door. His screens displayed the area around the ATV. Shifting his dish to the information satellite, he listened to the news broadcast. There was no mention of Rowan or an intrusion of the studio grounds. "John must be keeping it quiet," he muttered. He checked the liquid-nitrogen tank, which read full, and the emergency batteries, which were topped out at 50 per cent. "Water damage."

The door opened, and Rowan entered the bridge. She leaned against the wall, breathing hard.

"Sit down." Ryan leapt to her side and helped lower her into the co-pilot's chair.

"I don't know what's wrong with me. I can't get enough oxygen." Rowan's skin had gone pale. Ryan took her pulse. It was racing.

"You're probably still anemic from the toxin. It will take a while for you to replace the red blood cells it destroyed." Fumbling under his seat, Ryan pulled out a package about a decimetre square and passed it to her.

"What's this?"

"Breakfast. Eat up, your body needs the fuel. Then you should go back to sleep."

"I think I'm all slept out for a while. What's that?" Rowan pointed at the main screen where the steam pipe's trackway was displayed.

"A geothermic energy transfer line."

"Geothermic? That thing looks like it was put together by the same people who built Stonehenge. As far as I know, there's only one geothermic plant in North America, and it's in Yellowstone. Somehow I think you could have found a parking space for your ship closer than that."

Ryan began to sweat, and he gripped the arms of his command chair. "You should eat."

"What did my father think you should tell me?" Rowan's face was pure focus.

"You need to rest, regain your strength. Eat your ration pack. I'll explain everything when you're stronger."

"No way, buster! You'll explain now, or I... or I'll..."

"What? Rowan, trust me. I do have your best interests at heart. Now eat your rations and go back to bed like a good girl."

Red tinted Rowan's cheeks despite her pallor. "Don't you dare pull that little girl garbage with me, mister! You want me to eat, fine! Tell me what's going on, and I'll eat. Keep silent, and I'll starve myself. I swear, I will!" Rowan stared at him defiantly.

"I always did have a thing for strong-willed women." Ryan shook his head.

"I'll take that as a compliment, I think. Now spill!"

Ryan nodded. "After we're underway, I promise. I'd have to tell you eventually anyway, and I need you to eat. For now, only the short version. You need to recover your strength."

"I can live with that." Rowan released the tab at the side of the ration box. The box folded out into a tray. "Sausage and eggs with a side of toast, and it's hot!"

"You need the protein, and there's no excuse for bad

food when you apply good tech."

Rowan picked up the black fork from the side of the tray. It was cool to the touch and slick against her fingers. "What is this made of?"

"Polycarbonate. About a hundred times stronger than tempered steel."

"Stardust!" She stabbed her sausage and took a bite. It was pleasant, far from the best she'd had but better than her father's rare attempts at making breakfast. At the thought of Gunther, she hung her head.

Ryan saw pain cross her features. He wanted to ask why, but over half a century of marriage had taught him that sometimes it was best to give a woman her space. "I'm going to go out to prep the vehicle. I'll only be a few minutes."

"Then you will tell me everything?"

"Everything is an awful lot. One thousand five hundred and fifty-seven years is a long time."

Rowan's mouth dropped open as Ryan moved to the troop compartment.

The ATV jolted over the bedrock plain. The liquid-nitrogen feed masking its heat signature was perfect. The batteries were sinking fast.

Rowan stared at the man beside her, who kept his eyes on the screen in front of him. She felt sick, and she knew it wasn't from the poison's effects.

"All those people died so somebody could watch TV? Farley cheated on me, so people could have a cheap thrill?"

"Not like TV. It's a full experience, all five senses, plus emotion. They tried to do thought, but the process is too complex." Ryan's voice was flat.

Rowan shook her head. She couldn't believe it, wouldn't believe it. It was too big, though oddly it made sense of so much. Taking a deep breath, she focused on a minor point, hoping that if she took it in little bites, she could wrap her brain around it. "Why the early twenty-first century?"

Ryan manoeuvred around an area of sand that would show his tire marks. "By the mid-twenty-first century, any university lab would have had the equipment to spot some of the control vectors we use. They couldn't make complex nano-bots, but they could spot them and get a good idea of what they were for. The clones have to be kept in the dark for the system to work."

"You are a real bastard!" Tears came to Rowan's eyes. "We're people! You turned us into puppets."

"Rowan, understand this. You aren't a person, not on this world. You're studio property, and I've stolen you."

"Stardust! You can't own people, that's sl—"

"I know that! They don't admit it though. Rowan, you were grown in a tank until your body was fifteen years old. Your memories were compiled out of archives of other clones' experiences, then imprinted on your brain. The process took less than a year."

"Less... That time I fell off the horse, and my dad picked me up and put me back on it so that I wouldn't be afraid of them?"

"Stock file. I don't know the code designation, creation wasn't my department."

"When Amitose saved my mom from cancer by making her a cyborg?"

"Your mother was a perfectly healthy clone, except for the studio's tinkering. I wasn't in on the start of the series."

"She suffered so much. She hated herself for so long because she wasn't totally human."

"That's e-entertainments. I don't make the rules."

"How could you?" Tears trickled over Rowan's enraged features.

Ryan bit his cheek, then spoke softly. "I couldn't... not anymore. I couldn't let you die." He rubbed the back of his neck; the muscles were like ropes. "Look, there's over a thousand years of catching up you need to do, and we aren't going to do it today. Go to bed, let your body heal."

"I can't sleep with all this going through my head. I can't."

Ryan stopped the ATV, pulled his hand-held from his pocket and pointed it at Rowan.

"Don't you dare, you son of a bitch! I—"

"Goodnight, Rowan." He hit a button.

"Ryan, you bas—" Rowan slumped in the co-pilot's seat.

"It will be better soon, I promise." Ryan carried her into the troop compartment and lay her on her billet. He paused, staring at her. "Don't hate me. I'm just another fakey trying to get by." He kissed her forehead before activating the retaining field and returning to the bridge.

Mildred sat in a padded swivel chair before a console that consisted mainly of screens. Her feet dangled nearly thirty centimetres above the floor. She reviewed the time log her assistant had highlighted. A speck appeared in the top left corner of the screen in front of her.

"Gene, centre main screen on section A-ten," she ordered.

"Complying," spoke the soft, male voice of the studio computer.

The image shifted. Now, much of it was a blue screen.

"Gene, enlarge main screen centre."

"Complying. Mildred, you are half an hour past your scheduled departure time. Should I call your husband to prevent worry?"

"He's working tonight. Gene, can you enhance the image's clarity?" Mildred pulled herself closer to the screen. It looked like a roughly man-shaped blob standing on a rock.

"With a tolerance level for image inaccuracy, I can."

Mildred bit her cheek. "Belay enhancement, run the recording."

On the screen, the human-shaped blob pulled something out of the rock that might have been a power-bike. The screen went blank.

"Gene, what happened to the image?"

"The satellite moved out of range. Do you want me to bring up the next images of the area in the log?"

"How much later is the image?" Mildred stroked her chin.

"The surveillance gap was fifteen minutes and twenty-seven seconds."

Mildred shook her head. "Gene, bring up the most recent picture of this region on screen number three." Mildred peered at a screen to the right of her main one, then looked back and forth between them. "Gene, are you sure these are the same area?"

"Yes."

Mildred slammed her fist into the arm of her chair. "Stardust! The boulder is missing. Our Johnny has some kind of stealth vehicle! Gene, get me Running Deer, no use him checking bike rentals. Reset the satellite scans to expanding circles around the set region, look for tire tracks. Whoever took her went cross-country. This is one clever Johnny!"

"I require authorization from the chief producer to alter satellite scan areas."

"Gene, call Mike. If we're going to catch this one, we have to hurry." A gleam entered Mildred's eye. "This just got interesting."

⬤══✦

Greg sat in front of the show's control station. It was like the characters had gone mad. They'd fought almost constantly since his shift started, beating information out of alien clones, trying to find Hunoin. Out for blood would be an understatement, crazed better fit their condition. He'd tried to moderate them, but every time, their own biology overruled his manipulations.

On the main screen, a k-no-in threw a punch. The screen showed Fran's perspective. She ducked and lashed out with lithium grease coated claws. Greg adjusted her adrenaline to speed her reaction time. She leapt back from her stricken foe's final blow.

"At least one thing is going as I intended," observed John's voice.

Greg spun in his chair. His serpent-like tongue flicked out as his slit-pupil eyes widened into almost rounds. "Ssir, I didn't hear you come in."

"Evidently. This is why Rowan had to die. The rage, the aggression, this is a spectacular way to start the next season." John plodded up to the control station.

"They're mad, but, if you don't mind me ssaying sso, that'ss all they are. I don't think the fanss will like the ssingle emotion asspect."

"I do mind you saying so. This is my show." On a side screen labelled 'Angel's perspective,' a male otterzoid was falling toward jagged rocks. The perspective swooped down, caught the alien and carried him aloft.

"Where is Hunoin? Next time I won't catch you, scum. Read my thoughts if you think I'm bluffing." Angel's voice issued from a speaker. Her emotional monitors showed levels of pain and rage higher than she'd ever known.

"Magnificent. When we edit this down, we'll have at least six episodes." John rubbed his hands together.

"With nothing to counterpoint the violencsse and rage, people will dessenssatisse, and it won't fly with veteranss. It hitss too closse to home."

"You obviously know nothing about pleasing an audience!"

On the screen, the otterzoid male was screaming. "I don't know where she is. I don't, I swear I don't. Please, please, NO!"

Angel released the otterzoid and watched as it became a red splat on the jagged rocks below. "Next!" was all she said.

"There iss another problem. The casst aren't being csircumsspect. I've had complaintss from *The Sstation Housse*, *Paramedic Ssquad*, *Defenderss of the Crysstal* and *Detective Dave*. It iss becoming difficult to maintain sshow autonomy."

"Let them worry about their own show autonomy. This will blow over in a day or two. They're only fakeys. They don't feel the way we do." John waved his hand dismissively at the screens as he left the room.

Greg looked at the screen labelled Farley. The monitors registering anger and grief were almost topped out. He was holding the head of a felinezoid under the surface of a stream, screaming as tears flowed down his cheeks.

"No, they aren't like uss. They're more human."

DEDUCTIVE REASONING

Mildred crouched beside the tire track holding a hand-held. She ran it across the track then looked into its screen, which filled with information.

Possible matches - T 5 light troop carrier.
- AS 8 armoured fast assault vehicle.
- A 4 evac. ambulance.
- E 9 ground exploratory vehicle.
- C outdoorsman terrain master.
- C salamander series fire truck.

Mildred stopped reading the list after the first few possibilities. "Hand-held, eliminate all vehicles that do not have camouflage capabilities." The screen shifted, displaying a shortened list.

Possible matches - T 5 light troop carrier.
- AS 8 armoured fast assault vehicle.
- C outdoorsman terrain master.
- C naturalist class research vehicle.

"Better, but not good enough." She stroked her chin. Her body needed sleep, but the challenge was too exciting. After years of routine, her skills were getting a workout. "Hand-held, eliminate all vehicles incapable of carrying a power-bike inside them."

Possible matches - T 5 light troop carrier.
- C naturalist class research vehicle.

"Hand-held, get a list of all indicated vehicles currently on New Gaea."

The hand-held beeped. "Please stabilize for uplink," appeared on the screen.

Mildred set the device on a nearby boulder, then walked back to the tire track. She examined the area, pausing above a bit of discoloured dirt. She touched it and sniffed her fingers. "Hmm." Taking a bottle from her pocket, she scooped the soil into it and walked back to her hand-held.

The screen now read, "There is one naturalist class research vehicle registered with the New Gaea DMV. Ownership is by S.E.T.E., currently in use by Mildred Tallman, head of studio security."

Mildred looked over her shoulder at the black, seven-metre long by one hundred and eighty centimetres wide vehicle behind her. "Stardust!"

Taking her hand-held, she strode back to the van and stepped through its side door.

The front consisted of two swivel chairs behind twin controls, while the back was set up with four fold-down billets, situated two to a side, backed by a small refrigerator, microwave and sink. Behind that was a compact lab that could be closed off with a curtain. A fold-down toilet hung on the back wall.

Moving to the lab, she poured a portion of the soil she'd collected into an autoanalyzer and pressed the activate button.

"Analysis will take approximately five minutes," spoke a female voice.

"Let me know when it's done, Muriel."

Mildred moved to the driver's seat and settled herself. It was as far forward as it would go.

"I've stolen my dream clone. I know they can't see me with normal light. The infrared caught nothing... infrared caught nothing." She flipped open her hand-held. "Hand-held, previous list. Does either of the vehicles mentioned have infrared masking capacity?"

Match - T 5 light troop carrier.

"Oh, boy! Muriel, connect me with Planetary Defence."

"Placing the call."

"Hello, Planetary Defence, may I help you?" A man with dark-brown skin and round features appeared on the screen to Mildred's right.

Mildred swivelled her chair to face the screen. "This is reserve Major Mildred Tallman, Head of S.E.T.E. Studio Security. Give me a direct line to Colonel Burtch."

The line went silent for nearly a minute, then it picked up.

"Milly, what can I do for you?" The voice was deep and measured as if each word was carefully chosen. The face on her screen was of a balding, Caucasian man of late middle-years.

"Bob, we've got a big problem. Some nutcase is running around in a troop carrier. I don't know if its guns are active. If they are, we'd better get on it. This crackpot stole one of our clones. There's no telling what he'll do next."

The rest of the call passed quickly, then Mildred sat back in the driver's seat. "What is he up to?" she asked the air.

"I have completed the analysis," said the computer.

"What is the gunk, Muriel?"

"It's a mix of sand and Wellington 17 heavy-density hydraulic fluid."

"Hmm… 'Curiouser and curiouser, said Alice'," quoted Mildred as she stroked her chin.

Arlene recorded the phone conversation. The monitor feed

from inside the studio vehicle was giving her some nice shots of Mildred.

"The images the satellite caught of her outside will splice together nicely." Michael pulled a chair up behind Arlene and sat.

"I worry that without empathic feeds, people won't be interested in these clips." Arlene turned her attention to a side screen that showed the front of Ryan's ATV. The focus shifted to the power meter. It showed 40 per cent.

"We'll keep the non-empathic clips short, only enough to give context. It will work out."

"Won't Mildred object?" Arlene shifted her view to Rowan's screen.

"Her grandson is in university. I've found that moral outrage tends to dissipate in a direct ratio to the credits offered, especially when it is needed by one's family."

Arlene shrugged. "Tell me one thing. Am I being recorded? Am I part of your great experiment?"

Michael smiled enigmatically.

"I'm in a blasted fish-bowl," griped Arlene.

"Gives you a different perspective about what we do, doesn't it? Have you noticed something odd about Rowan's bio-readings?" Mike indicated the screen to Arlene's left.

"I think the nano-bots are having trouble keeping the toxin tied up. They were never meant to hold it dormant this long."

"Keep an eye on them. Hopefully, Ryan notices that something is wrong. Otherwise, this could be a very short series."

"We could help them."

"No. I've done for Ryan all I can. It's up to him now. I have to answer to the shareholders, and the public loves a champion."

"Wakey wakey, lunchtime." Ryan knelt by Rowan's billet

and gently shook her shoulder.

"Hmm." Half asleep, she nuzzled his hand. "Farley, I don't want to get up, I'm comfy."

"Rowan."

Rowan's eyes shot open, and she stared into Ryan's face. Her gaze took in the troop compartment. Her expression raced through confused, to scared, to realization, to anger. "Don't ever do that again!" She pushed Ryan's hand away. "I won't be your puppet! I'm an adult; I'll sleep when I please."

"I'm sorry," said Ryan.

"For what? Putting me to sleep, or for holding my strings for the last five years?" Rowan sat up. Her colour was better.

Ryan shook his head. "You know, you aren't the only one with problems here. You could try and show a little gratitude. The studio was going to kill you."

"Oh, sorry, master. Let your humble slave fluff your pillows for you."

Ryan stood up. "You're always like this before you think things through, then you always end up apologizing."

"How would you know?" snapped Rowan.

Ryan stared at her. "Come on, Row. I've been you. I didn't just make the show. I've experienced life through your eyes, through Farley's, through Gunther's. Through all of you."

"You've been… you experienced it when Farley and I…"

Ryan blushed.

"That is sick!" Rowan looked away from him.

"And you never watched video porn? Here's your ration box. When Her Majesty is done, it would be in her own self-interest to let me run a check on the nanobots that keep her from dying of cancer. Oh yes, I should mention that if I don't find a place to recharge soon, she might have to get out and push." Ryan stomped into the bridge.

Rowan hung her head. She didn't know whether to be angry, scared or embarrassed. She settled on all three. She closed her eyes and thought with all her might. "Daddy." For the first time in five years, no voice answered the call. "Stardust!" Reaching for the ration pack, she opened it to find a roast beef sub. "At least he feeds his slaves well." She bit into the sandwich.

Ryan stared into the screen of his hand-held. Worry furrowed his brow.

"What is it? Can't find the button to make me a sex slave?" Rowan sat in the co-pilot's seat scowling.

"Actually, making you become infatuated with me would be easy."

"What?" Rowan straightened in the chair. "When I first saw you, I felt... well... I felt something. Was that...?"

"Arlene probably altered your body chemistry so that you'd want to go with me."

"Arlene." Rowan's curiosity was slowly conquering her rage.

"Another tech. She was monitoring the shift when I rescued you."

"So why don't I feel that way now? Infatuated, I mean."

Ryan looked up from his screen. "Because maybe I'm not as bad as you'd like to believe. Rowan, I'm not going to lie. I'm stupidly, head over heels, puppy dog, in love with you. I've followed your life since my discharge. I know you don't know me. I don't expect anything, but that doesn't change how I feel."

Rowan sat back, staring at her benefactor for a long minute. "What exactly am I supposed to say to that?"

Ryan reached across and touched the back of her hand. "I'm hoping you'll say that you'll let yourself get to know me. No pressure, no expectations. Maybe we could, at least, be friends. I'm not such a bad guy." Ryan adjusted a setting on his hand-held and once more checked the screen.

Rowan stared at the floor. "I'd kinda like to get to know you, especially since it seems my life depends on you."

"Stardust!" Ryan slammed his hand down on his armrest. His face looked grave.

"Not the response I expected."

"What? Sorry, it's, well..." Ryan tapered off.

"It's about me, my body, isn't it?" Rowan pulled the screen around to examine it. The information was meaningless symbols and numbers to her.

"Why don't you let me worry about—"

"If you know me as well as you say you do, you know what I'm going to say to that." Rowan's face was grave.

Ryan sighed. "I didn't like being a puppeteer, but it takes a bit to break the habit."

"So?" Rowan touched his hand and caught his eyes with her own.

Ryan swallowed in a dry mouth. "It's the nano-bots holding the poison. They were only designed with a short operating life. They're beginning to break down."

"And this means?" Rowan bit her lip.

"They're slowly releasing the toxin back into your system. That's why your red cell count has been so slow in coming up."

"You have my permission to pull my strings, puppet master. Do something. Dying is not on my to-do list for at least another fifty years."

A shadow crossed Ryan's features, but Rowan missed it. "I can't do anything about it. I was hoping to get the poison purged when we reached the Switchboard Station, but you won't last that long."

"The what? Never mind, tell me later. So maybe you could use some of the other nano-bots swimming around in me to pick up the slack?"

Ryan shook his head. "There are limits on after insertion reprogramming of nano-bots."

"Stardust! So maybe a hospital? You still have hospitals, don't you?"

"We still have them, but your retina and voiceprints aren't on file and..."

"And?"

"You were the best-liked character on the number three rated e-entertainment. Your face is better known than the Chief Councillor of the United Earth Systems' Parliament."

"This is being a star? What can we do?"

Ryan fell silent. His eyes strayed to the charge meter in his dash. It read 10 per cent.

"First, I have to find a power source or none of this will matter. This piece of stardust is all that's keeping us clear of satellite pickups." Pressing a button, he scanned a map of the surrounding area. A smile split his face. "Kadar no radar. Could work."

"What's a Kadar?" Rowan scanned the screen but couldn't see the name anywhere.

"Kadar's an old space services buddy of mine. The man had no sense of dangerous situations. It got so bad he wasn't allowed to leave the ship without someone to steer him away from trouble. He was our ship's doctor when we did the offensive on Murack Five." A shudder ran up Ryan's spine, and he went pale.

"What?" Rowan rested her hand on his shoulder.

Ryan ignored the gesture and continued, "Last I heard, he was in Williamville. He owes me, big." Ryan turned towards the nondescript dot on the map and hit the accelerator.

AN OLD FRIEND

Henry watched the workpeople through the hangar bay's camera as they filled the space left by the ATV with crates and secured them in place.

"Any idea what this stuff is, Zack?" The smaller worker, a young woman with ebony skin and blonde hair dressed in sexless, green coveralls, extracted the grav-lift from a slot on the box she'd stacked.

"Manifest said coffee and orange-mist air freshener." The larger worker, a plump, Caucasian man of middle-years in green coveralls, adjusted the control on a grav-lift, and his crate drifted to the top of the pile.

"Don't put that there," Henry ordered through the intercom.

"What? Who?" Zack jerked around, scanning the room.

"Stack the coffee behind the air freshener."

"Why's it matter?" The woman looked directly into the video pickup.

"Well, sweet cheeks. The coelenteratezoids love orange-oil spray. It puts them in the mood. I'm sure you know all about that."

The woman blushed but couldn't quite stop a smile. "I'm called Ardra, not sweet cheeks."

"So, you're trading with the Zoders," said Zack.

"Coelenteratezoids, chubby. This was their system before they sold us this rock, and we still have to share their sun, so best show some respect."

"Okay, you're trading with the coelenteratezoids."

"Nah... that would be illegal, this is a gift for a friend."

"Yeah, right. No skin off my nose. Long as I get paid, it's none of my business. What's with the coffee?"

"We're going inter-system. My captain figures it will turn a bit of credit with the crowd on the Switchboard Station."

"Yeah. Can see how the poodycats would like it."

"Zack, they're felinezoids," objected Ardra.

"Thanks, sweet... Ardra. Please stack the coffee behind the air freshener." Henry continued monitoring as Zack and Ardra filled the vacant space.

Ryan saw the ledge coming up and turned the wheel. Nothing happened.

"What the?" he gasped.

"Ryan, that's a cliff!" Rowan clutched the arms of the co-pilot's seat.

"I KNOW THAT'S A CLIFF!" Ryan hit the brakes as the ATV careened forward.

"RYAN!"

"Stardust, stardust, stardust!" Half-panicked, he scanned the control console for the switch he needed. He'd found it when the ATV launched itself over the cliff face.

There was a silent moment that seemed to last forever, then the ATV crashed, throwing him against his safety harness. A screech filled the cabin, loose bundles of wire and fibre optic cable fell from the gutted consoles, and everything slid to the right. There was another crash and a sick, whining sound. The smell of burning insulation filled the air, then everything came to a stop.

"Stardust! Are you okay?" Ryan reached forward and tried to get a damage report from the computer. Almost everything was reading red.

"I THOUGHT YOU KNEW HOW TO DRIVE THIS THING!" Rowan sounded shrill even to herself.

"When did I ever say that? I was a space forces *engineer*!

I only learned to drive these things well enough to move them in and out of my repair bay."

"Great. Just great. Can you fly this fabled ship of yours, or is that supposed to take care of itself?"

"I have a pilot's rating. Not a great one, but I'm checked out for the *Star Hawk*." Ryan was returning heat with heat.

Rowan looked at him. "Sorry, I'm kinda scared."

"I know." Ryan smiled.

"What happened?"

"That I have to find out." Ryan stood. "Coming?"

"Can you fix it?" Rowan stood on the bedrock and broken-gravel barren that surrounded the ATV. A ledge of rock over three metres high was about fifty metres behind them. Bits of the ATV formed a trail from the base of the ledge to its present location. Ryan lay under the front axle muttering words she assumed represented profanity from several alien tongues. The vehicle was still blending with its surroundings.

"Oh yeah. Piece of cake. If I could get some industrial strength hydraulic hose, a new pump, and oh, let us not forget, hydraulic fluid, two electric motors with control circuits, not to mention tools and at least three days, none of which we have. I shattered both rear motor casings. Why did I gut the proximity alarms?"

"I'm sure you had a good reason."

"What bugs me is I did. I needed the parts to restore the *Star Hawk*'s internal sensors."

"Well, you see. What happened in the first place?"

"The hydraulics bled out. I'd gutted so many systems for parts I must have disconnected the warning monitors. We lost steering and brakes in one fell swoop."

"Oh, I... Oh!" Rowan collapsed against the side of the ATV.

Ryan crawled out from under the machine. "Nova blast!" Racing to Rowan, he helped her to sit, then pulled his hand-held from his pocket.

"The nano-bots are breaking down faster than I expected."

"Kinda figured that. Am I dead?"

"No! I won't allow that. No way, no how." Ryan picked her up and carried her into the ATV, heading toward her billet.

Rowan shook her head. "I want to see where we're going."

Ryan nodded. Taking her to the bridge, he secured her in the navigator's chair. Settling in his own seat, he began throwing switches.

"What are you doing?" Rowan painfully shifted position to watch him.

"I've killed the stealth."

"They'll see us!"

"Only if they look in the right place." Ryan pressed a button, and a discordant hum went through the cabin. The angle on the screen shifted, so the ground appeared to be sinking below them. "Come on, Come on." Ryan pushed forward on a lever, and the ATV jerked ahead.

"What?"

"Anti-grav and air turbines still work. At least well enough. Without stealth, I might have enough power to get us to Williamville."

"Suppose they see us?"

Ryan reached across and took her hand. "Then, they see us. We're in this together."

"May the Divine be with us."

"I'll take all the help I can get."

The ATV tilted dangerously to one side, and the smell of smoke filled the air. Ryan adjusted a control, and the craft levelled. "Though if the Divine has some mark-four grav-nullifiers it could lend us, it would be a real help."

Mildred had stripped to the waist, and still, sweat poured off her. The geothermic generating station was to her right.

She used the evening light to inspect a short length of cable that dangled against the cold-water supply track.

"Maybe not so dangerous after all."

Reaching into her pants pocket, she pulled out her handheld. A minute later, the image of Colonel Burtch appeared.

"Milly, so far our scans have turned up blank. Have you got something for me?" The colonel seemed nervous.

"Maybe. Focus your scans closer to the set region. I think our boy went to ground last night at geothermal generating station sixty-two."

"I'm getting stupid in my old age. It's a ground pounder trick, for when you need to recharge your heat dampening stores."

"He also stole power from the system." Mildred crossed her fingers. As an officer, she knew she had to report it, as head of studio security, it could lose her her military assistance.

"He stole... I see. Probably running on batteries. Not much of a threat."

"Bob," began Mildred.

"Not to worry, Milly. The studio is a major source of revenue for this planet, not to mention the United Earth Systems. I'll keep up the search. We can't have people stealing studio property, when would it end? This kind of thing could have us all up to our epaulettes in fakeys."

"Thanks, Bob." Mildred killed the line and inspected the ground.

"So where would I go. I've got full batteries, for now. Hmm." Mildred stroked her chin as she strode to the live steam track. There was a depression beside the track with a puddle of sticky goop on the rock. "Interesting." Pulling a plastic vial from her pants pocket, she scooped up some of the goop. "Bet I know what this is." She grinned as she returned to her vehicle. "For that matter, where did I get a T-five light troop carrier in the first place? One that leaks hydraulic fluid. Hmm."

Stepping into the vehicle was like diving into a cold lake,

and she paused to enjoy the goosebumps rising on her skin.

"Muriel, place a call to Michael Strongbow." Mildred was doing up the buttons on her shirt when the studio head's face appeared on screen.

"Mildred, what can I do for you?"

Mildred looked at her handsome, charming boss and didn't trust him as far as she could have thrown a planet. "Michael, are you still a member of that tech restorer's society?"

"Why, yes, I am. My old tank is nearly fully operational. She's the one I actually served on during the—"

"Fascinating. I need your help with something."

"What?"

"It's about the Rowan situation. I think I may have a lead."

Rowan's breath was ragged. Ryan's gaze kept shifting from her to his gauges and back.

"I'm not going to make it, am I?" Rowan could feel her pulse racing.

Pulling his hand-held from his pocket, Ryan hit a key with one hand as he held the steering with the other.

Rowan's pulse slowed. "I... What did you do?" Rowan took a deep breath.

"I released the oxygenated, artificial blood in your control pack. It should buy us time." Ryan glanced at his power gauge, then at his main screen. Beneath them were line upon line of orchards, pierced by a long straight road. He dropped his altitude to centimetres off the road. The lights in the cabin were dim, and the screens so dull he could barely see where he was going. The power gauge flashed at 1 per cent, then the console went black. Everything jolted, and there was a grating sound. Ryan threw a switch. A hum ran through the cabin, and the main screen lit up.

"At least that front engine's good for something."

"What?" Rowan looked at him quizzically.

"Regenerative braking, it's giving me enough to see."

"Speaking of brakes." Rowan gestured to the screen. They were drifting toward the edge of the road.

"Got none. I told you the hydraulics were dead. Only the regenerative is working."

"Stardust!" Rowan gripped the arm of her chair as the ATV skidded into a tree. There was a jolt that threw them back onto the road where they dragged to the left until they stopped. The lights went out.

"What now?" asked Rowan.

A flashlight beam split the blackness. Rowan found herself hauled up on Ryan piggyback. A moment later the flashlight's beam highlighted a handle on the troop section's exit hatch. Ryan's hand grabbed the handle, the door opened, and evening light flooded the ATV. Ryan leapt onto the road and took off at a jog.

"It's only a kilometre or so to Williamville. We'll make it, you'll see."

Rowan held on for all she was worth. Her guts were sore from bouncing up and down with Ryan's jog. She couldn't fault him for the ground he covered. The road came out from between neatly planted rows of orange trees into the midst of a collection of small, identical, 'huts' was the only word she could think of. Each was made of native stone, mortared in place and was about nine metres cubed, with a peaked roof of black tiles. Several people watched her and Ryan pass. They all wore an orange coverall with a pattern of chain links embroidered over the breast pocket.

In what could generously be called the town's centre was a large, stone building, nearly thirty metres long by ten deep and three stories tall, with a peaked, black roof. Ryan slammed through the glass and steel doors at the building's front into a reception room. Panting, he staggered to the main desk. A small woman with short, dark hair, wearing green coveralls with embroidered chain links, sat behind a computer screen.

"Can I help you?" she asked.

"I need to see the doctor. It's an emergency." Ryan leaned against the desk, still carrying Rowan.

"I can call for an ambulance, sir. The hospital in Ball Tower is much better equipped than our infirmary."

"No! I have to see Kadar. Tell him it's Ryan from the *Star Hawk*. Tell him... Tell him, Wesnakee."

The woman at the desk stared at Ryan, then pressed a button on a console built into her counter and spoke softly into a microphone. A moment later, her eyes widened, and she nodded.

"Doctor Kadar will be here as quickly as he can. I'm to escort you to the infirmary."

Rowan's head lolled as Ryan carried her. She was vaguely aware of passing a cafeteria and a little further on a kitchen. She felt Ryan lay her on an examination table, then a retaining field came down and held her in place. She heard a door closing. White lights glared into her eyes.

"I know you hate this, but you'll need less oxygen," said Ryan, then everything went black.

Ryan opened and closed the cupboards that lined the infirmary's walls until he found the portable oxygen rig. Attaching a mask, he started the feed and put it on Rowan's sleeping form. The infirmary was a large room with five narrow beds in addition to the examination table. A diagnostic monitor occupied the wall above Rowan's head, and everything was antiseptically white.

"Ryan. I didn't believe it until I saw you." The voice was little more than a whisper.

Ryan jerked around. A wizened, dark-skinned man, dressed in a green coverall that hung off him like a sack, stood in the doorway.

"Kadar, what happened?" Ryan moved to help support the man.

"The allowable treatments have proved less than effective. Why have you come, old friend?"

"I need your help. Ro... My friend has been poisoned."

Kadar pulled away from Ryan's supporting hand and shuffled to the examination table. He looked at Rowan, then froze.

"Please, tell me you didn't do this! Tell me she's one of those youngsters who get themselves altered to look like the character."

"I didn't think they permitted e-entertainments here."

Kadar sighed and looked towards the ceiling. "I'm in prison, not under a rock. We aren't allowed e-entertainments, but they do let us have magazines. By the Divine, man! Do you know the trouble you could get into, have gotten into?"

"I need you to help her." Ryan moved to the side of the examination table and took Rowan's hand.

"I can't be a party to this. This prison may not be a country club, but there are places that are far worse."

"Kadar, please!"

The wizened man turned away. "No. I'll not report you, but aiding you is out of the—"

"Do you remember Wesnakee? Henry and I disobeyed a direct order to get you out."

"I haven't forgotten."

"Neither have I. I still remember what it was like to have a felinezoid particle beam explode my eye. I still remember how much it hurt as you regrew it. I still remember bludgeoning that guard to death, all because you—"

"SHUT UP!" The shout was little more than a regular voice and left Kadar doubled over. He slowly straightened, taking deep breaths. "All right, I'll help you. What can they do in the time I have left? What do you need?"

"First, Rowan treated. Second, the ATV I was driving is

smashed up about a kilometre out of town. Can you get it camouflaged somehow?"

Moving to the monitor board, Kadar activated it. "An ATV? Is it inside the perimeter zone?"

"It's in the orchards."

The screen displayed Rowan's vital signs, blood gasses and cell counts, as well as starting a scan for infectious agents.

"Do you know what's wrong with her?" The doctor examined the readouts, his face a mask of concern.

"She was dosed with Virtion leech venom. Nano-bots have tied it up. They're degrading, releasing the toxin back into her system." Ryan stared at the readouts. He knew just enough to know it wasn't good.

"Markus, quick reference Virtion leech venom, effects on human biology."

Lines of text appeared on the screen sitting above a desk in the room's corner.

"This computer is incredible, far more than I need. The studio donated it to the correctional department when they upgraded. Never understood why they picked the name though." Kadar moved to the screen and read.

"Can you help her?" Ryan fidgeted, shifting his gaze from Rowan's readings to her beautiful, pale face.

"Let me read. Go out to Sara at the front desk. Tell her I've vouched for you. She'll be able to arrange for some people to hide your vehicle." Kadar became absorbed in his reading as Ryan left the room.

Minutes later, Ryan was back holding Rowan's hand.

Kadar looked up from his screen. "Stardust. This toxin is a thing of nightmare. Neurologic and hemoclasic. I'm sorry, Ryan. I'd need a selective-blood dialyser. Your only hope is to get her to a proper hospital."

"I can't do that. The show's producer is trying to kill her."

"My boy, she's already as good as dead. I cannot remove the toxin here, and when the nano-bots holding it degrade, she will die."

"You have to try something. Please."

Kadar stared at Ryan in mute compassion. "If we had control of the nano-bots, there might be something."

Ryan pulled his hand-held from his pocket. "We do. I have the nano-bots control codes. Only I can't adjust their program enough to get them out of her."

"How did you get the control sequence?"

"My hand-held is the deluxe unit, it has a decode function."

Kadar nodded. "Really. Understand, this is a long shot, and much could go wrong."

"Fine. What do we do?"

"First, order all the nano-bots carrying the venom to congregate in her left hand."

"They won't all go. There's an in-built concentration limit to prevent the amputation option."

Kadar moved to Rowan's right side and hung a bag of artificial blood. "I do not intend to lop off her hand. So, do it."

Ryan pressed a button that brought a diagram of Rowan's circulatory system up on his screen. He entered the code to control the nano-bots dealing with the poison, then tapped a go-to command and the left hand. "That's the best I can do. It's maybe 20 per cent of them."

"It will do. Now I go back to the earliest days of my profession." Kadar placed a collection tray beneath Rowan's wrist. "In ancient times, they believed the blood of a slave was impure, and that by letting it they could heal. Your lady here needs to be rid of the impurities." With expert ease, he placed a tourniquet around her upper arm, then slit the vein in her wrist.

"WHAT ARE YOU DOING?"

"Order the nano-bots into the blood. Let them purge, and be patient, this is only round one."

Ryan pressed a button on his controller and watched as the tray filled with blood.

Kadar placed a pressure dressing against the wound

and took the tray to his desk. "Now order these nano-bots to release the toxin and go into passive maintenance mode."

"We should do it in another room, so the signal doesn't reach the ones still in Rowan."

"Be quick about it, and bring the tray back here immediately."

Ryan took the tray and his controller out of the room. When he returned, Kadar had a beaker and a syringe sitting on his desk.

"Now what?" Ryan placed the tray of blood on the table.

"The nanobots' specific gravity is nearly double that of the venom. Thus, centrifugal force should separate them." Kadar poured the blood into the beaker and put a stopper in its top.

"Where's the centrifuge?"

"For this volume of fluid?" Kadar rummaged in his desk drawer, producing a ball of twine and a long, thin bag made to carry portable oxygen cylinders. "Put the bottle in this bag, tie the cord to it, go outside and swing it. Once it forms strata, pour off the top half. Bring me the rest."

Ryan rubbed his arms while Kadar injected the separated fluid into the flow of artificial blood going into Rowan. This was the seventh time he'd watched this show.

"I am pleased to hear someone managed to salvage Henry. He may be a polymer pervert, but he was a loyal friend."

"Keep it under your hat. I don't need any more trouble than I'm already in."

Kadar laughed; it was an unhealthy wheezing sound. "You couldn't be in more trouble than you're already in. The nano-bots are in place, activate their seek and capture program."

Ryan pressed a button on his hand-held. He noticed that

the infirmary's window was brightening with the coming dawn. "How's she doing?"

Kadar looked at the bio readings. "Much better, although I don't like using this much artificial blood. It puts a strain on the liver. Still, her oxygenation's good. What does your hand-held have to say about her little helpers?"

"Between those that wore out and the ones damaged by the spinning, only about half the venom grabbers are working. Only about 10 per cent of them have locked onto venom."

"Excellent! I think it is safe to let the remaining nano-bots keep the concentration down until you can have her treated properly."

"Should I wake her up?" Ryan smiled at Rowan.

"Just a tick." Kadar pulled the dressing off Rowan's wrist and glued the incision closed before applying a layer of artificial skin to finish the job.

Ryan pressed a button. The studio nano-bots in Rowan went to work collecting the sedative from her body and returning it to her control pack.

A long minute passed before her eyes fluttered open. She looked up into Ryan's exhausted but smiling face. She smiled back at him and said, "You look awful."

"You're not exactly ready for a photo-shoot yourself." On impulse, he kissed her forehead.

"Ryan, I'd prescribe sleep for you," said Kadar.

"Can't. We've got to keep moving."

"Hogwash. She can't be moved for at least a few hours. Now stretch out on one of the beds. I promise not to let you oversleep."

Ryan made to object. An enormous yawn stopped him. "A couple of hours. Are you sure the ATV is hidden?"

"My boy, half the convicts in this place were ground pounders. We'll be lucky if it hasn't been re-commissioned and flown into battle. Now go to sleep."

Ryan nodded and collapsed on the closest of the beds.

INJUSTICE IN THE STATE

Rowan sat on the infirmary bed and gazed at Ryan where he slept.

"A pleasant enough looking man." Kadar shuffled closer, holding a bulging gym bag.

"What? How'd you know I was..."

"Body language. You lean towards him, the set of your shoulders is quite relaxed, and your facial expression is extremely proprietary." Kadar seemed to pull in on himself, and he grimaced.

Rowan leapt to her feet and had to steady herself against the bed before she could grab a chair and pull it over.

"Thank you." Kadar lowered himself into the seat. "My people found this in the ATV. I'm assuming it belongs to you." He passed her the gym bag.

Rowan accepted it and opened the top zipper. A tear came to her eye. She hugged it to her. "Thank you, Carl."

"Mementos?" Kadar slouched in the chair.

"Treasures. Are you all right?"

"No, I'm far from all right."

"Can I help?"

Kadar smiled wearily. "I doubt it. I'm dying. Radiation-induced cancer. It can be quite painful. The medical nano-bots slow the process. It's the same thing that killed Ryan's old body."

"What?" Rowan glanced at the sleeping man. "His old body? You mean he's a clone, like me?"

Kadar took a deep breath. "Not exactly like you. Could you get me the blue bottle of pills from my desk? This is a rather bad session."

Rowan looked at the desk and reached with her mind. The pills flew into her hand. A brief ripple of pain creased her brow.

"Extraordinary!" said Kadar as she passed him the pills.

"Otterzoid DNA. So why is Ryan a different kind of clone than me? I can't believe I asked that. I can't believe he's a clone. Stardust! I can believe I'm one. Why have I accepted this so fast?" Suspicion marred Rowan's features.

"Necessity." Kadar took two of the pills. "And the fact it makes no real difference. People are people, whether they are born or grown in a vat."

Rowan smiled. "I'm getting a feeling that's a minority view in this galaxy."

"Only among humans." Kadar patted her hand. "If Ryan is doing what I think he's doing, I wouldn't worry too much. He has a place in mind where your origin won't matter."

"Nice to know. Why's he different? Why's he a clone?"

"Murack Five." Kadar's dark complexion blanched.

"I've heard the name, but I don't know what it is."

"It is a planet. There was a war. I do not wish to discuss the rest. Let us leave it that both Ryan and I received a massive dose of radiation. It so damaged us that only the most radical of treatments was a viable option. It was a death sentence. Ryan was only eighty-seven at the time."

"EIGHTY-SEVEN!" Rowan's gaze leapt to Ryan, then locked gazes with Kadar.

"My dear, did you think medicine would have failed to advance in the years separating the technologies we are accustomed to? The average human, without the use of cloning, can expect to live approximately two hundred Earth standard years. That's about one-hundred and ninety New Gaea years, give or take based on individual biology."

"Two hundred... Stardust!" Rowan's already pale skin grew even lighter. "He was eighty-seven. What was he doing in combat?"

Kadar smiled. "Paying his son's way through university. Rowan, you cannot think of him as an unaltered human of the age of eighty-seven. Think of him as a man who was just entering his middle-years. Perhaps thirty-five by your standards."

"Wow. So, he got a dose of radiation and needed a new body, so they grew him one."

"Then transferred his memories and consciousness into the new shell. That's the tricky part." Kadar coughed. It doubled him over. Rowan rubbed his back until he stopped.

"If they could save Ryan by cloning him—" began Rowan.

"Why couldn't they save me?" Kadar smiled sadly. He looked exhausted. "They could have, but I was a hundred and ten."

"So?"

"Humans Ascendant is a powerful lobby group in the United Earth Systems. They feel all cloning and genetic manipulation should be banned. Years ago, they pushed to have limits set on the use of medical cloning. An age was chosen beyond which the extreme measure of cloning a replacement body as a treatment was illegal. The politicians and environmental lobbies helped push the law through. You see, humans tend to breed, and keeping our population to manageable levels is a major concern. They picked a nice round number, with no regard to scientific reality."

Rowan stared at Kadar. "One-hundred."

"You are clever. I was left to rot in my cancers while Ryan was issued a new form, though...."

"Though?"

Kadar pulled himself to his feet and stepped away. "Are you hungry? The cafeteria is open for breakfast. I can have a tray brought in."

Having it mentioned was like throwing a switch. Rowan's stomach growled as her mouth began to water. "I'm famished."

"I'll call into the kitchen. The fewer people who know of your presence, the better. After you've eaten, I'll examine you again. If you check out, we'll see to sending you and Ryan on your way."

Mildred pulled up to the coordinates Colonel Burtch had called in to her. A young-looking man, wearing a ground forces field uniform with lieutenant's pips, waved her to a stop. Mildred moved to the side door and stared into the early morning light.

"I'm sorry, ma'am. You'll have to leave the area." The young lieutenant was polite but firm. His black hair was cut short. His Malaysian features betrayed no hint of compromise or threat. What he said was simply how it was.

"It's all right, Lieutenant. I'm Major Mildred Tallman, Planetary Reserve Forces. I'm also the head of studio security. Colonel Burtch should have told you to expect me." Mildred jumped down from the ATV and found herself staring straight into the bottom of the lieutenant's chest. She was used to being the shortest one in the room, but this made her realize how tall the lieutenant actually was. She looked up to find him looking down. He didn't smirk, which won him more points.

"Of course, Major. If I could see some identification?"

Mildred pulled her universal ident card from her pocket and passed it to the man. He pushed it into a hand-held, then pointed its lens at Mildred. A second later, he passed back the card. "Thank you, ma'am. The debris is this way."

The lieutenant began walking, slowing his natural stride as a courtesy to his guest.

"So, Lieutenant, what are you called?" Mildred hastened her stride, allowing him to walk a little more normally.

"Lieutenant Chen Chow, ma'am."

"All Colonel Burtch told me was that the satellite had

picked up a trail of debris." Mildred came to the edge of a shallow cliff. Below her, something large had slammed and dragged, leaving a scar on the bedrock while scattering bits of itself everywhere. Six men collected the debris into a central staging area.

"My tech says it's a polycarbonate used in some of the older armoured vehicles. There's no trace of the main vehicle. We're assuming these are cast-offs. We haven't found any tire tracks. I doubt we will."

Mildred looked up into Chow's serious face. "And why is that?"

"From the mission file, if this was our target, the vehicle had an anti-gravity flight capacity. If the ground drive was damaged, they might have been forced to use the anti-grav despite the energy drain. I've alerted local authorities in all the nearby towns to report back about any strangers."

Mildred stared at the rubble. "Did you find any hydraulic fluid?"

"A small amount. Now that you mention it, not as much as I would have expected." Chow turned and looked behind them. "No skid marks, no scuffed gravel from a failed attempt to turn. Hydraulic failure, the first cause of the accident." Chow nodded.

"Very good, Lieutenant. Now let's get down there. I need a map of this area. After a crash like that, they would need to find other transport. A fairly major centre would be best for that... unless there are elements at play that we don't know about."

"Yes, ma'am."

Rowan popped the last bit of toast into her mouth and chewed. She was sitting on the edge of her bed with a rollaway cart supporting her food tray. Kadar sat in a chair at the foot of the bed.

"Human honour was on the line. We couldn't let them

out drink us. The bet was one of their intoxicants, then one of ours. Ryan made Irish coffee. Did you have felinezoids in your series?"

"Yes. My best friend, Angel, was dating one." Rowan took a sip of her coffee.

"Lucky girl." Kadar sighed. "In any case, you know how caffeine affects them. By the next round, half of them were passed out. The felinezoid commander was hanging off the ceiling fan howling some 'song' the translator refused to interpret."

"I saw Toronk on an espresso binge once. I can imagine a room full of them." Rowan laughed.

"It is a night I will never forget. I am sure the pussycats will never forget the next morning." Kadar grinned.

"Kadar, do you mind if I ask you a question?" Rowan looked sheepish.

"Not at all. In fact, I enjoy having a new audience. The other inmates have all heard my stories."

"So, this really is a prison?"

"Is that the question?" Kadar leaned back in his chair.

"No. It's just different from what I would have expected." Rowan waved her hand to indicate the compound.

"New Gaea is still in the process of being terraformed. Criminals from all over the United Earth Systems are transferred here from regional holding facilities."

"But there's no way to keep you all from escaping."

Kadar smiled and tapped his arm. "Nano-bots keyed to a proximity transmitter in the village. If I go more than twenty kilometres from this town, I get a headache. At twenty-one kilometres, I'm rendered unconscious, and the nano-bots link together to form a homing beacon. It is quite effective."

"So, you stay put."

"Most of us work the farm, some, like myself, supply skilled services to the prison community. We also plant the perimeter out to new orchards, thus expanding the green zone. They pay us board and a fraction of what they would have to pay free men."

"Won't the guards report us?" Rowan bit her lip.

"The only guards are the perimeter patrol. Anyone entering along the road is inspected for contraband. Visitors are welcome though. Some of the inmates have their mates and children up for weekends. I'm assuming Ryan flew in cross country, thus avoiding the checkpoint."

"Isn't it, well... dangerous?"

"We're all chemically conditioned to make us non-violent. It's a standard part of sentencing, and we do police ourselves. Our sheriff was a detective on Frigga. He got caught taking a bribe. In this environment, he's quite effective. It isn't a bad life. We all have our own hut, and the food is good. Of course, there are some restrictions. We aren't allowed e-entertainments. The commissary sells a wide range of minor luxuries. There are worse places to die."

"I wish there was something we could do for you. You've been so good to us."

Kadar grinned at Rowan's use of the plural. "Don't be sad for me, my dear. I've found a kind of peace here. And as to how I've helped you, it is little enough payment for what Ryan did for me."

WAR STORIES

14

Mildred slammed her hand down on the cafeteria table. The remains of her brunch jumped on the plate. "It doesn't make any sense."

A Hispanic soldier, who looked to be barely out of his teens, stood beside her with a worried expression. "I'm sorry, ma'am, the security records show no unusual traffic. Only the regular commuters." The corporal's eye strayed to a left-over bit of toast on her plate.

Mildred caught the direction of his gaze. "Chow, they're your men, and you've all been most kind to me."

The lieutenant, sitting opposite her, nodded. "Rodriguez, get McDonald. The two of you chow down. Keep the receipt, we'll charge it to the discretionary fund, keep it reasonable, no lobster this time."

"Thank you, sir, ma'am!" Rodriguez snapped off a salute and stepped away.

"Lobster?" Mildred scanned the cafeteria of the mag-lev station. It was the end of a little-used line connecting a trendy village to the tower city.

"We were looking for some convicts that had managed to deactivate their nano-bots a few months ago. It was well past dinner when we came to a town, Harper's Vil."

"Beautiful place. A real getaway community. My husband and I vacation there," Mildred smiled.

"You earn a lot more than I do, ma'am. I let them have their pick of the menu before I looked at the prices."

"Oh my! The restaurants there are excellent, but you pay

for what you get."

"And then some. We caught the escapees, after which my company was dispatched to work off the money we owed for the meal."

"A valuable lesson on how tight to hold the reins." Mildred smiled at the young man.

"In a sense, it worked out. One of my men had an undiagnosed allergy to shellfish. He tried the lobster and started to react. There was a doctor at the next table over. He injected a histamine blocker and a nano-bot neutralizer for the protein causing the allergy. My man was back on his feet in minutes. If it had been my medic treating him, it could have taken hours."

"Medical attention..." Mildred drummed her fingers on the table. "After a crash like they must have had, they could have been injured."

"No offence, ma'am, those troop carriers are built to take a beating and keep the crew safe and sound." Chow sipped at his coffee.

"Still, or maybe for something else. The property had been injected with a poison that nano-bots were keeping dormant. It's a place to look." Mildred pulled her hand-held from her pocket.

"It couldn't be a major facility, or the auto scanners would have flagged the stolen property as non-listed."

"Hand-held, centre search on wreckage field. Locate all medical facilities without automatic patient recognition systems within a hundred-kilometre radius. Display."

Twelve possibilities appeared on the screen.

Chow moved to stand behind Mildred. "Ma'am, I suggest you pull in your field. Anti-grav eats a lot of power. Maybe fifty klicks."

"Hand-held, same search, fifty klicks." Mildred smiled when four places were listed.

"Now eliminate any that were un-staffed yesterday evening. There are a lot of part-time offices out here," offered Chow.

"Hand-held, you heard the man, do it."

Match - Williamville, minimum-security penal institution.

"They wouldn't have?" Lieutenant Chow shook his head.
"The unmitigated gall!" Mildred smiled. "It feels right. Lieutenant, tell your men to get a doggy bag. Don't worry about the expense. The studio's picking up the tab."

"What is Wesnakee? I remember Ryan saying something about it when we arrived." Rowan looked at Kadar, forcing her face to appear open and posture relaxed. She needed to learn all she could to survive, and right now, she needed to learn all she could about Ryan most of all.

"Wesnakee... Wesnakee is many things, a bar, the most embarrassing moment in my life, the worst thing that ever happened to me, and the best thing that ever happened to me." Kadar sighed and hung his head as a shy smile touched his lips.

"I'm sorry if it's too personal..." Rowan patted Kadar's knee.

Kadar laughed. "My dear, you are remarkable. After what society has done to you, you worry about my privacy? Wesnakee was where I fell in love."

"That's pretty personal." Rowan grinned.

"Extremely. You see, my dear, I have what is currently called a 'taste for fur'."

"You... ew... please tell me that's not what it sounds like?" Rowan closed her eyes against the images that came unbidden to her mind.

"I don't know what it sounds like. I can assure you, I have only been with consenting sentients of mature years." Kadar looked offended.

"Consenting sentients... you... aliens! Oh, stardust! Why should that matter? I admit when Angel and Toronk first got together, it seemed kinda weird, but I got over that years ago."

Kadar looked up. There was gratitude in his eyes. "It is considered rather questionable by many species. I'm glad to see you understand. An appropriate amount of life experience, a mind, a will and the ability to make informed consent should be the only parameters to where beings share their passion."

"You fell in love."

Kadar got a faraway look in his eyes and began speaking. "It was during the Murack campaign. The *Star Hawk* had been on constant duty for six months. When we made space dock for repairs, the captain granted everyone leave to explore the Switchboard Station."

Rowan closed her eyes. It was like some trickle of her father's ability touched her because as she listened to his words, she could almost see it in her mind.

"Kitoy was lovely. Cougar tan fur so soft you had to stroke her. Her legs were long, and her features were like a cheetah's. The firmness of her body, the coiled muscle, the way her whiskers tickled when we stroked cheeks. She was short, for a felinezoid, only ten centimetres taller than me.

"We met in Wesnakee. It catered to oxygen breathers, from small, rocky planets, who wanted to mingle with members of other species. The seating consisted of cushions that would configure to your body. The tables were on hydraulic pillars so that they could be set to any level.

"It was really a big room with images of various homeworlds on the walls and ceiling. It was always full of life forms flopped, seated and sometimes passed out. I loved the place. The smells, and they served the best pizza outside the United Earth Systems."

"Pizza?" gasped Rowan.

"It is mankind's great contribution to galactic cuisine. Otterzoids especially are passionate about it. Most creatures that can eat human food agree it's delicious."

"Carl would be happy." Rowan shook her head. "You were about to meet K..."

"Kitoy." Kadar smiled, and his face grew soft. "A k-no-in had marched up to her table and was trying to rent her for the night. They have abhorrent mating customs by most sentient standards. She wasn't interested. He wouldn't leave. I asked him to. The poor bastard nearly wet himself to have a human tell him to push off."

"Why?" Rowan opened her eyes.

"Humans have something of a reputation. I'm sure Ryan will explain it to you."

Rowan closed her eyes. She could picture a healthy Kadar standing by a table where a pretty, young felinezoid sat. Rowan grinned as she mentally added a silver sash falling off one of Kitoy's shoulders like Valaseau wore.

"I asked if she would like some company. I remember how the slits of her pupils widened. She swished her tail as she motioned me to a cushion. I'd studied felinezoid arousal signs."

Rowan looked at Kadar's face. His eyes were closed, and he was smiling.

"To make a long story short, we spent that evening talking. She told me she was a clerk working on the station and had an interest in Earth. Over the next few days, we became inseparable. At night it was magnificent. Humans and felinezoids are the closest matches in bedroom matters of the seven species humans can have relations with. I was so happy." Kadar fell silent.

"What happened?" prodded Rowan.

"The day for the *Star Hawk*'s deployment was coming up when I found out my beloved Kitoy was a spy. One moment I was lying sated in her bed, the next I was in an interrogation chair being questioned. The felinezoids had secretly accepted a contract to enter the Murack conflict. They wanted human medical scientists to help them develop bio-weapons that would be effective against our species."

"They sound like savages." Rowan's face hardened.

"They are only a little less aggressive and ruthless than humans. Thus, many species would agree with you." Kadar's voice held no animosity.

"Oh…" Rowan blushed and hung her head.

"In any case. The felinezoids were trying to brainwash me, make me betray my species. I had no way of knowing what was happening outside the little room they kept me in.

"Apparently Henry, the company military android, had been suspicious of Kitoy. He'd hacked the system and monitored her communications. He approached Captain Ackerman, my CO at the time, with his suspicions when I didn't return. Ackerman was too political to risk a diplomatic incident. The Switchboard Station is supposed to be neutral. You may not even wear a sidearm within it. Thus, he left me to rot.

"Ryan was the chief engineer and second mate. He and Henry disobeyed Ackerman's orders and came for me.

"I don't know how they found me."

"I knew a felinezoid in their sector admin. I'd been trading with him for parts. I swapped him a couple kilos of coffee for two blank entry passes for the felinezoid section and the location of your girlfriend's apartment. This guy had a two cup a day habit, so it wasn't hard." Ryan's voice issued from the bed.

"You're awake." Rowan jerked around to look at him.

"If you say so." Ryan sat up and rubbed the sleep from his eyes.

"How long have you been listening?" Kadar moved to his desk and pressed a button. The face of the woman at the front desk appeared on the screen. "Sara, has the kitchen finished with shift two's breakfast?"

Sara grinned. "Your other friend has woken up? I'll tell chef to prepare a tray."

"Thank you." Kadar turned back to Ryan.

"I taught myself to pay attention when someone mentions Ackerman. It helped keep us all alive if the officers knew what that idiot was up to," explained Ryan.

"He wasn't well-liked?" said Rowan.

"He was a politician with a reserve commission who thought an active stint would look good to the voters. He cared about his own skin and keeping it intact."

"He should never have been a line commander," agreed Kadar.

"How'd you find Kadar?" asked Rowan.

"The Switchboard Station is huge, but we only had to cover the felinezoid section, and humans exude a pheromone that's unique to creatures evolved on Earth. Henry sniffed him out." Ryan picked up the story.

"Most of the station corridors are three metres across and high. Henry and I bought a k-no-in costume in a novelty shop and put it on. I had to be the back because Henry had to smell where we were going."

"Wise move. I wouldn't put Henry in the back of anything if I were in the front!" commented Kadar.

"Agreed. At any rate, we found the apartment Kadar had been taken to. It was a standard unit, nothing to draw attention. I jimmied the lock, then it was like an asteroid collision on a viable biosphere.

"It was a good thing Henry was in the front of the costume. His body armour stopped the knife. Henry leapt into the apartment's main room, the costume tore in two. There were at least ten felinezoids there, all with monitoring equipment, most of which was illegal on the station.

"I charged in after Henry and nutted a big tom. That pussycat must have been two and a quarter metres. He dropped like a tree. Henry was under a pile of fur.

"We're lucky the felinezoids didn't have one of their battle mechs. They had us for numbers, in a fair fight we'd have been toast.

"The food prep area was the room next to the main one.

I dove in and grabbed this big, club-like thing felinezoids use to soften up their meat. A female came at me, claws out. I started a swing for her head when she moved to block, I punched her in the throat. She was too busy trying to breathe to get in my way.

"I went back to the hall and saw another female scrambling to unlock a door. I charged her. She turned and was holding the smallest particle weapon I've ever seen. How she got it past station scanners, I still don't know. I tried to duck. She caught the side of my face.

"One second, there was a blaze of light and pain, the next my left eye was black. It hurt worse than I can describe. I guess the particle beam was a one-shot unit because she didn't kill me. I reached up and felt liquid where my eye should have been. I went nuts!

"I was screaming 'Bitch! Bitch! Bitch!' as I slammed that club into her head. I..." Ryan fell silent. His eyes were haunted, and he was trembling.

Kadar picked up the story. "I heard Ryan in my cell. It was minutes later that the door opened. Henry must have scrambled away from the felinezoids because he released me. Ryan, the left side of his face burnt down to the skull, was at the end of the hall shrieking and swinging a club. The felinezoids were keeping their distance."

"Felinezoids don't have battle madness. They didn't know how to deal with this savage. They could see the corpse behind me. I'd..." Ryan hung his head.

Kadar continued, "Henry half-carried me from the apartment, then grabbed Ryan and dragged him out. I still don't know how we made it back to the human sector."

Ryan's voice was haunted. "The felinezoids had violated weapons and tech regulations, kidnapped a citizen of a member state of the Republic and were conducting spy activities on the Switchboard Station. They had more to lose than we did. If the elder species had found out what they were up to... I don't want to think about it."

Rowan looked into Ryan's haunted expression. At that

moment she could believe he'd lived over ninety years. Sara deposited a tray on the rollaway cart beside Ryan before turning to Kadar. "Doctor, Victor looked into that other matter. He says it would take at least a week."

"Thank you, Sara." Kadar lifted the tray's cover. Tantalizing aromas wafted up.

"What happened when you made it back to your ship? Was the captain mad?"

Ryan took a bite of his eggs and chewed before answering. "We let Ackerman take credit for the idea. Uncovering a spy station was a coup. Kadar regrew my eye on the way to our next duty assignment, and that's about it."

"Don't forget you and Henry being awarded the Martian Medal of Valour."

Ryan stopped chewing. "No one deserves a medal for beating someone to death with a stick!" He focused on his food, ignoring the uncomfortable silence in the room.

C.Y.A.

15

Greg's forked tongue flicked from his mouth. He'd been called in when Lee Ann, the technician who was supposed to be on duty, had run sobbing from the building. The main screen showed Fran's perspective. She was dismembering a k-no-in. Blood was everywhere. The alien's intestines were strung out around it. She'd hung it from a hook in the meat-packing factory they used in the *Vampire Tales* series.

"Where is she? Where is that otterzoid bitch?" Fran yanked out another metre of gut.

The k-no-in screeched, then passed out.

"Wimp!" snapped Fran.

"You can't do this! This is my show!" John's voice blasted into the control-room as the door was thrown open.

"You'll be lucky to have a show if this keeps up." Michael Strongbow's voice was just shy of a shout as he pushed into the room. "There isn't a program that hasn't had to do major diversions and patches to keep show autonomy. Stardust! *Day Care Days* has been forced to do a plotline about religious visions and tolerance because three of the kids saw Angel and that batzoid fighting. We're lucky batzoids look the way they do! The kids think it was a real angel fighting a demon or something. I'm shutting you down. I don't have a producer on staff who isn't behind me on this." Michael turned to Greg. "Start a sedative feed. I want all the characters in bed an hour from now."

"If you do it, I'll can you," snapped John.

"Shut up, John. I run this studio. I could have told you this would happen when you killed Rowan. She was the moderator of the group. Besides, we're almost out of alien antagonists. You've exhausted this season's stock in three days. Greg, my authority, dope 'em." Michael's eyes flashed, and the silver-haired executive locked gazes with John.

John swallowed and sweat beaded his fat body.

"Thank the Divine!" Greg started ramping up the sedative level in all the characters.

"You're finished!" John snapped at Greg, then turned on Michael. "When the shareholders see the numbers these episodes bring in, I'll have your job."

"Maybe. For now, I run this place, and your series is taking a breather."

John stormed from the room.

Michael took a deep breath and let it out before placing a hand on Greg's shoulder. "Sit tight for a little while. I'll bring you in on my new series. John can't hurt you."

Greg let out a breath he didn't know he'd been holding. "Thank you, Misster Sstrongbow."

"Michael, please." The older man grinned.

Greg smiled back. "With all that'ss happened, I haven't kept up. Have they found Rowan yet?"

Ryan sat on his bed and stared at Kadar as the sound of Rowan's shower issued through the bathroom door. "I won't do it."

Kadar sat in a chair shivering. "Please. The nano-bots can't save me. At this point, nothing can."

"Kadar, you're asking me to kill you." Ryan stared at his old friend.

"The accident on Murack Five killed me. It's just taken a while to do it. At least give me the deactivate codes. Let me have a choice. They won't allow me to stop treatment because I'm a prisoner. You know how much it hurts. Your old body was as bad as mine is now by the time your new one was ready. If you'd known there was no hope, would you have wanted to keep living?"

Ryan hung his head, then reached for his hand-held. "It might not work. This is keyed for the nano-bots we use in the studio. I'll try and get you the codes. I'll leave them with you. What you do with them is your choice."

"Thank you." Kadar heaved a sigh of relief.

Ryan sadly scanned his friend's body.

Rowan stepped out of the shower. The only major surprise in the bathroom fixtures had been the lack of towels. She gritted her teeth and looked into the mirror. Her short, brown hair was now honey-blonde and shoulder-length. She traced her eyes down her body. The only hair visible was a neat triangle over her mons Veneris. It matched the hair on her head.

"Nobody's going to guess the colour came out of a bottle, that's for sure. Programmable nano-bots. Leg hair to hair extensions. Stardust, I'm living in an SF novel." She shook her head and pressed a button above the sink. Warm, dry air came from vents in the walls. She revelled in the feel of it as it caressed her skin, drying both the bathroom and her.

"Rowan, can you hurry it up? You're not the only one who smells." Ryan's voice blasted through the closed door. She slipped on the hospital robe Kadar had given her and left the bathroom.

"Whatcha think?" she pointed to the new hair.

Ryan forced his eyes up from her legs, which the robe left exposed to mid-thigh, and focused on her face. "You look better as a brunette. You're still beautiful."

"Thank you." She stepped into the infirmary's main room

as Ryan disappeared into the bathroom.

"I purchased some clothes from an associate of mine who's about your size." Kadar indicated a pile of clothes on one of the beds. "My old suit should serve Ryan well enough. I also made this up." He held out a petri dish with two brown contact lenses floating in it. "They're simply ornamental, but to a casual observer they should prove effective, and they will blur any long-distance retinal scans."

"I've never worn contacts."

"Put them in. They'll dissolve on their own after a day or two."

Rowan turned to the pile of clothes and, picking up the French cut panties, blushed. "This associate... she, well... I mean..."

"You must keep in mind that our casual clothing is prison issue. This is her evening wear, purchased as a luxury from the commissar. We hold a formal dance on the first Saturday of every month. It gives us something to look forward to."

"Wow. Could you... well?" Rowan blushed.

"Oh, yes, of course. I'll step out. I promised Cathy I'd purchase her replacement clothing in time for our next dance. I believe she's selected the most expensive outfit in the catalogue. Such is life."

Ryan stepped out of the bathroom wearing a robe identical to the one Rowan had worn. He froze. The vision before him was a thing of fantasy. The black, knee-length dress hugged Rowan in all the right places, and her newly blonde hair counterpointed the dark dress like living sunlight.

"Kadar left clothes for you," began Rowan, then she saw the look on Ryan's face. "What?"

"You... You're magnificent! You..."

Rowan blushed. "I need to put in the contacts he made

me. Do you want me to leave while you dress?"

Ryan pulled himself together. "No. I... I'm not modest. Serving in the forces knocks that out of you pretty fast." Moving to the blue suit draped over the bed, he began dressing. Rowan tried not to peek but couldn't help herself. What she saw made her smile and blush, in that order.

Mildred glared at the prison guard. He was an older man carrying a few extra pounds on a frame that had once been pure muscle. His blue and black uniform was somewhat scruffy, and the name tag over his right, breast pocket read Swen Thorson. He spoke with a thick, Mielkkien accent.

"I don't be carin' if yur be the grand high commander of all the human forces. You aren't gettin' in me prison with weapons or stealth technology."

"A dangerous convict has already breached your perimeter with stealth technology," stated Lieutenant Chow.

Swen stood in a stone guardhouse almost identical to the prisoners' huts. He leaned out the window as he spoke. "So yur sayin'. Where's yur proof?"

Mildred buried her face in her hands. "It's deductive reasoning."

"Yur can be goin' in for a look-see if yur like. Yur can't be takin' yur equipment."

Lieutenant Chow clutched his hand into a white-knuckled fist. "Listen to me, you—"

"Lieutenant, I have an idea. Call the correctional facility monitoring station. Ask them to have a satellite scan this area." Mildred turned to the guard. "If I show you a satellite picture that shows your facility has been compromised, will you let us in?"

"Shurin' that would be proof." Swen disappeared into the shed and closed the window. Reaching under his desk, he pressed a button, then spoke in a whisper. "Whoever be listenin', we got visitors. Make the place look good."

Sara burst into the infirmary as Ryan did up the last button on his shirt.

"You need to get out of here! Someone's at the gate."

"Who?" demanded Ryan.

"Don't know. The guards and us have an understanding. They let us know when someone official shows up, and we make the place look good. We have a hardwire intercom set up. Now move."

"Where's K—"

"Ryan, Rowan, you have to get out of here, right now!" Kadar burst into the room at as close to a run as his body could manage.

"My ATV?" asked Ryan.

"It's not mobile. I've got one of the farm runabouts waiting outside. The driver knows where to take you. There's a town about three hours walk outside the farm's perimeter. It has a mag-lev link."

"If they find my ATV and check it? My DNA is all over it. They'll block my flight clearance." Ryan wrung his hands.

"It's hidden, and I have some friends who are rigging up a little surprise. I think we can buy you a few hours."

Ryan nodded as Rowan grabbed her gym bag. Kadar picked up their old clothes and stuffed everything but their shoes into a chute on the wall. "Medical waste disposal, it should destroy any DNA traces."

"Thanks, Kadar," said Ryan.

"Don't mention it. It's nice to have a chance to make up for some of the ones I owe you. Get her off this rock, and have a good life, my friend." Kadar hugged Ryan. "And tell that polymer pervert I said to look after you."

"I will."

"Thank you for everything." Rowan kissed Kadar's cheek, then followed Ryan. They raced through the prison's common building and out the large, glass doors. A small, six-wheeled, open-topped vehicle waited on the main street. A fit, silver-haired woman, dressed in a prison-issue coverall, sat behind the driver's station. A day-pack and two water bottles occupied the cargo space behind the back seat.

"Hurry, the guards can't stall them much longer," Sara called from the main building's door.

Ryan and Rowan jumped into the runabout and were immediately jerked back into their seats as the vehicle accelerated.

"I'm Cathy. Glad to see old Kadar hasn't lost his eye; my dress looks great on you," the woman driving said as soon as they were behind the cover of the orchards.

Rowan steadied herself and hunted for a seat belt as the runabout jolted over the uneven ground. "Thank you for the clothes. They're lovely."

"Kadar said you were forces. Where'd you serve?" Rowan looked at Ryan, her face full of confusion.

"I was Space Combat Corps," said Ryan.

"'Sanguinis abl planeta!'" Cathy turned her attention back to her driving.

"Sanguinis abl planeta!" Ryan sank his fingers into the padded seat to hold himself steady as they jolted along.

"What?" whispered Rowan, who was still frantically looking for a safety belt.

"Motto of the Space Combat Corps. What are you doing? You're squirming around like someone dropped a snake down your skirt."

"I can't find the safety belt."

A bark of laughter came from the front seat. "You've been watching too many e-entertainments. Trust the suspensor fields. They'll hold you fine."

"Sorry, I—" began Rowan.

Ryan cut her off. "She was raised on Silvanus. You know what it's like there. When you're dirt poor, a strip of cloth is cheaper than replacing a suspensor projector, and it works almost as well."

Cathy looked into the back seat. "Enjoy the nice clothes, girl. Coming from Silvanus, you deserve a break."

"Thank you." Rowan waited until Cathy was looking forward to shoot Ryan a glance. He silently mouthed the word 'later' and passed her a wide-brimmed, straw hat that was sitting on the seat. "Put this on."

"Why?" Rowan took the hat.

"After changing your hair, it would be a shame if a satellite photo tipped them off."

Rowan shuddered. "I feel like I'm in a fishbowl."

"Welcome to the school, don't flounder." Ryan smirked.

"Do you see it?" Mildred stabbed the satellite photo with her finger. The image depicted a break in the trees beside the road. It looked like a strip of freshly laid sod.

"It don't be much. I'll send me guard to have a look-see." Swen stared at the image.

"This is ridiculous! It's obviously an attempt to camouflage a crash site," snapped Chow.

"Could be the prisoners got rowdy and were racin' the farm vehicles. I'll send a guard for a look-see." Swen smiled, then a beeping sound called him into his guard-shed.

"What is he trying to accomplish?" snapped Lieutenant Chow.

"He's covering his butt. He probably hasn't done a contraband sweep in years and doesn't want us seeing what the good little convicts have gotten up to." Mildred looked at the picture again. "How fast do you think they would have been travelling to do that kind of damage?"

Swen threw open the guardhouse's window. His face was pale, and the whites of his eyes were showing. "You can be goin'. Sorry I kept you waitin'."

The fence across the road rolled back.

"About time!" Mildred moved back to her ATV with Chow in tow.

"Why'd he change his mind?" Chow settled in the navigator's seat.

Mildred smiled as she pulled the studio vehicle ahead. "That second call I made might have something to do with it."

"Pardon?"

"My husband plays golf with the head of the planetary corrections department."

"Oh."

"Never forget that often who you know can work for you." Mildred watched Chow out of the corner of her eye. He nodded as if taking mental notes.

"I think you should contact Colonel Burtch. See if he'd be willing to divert a couple of satellites to scan the prison's perimeter. Just in case," she added.

"I'll get right on it, ma'am." Lieutenant Chow smiled as he opened his hand-held.

Ryan scrambled out of the runabout, donned the day-pack, threw one of the water bottles over his shoulder and passed Rowan her gym-bag.

"End of the line. Any further, my nano-bots give me a migraine," explained Cathy as Rowan climbed from the back seat.

"I appreciate this." Ryan scanned the rocky terrain. Scrub grasses and lichens grew up in patches from a boulder-strewn field. The orchards were a line of green nearly two hundred metres away.

"No sweat, I owed Kadar, glad to pay him off while I still can. Hate to have to deal with him in my next life."

Rowan looked skyward.

"Keep your face down!" snapped Cathy.

Rowan obeyed. "Why?"

"Satellites. They probably aren't focused on us, but if they happen to be, a facial scan could identify us." Ryan passed Rowan the other water bottle, which she secured over her shoulder.

"You know your stuff, for a sky jockey," said Cathy.

"I spent enough time with ground pounders I picked up some tricks."

"I don't know why you're hot, but take my advice. Get out of the United Earth Systems. You don't want to be stuck on one of these Divine forsaken farms. I better race." Cathy shot Ryan a salute, then peeled out in a hail of gravel.

"Now what?" asked Rowan.

"Now we walk. Kadar said there was a hiking trail going in the direction we want a hundred metres past the prison perimeter. If we make that, a casual satellite sweep won't catch us out."

"Just a second." Leaning against a boulder, Rowan pulled off the high-heeled pumps that she'd donned with her dress and replaced them with her running shoes, which she'd stowed in her gym bag.

Ryan watched her, a smile playing over his face.

Rowan noticed his gaze. "What?"

"Evening wear and running shoes." Ryan pulled off the daypack and opened its zipper.

"You don't think I'm going to wear heels to hike cross country, do you?"

"No. Your practicality was one of the things that attracted me to you in the first place."

Rowan finished changing her shoes, then hooked the heels of the dress shoes through a loop on her gym bag. "What do we have?"

Ryan pulled a compass and a map out of the bag. "Emergency ration bars, matches, a first aid kit, an emergency blanket and an umbrella."

"Kadar's a good friend."

"This time." Ryan took a compass reading, checked the map and started walking.

"Whatcha mean 'this time'?" Rowan threw her gym bag over her shoulder and matched his stride.

"Wesnakee wasn't the only time Kadar got into trouble, and Henry and I had to bail him out. He was always falling into holes, and we were always digging him out. This one time on Petteron, the batzoid homeworld, he got involved with a local crime boss, and..."

WALK AND TALK

16

Kadar felt giddy. Focusing his thoughts through the pain medications he'd taken was hard. Dots swam before his eyes. He'd used the deactivate codes before he left medical and knew it was only a matter of hours. Each step was an effort as he made his way between the trees of one of the oldest orchards. A green mound rose before him. He felt along its face to where a camouflage tarp came up against strips of sod. He slipped under the tarp where it was supported on the trees. The battered ATV sat on the ground, its nose and tail buried. The side door hung open, and there were gouges and scratches in the craft's hull.

"Kadar." A chubby, middle-aged, blond man in prison orange appeared in the vehicle's doorway.

"Victor." Kadar slumped against the craft's side and took a rattling breath.

Victor moved to Kadar and helped him sit on the ground. Kadar trembled with the effort of the last few hours. "How much longer?"

"This thing's a mess. We've scavenged it for ration packs and some other stardust. None of the tech is compatible with our units."

"To make it operational, Victor."

"Forget it. The ground drive is a lost cause, and the forward grav-nullifiers are toast. The lower wind turbine on the port side is tangled metal, and it only has about 20 per cent of its emergency batteries that can hold a charge. Plus, the control and sensor systems were gutted by a pro.

The thing can't even camouflage."

Kadar hung his head. "It's hopeless. You can't get it into the air."

Victor grinned. "Never say can't to a ground-forces-service tech. There were some grav-lifts inside. I've bolted them to what's left of the forward undercarriage. They won't last long, but this beast should get off the ground. The topside wind turbines still have a little life in them, though the velocity control is gone. They're full on or nothing and forget about brakes. I wouldn't risk it, but if your friend wants to—"

"My friend is already gone. Show me the switches to throw. Do I have a compass?"

"That you do, but... Kadar, you can't mean to..."

"I owe the man. If it wasn't for him, I never would have survived Swampla."

"I don't think I've heard that one."

"We were serving as a diplomatic escort to the Swampla Planetary Council when I met Splorta. She was an otterzoid, and so beautiful, sleek, compact." Kadar's voice became soft as he remembered. "She loved to buy me gifts. How was I supposed to know she considered her gifts my husband price? It ended badly when I found out she expected me to stay with her for life. The matriarchs of her clan charged me with false promise. It looked like I was going to be spending time in an otterzoid prison. Ryan did some investigating and found out that Splorta had secretly married years before, then abandoned her husband. Since otterzoids are monogamous, she couldn't pay my husband price, so I was off the hook. Though I never managed to patch things up with Splorta.

"Now help me to the pilot's seat. Then stand by to turn on those grav-lifts."

Chow lifted a flap of sod and looked at the ground

beneath. "In another day, this would have been impossible to spot."

Mildred watched Rodriguez and McDonald as they rolled the sod strips and piled them next to her ATV. "Have the rest of the squad reported anything?"

"I've recalled the ones at the more distant transport stations. They should be here within an hour. Those at the nearby links all have a description of the property. They're keeping an eye out."

"Good. Have you contacted the convict sheriff?"

"I got his deputy. She said he was fishing and had left his hand-held at the station." An expression of resolved disbelief crossed Chow's face.

"Cheer up, we nearly have them." Mildred scanned the exposed dirt. "What do you see?"

Chow scanned the area. Shallow soil covered barren rock. "Nothing, what should I see?"

"Nothing." Mildred grinned. "What does that tell you?" She watched the young lieutenant as wheels seemed to turn in his head.

"The camouflagers were thorough. They picked up any debris and masked the gouges, so you'd have to clear the entire area to see them."

"Yes. Who's that thorough?" Mildred started back to her ATV. Chow followed her and motioned for his men to join them.

"Stardust! Ground pounders, maybe even elite squad. This guy is dangerous. I'd better warn my men." Chow started pulling out his hand-held. Mildred stopped him.

"Not so fast. Remember where we are. A lot of line personnel have a hard time adjusting to civilian life. This was probably done by the convicts. Now ask yourself, why would they?" Mildred and Chow were at the ATV's door, and Mildred climbed the steps.

"A favour?" Chow followed her as they made their way to the cockpit.

"A debt. You know the code, guard your squad and

remember your friends." Mildred settled into the driver's seat, while Chow took the navigator station.

"Our Johnny knows someone at this facility. Someone with enough clout to get all this done."

"That's the hypothesis. It fits with the other facts we have."

Chow considered. He yelled into the back of the vehicle when a red light turned green on his dash. "You two secured?"

"Stowed away, lieutenant," called Rodriguez.

"Good. I want to get to the town. It's likely that our quarry will still be there. If the prisoners are on their side, they'd want to get their vehicle operational in a place with friendlies." Mildred started driving.

"With your permission, I'll cross-reference the prison records with service files and the rest of our facts, see what comes up." Chow pulled his hand-held from his pocket.

Mildred smiled. "Use my system. It will be faster. Muriel, grant the lieutenant full access."

"As you wish, Mildred. Hello, Lieutenant Chow. I am Muriel, the vehicle's interactive computer interface. What can I do for you?"

"You studio people have nice toys," commented Chow. "Muriel, download the prisoners' portfolios for the Williamsville Penal Facility, and discard all those without a history of military service."

"Muriel, while you're doing that, cross-reference the work histories of studio personnel for military service. Also, place a call to John Wilson. I'm beginning to think whoever did this must have had some in with the studio. I need his take on disgruntled employees."

⊶✦⊷

John lurched across the living room of his mansion. The furnishings were all ultra-modern, expensive and devoid of charm. Nude pictures of e-stars, of both genders, decorated the walls. He reached the beeping vid-phone and slammed his fist into the control plate, bloodying his knuckles.

"SHUDDUP," he yelled, then leaned heavily against a counter beside the vid terminal.

"Gin and tonic," he slurred.

The auto-bar emitted a hissing sound as a rotary tray at one end turned, and the drink appeared. John downed it in one gulp.

"Little fakey slut!" He hoisted the crystal goblet and sent it careening against the wall. "Bitch, frigged bitch!" His chest heaved, and he began to sob. A minute later, he yelled. "LUBA, GET YOUR ASS OUT HERE!"

"My ass is present, master," spoke what appeared to be a short, large-busted, blonde woman. Her hair touched her shoulders, and her body was fit. She was dressed in a see-through white, lace teddy.

"Why in the divine's myriad names are you like that?" slurred John.

"Information request format not recognized," replied the female.

"Why are you in CG-F emulation mode?"

"You ordered me to service Mr. Jastrow's preferences."

"You're the best investment going, you mechanical slut. Get my gardening done for free. AS-F emulation mode, execute."

John watched as the robot shifted form, growing taller. The hair shortened and changed colour, and the breasts shifted up and shrank. The face swam as the features rearranged themselves. In moments, John stared at the image of Rowan, wearing an ill-fitting white, lace teddy.

"Are you at maximum height?" demanded John.

"This module can only emulate up to one-hundred and sixty-five centimetres. Post-market products are—"

"Silence. Luba, access my preference file. Execute blow job." John smiled as the robot approached him and placed its hand over his crotch.

"Oh, Mr. Wilson. It's so big! I know I'm a filthy fakey, but may I suck it, *please*, my master," breathed the robot in Rowan's voice.

"You may, you little fakey slut. You may."

Arlene watched the screen. Ryan's perspective showed a terrain of scrub bush and boulders. His gaze kept slipping to Rowan's backside. Arlene glanced at Ryan's empathic readings and shook her head. "I hope it works out for you. Brother, I only expect readings like this from a horny fifteen-year-old. I'm surprised you're not walking funny."

She shifted the big screen to Rowan's perspective. At that moment, she stumbled. Ryan caught her arm to help steady her. Arlene checked the empathic levels. "Forget I had doubts. It's always the quiet ones. Hope he can keep up with her. Better all the way around if she owns up to it soon."

Arlene's fingers itched to tweak Rowan's biology, but Michael had told her that that wasn't part of the series in anything short of a life or death situation.

"It looks like something is brewing," commented Michael's voice from behind her.

Arlene jumped, then swivelled her chair to face him. "How do you do that?"

"Do what?"

"Move so quietly."

Michael grinned. "Twenty-five years as a ground pounder. It's hard to break the habit."

"That was fifty years ago, wasn't it?"

"Sixty-two, actually. How are things progressing?"

"I had a satellite follow Kadar until he disappeared under the camouflage tarp. The pickup in the studio ATV has caught some nice moments between Chow and Mildred. I thought she was in a closed twosome."

"She is. She's been looking for an assistant she feels confident in. Her husband wants to run for a seat in the United Earth Systems' Parliament. If he wins it, she wishes to take a leave of absence and go to Earth with him."

"Oh. It's a mentor kind of thing."

"Exactly. You'll be happy to know I've made an overture to Greg about transferring to our show. When we go to season two, I'll be bringing him in."

"Thank the Divine. Just staying on top of perspective shifts and weeding out waste time is too much for one person."

"It is necessary to keep secrecy at this stage."

"I understand, but it's a lot of work."

Michael glanced at Rowan's empathic feeds. "Aw... I think Rowan is learning some things about this brave new world, and the creatures in it."

"The ecology of Silvanus never stabilized. The colonists still rely on imports for food. The economy can't get off the ground. The case went before the Republic Justice Committee. They agreed that the chameleonzoids were guilty of introducing the mould into the ecosystem, but we couldn't prove it wasn't an accident. The lizards got a slap on the wrist.

"Personally, I think it's stardust. The chameleonzoids are one of the oldest species. They know how to check for a bio-hazard better than anyone. They were pissed that we'd won the right to terraform Silvanus and not them.

"Long and short. We're stuck with a hunk of rock. All the planet's resources get gobbled up trying to neutralize the mould and keep an Earth-like ecology going. The population are dirt poor by interstellar standards."

"That's so sad. To have all that hope then have it shattered because some lizard has a grudge."

"Pettiness isn't only a human trait. On the other hand,

multi-generational vengeance is. That fact has led the chameleonzoids to reconsider their stance on reparations. They've even sent some scientists to help find a counter for the mould. They see the writing on the wall."

"Whatcha mean?"

"When human tech is up to it, the lizards are afraid that we might pay them a visit of the gunship variety. They pulled their stunt on Silvanus before we were well known as a species."

"I get the feeling humans don't have the best of reputations." Rowan's brow wrinkled. A pebble floated into the air and flew towards a boulder.

"WHAT ARE YOU DOING! ARE YOU CRAZY?" Ryan's shout held panic. He grasped her by the arms and stared into her face.

"What did I do? Let go of me!" The pebble fell to the ground as she jerked away from him.

"I... Oh, stardust! Rowan, swear to me you won't use your power unless it's a matter of life or death. Please!"

Rowan saw real fear in his face. "What's going on?"

Ryan swallowed in a dry throat. "I was hoping to have you on the *Star Hawk* before I had to get into this."

"Give me the short version." Rowan started walking again. Ryan took a compass reading and followed her example. Soon they were side by side.

"The short version. If you use your power, you could die," explained Ryan.

"This is becoming a repetitive theme. Why?" Rowan sounded annoyed.

"The best human telekinetics, that can control the ability, can only move a few grams over short distances. When they engineered your genome to incorporate the otterzoid level of the ability, it put an incredible strain on parts of your brain."

"My headaches."

"Right. On set, do you remember how there'd be a slow period every year, and you always got sick for a few days during it?"

"On set... that 'set' was my home, buster." Rowan looked straight ahead, refusing to acknowledge Ryan.

"Sorry. In any case, those times you were recovering from a bio-intervention."

"Huh?" Rowan looked puzzled.

"At night we'd knock everyone out, kidnap you, take you to the studio facility and do repairs. The main one with you was to inject stem cells into your brain, to replace the brain cells that died every time you used your power. We'd also replace your control pack."

"Oh, Divine! What about my father?"

"He isn't as much of a problem, human telepathic levels are naturally higher than the telekinetics, so we didn't have to repair him as often."

"We were... are, pieces of meat to you!"

Ryan scuffed his feet. "Not to me."

They walked in silence for a long time before they topped a hill. Rowan pointed into the distance. "What's that?"

Ryan gazed in the direction she indicated. There was a line of dark green. "That's a green belt. An area around a human habitation where the terraforming has reached stage four. In the middle of those trees is the town we're looking for. With luck, we'll be able to catch a mag-lev and be at the *Star Hawk* before nightfall."

"Then what?" Rowan paused to stare at him.

"Then we leave this world and take you someplace where who you are is more important than how original your genes are."

Rowan nodded. "Ryan. I'm sorry if I'm bitchy to you. My world is upside down, I'm scared, and I want to blame someone."

Ryan smiled and touched her cheek. "You have a right. Just please try and remember, I hate the studio almost as much as you."

"Why?"

Ryan started toward the line of trees. "Lots of reasons. I know Kadar told you I'm a clone. That's one of them. I hate how they make us second class citizens. Another." Ryan looked at the ground and took a deep breath before continuing. "I guess I'd have to tell you sooner or later. I have a wife."

"WHAT? YOU'RE MARRIED!" Rowan's face reddened to almost a healthy shade, despite the fact that she was living on artificial blood.

"It's not what you think. My marriage ended long ago. I was just too stubborn to admit it. Maybe it was because I was away so much during the wars. Joslin got lonely, I guess. She started obsessing about e-entertainments. You see, e-entertainments can be addictive. When I got out of the hospital, after my discharge, it went from bad to worse. You see, she..."

INTERVIEWS

H enry kept the illusion of Ryan's face on the screen and answered with Ryan's voice.

"Helen, read my lips. I'm not coming in for an interview!"

On the screen, the earnest young woman, in a studio security uniform, blanched. "Ryan, I like you, and I know you've had it rough with Joslin. Please don't make me sic the real police on you."

"On what grounds? I know my rights. You tell the cops I don't want to be bothered with my ex-employer. See how much they want to face a harassment charge. Look, hottie..."

"Pardon?" Helen seemed shocked.

Henry felt a quiver go through his processors and tried to think of how Ryan would cover a slip. "I'm sorry. I've been up for days. It must have slipped my internal filters. Could you take it as a compliment?"

Henry plastered an open smile on the image of Ryan and added a slight blush to his cheeks.

Helen lightly bit her lower lip. "Are you sure you aren't available for an interview?"

"Not today. I'll be free Friday. We could meet and chat. I'll come by the studio, say two-thirty?" Henry dilated the pupils of the Ryan image and added a trace of heat to his voice.

"Can't you make it sooner?" Helen smoothed her dark hair. A smile touched the corners of her wide, full-lipped mouth.

"I wish I could. I'm prepping my ship for a trip to Earth."

"Earth?" Her brown eyes sparkled. "I've always wanted to visit the homeworld. You must have done well for yourself to afford a trip like that."

Henry nearly laughed. He had her number now. "It isn't that expensive, if you own the ship. My cargo will cover the costs."

"You own your own interstellar freighter? Why did you ever work here?"

"I needed to do repairs. This planet is a cheap port. I've got some finishing touches to do, then it's to the stars."

"Congratulations. You should have told me. I've always dreamt of seeing the galaxy." She fiddled with the top button of her blouse.

"I do have some crew openings. We can talk Friday."

"I'd like that." Helen licked her lips.

"Until then." Henry made Ryan's face smile, then disconnected and shook his android head. "I finally get a date, and I'm either going to be in space or on a scrap pile. Stardust!

"Come on, Ryan, get here. I can't fool all of the people all of the time."

"Thanks, Melissa, I appreciate this. Tell Petra that if he comes by next Tuesday at eleven hundred, I'll set him up with that internship." Mike closed the vid-phone line on his office desk and moved to the lounge area. Greg sat in one of the loungers, his green skin a striking contrast against the brown chair.

"I'm sorry for the interruption. That was General DeFranko. It seems that Mildred had arranged for rather intensive satellite surveillance of the prison area. The general has seen to it that the images will be mislaid long enough to maintain Ryan's lead."

"I can't believe you're actually doing thiss," remarked Greg.

Mike settled in the other lounger. "People have become too complacent. It's been too long since anything shook their views of clones and how we treat them. This show will challenge a thousand preconceptions."

"If it doessn't get uss all arressted."

"There is a risk of that. A price must be paid to make great art. Don't worry, I had it prearranged with the planetary and system defence commanders. Officially, we are assisting the military in a double-blind training mission to seek out weaknesses in joint actions between them and other enforcement agencies. At worst, we are accessories in a theft. I'll pay for the lawyers, if it comes to that. Are you in?"

"You bet! I like Ryan. He alwayss treated me like one of the guyss. That issn't too common among unaltered humanss. They tend to look at uss as freakss."

"I thought that was the effect you wanted?"

"My parentss made the choice to be altered, I inherited it."

"I'm sorry."

"No ssweat. My girl is a norm. The docss ssay that the altered geness will be neutralized for the next generation."

"I'm glad it's working out for you. I want you to stay with *Angel Black* while we wrap up the crossover elements, then I'll bring you in under Arlene."

"That ssounds accseptable."

"Welcome aboard." Michael and Greg stood and shook hands.

Sara drummed her fingers on the cafeteria table and stared at Mildred, who sat opposite her. Lieutenant Chow sat beside Mildred with his hand-held pointing at Sara and stared into its screen. The large, clean room echoed with every word. The convict sheriff, a slender man with greying black hair and a hooked nose, stood to one side watching the proceedings. He was dressed in a tan uniform, shirt and slacks, with the linked-chain prisoner's emblem over the left breast pocket and a badge hung over the right. A belt with a stun pistol, a nightstick and hand-held completed the outfit.

"You saw no one?" said Mildred.

"I saw lots of people, this is the common building. People are always coming in and out of here." Sara smiled.

"Can the stardust. You know what I mean!" Mildred slapped her hand down on the table.

"That's enough of that," said the sheriff. "If you ask reasonable questions, you'll get reasonable answers, or you can stop scanning her for anatomic responses. I won't allow a fishing expedition on my beat."

Sara looked at the sheriff gratefully. Mildred glared at him.

"Let's try it this way." Mildred bit her cheek. "Have any strangers visited the prison in the last twenty-four hours?"

"They wouldn't be strangers after I met them." Sweat beaded Sara's brow.

Mildred gritted her teeth. She mentally counted to ten, then a cold smile crossed her face. "Did anyone you hadn't seen before yesterday enter the facility? Answer yes or no."

Sara bit her cheek.

"Seen in person," Chow rushed to add.

"Good point," agreed Mildred. "Well, Sara?"

"Yes," admitted Sara.

"Who were they?"

Sara smiled. "Who were who?"

"Stardust! Who were the visitors we were talking about?"

"Well... they seemed nice. Very polite and friendly. They..."

"Their names?" demanded Mildred.

"I'm horrible with names, I can never remember them."

"She's telling the truth. It took her three months to remember mine," commented the convict sheriff.

The cafeteria door opened, and Corporal Rodriguez

stepped in.

"What is it, Corporal?" Chow didn't take his eyes off the hand-held's screen.

"Sir, we've completed our check of the prisoners' ident codes. Two are missing."

"Which two?" demanded Mildred.

"A Doctor Kadar Hadi Al-Qahtani and Victor Edwin O'Hare. I took the liberty of cross-referencing them against military service. Both were line personnel. Victor O'Hare was a ground forces service tech."

"Good work, Rodriguez. Get me their files," said Chow.

Rodriguez held out a data wafer and passed it to his lieutenant.

"You really do want to make sergeant." Chow took the wafer and plugged it into his hand-held. "Have the others arrived?"

"Yes, sir. We have ten personnel awaiting further orders."

"Well sheriff, it appears you have some lost sheep. Perhaps we should try and find them. I want the locator frequency for this Kadar and Victor, right now!" Mildred stared at the sheriff with unveiled hostility.

"I've extended you every courtesy. You're only a studio cop. You can't order me to do anything."

"Sheriff, give my men the locator frequencies. I have the authority to order you to do so, and I am," said the lieutenant.

"Technically," began the sheriff.

"Now!" Chow stood and glared at the sheriff.

"To the letter of the law, sir. They're in my office safe. Shall we?" The sheriff sauntered from the room.

"I'd better go with him." Chow hurried to catch up with the sheriff.

"Rodriguez, could you stay a moment?" called Mildred.

"Of course, ma'am. How can I help you?"

"Could you arrange for the men to look for traces of the ATV? It must be someplace. Without transport, our quarry is as good as caught."

"Of course, ma'am. The lieutenant told me to follow your orders. I'll get the troops looking."

"Thank you." Mildred watched Rodriguez leave the room, then turned to Sara. "And that leaves us."

"I don't know what you want me to tell you." Sara looked pale.

Mildred smiled. "Anything you remember. First, what did they look like?"

"The man was cute. Big hands, I always notice peoples' hands, you can tell so much about them. Take yours, for example. They're square, which means you're very practical, and your nails are short, so fashion isn't important to you, and—"

"Tell me about his hands." Mildred massaged her temples.

"They were big, and you know what that means." Sara gave a knowing smile. "And they looked strong, like they could hold onto a star and keep it from falling into a black hole. His nails were short and clean, but not filed. That told me he cared about cleanliness but didn't want to waste time on fussy things. I like that in a man. I never liked sissy fashion plates with every hair in place."

"We share that in common. Now, what did his face look like."

"Hmm... You ever experience, *Kids in the Band*?"

"I reviewed a few episodes."

"He looked a little like Trevor, only his hair was a different colour, or maybe he looked more like Andy. I guess he could be a cross between the two." Sara fixed her inquisitor with a vacant gaze.

"Fine, what did the woman look like?"

Sara snickered, intelligence filling her expression like water flowing into a picture. "You know what she looked like, Mrs. Studio Security Officer."

Mildred shook her head. "Why are you doing this? What are they to you?"

Sara smiled. "My father fought in the Swampla defensive. He took a dose of neuro-toxin. The only way to save him was a new body. I watched him work every nova-blasted job that came along after that. Then one day he died cleaning a defective waste conduit for a tower city. Drowned in a river of human shit. He should have been doing maintenance on mag-lev systems. He had the qualifications, but they wouldn't hire a fakey.

"I know what you are, and I know what she is. If someone wants to try and do the right thing by her in this miserable, unjust universe, then I'm all for it."

Mildred stared at the other woman. "I'm wasting my time here."

Sara smiled pleasantly. "Nice that you figured it out. Now can we finish this, it's getting close to dinner time."

Rowan tore the wrapper off the ration bar and took a bite. "This is good!" she commented. The trees surrounding them allowed the late afternoon sunlight to dapple the ground, and a soft loam of dead leaves and other organics cushioned the bedrock.

"I hate the nova blasted things," grumbled Ryan as he bit into his own bar.

"Come on. When you said emergency rations, I expected something dry and disgusting. These taste like cake." Rowan stopped at a stream that crossed their path. The water bubbled and gurgled between moss-covered rocks.

"You try eating them for three months straight."

"Three months?"

"We were pinned down on Murack Seven C. The felinezoids had cut our supply line. Emergency rations and recyc water were all we had for three months."

"That must have been awful. I thought the battle was on Murack Five."

"Murack is a star with ten planets. Murack Seven is a

gas giant with seven moons. C is the third largest. The war encompassed the entire system."

"So Murack Five is the fifth planet out from the star Murack."

Ryan moved to the stream's edge and spoke with a waver in his voice. "We should cross. I want to be at the station before we lose the light."

Kadar sat in the driver's seat of Ryan's ATV. The pain was less when he didn't move. Victor entered the cockpit and passed him a wire with a switch on its end.

"If you throw this, it will turn on the grav-lifts. I still say you're nuts."

"Perhaps?" Kadar sighed and looked up at the larger man. "Better to die in a final blaze of glory than waste away beyond any hope of doing so."

Victor nodded. "My ancestors on old Earth believed in a place called Valhalla. The bravest of warriors who died in battle went there."

Kadar smiled. "My parents were Muslim. I haven't really thought much about an afterlife. Perhaps a beautiful garden with young, nubile felinezoids and otterzoids to see to my every whim."

Victor settled in the co-pilot's seat. "I have to ask, why fur?"

Kadar closed his eyes. "I guess because they were as unlike my mother as I could find. You should go."

"Why?"

"Because you could get into trouble, and your tracking nano-bots are still active. Head for the swim-hole I showed you when you first arrived. If they say anything, tell them you didn't know they were looking for you."

Victor stood. "You're a good man, Kadar. We'll miss you. I'll wedge the door closed after me so that it doesn't affect the aerodynamics."

HUNTER THE HUNTED

Ryan stared out from between the trees as wind blasted out of vents at one end of the mag-lev station, marking the train's arrival.

"That's thirty minutes." Rowan checked her watch.

"Yup. Remember, we want to be in the station for as little time as possible. Once we're on the train, we should be all right. If anyone challenges you, you're Joslin Chandler, and you had a major reconstruction done as an early ninety-fifth birthday gift."

Rowan looked at the card that Ryan had passed her. The picture on it was of an emaciated woman in her middle years. "This is your wife?"

Ryan looked at the picture. "She's married to an e-rig now. That was taken when she turned ninety-three. It was the last time I got her out of our apartment. Don't let anyone get the card. If they scan you against its data files, they'll know you aren't her. Don't use it for anything if you can help it. I'll use my card to cover our fares."

"Right. Should we go in now?"

Ryan checked his hand-held for the time. "Just like we planned."

Standing, Ryan and Rowan stepped onto the trail and walked into the town. Adobe buildings flanked a network of streets. The large, white, stone structure of the mag-lev station occupied the end of the main street. When they reached the pavement, Rowan kicked off her shoes and put on the heels that she had hooked to her gym bag. Ryan took her hand and both plastered smiles on their faces as they followed the main street to the terminal.

By the time they reached the terminal lobby, the train was pulling in. Taking her arm to steady her, Ryan ran with Rowan through the lobby. Rowan barely had time to notice the vending machines that lined the wall and the spattering of people occupying the rows of seats before she was rushed to a platform. The mag-lev car stood on the track, its doors starting to close. It looked like a tubular subway car. Ryan half-carried her the last few steps and jammed his leg against the door. It automatically slid back. Stepping into the car, he ran a card with his picture on it through a scanner unit, twice. Rowan watched as a bored-looking man in a ground forces uniform glanced at her, then leaned back against the wall.

"Good afternoon, Doctor Chandler. Your travelling account is down to 10 per cent, do you wish me to request a funds transfer from your general credit balance?" spoke a soft female voice.

Rowan felt a gentle pull towards the back of the car, and the platform disappeared.

"No, thank you."

"Enjoy your ride. We will be at the Ball Tower Link Station in ten minutes."

Rowan looked out the window on the door. The tunnel wall was a blur.

"How fast are we going?"

Ryan glanced out the window and half-dragged her toward the closest of the rows of seats that filled the train. "Only about eight-hundred kilometres per hour."

"Only?" Rowan's voice squeaked.

"The main inter-tower line travels at sixteen hundred."

Rowan swallowed and took a seat. She fumbled for a safety belt and found none. "Has there ever been an accident?"

"Of course, nothing is foolproof." Ryan leaned back in his chair and closed his eyes.

"Were there any survivors?"

"Nah. They did manage to collect some of the liquefied remains for burial."

"Stardust!" Rowan stopped looking for safety belts and tried to think of anything else.

Mildred bent down and examined the side of a tree where the bark had been scraped away.

"Do the convicts have anything that could lift an ATV?" She turned to the convict sheriff.

He smiled coldly. "No."

Lieutenant Chow examined another damaged tree farther along the gap that allowed farm machinery into the orchards. He moved to Mildred's side before addressing the sheriff.

"Do you have portable, electric generators with a twenty-thousand watt or better generating capacity?"

The sheriff pretended to consider. "No."

"Could they have recharged the batteries with a lower output generator and moved it?" Mildred rubbed the back of her neck.

"Probably not fast enough to avoid detection." Lieutenant Chow pondered the mystery.

"If that thing is still operational, they could be long gone," said Mildred.

"Sir, ma'am, I've found something," called a woman in a private's uniform with her blonde hair pulled into a bun.

Chow and Mildred moved to the discovery and stared at a piece of blue plastic embedded in the tree.

"ATV debris?" Mildred touched the scrap. It flexed under her hand.

"No. It doesn't have the rigidity, it..." Chow paused and stroked his chin. Mildred watched him, a smile coming to her face.

"Sheriff, could a combination of the suspensor vehicles

you have on the farm carry an ATV?"

"They aren't designed to do that, and none of the control systems could be linked, and—"

"Thank you, Sheriff. That's how they did it. They hoisted the thing onto multiple suspensors. It's a good bet that the ATV is, at least for now, out of commission." Chow moved to where the passage between the trees made a four-way juncture.

"Sir, this side. I've found another damaged tree," called a large black man wearing sergeant's stripes. Chow and Mildred rushed to join him.

⊶

Kadar sat alone in the ATV's cockpit. He watched a hand-held as pictures paraded across the screen. A middle-aged Ryan with a fully-functional Henry and himself standing in front of the Swampla Capital building. Another image, him and Kitoy in a felinezoid green space on the Switchboard Station.

"It has been a good life." He checked the time. Eighteen hundred. "They are taking their time to find me."

He leaned back in his chair and closed his eyes.

"Deeeeeeeeeeeeee," sounded in the cabin. Kadar's eyes jerked open.

"Finally." His voice was little more than a whisper. "I'm glad they threw Victor's tripwire. It will make it all much safer."

⊶

Arlene watched the feeds from inside the ATV and the satellite downlink.

"What I wouldn't give for an empathic download on Kadar," she muttered. Rowan and Ryan were delegated to a side screen, where they waited impatiently in a mag-lev terminal to catch the connecting train.

The satellite showed Chow's troops stalking up to a low, grassy hill.

"This is so much easier when you can manipulate the characters," griped Arlene.

⚬═══⊷

Mildred watched the troops approach the mound of dirt that bisected an intersection of the access tracks.

"My hand-held has the sonar attachment, and it says that mound is hollow," stated Chow.

"Big surprise. I will hand it to them. From satellite, you wouldn't think anything of this." Mildred examined a magnification of the mound's surface on her hand-held.

"Do you think they'll be in there?" Chow checked his troop's location, then a thought crossed his mind. "Stardust." Tapping the screen of his hand-held, he changed its mode.

"What?" asked Mildred.

"Tripwires. If I was hunkered down like..." Chow never finished his sentence.

⚬═══⊷

Kadar pulled himself forward on his seat and tapped the screen of his hand-held, bringing up a set of instructions.

"Grav-lifts on." He threw the switch connected to the wire that Victor had given him. "Activate all grav-nullifiers." He threw a set of switches on the console. The smell of hot circuits filled the cabin, and an unhealthy humming sound assaulted his ears.

⚬═══⊷

Arlene watched via satellite as the battered ATV shuddered into the air like some grotesque blimp. Soil and bits of sod clung to it as the troops ran for cover.

"Go, you crazy old pervert, go!" Arlene was bouncing in her seat.

The unhealthy hum of malfunctioning grav-nullifiers made speech impossible. Chow and Mildred watched the ATV climb into the air, like the remains of some horrid beast of legend risen from its mouldering grave. Its hull was fractured in so many places it looked like scales. The front end was nothing but shattered polycarbonate.

The broken machine lurched, leaning dangerously to one side. A new whine joined the hum of the grav-nullifiers, and it blasted forward.

Still deafened by the noise, Mildred activated her hand-held and made a one-sided call. "Satellite tracking, follow an illegal ATV leaving Williamsville Penitentiary!"

Kadar gritted his teeth against the noise. Everything was shaking around him. It took all his remaining strength to wrestle the control wheel so that he flew in a straight line. The compass on his secondary screen had two red lines drawn on its face, and he kept the needle between them. The wind turbines were screaming, and the numbers on his power gauge were scrolling down.

"WE HAVE THEM," shouted Mildred.

"THEY WON'T GET FAR WITHOUT CAMOUFLAGE," agreed Chow in a parade yard bellow.

"Let's get back to the vehicles. I want to question this Johnny myself." Mildred started down the access road.

Chow turned to his troops, who were brushing dirt and sod off themselves. "COMPANY ASSEMBLE," he bellowed.

Several of them seemed not to notice.

"COMPANY ASSEMBLE," he called again.

Rodriguez looked at the lieutenant, touched his ears and shook his head.

"Stardust!" Chow went to collect his people.

Kadar hung on. The strain of steering the ATV was draining him, but he hadn't felt this alive in years. He looked at the front viewer. Blue sky stretched before him in an endless panorama. He checked an auxiliary screen that showed the terrain below. It was barren and rocky. He glanced at the timer on his hand-held. The flight had lasted less than ten minutes.

The ATV pitched nose down and started to lose altitude.

"Stardust, the grav-lifts." Kadar cut the power to the turbines, allowing his momentum to carry him forward. The main screen filled with green, then blue.

"Lake Doig, you are a beautiful sight."

Arlene recorded everything with the hidden cameras in the ATV. Kadar was shaking like a leaf and seemed to be unaware of the blood that dripped from his nose.

Mildred looked up as a Civil Air Defence Unit rocketed overhead. The five sleek, atmospheric-assault aircraft glinted in the sun as they accelerated toward their target.

Kadar watched as the atmospheric assault aircraft overshot him. Their wing lights flashed a warning, which he ignored. The jets turned, and as they approached, a missile sped away from the lead aircraft. The ATV jerked with an impact. The smell of burning circuits became worse. Kadar started to lose altitude at a faster pace.

"Let me get a little further. A few more seconds." He stared at the power metre, which read 2 per cent, then at his forward screen, which now showed blue waves with white caps.

He nodded. Picking up his hand-held, he pressed a button.

"Hello, S.E.T.E. head office," said a pleasant female voice.

"For that which is most human and high in us all. Freedom, equality, love. In service to true humanity."

The ATV jerked with another impact.

Kadar smiled. "For the love of Rowan. Sod you!" Reaching forward, he threw the switch that activated his turbines, then killed his grav-nullifiers.

⊂═◈⊱

"Divine be with him!" Arlene watched the satellite feed, which showed the ATV plummeting toward the lake. The internal feed showed Kadar, eyes closed and smiling. There was a jumble of light, and the internal feed cut out. The satellite showed a plume of water rocketing into the air, then settling in a shower of rain. A small, quiet part of Arlene's mind noted how pretty the falling water was. It resembled a billion airborne diamonds, each to reflect a facet of a life now gone.

⊂═◈⊱

Mildred received the report while she was waiting for Chow and his men. She sat in silent disbelief. Hands trembling, she activated her hand-held.

"Helen," Mildred spoke as soon as the other woman's face appeared on the screen.

"I heard. I've accessed the web and am requesting bids from retrieval diving firms."

"Good. Don't take the lowest one. Go with the low end of average. If it's too good to be true, it is. I want quality work here."

"Yes, ma'am."

"Have you completed the in-house interviews?"

"I've got everyone but Ryan Chandler. He's agreed to meet with me this Friday."

"Friday. Why so late?"

"He recently quit and is preparing to take a trip to Earth. It's the earliest that fit his schedule."

"Oh. I'm going to the crash site. Contact me with the name of the retrieval company."

A TASTE OF THE MASTER'S LIFE

19

Mildred drove in silence. Chow sat in the navigator's seat while four of his men occupied the seats in the back. The rest of the squad followed along in their military transport vehicle.

Chow sadly flipped through the satellite images. His breath caught. "Muriel, compile a timeline from the satellite image now on the screen. Follow the human figures forward and back."

"Did you find the convicts hiding the ATV?" Mildred glanced at the image.

"Even better!" Chow pressed a button, causing the image on his screen to appear on Mildred's secondary screen. "These were taken about thirteen-thirty hours, on the west side of the prison grounds."

The image showed two people in wide-brimmed, straw hats walking across the prison perimeter towards a hiking trail.

"They could be some day-trippers who decided to picnic under the trees," said Mildred.

Chow worked another control, zooming in on the image. "I don't think they're wearing hiking clothes, and that bag the smaller of them is carrying seems awfully bulky."

Mildred stared at the new image Chow brought up and slammed on the brakes. "Muriel, call the studio. Tell them it will be a while before I meet up with the salvage team."

Turning the wheel, she hit the accelerator and started toward the sector shown in the satellite image.

"Maybe I should renew the alert in the travel stations," remarked Chow.

"We should check the area first. I want to know which direction those day hikers came from before I risk my reputation. Remember, 'cover your ass' in all things."

Chow nodded. He could feel the enthusiasm returning.

"Muriel, interface with the planetary travel grid. Check to see if Ryan Chandler is currently on any form of public transit." Steering one-handed, she flipped open her hand-held and tapped its screen. A moment later, Helen's face appeared.

"Mrs. Tallman?" said the younger woman.

"Helen, call Ryan Chandler, then call me back and let me know if he's in." Mildred closed the line.

"A suspect?" Chow grinned.

"Possibly. If he is, studio security really fell apart at some point. It would mean that this was an inside job, and we screen all our people."

"It happens."

"Not on my shift, it doesn't!" Mildred focused all her attention on driving and sped up.

Ryan settled into his seat beside Rowan on the mag-lev to the Duchovny Tower. They'd been forced to wait for over an hour in the terminal. Being on the move again was a relief.

"How long will this take?" Rowan fidgeted uncomfortably.

"Forty minutes, give or take. Relax, mag-levs are statistically the safest mode of on-planet travel."

"And if something goes wrong?"

"You don't live long enough to worry about it." Ryan patted her hand and smiled.

The train pulled out and started to accelerate.

"Are there magazines or anything?" Rowan fidgeted.

Ryan looked at her sadly and nodded. "You'd come across it sooner or later. Each seat is equipped with an e-rig. They only do PG non-specific-viewpoint programming on the trains. It would be a good idea for you to use it. It covers your face, which means that you're less likely to be recognized."

"Fine, anything! So long as it takes my mind off how fast I'm going."

"The nano-bots they used to construct your memories are the same type that the e-inputs use. You should be good to go. Lean back and press the green button on your armrest. The service is included in the boarding cost. The computer will pull you out five minutes before we reach our destination."

Rowan did as instructed and watched as the e-helmet descended out of the top of her seat.

She found herself staring into a selection screen listing various shows.

"*'Detective Dave'*. They have got to be kidding!" She read down the list.

'*Angel Black* - Gamble and Lose - Angel and Toronk reconcile after her tryst with Farley, while Farley tries to win back Rowan's affections. Meanwhile the chameleonzoid pirate Hussut and Valaseau plot to access the escape pod and summon the pirates' battle cruiser into Earth orbit. - Warning: adult themes and violence.'

"Been there, done that, once was enough. This is sick!"

She settled on a tourist piece that was a tour of the studio museum and triggered activate.

Questions came up asking her gender, age and sexual orientation. She was tempted to lie but really didn't want to find out what that might result in. Rowan found herself standing at the doors to a large, one-story building fashioned out of rock. The roof was covered with black panels. She entered, stepped up to an automated ticket booth and swiped an ident card before moving forward.

She could feel the brush of her clothing against her skin; smell the mild hint of lavender that was in the air. Every sense was alive, but she had no free will. She couldn't control her actions. The first wave of emotion hit her as she looked at a hologram. The image looked like her father, perhaps age thirty. She felt lust for the man. She tried to feel ashamed but couldn't. She was filled with the emotion of some other woman who'd once done this tour.

"Hi, I'm the image of an ASH-M series clone. I'll be your guide as we explore the fascinating history of e-entertainments." The image looked at her with smouldering eyes, and the tour commenced.

John's vid-phone bleeped. He rolled over where he'd fallen in a puddle of his own vomit.

It bleeped again, then the record function triggered. Helen's face appeared on the screen.

"Mr. Wilson, if you're there, please pick up. We need to speak with you about possible security issues with your staff. Anything that you could tell us would be a help. Mrs. Tallman thinks the ATV that crashed into Lake Doig is the vehicle that was used to transport Rowan. She needs to figure out who the thief was. Please call the studio as soon as you get this." The screen went blank.

John rolled his obese form over and belched.

Mildred stared at the tire tracks. Even in the evening light, it was obvious that one set came from inside the prison and another went back the same way. No footprints came from the hiking trail, but two sets went toward it. "It was a diversion. I've got to learn to stop underestimating this Johnny."

"I've re-instituted the travel watch. Any idea who the thief is?"

Mildred held her hand-held focused on a print in a patch of moist dirt. "He wears a size-ten shoe. Hand-held, connect me with Helen in studio security."

"Mrs. Tallman, I haven't been able to get through to Mr. Wilson. I did reach Ryan. He's getting really annoyed about us harassing him."

Mildred smiled and ran into her vehicle. "Muriel, where do the records place Ryan Chandler's location?"

"Ryan Chandler is currently on the express mag-lev from Ball Tower to Duchovny Tower. He's listed twice."

"We have him." Chow stepped into the vehicle.

"It's indicative, but not enough to revoke his travel privileges. There's no law against having a sophisticated answering machine...unless... Muriel, put in a call to Justice Fred Edwards at the Duchovny Tower. Bleep me when you get through to the man himself."

Mildred returned her attention to Chow. "I've met him at some studio parties. He might be willing to issue a freeze on Chandler's travel privileges."

"Oh. Now what?" Chow looked out the door toward the setting sun.

"Now we hope that someone catches the property in a travel station while we go check out that ATV. Our Johnny, Ryan, was living in it for the Divine knows how long. There's bound to be DNA left if the ATV didn't disintegrate in the crash."

"Ma'am, those troop carriers wouldn't disintegrate in a sun. They may break down, but they are tough puppies. We'll find it."

"Good. We'll have to set a watch at the Duchovny mag-lev station. I want anyone that looks remotely like the property checked. Double-check that the property's particulars have been logged at the spaceport. He's going to have to take her off-planet. When he tries, we'll get him. Unless... Hmm." Mildred started for the driver's compartment.

"What are you thinking?" Chow fell into step beside her.

"I'm thinking I'm going to check a hobbyist website, then call a man about some scrap. Can you arrange for a military airlift to pick us up?"

"Yes."

"Call it in. We may be in worse trouble than I thought."

"The emotional surrogates provide a template that is translated into an input matrix and sent to the e-rigs." Rowan listened as her father's image lectured as she watched a display demonstrating an emotional transfer.

"Excuse me, where did the genetic material for the emotional surrogates come from?" Rowan felt her lips move, her throat vibrate, but it wasn't her voice that issued out.

The image of her father smiled. "That is a good question. This display addresses that issue." The holographic guide vanished, then reappeared beside another display. Pictures of various e-stars were up on it. Rowan noticed her own image there. Her eyes refused to fix on it, instead preferring a picture of a well-muscled, black man.

At least she had good taste, thought Rowan. The tour focused her attention on what the guide was saying.

"Way back in human history, during the era known as the twentieth-century CE, humans had a primitive form of entertainment. Dramas were performed and recorded, then shared with an audience through a variety of means." The hologram smiled condescendingly. "They were restricted to the senses of hearing and sight and had no emotional input."

Television and movies. He's talking about television and

movies like they were hieroglyphs, thought Rowan.

"Some examples of these early attempts at entertainment have survived to this day. Copies of these can be viewed in the archive sections of this museum and purchased in the gift shop.

"The actors and actresses that performed in these entertainments were deified by primitive humans, who worshipped them as incarnate gods. The main temple of this strange faith was in a region known as California.

"Sometime in the ninth century before contact, a natural disaster struck this region. This disaster destroyed the temples and bankrupted many of the entertainers.

"This period in history corresponds with human kind's first major advances in biotechnology. Many performers sold their DNA to the emerging biotech firms. These firms made perpetual cell cultures and extrapolated products that allowed people to alter their appearance to approximate that of their favourite deity.

"Centuries later, the studios obtained the rights to these cell cultures. These cell cultures, coupled with samples revived and added from archaeological digs, have provided the DNA templates to create the emotional surrogates."

"How do they create the surrogates' quasi-personality?"

"We are sorry to cut short your entertainment. The train is approaching the Duchovny Tower station, please prepare to disembark."

Rowan blinked as the interface lifted off her head.

"What did you think?" Ryan reached over and took her hand.

"It's horrid! TV was bad enough! And they talk about clones like we're pieces of meat, property. I..."

"Keep your voice down." Ryan's face looked panicked.

An elderly couple in the next seat over stared at Rowan with distaste. "I don't know why they let fakeys ride with decent people," said the woman who was resplendent in a fur coat.

"Maybe because it was the lives of our first bodies that

bought humanity's worlds from the day we joined the Republic," snapped Ryan.

While the woman looked away, the man leaned into the aisle and whispered, "Terra noster sors."

"Sangunis abl planeta," Ryan whispered back.

The man nodded gravely and shot Ryan a thumbs up.

Rowan shook her head.

Ryan turned his attention back to her. "So, you didn't like e-entertainments?"

Rowan spoke softly. "I don't like not having control. It was creepy not being able to decide anything. I hated it."

Ryan took a deep breath and beamed. "You can't imagine how glad I am to hear that."

CELEBRITY

Michael lay in his king-sized bed with his wife's back spooned against his front. She felt warm and, even after their fifty-three years together, he knew there was no place he'd rather be.

"I love you so," he whispered.

"Hmm," was her sleepy, post-coital reply.

"Sir, you have a priority message from the studio. It's Mrs. Tallman," said the house computer.

Michael sighed. "Mr. Wells, please ask her to hold the line. I'll take it in the living room."

"Very good, sir. Should I block the video feed?"

"No, I'll put on a robe." Mike gently extracted his arm from under his wife and kissed her cheek. She murmured, then rolled onto her back. He paused to smile at her. She was as beautiful as the day he'd first seen her. He climbed from the bed and donned a heavy, hemp robe. "Mr. Wells, what's the current status of Project Exodus?"

"As of Arlene's last report, the protagonists were in an inter-city mag-lev. Shall I call for an update?"

"No. Things are going about as well as they can. It's time to let the cat out of the bag." Michael strode out of the bedroom and down the hall to the classically, but comfortably, furnished living-room. He settled on his couch before he spoke. "Mr. Wells, please activate the vidscreen."

Mildred's face filled the wall-sized screen in front of the couch. "Michael, the property is still on the move, as is the fugitive."

"Really? Well, that is more a matter for John to deal with. Why aren't you in touch with him?"

"Because I don't like him, and I do like you. If you're involved, this may be your last chance to cover your ass. Why didn't you tell me Ryan Chandler had a stargate rated space vessel?"

Michael straightened on his couch. "Does it matter?"

"Our Johnny has to get off-planet somehow. That ATV was old military scrap."

"Ryan was never listed in the club files as having an ATV. He never received a rating to operate one. I took a quick look at his records when all this began and dismissed him for those reasons. Do you suspect him? Didn't Helen speak with him a few hours ago?"

"The vid-phone messages were faked. He was on a mag-lev and answered his ship's pick up the last time we called."

"You really believe that Ryan is behind the theft? He always seemed a moral fellow." Mike smiled.

"I've placed a request with the Duchovny City Justice Department to block his travel account."

Mike looked astonished, then concerned. "That was not advisable. You don't have any physical evidence, and the studio would not look kindly on a harassment charge. Ryan hates us, with reasonable justification. Perhaps you should wait until you have something more solid."

"Mike, so help me, if you're behind this…"

"Mildred, I'm on my own time, and you called at an inopportune moment. Please don't rant at me." Mike smiled.

"Fine, I'll try to get through to John again. I need Chandler's complete file. You wouldn't happen to know his shoe size?"

"Not a clue." Michael shrugged. "I think the more distant from this I am, the better. If I'm not directly involved, I might be able to talk Ryan out of suing us. We have a tentative friendship. Are you still on for the launch party next month?"

"I'll be there. Why is it so hush-hush? What's your new show about?"

"You'll be pleasantly surprised, I think. I'm signing off now."

"Say hi to Marcy for me. If he slips past us, I warned you."

"Understood." The screen went blank. Mike drummed his fingers on his knee. "Mr. Wells, contact Fred Edwards at the Duchovny Tower, flag it as urgent."

The screen filled with the image of a handsome, Caucasian man with strong features and black hair greying at the temples. "Mike, if this is about the request for the travel stoppage by your security head, I was about to rubber-stamp it."

"Oh." Michael pursed his lips. "I have to ask, if it wasn't my studio security officer, would you grant the restriction?"

Fred stared out of the screen. "Hmmm... The evidence is light. I know Mildred, and she is good. Still, if a city cop came to me with this for a warrant, I probably would have asked for something more solid. This sort of thing is always a judgment call. Why?"

"Fred, I'd be much obliged if you treated the request *exactly* as you would if you didn't know Mildred or me."

Fred smiled. "Up to your old tricks, are you? Say hello to Marcy for me. I'll disqualify myself and pass it to Justice McFly. He's a bit of a stickler for individual rights. I really should have stepped aside at the start because of our history."

"Thanks, Fred. Terra noster sors."

"Terra noster sors." Fred broke the connection.

"There you go, Ryan, that's the last bit of help I have to give." Mike stood and stretched before making his way back to bed.

Ryan guided Rowan across the platform. Wall screens advertised a variety of products she never would have believed were possible, and vending machines dispensed a seemingly endless supply of junk to the people that lined up at them. A humming sound drew her attention to the back of the train. People on power-bikes were pulling onto the platform from a train car and exiting down a ramp.

Ryan watched the direction of her gaze. "Commuters. I used to do that grind three days a week. One thing I won't miss."

"So much is different, but so much is the same. I'd expected, with all your technology, things would be a lot stranger." Rowan turned her gaze forward.

"The tech has to serve humanity. We learned after the Gene War. If you change a human too much, they're no longer human. Technology has to adapt to humanity, not the other way around."

"The Gene War?" Rowan walked with Ryan into the station's lobby.

"Happened about six hundred years before contact. They tried to engineer speciality humans. Problem was, the speciality humans didn't think of themselves as human. They tried to take over. It got messy! After that, laws were passed about the limits on genetic engineering. That's when Humans Ascendant got its start."

Rowan stopped. She was staring into the corner of the station and couldn't believe her eyes. Gunther was locked in a passionate embrace with Rowan, herself. "What...? what...? what...?"

Ryan followed the direction of her gaze. "Oh that. Some people..."

"Wow!" commented a middle-aged, Filipino-looking man in a suit.

Rowan turned to look at him.

"I haven't seen a Mary in years. Your doctor is an artist."

"I... Um."

"The lady is with me," explained Ryan.

"Hey, wow, sorry. Misunderstanding time. I didn't mean it like that. It's just, she looks so much like the fakey. I'm thinking of getting a Rick, from *Defenders of the Crystal*, done. I'd really appreciate it if you could give me your doctor's name. Yours is the best work I've ever seen." The man pulled his hand-held out of his pocket and held it up to record the name.

Rowan's hand trembled where Ryan had taken it.

"I... well... I..."

Ryan mentally groped, then a thought came to mind. "Kadar Al-Qahtani, though you'll probably have a hard time getting in to see him. He's an old space forces buddy of mine. That's the only reason he saw Joslin at all. He's semi-retired."

"Tell him from me, he's an artist. I have the deluxe disk version of every episode of *The Castaways*. You could be Mary the way you look." The man turned to Ryan and smiled. "You're a lucky man. Thanks for the name. I'll try to get a referral." He walked off into the crowd.

"What?" Rowan looked like a deer caught in headlights.

"Come on." Ryan took her arm and started toward the station's doors.

"Who's Mary?" whispered Rowan.

"She was a character on an old show called *The Castaways*. I'd forgotten that they made her blonde. She was an AS-F series, like you. With the hair and the skirt, you look like her. I'm an idiot! I should have seen it from the start." They were almost at the doors.

"Great. So how about the incest fest in the corner? Me and my dad, like, please. There are things I don't do!" A shudder passed through Rowan.

"Some people get themselves altered to look like e-stars. The looks from *Angel Black* are very popular."

"Stardust! You people are sick!"

Ryan and Rowan had reached the door when a siren sounded. There was a clicking noise, and the doors all slid shut.

"We apologize for the inconvenience. General visual scanning has detected a possible felon. Please bear with us as security forces investigate."

"What?" Rowan looked around panicked. The facial expressions around her ranged from angry to curious.

"Do nothing," whispered Ryan.

Two dark-haired, muscular men, dressed in black shirts and slacks and wearing badges, pushed through the crowd. Each wore a thick, black belt on which was hung a hand-held, a nightstick, a stun gun and what looked to Rowan like a semiautomatic pistol.

Ryan tensed and tried to remember his unarmed combat training.

The two cops pushed by them and strode up to the woman that looked like Rowan. They spoke to her, but their words were lost in the crowd's babble. She passed them a card. The larger of the cops slid it into his hand-held. He smiled and said something as his partner spoke into his hand-held. The woman laughed, then the intercom came to life.

"Thank you for your cooperation and for your use of inter-city mag-lev services. Have a nice day."

The doors opened. Ryan let the flow of people carry Rowan and himself into the parking garage. Small, boxy cars filled the spaces. Ryan led Rowan to the closest of these and held the door for her. When they were seated in the front seats, he swiped his travel card through a scanner and pressed his thumb against a plate built into the dash. These were the only controls.

"Hello, Doctor Chandler. Your transport card is showing only 3 per cent. Would you like me to auto-transfer funds from your primary account?" asked a pleasant female voice.

"No."

"Where do you wish to go today, Doctor Chandler?"

"Hogan's airstrip, most direct route."

"Plotting course. There is congestion on Shatner

Boulevard. Should I divert to Straczynski Drive?"

"Use the fastest route, taking into account current traffic conditions."

The car pulled out and drove itself into a long concrete corridor.

"We want an old landing site called Hogan's field," Mildred told the pilot of the military air transport as she boarded. Chow took the seat beside her. Four of his people filled the two rows of seats behind that.

"I have it on the computer. It's on the northern continent," said the pilot.

"Get us there as quickly as possible," ordered Mildred.

"Aye, ma'am!" A grin split the pilot's face.

Mildred and Chow jerked back in their seats as the aircraft accelerated at six Gs.

"Sky jockeys!" muttered Chow when he could speak again.

"Chandler wears size ten shoes." Mildred wiped a dribble of saliva from the side of her mouth as she scanned her hand-held.

"I've called a reservist I know on the Duchovny Police Force. He's watching for Chandler on the QT and is going to do a drive-by to see if he can spot the property." Chow stared into his hand-held. "Chandler must be up to something. He's registered as owning a power-bike, but he logged on in a ground car."

Mildred pressed a button on her hand-held. "Helen."

"Yes, Mrs. Tallman," came from the small speaker.

"I want you to look around for Ryan's power-bike. The tracking code will be with studio parking. Call me if you find it."

"I'm on it. I don't think he could—"

"Do it!" Mildred ended the call. "That girl does her thinking with her ovaries."

"Do you think we have enough to block his flight clearance?" asked Chow.

"Only if you have some friends in Space Traffic Control. After being turned down by that Justice, I don't want to file another request without something solid to back it up. What we have is all circumstantial. He could have given his bike to a friend. I wish I had that blasted ATV. One shred of his DNA and we'd have him."

"Who do you think is in on this with him?" Chow brought up a list of names from Ryan's old squad. Most were coloured red to indicate that they were dead. Over half of those left were orange, indicating that they were in prisons. Others were yellow, meaning they were living on other planets.

"I don't know. I'll say this much. If it is him, I want to shake his hand before I put him in restraints. I haven't had a challenge like this in years."

"He is good," agreed Chow.

"Call into the Duchovny Tower Police again. Have them check the lease car for the property's DNA ASAP. If it's there, that would be enough to put a hold on his flight clearance."

"On it."

Rowan gazed through the car window as they emerged from the concrete tunnel into a forest. Turning, she looked behind them and saw the tower city rising into the clouds. "I'm definitely not in Sun Valley anymore."

"You should try and relax. It will take about a half-hour for us to reach the *Star Hawk*."

"I do feel tired. Why is that? I haven't been up that long."

"You're running on artificial blood, and we've crossed five time zones. Rest. If you like I could..." Ryan patted the pocket containing his hand-held.

"Forget it. Besides, I'd like to see some of this planet

before I leave it forever."

"I'll kill that fakey!" John stared blurrily into his vidscreen.

"You agree with my assessment?" Mildred looked out of the screen at him.

"I didn't say that. If it was him, he certainly fooled your security screenings. It shouldn't fall on me." John sat back on his couch. He was dressed in a robe with his hair still damp from the shower. The glass in his hand contained a Sober Quick prescription.

"I need any information we may have on him. The medical release forms don't apply to security, and the clerk won't give me the data without your authorization. I need his DNA profile for a quick match and his psych assessments."

"I'll make the call. Just get Rowan back. We can't have it getting out that someone stole our property, it would never end." John cut the line and sat thinking.

"Jena, call the studio medical records division."

INTO THE STARTING GATE

Ryan stepped out of the car onto the landing strip with Rowan's gym bag slung over his shoulder. Rowan stood by the car, slack-jawed, staring at the mass of the *Star Hawk*.

"Computer, return to nearest recharge station and auto-connect," Ryan ordered into the vehicle.

"Projection, after this action, your travel account will be in deficit. Interest charges will apply, and a usage ban will be in effect. It is strongly recommended that you transfer funds into your travel account."

"Computer, go!"

The car drove away empty.

"What do you think?" Ryan gazed at Rowan's profile.

"It's magnificent. It... it's beautiful, like an ebony cabochon. I... this is what I always thought the alien technology would be like from the broken bits I've seen."

"It's human. Sure, we bought a lot of it from other species, but we made it our own. We should get in."

Ryan took Rowan's arm and led her to the hangar's ramp. As they drew close, her heel caught in a crack in the rock and broke.

"Nova blast! I..." Rowan hobbled forward a couple of steps then felt herself swept off her feet. Ryan grinned at her as he carried her into the *Star Hawk*. He set her down amongst the small forest that occupied his hangar bay.

"Henry, we're home. Close the ramp and give me pre-flight status." Ryan lowered Rowan's gym bag to the floor and passed her her running shoes.

"About time! When I heard about that ATV crashing into Lake Doig, I almost browned my shorts." Henry's voice was scolding. The hangar ramp lifted into the hull and the bay doors closed.

"That would be a trick. What ATV crashing?"

"You didn't hear the news? Hangar pressure check, positive seal."

"We've been on public transport. How's the pre-flight?"

"I've been updating it since yesterday. How in the divine's myriad names did you end up on public transport? You were supposed to catch a lift with Yancy."

"ATV clapped out before I reached him."

"If they cross-reference when you were on transit with when I was on the vid-phone—"

"I know, I know."

Rowan straightened from tying her laces. "Who is that?" She glanced at the intercom.

"That's Henry. At present, my ship's operating system."

"Hubba, hubba, sexy lady. You are even hotter in person. Yummy. Why not blow off the fleshy and give plastic a try?" Henry sent a growl through the speakers.

"HENRY!" Ryan shouted.

"At least bend over and tie your shoe's laces again, sweet thing."

"Is this the Henry from Kadar's story, the robot?" Rowan self-consciously tried to tug her dress lower.

"Oh baby, you hurt me so bad. Humanoid artificial intelligence, please."

"I'm sorry."

"Make it up to me with a big, juicy snog."

Ryan took Rowan by the hand and started toward the lift. "We need to get out of this planet's jurisdiction. I'm guilty of about a dozen offences on this rock. Henry, heat up the systems."

Rowan allowed Ryan to guide her. The inside of the *Star Hawk* was as impressive as its outside had been. The walls seemed to meet without seams, and where panels were visible, they glowed in green lights and digital displays.

"Mrs. Tallman, divers have found the ATV. The front of it is caved in. The crew area appears to be largely intact. The contractor says it's too dangerous to raise it until morning." Helen's face gazed out of Mildred's hand-held, wearing an earnest expression.

Mildred rubbed the back of her neck with her free hand. "Tell him to use suspensor lights; he knew it was a rush job when he took it. If he refuses, offer a 10 per cent bonus if he has the craft on the surface within the hour. Have you got through to Chandler yet?"

"Both his hand-held and his ship's system are locked out to public frequencies. He's probably sleeping. He said he was planning a trip to Earth." Helen looked pouty.

"Earth...?" Mildred closed the frequency without saying goodbye. "Chow, where is Chandler right now?"

Chow checked his hand-held. "Hogan Field. The car dropped him off, then was sent to recharge."

"He's definitely our man, and he's about to launch."

"How do you know?"

"Chandler is a clone. He told that twit Helen that he was going to Earth."

"And she didn't catch on?" Chow looked amazed.

"She's one of the producer's pieces on the side. I hired her for political reasons, not her brains."

"Oh..."

"Pilot, how long will it take Chandler to get launch clearance?" Mildred shouted into the front seat.

"What's he flying?" asked the pilot.

"An H.L.T.C. two-one-seven. Whatever that is."

"Heavy Lander Troop Carrier. That's one of the old Hawks. Stardust! I'm calling for backup."

"Why?" Mildred leaned forward in her seat.

"Those were the toughest birds ever built. I don't look forward to trying to stop one in this thing."

Mildred balled her hand into a fist. "How long for flight clearance?"

"If he bothers, half an hour. If traffic control is slow."

Mildred considered. "Hand-held, put me in touch with Space Traffic Control, North-Western Quarter Head Office."

Ryan ran onto the *Star Hawk*'s bridge and turned to the engineering panel.

"Can I help?" Rowan stood inside the door.

"Hey, sweet thing, you can come over here," said Henry.

Rowan stared at the mutilated android. "Stardust! What happened to... I'm sorry, what can I—?" She started toward the console.

"Rowan, be careful, he—" began Ryan.

"HEY, WATCH IT BUSTER!" Rowan jumped away from Henry. "Keep your hand to yourself!"

"Gets grabby," finished Ryan.

"Would do if I had hips, cutie."

"Engineer's pre-flight complete. Henry, behave yourself. Rowan, take the captain's chair in the middle of the room. Henry, prepare for antiproton reaction." Ryan moved to the gunner's console and reached underneath it, undoing the clips on his makeshift control circuit. "Just until control finishes checking our telemetry. We don't need any more trouble."

"Amen, Blessed Be, Aunk em Matt, and the Prophet be praised to that," said Henry.

"Where in the cosmos did you get that?" Ryan moved to the navigator's console at the front of the bridge.

"I've been experiencing a documentary on sex and human religion through the ages. Gotta love the Bacchanal."

Arlene looked at the empathic readings. Ryan was stressed. "Must know they're almost onto you. I'm surprised you made it this far." She shifted to Rowan, who was awed, scared and excited at the same time. Henry was horny, as always; underneath that, his readings reflected fear.

She had the overview from the bridge monitor on her main screen. Ryan moved to the last console, other than the one Henry was wired into.

"Pre-flight status is confirmed, green across the board. Henry, give me flight plan B. Have the file for C prepped to transmit to Zod traffic control on a tight beam as soon as we're out of Gaea controlled space." Ryan pressed a button on the console in front of him and spoke.

"Gaea Space Traffic Control, do you copy?"

A pleasant female voice came from the speaker. "This is Space Traffic Control, proceed."

"This is H L T C- two-nine-seven - D - R C named *Star Hawk* on the Hogan landing strip, requesting launch permission. Am attaching a flight plan to transmission." Ryan pressed a button on his console.

A minute passed before the female voice spoke. "*Star Hawk*, you are cleared to launch in T minus thirty minutes. Please open your systems for control pre-flight."

"Roger." Ryan moved to the pilot's seat, hit a button and set a timer.

"Is it sick of me that I get hot when he talks like that? Nova blast, it's too bad I couldn't get him into the group." Arlene spoke to the empty control room.

"So, now what?" Rowan fidgeted in the captain's chair.

"Now, we wait. I don't want to violate space traffic control regulations."

Rowan shook her head and looked around the six consoles that filled the bridge walls, her eyes coming to rest on Ryan's back. "Why? I mean, you already committed grand theft, trespassing, stealing power and all that other stuff. I'd have thought that air traffic control regulations wouldn't be much."

Henry snorted. "Really is a fakey, ain't she?"

Ryan swivelled his chair to glare at the android. "I've told you. I don't like that word, ROBOT!"

Arlene watched Ryan's anger levels spike. "Boy-o, I didn't think they made 'em like you anymore. Take anything about yourself. Let the mech diss your lady fair, and you're a tiger."

Henry's metres showed his equivalents for hurt, then rage, then emotional quiet in the space of three seconds.

Arlene pressed a button on the console. "General note: slow and adapt Henry's emotional process before market. The AI processing speed is too fast to make good human entertainment." She thought for a moment. "Keep a version in original format with a view to breaking into the AI market."

"I'm sorry, hottie. Ryan, point taken." Henry gazed at Ryan.

Ryan nodded, then turned his attention to Rowan. "So far, I've only committed crimes of a planetary nature, aside from a weapons violation they don't know about. Once we're away from Gaea, the theft charge doesn't apply because of ambiguity about your status in the United Earth Systems and Republic spheres. The trespassing charges are petty, and they'd have to deport me to prosecute. The power theft might apply in the United Earth Systems, but it's iffy, it wouldn't apply to the Republic."

"Interstellar law is nova blasted," added Henry.

"So away from this planet, am I legally a person?" Rowan seemed hopeful.

Henry let out a bark of laughter.

Ryan hung his head. "Only on Silvanus and Frigga. On Earth, you'd be killed the minute you left the ship. Even on Silvanus and Frigga, you'd be deported unless you managed to evade detection for five standard years."

"Stardust, so where are we going?"

"Geb," supplied Henry.

"Geb?"

"It's a new colony world. The only reason it's accessible is that a stargate is being towed by it on its way to another system. That means that for a few years, it's not too far from the Switchboard system. As soon as the transit time to the stargate is over a year, it becomes an independent planet with no ties to the United Earth Systems or Republic. The colonists' constitution recognises all classes of clone as full citizens."

"Don't forget AIs. I'll be a person. Then I can get a body and open a brothel! It's my life's ambition," remarked Henry.

Rowan looked from the mutilated android to Ryan in disbelief.

"I thought your life's ambition was to watch all the pornography ever made?" said Ryan.

"That's only until I get a body. Why watch when you can do, sexy?"

Rowan lowered her face into her hands and spoke through her fingers. "I guess it's good to have goals."

John wiped sweat from his brow and stared at his vidscreen. A thin, balding man with weasel-like features stared back at him.

"What can I say, John? Your contract is very well written. You cleared Ryan, as such you share culpability for his actions. I'm sure we can avoid criminal charges. As to the studio honouring your work contract? That is up to Mr. Strongbow. If Ryan makes good his escape with the property, Strongbow could seize the rights to *Angel Black*."

"And if Rowan is recaptured or her death proven?" John stared beseechingly into the screen.

"Then the situation is null and void because dramatically, it wouldn't affect the direction of the series; thus she would no longer constitute a risk to the studio."

"I've got to get that fakey!"

"Can I be of any further assistance?" asked the lawyer.

"What? No, I'll call later if I need you." John hit a button that closed the view screen. "What to do? What to do? If they get off-planet, I'm screwed. I need a bounty hunter that will follow them, but the expense..."

John stopped pacing as a cold smile spread across his face. "Yes. He'll do nicely. After all, it's what he was created for." John strode toward his bedroom to dress.

AND THEY'RE OFF

"**W**hy is it taking so long?" demanded Rowan.

"The tower is double-checking our pre-flight. Space is not the place you want to find out you didn't close all the windows." Ryan smiled at her.

"How much longer?"

Ryan glanced at his console. "Ten minutes."

"Then we're off to Geb. Nice name. Ancient Egyptian, isn't it?" Rowan fidgeted in the captain's chair.

"The Egyptian earth god, who slept with his sister Nut, who happened to be married to the sun god Ra at the time. Ra was her grandfather. Thus, Geb fathered the Isisens. His penis was usually depicted as being proportionally over a metre long. Who can blame Nut? Ra was pissed off. He got over it and eventually remarried. A hot little number named Remit," explained Henry.

"Who picks the planet names?" Rowan's eyes kept straying to the display counting down on Ryan's console.

"The convention is that when humans take possession of a planet, we name it after one of the earth Gods or Goddesses from ancient religions. Beyond that, it's up to the colonists. To the other races, it remains star name whatever number out it is. To us, we feel a need to personalize it. Several of the older races think it's the most hopeful thing about our species." Ryan absently triple checked his instruments.

"Director Conway, I know the area is being cleared for a space launch, that's what we're trying to prevent!" Mildred glared into the screen of her hand-held. A harried-looking woman with light-brown skin looked out from the screen.

"If you think he's a criminal, get a travel stop order. Otherwise, he's obeyed all procedures, is an experienced pilot, and frankly, I don't like people who try to bully me."

"Listen here, you—"

"No, you listen! You may be some big hotshot at the studio, but I run this launch control facility. If anyone is guilty of an infraction, it's your pilot for skirting so close to a cleared zone. Now don't bother me again until you have a travel stop order. Good day!"

Mildred's screen went blank. "Bitch!"

"No luck?" Chow was watching on his hand-held as a group of men dusted a city-transport car for fingerprints.

"None. How about you?"

"My contact told me it would be faster to look for prints in the car. They've found lots of them. It's going to take a while to process them all."

"You have told them to only look for the property's and Chandler's prints, haven't you?"

"Yes. Even so, the system has to check and discard each sample."

Mildred tapped her hand-held and waited a minute for the screen to light up. "Helen, did you find Chandler's power-bike?"

"I was about to call you. It was in the parking facility." Helen looked chagrined.

"That's it." Mildred drummed her fingers on her thigh. "Blip Chandler's credit file to my hand-held. Hurry! After that, get out to the salvage site. Be ready to report when I arrive."

"Yes, ma'am."

"What are you thinking?" Chow stared at Mildred.

"If I were doing a run-up, I'd max out my credit, so I could buy things to trade out there." She gestured to the sky. "If Chandler's debt exceeds his total planetary assets, the justice department may freeze his travel privileges to keep him from skipping out on the loan."

"Brilliant! That will buy us time to get the prints and DNA evidence." Chow turned back to his hand-held.

"*Star Hawk*, this is Linda Conway, head of Space Traffic Control, Northwestern Quarter. You are cleared for launch. Please keep to your logged flight plan until you are clear of possible atmospheric collisions. Have a nice day."

"Five minutes early. That's strange." Ryan pressed a button on his console, moving the timer to zero, then worked some other controls.

"Up and away," said Henry.

Rowan felt nothing. When she looked at the front monitor, it showed the planet slowly retreating as they lifted straight up. Her lip trembled, and a tear formed in her eye. "Goodbye, Dad, Mom. Goodbye, everyone. Divine, why can't I have a choice?"

"When we get into thinner air, we'll accelerate to orbital speeds," explained Ryan. "Henry, watch the pilot's station."

"Sure thing, boss."

Ryan moved to the weapons console and reconnected the clips to the control circuit. "Like old times," he muttered.

"Outnumbered a hundred to one and about to get our asses blown off. Yup, that's old times," agreed Henry as Ryan returned to the pilot's station.

Rowan shook her head and focused her attention on the screen.

"You can see, Justice Haynes. There is no way Mr. Chandler's planetary assets can equal his level of debt."

The grey-haired, Chinese-looking man on the screen nodded sagely. "I am inclined to agree, though we cannot know what monies may be owed Doctor Chandler of an informal nature."

Mildred tapped her foot and tried not to let her impatience show.

"Though the right of an honest citizen to free movement is a sacred pillar of our society."

"Ma'am, the *Star Hawk* is airborne," said the pilot.

"The *Star Hawk* is airborne?" Mildred turned her attention back to her hand-held, where Justice Haynes was still droning on.

"The right of the creditor to have the debtor honour the contract is important for the smooth functioning of our society."

"Sir," interrupted Mildred. Justice Haynes looked shocked but fell silent. "Chandler's ship has launched."

"Oh? In that case, I am inclined to grant the travel restriction based on his debt load. I will have the file sent to Space Traffic Control. It shouldn't be more than ten minutes to draft the warrant and have it delivered."

⌖──◆

Director Conway stood up from the computer override station she'd used to expedite the *Star Hawk*'s departure. She was a tall, slender woman with small, high-set breasts. She ran her hand through her short, kinky hair. "Good luck *Star Hawk*, whoever you have aboard."

A small, Caucasian man, dressed in service tech coveralls, moved to her side and passed her a steaming mug. "Why'd you do that, Lin? Suppose they are criminals?"

"I asked myself, why would the head of studio security be so hot and bothered over some guy leaving the planet? What could he have taken that could be that valuable?"

"Don't know. Unedited e-files."

"Those boys surgically implant the disks and take them out on the big commercial ships. It was in that memo they sent around last week."

"So, what's he stealing?"

"As far as I know, nothing." Linda smiled.

Barr returned her grin. "If he were stealing something, what would it be?"

"You ever read ancient novels, Barr? Pre-contact stuff?"

Barr waved his hand dismissively. "Nah, never got into it. I'd rather do an e-entertainment."

"You're missing a lot. I did a minor in ancient Earth literature while I was training for traffic control. All stuff translated into modern language, it's not like I wasted my time learning to read English or anything. Those books tell you a lot. The works of Aldous Huxley or Mark Twain, from the earliest days of humans as technological creatures. I've got a word for how the studios treat their clones, and it's not a pretty one."

"Whatever you say." Barr turned his chair so that he faced his console.

Linda stood up and started toward the door.

"Where are you going?"

Linda smiled and laid her hand-held on the counter. "Don't change anything except as a matter of public safety. I'd like to confirm things. I'll be in the ladies' room at the end of the hall."

❦

"He's still lifting. We have him! Disobeying Space Traffic Control is a Republic level offence. They'll pick him up no matter where he goes, then deport him back to us. We have him!" Mildred nearly danced in her seat.

"Ma'am, I've been monitoring STC, and... well... No one's informed the *Star Hawk* of a flight status revocation. They probably don't have the warrant yet." There was an amused undertone to the pilot's voice.

"WHAT?" shouted Mildred.

"Nothing's been transmitted to the *Star Hawk*. Until the log shows that the message has been transmitted, it doesn't apply."

"I..." Mildred took a deep breath. "Get him, force that antique down."

"My standing orders don't authorize my taking on a combat role, or disregarding Space Traffic Control." The pilot kept looking into his screen, which showed the *Star Hawk* ascending. The landing legs had retracted into its hull. It now truly did resemble an obsidian cabochon. "Sangunis abl planeta," he whispered.

Mildred tapped the face of her hand-held and waited.

"Hello, Planetary Defence main reception, may I help you?" The screen filled with a mandala pattern.

"Put me through to Colonel Bob Burtch."

"I'm sorry, Colonel Burtch has gone home for the day. Would you care to leave a message?"

Mildred closed the connection, then spoke. "Hand-held, connect me to Colonel Bob Burtch's hand-held."

"Searching. There are eight hundred and ninety-seven B. Burtchs listed in the Gaea contact directory. Would you care to narrow the search parameters?"

Mildred gritted her teeth. "He's so close I can taste him, and he's getting away. Hand-held, narrow directory search to the Hannigan region."

⌑⟶

Ryan shifted the view on the big screen to a small aircraft circling the edge of the launch clearance zone. "I think they aren't too happy to have missed us."

"Can't have enough to do you in yet, boss, or they would have cancelled our flight clearance," said Henry.

"Too true, too true. Accelerating at one-tenth G. Inertial dampers working at optimum. I think we've actually done it."

"We've gotten away?" Rowan sat in the captain's chair, obviously fatigued.

"Stardust, no! At least now I know what I'm doing."

"Why doesn't that reassure me?" Rowan slumped.

"You haven't known him long enough to panic when he says he knows what he's doing. I'll panic for both of us," said Henry.

Ryan locked his eyes on the control board. "Polymer prat!"

Mildred passed her hand-held to the pilot, who spared the screen a glance before returning his eyes forward. "Sir," said the pilot.

"Commander, I want you to bring that bogey down," ordered Colonel Burtch.

"Sir, the craft is one of the old Hawk class heavy landers. I'm only flying an atmospheric personnel transport. Are you saying you want me to fire on the target?"

The colonel was silent for a long moment. "Give me back to Major Tallman."

The pilot handed back the hand-held. Mildred took it.

"How sure are you of this?" demanded Burtch.

"Positive. But all I can get legally, at the moment, is debt evasion."

"I can't order someone fired on because they're behind on paying off their credit line, Milly."

"But..."

Burtch held up his hand to silence her. "Get more evidence, then have the orbital patrol pick him up."

Chow's hand-held bleeped. He opened it, then after a moment, he spoke. "Sir, ma'am. They've found the property's and Ryan Chandler's fingerprints in the ground car."

"Is that enough for you?" demanded Mildred.

"Give me back to the pilot."

Mildred passed her hand-held forward.

"Sir?" asked the pilot.

"No weapons. I order you to try and bring that ship down," said the colonel.

"Yes, sir. If I may be so bold, sir? How would you suggest

I do that, sir? They'll be above my craft's ceiling in three minutes, sir."

On the small screen, Burtch massaged his temples. "Use your imagination, commander." The screen went blank.

"Use my imagination. Helpful, so helpful. Brass! Here goes." The pilot turned into the cleared zone and accelerated toward the *Star Hawk*.

"Incoming," called Henry.

"Stardust! What do they think they're doing?" Ryan watched on an auxiliary screen as the small, atmospheric craft shot toward them. It overflew his craft, missing it by less than twenty metres.

"He's turning around," commented Henry.

Ryan and Rowan watched the craft arc around and speed back. It overflew them again. Rowan closed her eyes and cringed when it looked like the jet was going to ram straight through the *Star Hawk*'s front screen.

"Is he trying to commit suicide?" asked Rowan.

"He's making another pass. Shoot him!" suggested Henry.

"No, this isn't a military mission," said Ryan.

The jet roared over them, close enough that the turbulence registered on the pilot's control board.

Ryan's mind raced. "He does constitute a clear and present danger in our flight path. We haven't heard anything about grounding us yet, right?"

"Right," said Henry. "He's turning for another pass."

"Let him. Inertial dampeners to full. Henry, sensor scans, is there anything above us?" Ryan's hands flew over the pilot's console.

"Some space junk too small to be a threat and an unmanned studio satellite."

"The studio can eat the cost. Hang on to your hats. Henry, give me a count for when that nut case is past us."

The android's voice became a near monotone. "Three, two, one, now."

Rowan felt a tremor run through the ship as the inertial dampers reduced the turbulence caused by the jet's near-miss to one-tenth.

"Full lift." Ryan slammed down on a control, and the *Star Hawk* jerked upwards.

"Space Traffic Control. This is the *Star Hawk*. I am deviating from flight plan to counter a clear and present safety hazard. Doing emergency ascent, running full scram-jet acceleration with zero gravity effect." Rowan listened to Ryan's voice as she felt herself pushed into the padding of her chair. On the screen, the sky turned dark purple, then black.

⌖

The pilot turned his jet around for another run at the *Star Hawk*, then a blast of displaced air sent a shudder through his aircraft. The *Star Hawk* rocketed into the sky.

"Go after them," ordered Mildred.

The pilot smiled as he plotted a course back to his home airstrip. "Unless you have an orbital launch vehicle in your pocket, ma'am, that's going to be a little hard to do."

"Nova blast! Get me Space Control."

⌖

Arlene watched the ebony form of the *Star Hawk* race towards her screen. She'd done her best to move the satellite, but there was still a chance it would get clipped. She shifted her gaze to Rowan's perspective. She stared into the ship's main screen, and the empathic monitors showed an incredible sense of wonder. "That's going to fly. She's like a virgin with a partner who actually knows what they're doing."

The door at the back of the control room opened. Arlene turned to watch Mike step in. "We're nearly at the end of stage one."

"Nearly. Once they shift to stealth, our telemetry will be blocked. Are you sure your lackey will keep its word?"

Mike grinned at his employee. "I have no doubt. You see, I still have to pay my agent on the *Star Hawk*. He'll trust me to keep our bargain. Do you think we have enough to do a full season?"

"Easily." Arlene turned back to her control boards. The satellite had survived. She altered its angle to watch the *Star Hawk* fly into the void.

Barr looked at the legal notice of travel restriction on his screen. The *Star Hawk* had just announced its deviation from the flight plan, and he'd logged it in the deviations file. Given the military craft's behaviour, the computer wouldn't even place a charge against the *Star Hawk*. He leaned back in his chair and read the legal notice from start to finish, including the small print. After that, he brought up the written protocols for dealing with a travel restriction. Clearly written in Subsection C was the order to pass the responsibility over to his shift supervisor in a timely manner. He pressed a button on his console and spoke.

"Southwestern Control, do you copy?"

"We copy, Northwestern Control. What's up, Barr?"

"I have to pop out for a couple of minutes. Can you cover my station, Val?"

"Sure. It's quiet down here. Send me your telemetry."

"Thanks. Catch you later." Barr pressed the button that routed his station's data to the southern facility, then stretched. Standing, he sauntered down the hall that led to the men's room at the far side of the building.

The travel restriction order blinked on the screen, awaiting a supervisor to implement it.

SEASON TWO

"Shifting from scram-jets to grav-laser drive. Course target locked and activated." Ryan hit a switch, then swivelled his chair.

Rowan sat in the captain's seat, staring at the main screen.

"Press the green button by your right hand, then turn the knob beside it a hundred and eighty degrees," suggested Ryan.

Rowan followed his instructions. The image on the main screen shifted to that beneath the ship. Gaea spun below them in blues, browns and whites. "It's beautiful. Can I see Sun Valley from here?"

"No, it's hidden by the horizon."

"It's so weird."

"What is?"

"I know I've lived on Gaea all my life, but, well... I always thought I was on Earth. All the pictures I saw were of Earth. I... I don't feel like I'm looking at home. I know that my dad and mom and everyone are down there, but I can't imagine it."

Ryan smiled and nodded. "You're probably a little numb. It's a lot to take in, and it's been a rough three days." Ryan paused in thought before continuing, "Henry, at our current velocity, how long until we're out of Gaea's territorial space?"

"One hour, three minutes and twenty seconds."

Ryan turned his chair and reset the screen to a forward

view. "Too long. Have we entered the Orbital Station's control sphere yet?"

"Yup."

Ryan moved to the communications console and opened the traffic control channel.

"Orbital Traffic Control. Request permission to change flight plan. I'd like to increase acceleration to craft rating of twenty-five Gs."

A male voice answered the call. "Your sector of space shows clear, and your flight plan has come up from the surface. Permission for plan deviation granted. Opening the old girl up, are you, *Star Hawk*?"

"I want to see what she'll do." Ryan closed the channel and moved back to the pilot's seat. "I didn't think they would."

Rowan felt a pressure pushing her back in her seat.

"Henry, what's our time now?"

"Ten minutes until we're in unclaimed space."

⟺

Mildred stared at the face of a dark-haired, Caucasian, early-twenties man on her hand-held's screen.

"You have to believe me." She fought to keep her voice even.

"I'm not saying you're lying, ma'am. Until the file gets transmitted to me, I can't do anything. OTC regulations are clear. We're to expedite the safe and swift disposition of all space vehicles. If I had a travel restriction order to transmit, I'd transmit it."

Mildred buried her face in her hands. "Why me?"

"I don't bother much with metaphysics."

"I'm sorry. As soon as you get the order, would you transmit it? This Chandler is dangerous."

"I'll send it the minute it comes in. Don't worry, ma'am. He has to land somewhere, sometime. What he do, kill someone?"

Mildred almost chuckled at the traffic controller's eager tone. "All I can say is, it was a major felony. Contact me on my hand-held once you've transmitted the message, please."

"Of course, ma'am. Over and out."

"Were we that green once?" Chow shook his head where he sat beside Mildred. The jet was on final approach for a landing strip by Lake Doig.

Mildred glanced out the front window and saw dust from where the studio's ATV sped to pick them up on auto-drive.

"I was never green." Mildred sat back in her chair. "How, in the divine's myriad names, am I going to tell that prat John that Rowan got away?"

"The travel restriction—" began Chow.

"Will never get through in time. Even if it did, Chandler might be desperate enough to risk a petty Republic violation. He could claim sanctuarial incarceration with one of the other species. That man is nothing if not gutsy."

Chow nodded. "In a way, you have to admire him."

"That's the problem! The man's Robin Hood! If the story gets out, the studio is in deep kimchee. People love a rebel hero."

Mike watched the screen over Arlene's shoulder. "It looks good. I'm glad he's avoided Republic involvement."

"I would have thought getting the Republic forces involved would have upped the drama." Arlene cut to the image coming from the military monitoring system. It showed Mildred laying in her seat. Chow watched the salvage team on his handheld as they placed Ryan's shattered ATV on the barge.

"I have considerable influence on Gaea, some with the United Earth Systems. At the Republic level, I'm 'Michael who?' I'd rather see this play out to a happy ending."

"I'm surprised you care."

"Why? I've told you I consider Ryan a friend, and I have a soft spot for Rowan. She reminds me of somebody. Doesn't look like her, but very similar personalities."

"Who?"

Mike looked at the side screen that gave a satellite shot of the salvage operation. "I hope some of the grav-nullifiers survived. I could really use them for the *Lucky Seven*."

⚓

Linda sat in her work chair at the control centre and carefully read the travel restriction. "It seems in order. Has the *Star Hawk* shifted to orbital control yet?"

Barr checked his console. "Quite a while ago."

"Hmm… We should forward the travel restriction as per procedure. Mark it, 'Attention Director of Orbital Control'."

Barr readdressed the file and made ready to send it.

"Wait." Linda chuckled as a conniving expression came to her face. "Send the day's standard dispatches as well. No use in under using the connection. Send the lot chronologically."

Barr chuckled. "Have I ever told you that you're an evil woman?"

"I'm only keeping the memo about the effective use of our allocated electromagnetic wavelengths in mind. Procedure is there for a reason."

Barr transmitted the files.

⚓

Ryan felt fatigued. He glanced back at Rowan. Despite the wonder and excitement, she was asleep in the captain's chair.

"We're clear. We're in unclaimed space," said Henry.

"Tight beam transmit the new flight plan to Zod control," snapped Ryan.

"On it. Blip transmission complete."

"Activate stealth."

"Stealth is going to eat power, and we're low on antiproton," warned Henry.

"We need to be invisible. If I know John, he won't stop the chase. That man hates to lose, as long as someone else bleeds for the victory."

"I think you're overreacting."

The communications console squealed, and a message appeared on the screen. Ryan moved over and read it.

"It's a travel restriction with an order from Space Traffic Control to dock at the space station. Fortunately, it's only binding for vessels in Gaea's space."

"All stealth systems active, sir." Henry shot Ryan a salute.

"Good." Ryan worked his control panel, changing the *Star Hawk*'s angle of flight so that they moved sunward and forward of Gaea's orbit. "Henry, the con is yours. Keep us invisible. Call me if anything comes up."

"As my sexy captain commands."

Ryan rubbed the back of his neck, stood and moved to Rowan. He stared at her for a long minute.

"She is a hottie. Whose quarters you gonna be in, boss?" Henry leered and half-heartedly pumped his arm.

"My own." Ryan slipped his arms under Rowan and picked her up. Her head rolled into his chest. She settled in his arms and murmured.

Ryan held her. Something in him felt alive. A strength he'd almost forgotten flowed through him, and he knew he could support her forever. His own exhaustion wasn't so much gone as it no longer mattered. He carried her from the bridge to the door of her quarters. The door slid open.

"Thanks, Henry." Ryan laid Rowan on her bed and removed her shoes before taking a blanket from one of her drawers and laying it over her. He paused, staring at her as she slept, then bent and kissed her forehead.

"Ryan, you crazy fakey, what are you doing to yourself?"

he whispered, then left the room.

"I am very disappointed in you, Mildred. Allowing Chandler to escape is—"

"I didn't allow him to do anything. Why didn't you transfer him when he started showing an obsession with the Rowan character?" On the screen, Mildred's face was florid. The back wall of the studio ATV's driver's compartment could be seen behind her.

"You can't shift the blame for this one onto me." John violently tugged the lapels of his suit straight.

"There's enough blame to go around." A beeping sound came over the channel. "I have to go. I'm on hold with the coelenteratezoid liaison office. I'll call back." The screen went blank.

"Coelenteratezoids, jellyfish, useless drifters. They don't have the spine do what needs doing," John commented to himself. Moving to a mirror, he examined his reflection. He could have been an executive from the set region. "Luba, come."

"Yes, oh, yes. It's so good, so good. Yesss!" cried a sultry, female voice from the other room.

John rolled his eyes. "I should have bought the contextual upgrade. Luba, transport yourself to within a metre of my present location."

The robot, now appearing as a beautiful woman with short, dark hair, a fit body, medium-sized breasts and huge, brown eyes sashayed into the room. Her skin was tan, and she looked like someone had deliberately picked the best features from all the branches of the human family tree and combined them. Her legs were solid muscle, and the knee-length black dress she wore showed them off from the calves down to her feet, which were encased in high-heeled pumps.

"Luba, prepare to accept expansion programs and short-term, post-market ram expansion. Keep full obedience protocols."

"Yes, my lord and master. I will serve you in all things." Luba stood completely still, awaiting further instructions.

"It is a wonder humanity survives. Who would want a woman when this machine does all I need and doesn't talk back?" John smiled and extracted three slender tubes from his jacket pocket.

"I'll have to get by without you for a few weeks. It can't be helped."

"Would you like a blow job?" The robot smiled vacantly.

"After this mission, my slave. Of course, I could always buy another Luba-bot. The larger chassis may cost more, but an Amazon type would be pleasant."

"Two Lubas are fun. With the post-market expansion program, two Luba-bots can perform for our master or entertain your guests. Never forget there is a wide range of after-market—"

"Silence," ordered John.

The robot froze.

John slid one of the tubes into the robot's right nostril and felt it click home. The base of the tube extended out of the nose. "Download, then delete all personal files. Password, sodomy."

The robot blinked three times, then spoke. "Download and delete complete."

John extracted the tube and pushed the other tubes up her nostrils. The base of the tube on the right remained exposed; the other was completely hidden.

"Warning, the data here contained exceeds this unit's current carrying capacity. Operating files will have to be deleted to accommodate this data."

"Nova blast! Why didn't I get a memory expansion for this thing?" John gritted his teeth in frustration.

"After-market expansions can give your Luba much greater versatility and make her a more re—"

"Silence, Luba." John scratched his head. "Delete after-market sexual-response additions. Password, sodomy."

"Complying with instructions. Deleting: she-male adaptation post-market expansion. Deleting: lesbian adaptive response. Deleting: group sex files. Deleting: sadomasochism file. Deleting: voyeur recording protocols. Uploading. Opening file: ship defence station operations. Opening file: batzoid language. Opening file: yacht operations. Opening file..."

Mildred watched the creature on the ATV's screen. She'd pulled to the side of the road for this call. The coelenteratezoid floated in an orange mist, its translucent, bubble-like bell pulsing. It looked like a jellyfish, except for the shadowy outline of complex organs that could be seen through its outer skin. A line around the edge of its bell blinked with multi-coloured lights. The tentacles beneath it writhed as it communicated.

"You must remember, honoured keeper of order, that the agreement that granted your species Gaea assured the autonomy of both our worlds."

"Most respected liaison officer Green-Blue-Red-Purple-Yellow. All I'm asking is for you to revoke his flight clearance."

The lights on the bell blinked out a complex pattern.

At least it's a pretty language, thought Mildred.

"The deed to Gaea specifically included free passage to any ship that had not committed a crime against the coelenteratezoid people or the Republic. We cannot, in good conscience, detain a free sentient when even his own government will not acknowledge his guilt." Green-Blue-Red-Purple-Yellow puffed its bell dramatically.

"In the human justice system, he must be present to be tried for his crime."

Green-Blue-Red-Purple-Yellow waved its tentacles. The translator made a laughing sound. "The foolishness of human justice is not a concern of my people. This Ryan Chandler is permitted free passage, though..."

"Though?" Mildred found herself almost hypnotized by the blinking lights.

"As a gesture of goodwill, if his crime is of a nature the people of Zod would acknowledge, we could see our way fit to detaining him. What did he do?"

Mildred shook her head. She'd known it would come to this. "Trespassing."

"The currents carry you where they will. One cannot always shelter against them. That is no crime."

"Power theft."

"When being or machine must feed, the plankton of the air is the plankton of the air. The reflections of Blue-Green-Green-Purple-Red-White-Yellow-Yellow, the most exalted, forbid denying another the necessities of existence. You humans could learn much from our holy records."

"He, he stole studio property other than food and power."

"A thing of matter? That is a theft we recognize. What did he steal?"

Mildred braced herself, knowing the likely reaction. "He stole one of our emotional surrogates."

Green-Blue-Red-Purple-Yellow floated still for several moments. The lights on its bell blinked, but the translator said nothing. It was obviously speaking with someone out of the camera's field of view. Green-Blue-Red-Purple-Yellow's entire communications ring blazed white, then the translator came back on.

"You disgust me! Blue-Green-Green-Purple-Red-White-Yellow-Yellow's most sacred law was that none may own the life of another. Ryan Chandler has free passage in all coelenteratezoid space. If you want him, send your own ships to get him. Do not enter my people's territorial space to do it. Your pursuers are unwelcome among us. I pray that Chandler sends you to the cold regions of oxygen you so richly deserve!" The screen went blank.

"What was that 'cold regions of oxygen' remark?" Chow leaned back in the navigator's seat.

"Green-Blue-Red-Purple-Yellow told me to go to hell. This is bad. Without them to stop Chandler at the stargate, he could get away, even if the studio manages to persuade the Orbital Defence to launch pursuit vessels."

"That's bad. In unclaimed space, Chandler is free to fight back, and no coelenteratezoid or Republic charges apply."

"At least that cuts both ways. Now we need to find him."

"I'm afraid you need to find him, ma'am. I've been ordered back to base as soon as we reach the salvage site."

Mildred looked at the young officer. "I regret that, Chow. I really do."

"As do I, ma'am. I've learnt a lot."

Mildred nodded. "Give the dust from this mess a couple of months to clear, then stop by the studio. I have a proposition for you that could give you a much more lucrative future than the military."

Chow looked thoughtful. "I'll call you. My hitch is up in under a year, and I was debating on reenlisting."

PROFESSIONAL HELP

John led Luba into the set region transfer station. The roller-coaster-like cars sat empty on their track, and the place was deserted.

"Gene, activate transfer car and arrange with the on set luxury-vehicle service to meet us at the sewage treatment plant's gate. Authorization, John Wilson, producer of *Angel Black*."

"Voiceprint and retinal scan recognized. Mr. Wilson, entering the set at this time constitutes a violation of studio policy," said the computer.

"Understood, thus keep this trip secret, Gene, on my authority."

"I will comply with all procedures your authority authorizes, Mr. Wilson. Enjoy your visit to the set, your limo will be waiting for you."

John guided Luba to a seat in a transfer car and pressed its activate button.

Greg sat in front of the *Angel Black* console. He'd done so much overtime since John had fired him that he felt ready to drop. It was past midnight, set time, and with the number of techs who'd quit *Angel Black*, it looked like he'd be there through the night.

"We could kill every otterzoid in the universe, and it still wouldn't bring her back." Angel's empathic monitors showed fatigue, emotional exhaustion and despair. All the

Angel Black primary characters were gathered in Gunther's living room.

Greg looked at Gunther's emotional monitor. It was a flat line, as if he were purposefully blocking all feeling.

"We still have to find Hunoin. Rowan must be avenged!" Toronk sat in a lounger with Angel cradled in front of him. His tail-tip lashed back and forth.

"I think we need to sort it out in our own heads first." Carl's monitors showed a quiet resolve.

"Greg, as per Mr. Strongbow's instructions, I wish to inform you that John Wilson has made an unauthorized entry into the set region. He's arranged for transport to meet him at the incursion point," spoke the studio computer.

Greg sat up straighter. "He hass, hass he?" Greg operated a control, zooming in a satellite image of the sewage treatment plant's gate. "Gene, sshunt thesse imagess to Misster Sstrongbow'ss control and recording fasscility, then wipe all record of them from thiss terminal."

"I will need Mr. Strongbow's or Mr. Wilson's authorization to wipe this terminal."

"Gene, call Mr. Sstrongbow and get authorizsation. Methinkss the game iss afoot."

Mildred stepped onto the barge supporting Ryan's shattered ATV. The barge was moored at a small recreational marina on Lake Doig. Suspensor lights hovered over it, making it as bright as day. The water made a gentle slapping sound against the floats that was at odds with the tension that emanated from the investigators standing around the broken vehicle. The ATV's front end was a tangled mass of polycarbonate. Its rear wheels were missing, as was the side door. The front wheels were mangled.

"The techs have been going over the ATV with collector

nano-bots. They found some recent DNA. I had them send it to the lab in Ball Tower. They should be back to us soon." Helen approached Mildred from the far side of the barge.

"It will only confirm what we already know. Ryan Chandler is the thief. What's under that tarp?" Mildred pointed to where a lump was covered with a plastic sheet.

Helen swallowed. "They found a finger. The print identified him as Kadar Al-Qahtani. They had to pry the driver's compartment apart with suspensor fields to get him out."

Mildred nodded, then indicated a tarp beside the one she'd pointed to. "And what are they hiding under that one?"

"I think his legs are under there, or it might be his shoulder. I don't... excuse me." Helen sped to the side of the barge and was sick.

"Stardust!" Mildred walked to the hole in the ATV's side that used to be its entrance. "Is it safe to go in there?" she asked a short, stocky, man who stood by the door.

"It's not about to collapse, if that's what you mean. I'll tell you this for nothing. You won't find much."

Mildred nodded, then stepped into the ATV. Two cots had been pulled down. The floor had mud on it, and an unpleasant smell permeated the air. She moved to the nearer billet and ran her hand over the soaking mattress. She knew the vehicle had a story to tell; she just couldn't hear it. The beeping of her hand-held pulled her from her reverie.

Opening the device, she bit down on a short reply. "Mildred Tallman, head of S.E.T.E. security."

"Mrs. Tallman, I'm Admiral Newton. The night watch commander called me. She said it was urgent. What can I do for you?" A sleepy-looking, bald man with medium-brown coloured skin and blue eyes stared out of the screen.

"Sir. A man named Ryan Chandler has stolen one of the studio clones. He is currently escaping through space in an

H L T C called the *Star Hawk*."

The Admiral whistled. "Tough ship! Ryan Chandler. Captain Ryan Chandler?"

"Yes."

"He got that old bucket of bolts up in the stars. Hell of a good engineer. My XO served with him. I met him at an air show his club came out to. Your studio head, Mike Strongbow, is their military liaison." The Admiral rubbed his temples.

"Admiral, if you could try to apprehend Chandler—"

"What do the coelenteratezoids have to say?"

"They say it's our business."

"Typical. Who'd Ryan swipe?" Alertness and intelligence were slowly growing in the Admiral's sleepy eyes.

"Rowan from *Angel Black*." Mildred tapped her foot. She felt her own exhaustion pulling her down but needed to finish this before she slept.

"Man has good taste; I'll grant him that."

"Sir, if you could send some ships from the Orbital Defence Force..."

The admiral closed his eyes and sucked on his cheek as he thought.

"Send me your downloads. I'll hand them over to whatever defence squad is mobilized at this hour. It will be a few hours before we can launch a mission. We aren't at alert status, and our forces are only meant to defend the orbital territory. Equipping one of the frigates for an extended mission will take a bit."

"Thank you, Admiral." Mildred felt a knot loosen in her guts.

"Don't thank me yet. If that Hawk is stealth capable, there's a good chance we won't catch it until it approaches the stargate, and that region is a Republic no-fire zone."

Mildred nodded as the admiral closed the channel. She moved to the open billet farther from the cockpit and touched it. "Chandler, if you'll do this for a fakey, I'd have loved to have introduced you to my sister."

Exiting the ATV, she turned to Helen. "I'm going to the studio vehicle to get some sleep. Wake me if anything mind-shattering comes up. Otherwise, wake me in eight hours with a progress report and breakfast, two eggs, bacon crisp, toast and coffee, black."

"Yes, ma'am," said Helen as Mildred swept past her towards the shore.

John ordered the limo driver to pull to the side of the road and exited the car. The first glimmer of false dawn was lighting the horizon. Only because he knew where to look, he could make out the dark opening of a cave in the cliff face to his right.

"Luba, co... join me." John waited as the robot climbed from the car and stood at his side. He then stuck his head into the limo. "Driver, you are to depart. I will expect you back here in exactly three hours. Do you understand?"

"Yes, sir," agreed the Korean-looking man behind the wheel.

John slammed the door and waited as the driver pulled away.

"Mike iss going to love thiss," remarked Greg in the control room. All the *Angel Black* principals were asleep, and he was devoting his full attention to John's activities.

Taking a deep breath, John stepped onto a nearly invisible trail that followed a narrow ledge up the cliff face.

"Luba, follow me," he ordered.

It was full light. Sweat poured down John's fat face by the time he reached the cave mouth and climbed in, with Luba close behind. He swallowed and tried to quiet his racing heart before calling.

"Croell, hatched of Creen, flown by Brock, by the Great Flyer of the Skies I seek you with a fair offer of payment, hear my words." John turned to Luba. "Repeat exactly that in High Batzoid."

Luba made a series of hissing and screeching sounds that put John's teeth on edge.

Greg recorded Croell's response. The first rush of annoyance at being woken. The process of slowly extracting himself from his wife's sleeping form as his injured ribs throbbed. The surprise at hearing the traditional words changed into Low Batzoid from the human's language by his translator nano-bots. Then utter shock at hearing them spoken in High Batzoid, his ritual tongue.

"I hear the words and so am bound to listen by the Great Flyer of the Skies' law. Enter my home. Let us all be barred from violence until the sun sets upon this day."

Greg watched through Croell's eyes as he moved into the front chamber of his cave and examined John and the Luba, who were backlit by the rising sun. The empathic monitors indicated curiosity above all else.

"Come in. Please accept my hospitality as we discuss your business, and perhaps, how a human comes to know High Batzoid," greeted Croell.

Minutes later, Croell threw his neck back and bellowed, his wings spread wide. He picked up the low table that occupied the centre of his sitting area and smashed it into kindling. The cushions that had surrounded the table were already torn and scattered around the chamber. John huddled behind Luba with his back pressed against a tapestry depicting a sky-scape that covered the cave wall.

A slightly smaller batzoid rushed from the back chamber, throwing aside the curtain that separated the rooms. This second batzoid had bright red scales on its serpentine head.

"Croell, my husband! What is this? What have these done to you?" The female batzoid hissed at John and Luba, revealing a pair of fangs.

"My Zandra, the shame! The shame!" Croell bent and picked up John's discarded hand-held. On the screen was a picture of him and Zandra being extracted from incubation chambers.

"I do not understand, my husband?"

John inched toward the cave's mouth, keeping Luba in front of him. He had underestimated the level of the creature's rage.

"We are abominations! We were not laid but grown by these humans. We are perversions of life!"

"Humans do not yet have the technology," objected Zandra.

"It is not the time we have been led to believe. We were brought into being as an entertainment, a foolish waste of time. WE ARE NOTHING!"

Zandra stared at the picture. A drop of yellow liquid fell from her fangs. "We are abominations. We have no life to call our own. There is no place for us with the Great Flyer of the Skies. We are condemned to grovel with the things that crawl under the earth, never knowing light or wind." Zandra let out a high-pitched keen that shattered a crystal drinking glass.

Croell turned his full attention to John, who was nearly at the exit. "Human, if I were not oath-bound to harm you not before the sun sets, I would kill you where you stand. At least tell me whose body you violated to gather the cells that were our abominated origin."

John swallowed and tried to speak. His voice came out as a squeak. He took a deep breath and tried again. "They were convicts charged with knowingly telling a falsehood. The Batzoid Theocracy surrendered the cells to us because the criminals had no family to pay for the execution."

"LIARS! Great Flyer of the Skies, NO! What foul creatures we are drawn from! What dark fate must embrace us? We will be devoured by Sisss in the bowels of Petteron." Zandra made a quiet hissing sound as drops of venom fell from her fangs.

Croell hung his head and stood silently for a long time. The cave stilled. John felt his pulse slow.

"We are not fully lost to the Great Flyer of the Skies, my wife. Do not despair."

"How?" Zandra looked at her husband.

"Remember the story of Verk and Kilet. Twins hatched of the same egg. Verk lied and betrayed his own clan. Kilet was true."

"Yes! By dedicating his life to the winged way, Kilet found forgiveness from the Great Flyer of the Skies and was permitted to drink from the blessed river Ratwaaa. He was not banned from new life because of the weakness of his flesh."

"We are like Kilet. We are of one flesh with," a grimace crossed Croell's face as he spoke the word, "liars, but if we live an exemplary life, the Great Flyer of the Skies may let us drink of Ratwaaa's waters and be spared the lower regions. It may be centuries before we fly again, but we can still find new life."

"But the sin of our creation?"

"That rests on these humans. We had no choice. We did not use the forbidden technologies; they were used upon us. The priests have decreed that that is excusable. These humans can grovel in the mud for their sins, not us."

John smiled. His computer projection had given this scenario a 72 per cent likelihood, so he was well prepared. "Croell, you haven't lived a perfect life. The sin of deception is upon you."

"What are you saying, human?" Croell's tongue flicked out, tasting the air for lies.

"You were contracted to poison Rowan, to arrange for Hunoin to kill her."

"And I did as I said I would. The venom I gave her is lethal."

John smiled, and a cruel light came into his eyes. "She was stolen and healed by a subordinate in the studio. At this moment, she is off this planet heading to someplace unknown to me."

"What?!"

"Husband, surely you acted in good faith and..."

"If we were true children of the Great Flyer of the Skies, that would be enough, my wife. Such as we are..." Croell flicked his tongue.

"I can help. I need Rowan's body. If you agree to return her remains, I can lend you a ship to pursue her in."

Croell looked warily at John, then to his wife. "Not for myself, but for my wife, whose fate is tied to mine. Who will pilot?"

John pushed Luba forward. "Luba, you are to obey Croell and Zandra in all things until Rowan's body is onboard the yacht. That accomplished, you will return Rowan, Croell and Zandra to me. Accept instruction. Password, sodomy."

"Instructions accepted." Luba stood perfectly still in front of the batzoid.

"Mechanical," said Zandra.

"Yes. She'll serve as an interface between you and the controls of my yacht, which is designed for a human pilot. She will also guide you to the yacht's location."

"We have no choice," said Croell.

"We will do this together, my husband."

John smiled condescendingly. "Heart-warming. I should go. I'll make arrangements for you to penetrate space-port security. The Luba knows my plans and will brief you." John picked up his hand-held, tapped in a code and pointed it at the two batzoids. "That will make it possible for you to leave the set region. If you aren't back here a year from now, you'll regret it." John left the cave.

Greg stared at the main screen. It was Croell's perspective. "I almost feel ssorry for the Ss. O. B." The empathic metres were off the scale.

"My husband, what are we to do now?" asked Zandra.

"Now, we prepare. When the sun sets, we must begin our hunt."

Greg's hand hovered over a control. A single press of a button would still the nano-bots that kept the cancers that threatened Croell's life at bay. Greg's hand trembled, then he pulled it away. "I'm ssorry, Ryan. I can't. I hope you can take Batty, becausse I can't kill him in cold blood."

Mike leaned back in his office chair, facing his vidscreen. "Don't look at it as a lie, Helen. You are simply omitting an unimportant detail that would otherwise clutter your superior's thought processes."

The dark-haired, studio security assistant stared out of the screen. "She should know about the extra video and audio pickups they found, and that studio telemetry booster. I don't know what Ryan's doing, but she might be able to track the signal."

"I've seen the latest reports. Ryan has been operating his ship in stealth mode. There is no signal to trace. It is meaningless information. I'll see to it personally that the studio property is returned."

"Sir—?"

"I heard a rumour that you applied for a job as a show tech?" Mike leaned back in his chair.

"I... I've always dreamed of making e-entertainments."

"Drop by my office. A training position has opened up on

one of the half hours. I believe in hiring from within."

Helen seemed to consider for a moment. "I'd like that. I guess the studio equipment can be slipped back into inventory. Ryan's in enough trouble already."

"I'm glad you see it that way. Remember to drop by my office. Goodbye." Mike broke the connection, then rubbed his temples. "If Sidney wasn't such a talented producer, I'd can that little fool personally. A man who cheats on his wife makes himself so vulnerable. There has to be someone you can be completely honest with. Now, where were we?"

Arlene fidgeted where she stood in front of the desk. A message had greeted her when she arrived at work asking her to visit Michael. "I was asking, what now?"

"What do you mean?" Mike rose and motioned her to the lounge area.

"Well... with Ryan out of communication, you don't need Greg or me anymore, and... I... well... I need this job."

"Good, because there is a lot more to do."

"What? The feeds are in. Sure, editing it will take a few weeks, but after that?"

"A few weeks? Arlene, a lot of the shots don't have an empathic component. It's third-person perspective. There are sections of the story we didn't record at all."

"So?"

"So, we're hardly in the early days of human technology. Your concerns about the audience not accepting the lack of emotion are well-founded. Plus, there are sub-stories to be shown and parts where the various devices I planted on Mildred's equipment missed elements."

"So, how do we fix it?" Arlene looked perplexed.

Mike smiled. "Good old-fashioned acting. We interview everyone involved on the pretext of developing a documentary. We'll do that as well as a making-of piece. After we have the whole story, we develop scripts for the bits we missed and use actors to enact them. Then we graph the images of Mildred, Chow, and the rest over the actors to keep consistency."

"Actors? That's so primitive. Where are you going to find actors?"

"The Spielberg Tower Historical Players Club. They've agreed to play the roles in exchange for me dealing with a rather staggering amount of debt. Marcy, my wife, was thrilled by that. She isn't much for e-entertainments, but she loves stage performances, and they're nearly a lost art."

"Marcy?" Arlene glanced at the picture on Mike's wall. "Um... So how does that solve the lack of empathic feeds?"

"It doesn't. That is the next element of my brilliant, if I do say so myself, scheme." Mike grinned.

"What?" Arlene sat forward on her seat. Everything about this project was radical. She couldn't help being excited. It would either be the masterwork of a master producer, or the biggest disaster in the history of e-entertainments. Either way, it was her place in history.

"You are aware that we provide television and movies to the studio region for authenticity's sake."

"Jack, from my group, works on dubbing the soundtracks on those relics, so the fa... emotional surrogates, will have something to waste their evenings on. So?"

"Up until now, we've only used those entertainments that we had surviving examples of. Scattered episodes strung together as best we could manage. No one has made a commercial television program in eight-hundred years."

"This matters because?" Arlene drummed her fingers on her knee.

Mike's smile made his face glow. "As I said, much of the show is third-person perspective, like those old television shows."

"So?"

"What isn't third-person can be done that way by selecting other cuts."

"Hold on... You're going to make a TV show for the

surrogates on set. What...?" Arlene looked perplexed.

"You're getting it. We make a show for the surrogates, and we can enter it in the archaic arts competition."

"So, we could win an award. It seems a lot of work to put a plaque on your wall."

"That's credits for empty antiproton containers. Do you remember a short-lived program called *SF Geeks*?"

"About three years ago. Horrible show! A poorly done rip off of *Kids in the Band*. I couldn't get into any of the characters. Your show was much better."

"Thank you. I agree." Mike settled contentedly in his chair.

"Why did you let it go forward?"

"The producer's father was a major stockholder. I needed his support in a vote. I knew the show would flop the moment I saw the concept. The producer was a spoiled, rich boy, who had an active antagonism to what he called 'losers'. You must have compassion for what the kids go through to make a show like that; he didn't. It only lasted half a season."

"I'm glad I'm not in management."

"It has a downside. I did manage to transfer the Jessica character over to *Defenders of the Crystal*. Dalbert was a victim on *Vampire Tales*. We did a little after insertion work on Carol. She's working the *Orgy Girls* special features now. Irwin has been co-opted for a minor role as a human slave in *Angel Black*. The other cast members are all extras, except for Sidney. There was a problem with his nano-bots; he died last year."

"So?"

"So, we produce the show. The characters left from *SF Geeks* are fanatical about the science fiction genre. We tell them they're a focus group reviewing a new show before its broadcast. Watching the show will be a dream job for them, and they're all rigged to give full empathic input."

"I get it. We record their empathic reactions, then dub them onto the non-empathic sections of the e-entertainment."

"If it works, we may even develop a spin-off series. *SF Geeks* wasn't a bad concept, it was simply done poorly and had too many characters. Now that the remaining characters are a bit older, I think something could be developed. Maybe them coping with higher education and slowly coming into their own."

"You are a genius," remarked Arlene.

"Flattery will get you a dinner invitation. Marcy does a marvellous stir fry. She asked me to invite you and your group over this Saturday. She likes to get to know the people I work with." Mike grinned, then his face became serious, and he pulled a data disk from his pocket. "I want you to input this into the control board. It's a monitor protocol for another ship."

"Whose?" Arlene took the disk.

"John's space yacht."

"What?"

"Greg called me last night about some shenanigans John's getting up to. I was expecting him to do something stupid, and he hasn't disappointed me. It's all recorded. I need you to work late tonight. We need to intercept Croell and Zandra for a couple of hours to prep them for their roles in season two. We also need to add a pickup to John's Luba bot."

"Why doesn't it surprise me that he has one of those things? What's this with Croell and Zandra? We are talking about the batzoid couple from *Angel Black*?"

"Watch last night's feed; you'll have all the answers you need."

"If you say so."

"I've hired a third tech. She was looking to move up from *A Cat's Life*."

"I love that show after a hard day."

"Most people do. I never thought the idea would fly. It was cheap to make, so I said, why not? Six seasons, and it's still the strongest half-hour we have. Go figure."

A RUDE AWAKENING

Rowan stirred on her bed. The mattress felt wrong. Her sleepy mind refused to process why. She was exhausted, as if she'd been up far too late and drank a little too much. There was an odd taste at the back of her throat, and her eyes felt grainy. She rubbed her eyes, and a heavy coat of fine grit came off on her fingers. Finally, her bladder forced her to fully awake. Her room surrounded her. A finch sang in the chestnut outside her bay window.

"Just a dream. Thank the Divine! Though Ryan was cute." She scanned the room again. The dresser sat in front of the window instead of in the alcove. Two doors opened off the wall to her right.

"Oh boy…?" Rowan sniffed. The air was impossibly clean, no odours. She sniffed the comforter. It smelled brand new.

"Please, it had to be a dream! It…" She swallowed when she realized that the room around her was smaller than the one she was used to and that the ceiling fan was an image. "Divine! It was real. Stardust!"

Biology forced past Rowan's shock. "Henry."

"Hiya, sweet thing. Want to give your teeth a brush before we snog?" Henry's voice issued from the speaker.

"Um… can you see me?" Rowan pulled the comforter over herself.

"Captain Killjoy barred my visuals, unless you request them. Wanna give me a show?"

"No! Where's the bathroom?" Rowan threw off the cover

and stood. The carpet was warm under her feet.

"I can't see you, sweetness. Look for the wall with two doors; one's the bathroom, the other's your closet."

Rowan shuffled to the doors and pressed a button by the closest. The door slid into the wall, revealing a small room with a toilet and sink of the kind she'd seen in movies set on airplanes. The fixtures flanked a small open area in front of the door. A human-shaped depression dented the wall opposite the entrance. There was a control panel beside it.

Taking a seat, Rowan sighed. Finishing, she stood and looked for the flush lever. Her eyes opened wide, and she cried out. "It's orange!"

"Sure thing, hottie, what you expect, plaid?" Henry replied through the speaker.

"I expected clear or yellow. What's going on?"

"Didn't Captain Cutie tell you?"

"Tell me what?"

"You're full of artificial blood. As it breaks down, it comes out orange. Sheesh, girl, you do have catching up to do."

"Stardust!" Rowan moved to the sink and stared at her reflection. "My eyes are blue again."

"Old Kadar did contacts for you, did he? You probably had crusty eye this morning. That was the broken-down contacts. No harm done."

"Thanks."

Rowan left the bathroom and opened her closet door. She pulled out a plastic-wrapped skirt and examined it.

"The Rowan collection, look like an e-star?" She read the label aloud. "They have got to be kidding!"

A buzzer sounded. "What?" gasped Rowan. The twisted normalcy of the room was shattered.

"It's prince charming. Could have asked me to open the door, but noo, has to go all gentlemanly," griped Henry.

"Let him in." Rowan hung the dress back in her closet.

"Henry told me you were awake." Ryan stepped through the door. He was groomed and wore a T-shirt and slacks. Rowan realized he could have easily passed for someone from Sun Valley.

"Yupper. I... did you do all this for me?"

Ryan smiled. "Like it? I tried to only get copies of the stuff you liked."

Rowan closed the closet door and smiled. "Is everything... well... what I mean to ask—?"

"Where you kept it in your old room."

"It is so weird that you know where I keep my underwear."

Ryan shrugged. "Henry said you were having some trouble adjusting."

"Orange pee takes a bit of getting used to."

"That should clear up once your liver and kidneys purge the artificial blood."

"I do have two questions."

"What?"

"Where's the shower, and why wasn't there any toilet paper?"

Henry let out a guffaw over the speaker.

"You shut up," ordered Ryan.

"Got yourself a baby, boss."

Ryan looked at the speaker. "And I'm sure you know how to use a batzoid WC."

"I know lots of things about batzoid." Henry made an odd squeak hiss sound.

"Why am I not surprised?" Ryan shook his head disparagingly, then led her into the washroom. There was barely room for the two of them to stand inside it. Sweat prickled Ryan's brow. The scent of her tightened his throat and caused his heart to throb.

"First..." Ryan's voice cracked, and he cleared his throat. "First, this is a spacecraft. We don't have disposables. The cleansing wipe comes out here." Ryan pressed a button on the wall; a strip of cloth two decimetres long appeared. He pulled it away from the wall and let Rowan touch it.

"It's moist."

"Disinfectant. When you're done, put it here." Ryan

dropped the cloth into a chute above the dispenser. "Nano-bots remove all the refuse, bacteria and viruses, then repair any fibre damage and put it back into the dispenser."

"Hold on... That was used!" Rowan grimaced.

"It's sterile and perfectly clean." Ryan shrugged.

Rowan shuddered. "Where can I get a shower? I smell like I haven't bathed in a week."

Ryan smiled proudly. "It took a lot of work to get these up and running. I salvaged this one from the captain's quarters of my junker." He shuffled slightly to one side and gestured at the depression in the wall.

"That?" asked Rowan.

"Set your levels here." Ryan pointed to the control panel. "I've left them at a general default. If you have dry skin, you might like to tell it to leave a bit more oil behind or vice versa."

"Ah-huh." Rowan took a deep breath. Of all the technology she'd seen this was, for some reason, the most disturbing.

"All you do is strip, press your front into the depression, and hit the activate button." He indicated the big green button on the top of the console. "Billions of micro-bots, they're about flea-sized, swarm out and clean away the oils, bad bacteria and dead skin. It takes about a minute each side, then you're cleaner than you've ever been. It took me weeks to configure micro-bots to replace the ones that were damaged when the junker got hit."

Rowan looked into Ryan's beaming face and forced herself to smile. "It's, um... interesting. You don't use showers or baths or anything on board?"

"Nope, it's one of the best parts of space travel. No muss, no fuss and clean as a whistle."

"Goody. I'd better clean up now."

Ryan smiled and tried to step by her. He couldn't help but brush their bodies together. He felt heat come to his cheeks. "I... yes. I'll be on the bridge. When you're done, I can show you around the ship."

Rowan smiled and nodded, not trusting herself to speak, then closed the door behind him. "No cold showers, stardust! Maybe I'll bury myself in ice."

Henry shifted the feed's perspective from Ryan to his vid pickup. The override circuits Mike had installed on the monitoring system were working perfectly. He watched Rowan strip and recorded her physical responses as the micro-bots cleaned her. He let himself enjoy the show as it played on his internal ram, while at the same time controlling the ship's systems and directing over fifty automated maintenance droids. He dedicated another sliver of his ram to watching an old pornographic e-entertainment. At the same time, he scanned the EM spectrum for any interesting communications.

He was bored. To say he was smarter than an exceptional human would be a misconception: smarter no, faster yes. A chain of thought that might take Ryan an hour to complete he would finish within seconds. He knew he could miss things because of his processing speed, not see side avenues that a biological, with their untidy organic minds, would see. But he was what he was.

"How's the hottie doing?" he asked as Ryan stepped onto the bridge.

"Fine. When she's ready, guide her to the bridge, please."

"Sure. Ryan..."

Ryan turned to face Henry's humanoid body. "Bad news?"

Henry nodded his mutilated head. "I picked up a transmission from Gaea. A news broadcast... Kadar—"

Ryan lifted his hand as he spoke. "Is dead."

"You knew?"

"His cancer was final stage. He asked me to give him the deactivate codes for his nano-bots. When you told me about the ATV crash, I suspected." Ryan slumped into the captain's chair.

Henry nodded. "He was a good friend."

"The best." Ryan traced his fingers over three brass plaques mounted on the side of the command chair. "Medical was the only room without a plaque."

"He died helping a friend."

Ryan nodded. "Sangunis abl planeta."

"Sangunis abl planeta," echoed Henry.

Helen sat opposite Mildred at the studio ATV's fold-down table. There were dark circles under the younger woman's eyes, and her hair was mussed.

"Good coffee." Mildred took a sip and turned her attention to her hand-held, where the report Helen had served with her breakfast was displayed.

"The cafeteria at the end of the dock is really nice," Helen agreed.

"DNA proves it. Ryan Chandler is the thief. His and the property's DNA were all over the bunks."

"Are you going to go after the other prisoner who was in the craft?"

"What would be the point? He's already in prison, and all he has to say is that he saw it and went in to see if someone was hurt. What's this about the antiproton power link being functional?"

"Is that important?"

Mildred drummed her fingers on the table. "Why run on batteries if you can use an antiproton pack? Unless…" Mildred straightened as her expression became sly.

"Muriel, download all flight records for Ryan Chandler and all purchase records for antiproton under his name."

"Accessing."

Mildred turned back to the report on her hand-held's screen. "Is this everything?"

Helen swallowed, then nodded. "Yup, everything. Can I go now? I'd like to get some sleep."

"Fine, thank you for the overtime."

Helen shuffled from the vehicle.

"Muriel, when was the last time Ryan Chandler purchased a charged antiproton pack?" Mildred took another sip of coffee.

"Ryan Chandler is not recorded as ever having purchased an antiproton power unit from either the orbital station's stores or the coelenteratezoid generating station."

"Muriel, connect me to Admiral Newton."

Admiral Newton leaned his elbows on the polycarbonate desk that filled half his space station office. His uniform was immaculate, and he stared into the vidscreen.

"He may be heading for the coelenteratezoid antiproton plant." Mildred stared out of the screen, her face serious.

"Or he might wait until he reaches the Switchboard Station. Antiproton is usually cheaper there." The admiral smiled condescendingly.

"I realize that. I'm betting he doesn't have enough power to maintain stealth all the way to the stargate."

"All right. I'll order the frigate to take up a position outside the antiproton generator's controlled space."

"Thank you, Admiral. I wish I could be there. This Chandler is a slippery one."

Admiral Newton's expression became sly. "If you can be at the spaceport in two hours, we're taking aboard a company of ground troops in case we have to board the *Star Hawk*. You are welcome to come along as a civilian advisor."

"Really!" Mildred's face lit up.

"Of course. You've almost had Captain Chandler on several occasions. Your input would be valuable."

"I'll meet your team at the spaceport."

"Good. It's convict retrieval unit three under the command of—"

"Lieutenant Chow," finished Mildred.

"You know him?"

"He helped with the on-planet pursuit."

"I'll leave you to your preparations." Admiral Newton closed the connection and sat up straight. "Alexander, connect me to Mike Strongbow."

Seconds later, the vid displayed Michael's face, which broke into a smile. "Jim, how's it going? How's Jesse?"

"Good, in both cases. I thought you might like to know, you were right. Mrs. Tallman expressed interest in staying with the hunt. I've arranged for her to be a civilian advisor."

"That's excellent. Milly's like a dog on a scent, that's why she's so good."

"I also arranged for the same ground pounder squad that Colonel Burtch assigned to hunt Ryan for our boarding support. Why you wanted that I don't know, but one hand washes the other."

"It's for my documentary. People like to see the same faces go from start to finish on a project. Don't worry, Lieutenant Chow is no slouch."

"You've been right so far. This is turning out to be one supernova of an exercise. The analysis boys have found more holes in our inter-agency coordination than a Swiss cheese. Chandler hasn't lost a beat since he was pensioned out."

"Glad to hear it's working out on all sides."

"I am concerned about the Kadar situation."

Mike nodded. "He wanted to end it, Jim. In a way, I'm glad that scenario was the one that panned out. I never met him. He seemed a good soldier."

"He was a great healer. He deserved one last flight, and a chance to go out swinging. I'll square it with the prison authority. I'm owed a favour or two. Kadar saved my brother's life on Murack Five, you know?"

"How is Sam anyway?"

"It's Samantha now. He… she's expecting her first child. I think she's happy, though it takes some getting used to."

"I'm glad."

"Me too. You know, Mike, when you first suggested this exercise, I thought you were crazy, but you were right. The system needed shaking up. Be sure and thank Mr. Wilson for the loan of the Rowan property. We'll try and bring her back undamaged."

"I'll do that. Just remember, I get full video and audio feeds of the mission."

"You'll have them. I better go. Take care, say hi to Marcy for me. Oh, by the way, thanks for moving Ulva up from *A Cat's Life*. I haven't seen her this happy since she was ten, and I gave her a junior editor e-adaptor for her birthday."

"Your daughter deserved the promotion. I just needed a job for her to move into. Take care, Jim."

"Same to you, Mike." The screen went blank.

John sat in the control room staring at the main screen. He hated the work, but so many of his techs had quit that he had to take a shift or leave the monitor unmanned. After a thirty-hour shift, Greg had insisted on leaving.

"No gratitude. He should have realized I was only blowing smoke when I fired him." John checked Croell's perspective. The batzoid was packing its most prized possessions. The Luba bot lounged provocatively on a pile of pillows. Zandra was nowhere to be seen.

"I wish you could leave earlier, but if someone sees a batzoid at the studio's spaceport, there will be questions." John shook his head and shifted the main screen to Angel's perspective. She was following one of the human slaves through the streets of Sun Valley. He completely missed Gunther, who sat in the Garlic Palace, his emotions artificially blank, his telepathy probing every mind that entered the room.

IN DAYS OF YORE

"I gutted the holding clips and used the parts to get some of the landing legs up and running. Originally this section didn't have life support. I routed in a feed." Ryan gestured about the dimly lit compartment.

Rowan scanned the large room. Crates, pieces of hull plating and other spare parts filled it. She could tell the moment she stepped into it that the gravity was substantially less than in the rest of the ship. "This was the bomb bay?"

"In all its destructive glory. We carried enough explosives to turn a medium-sized moon into dust."

"And I always thought humans would outgrow war." Rowan leaned against a crate marked 'control circuits.' "Why hasn't everybody blown everybody else up? I mean, if you can blow up planets."

Ryan sat on a crate labelled 'optic sensors.' "That's one of the reasons the Republic was formed. The older races did destroy some planets, a few million years ago. Then the Republic was formed. There's a ban on planet busters. Any species that uses a planet buster will be reduced to a Neolithic level. All the other species will join together to accomplish it. The guilty race also forfeits its stargate."

"Divine. Was that ever done?"

"Three times in the history of the Republic. The first was the oryceropuszoids. They redeveloped technology and re-joined the Republic about fifteen thousand years after they were set back. They're one of the oldest races in existence.

They have a contract with the United Earth Systems. We defend their cargo ships, they sell us advanced technology."

"How did they make them forget their tech the first time?"

"The Republic forces massacred their population. They only spared beings too young to know any technology. They dropped these on the species homeworld, after stripping it of all cities and towns. Those that survived formed the basis of the new race."

"That's awful!" What little colour there was in Rowan's face drained away.

"The Republic doesn't meddle much. The few laws they have are adamant, and very harsh. The elder races say it's the only way to maintain safety in the galaxy and species autonomy. The worst part is the target species loses all its colony worlds. That worked out well for the otterzoids and felinezoids. They evolved on worlds taken from the oryceropuszoids."

Rowan shook her head. "It's so hard to conceptualize a society that spans millions of years."

"You get used to not thinking about it. Most humans, unless they join the forces, never see another species close up."

"You said three races were 'set back'."

"Yeah, for any more you'll have to check the ship's data store. It's been a long time since high school history. I only know oryceropuszoids because they spoke for humans at the trial after Murack Five." Ryan shuddered and looked at the floor.

Rowan moved to his side and squeezed his shoulder. "You know, if you—"

"I don't! Not about that. I'm sorry, Rowan." Ryan looked up, and there was a long silence before he broke it. "Let's get on with the tour. Why don't I show you to the ground pounder quarters, then I should get back and make sure that Henry hasn't arranged for a thousand felinezoid dancing girls to meet us at the antiproton generating station." Jumping off the box, Ryan took Rowan's hand and led her back to the elevator.

"I've been meaning to ask, where do the species names come from?" asked Rowan.

Ryan could feel his tension draining away now that they were back on a safe topic. "That? It's impossible for most species to communicate without the translator nano-bots. You had a set installed on set so that you could speak with the alien races there. The human throat can't produce the frequencies otterzoids, for example, use to communicate, and the human ear can't hear them. The other species are limited in the same sort of way."

"I have a universal translator installed in my head. I think I'm moving past the ability to be surprised."

Ryan pressed the button for the level that had housed the ground troops. "Universal translator? Now there would be an invention. Only the languages of neurologically mapped species can be programmed in. The translator nano-bots connect to the speech and language recognition parts of the brain. The ones on the speech centres take the raw impulses and convert them to a binary language. These are transmitted using the brain's own bio-electric energy. The nano-bots on the recognition centres pick up the signal and insert it, so you perceive it as being your primary language. They also block the nerve impulses that come from the actual sound the alien is making."

The lift doors opened, and Ryan led Rowan into a huge room with a two-metre high ceiling. The entire floor space was taken up by potted saplings and automated support systems.

Rowan rubbed her forehead. "How many people did this ship hold?"

"This space was for the enlisted men. It used to be full of bunk beds. When I converted to cargo, I sold them off. There were three hundred ground forces. I gutted the mess and added it to this room as well. I needed the parts to get the space crew and officers' messes up and running."

"Three hundred?" Rowan sounded awed.

"Enlisted. There was one lieutenant for every twenty-five enlisted and the ground forces commander. Not to mention the medical crew, there was another dozen or so of them. They were all in officer country. The *Star Hawk* was designed to serve as a mobile HQ, a MASH and a troop transport all rolled into one. An entire campaign could be conducted from this ship."

Rowan rubbed her forehead. "I'm getting lost."

"It will make sense eventually. It's mostly stuff you don't have to think about. Life is what it is."

Rowan looked at the trees. "Are they life-support or something? The major ship systems are working, right? You aren't compensating with some makeshift." Rowan looked hopeful.

Ryan snorted. "The *Star Hawk* is spaceworthy. Just because I've converted her to cargo doesn't mean she's not safe. The trees are for sale when we reach Geb. It's a new colony world, trees always go for a premium. Think of it this way. Each one of these," Ryan gestured at a sapling, "we get to Geb alive is equivalent to a new luxury ground car."

"Wow!" Rowan did some mental math. "You're rich."

"It's a start. Enough to finance me getting up and running as a space hauling service. You see, Geb is only a stage one world, and when it's cut off by the stargate moving out of range it will have to supply all its needs from in system."

"And that means?"

"It's a desert planet for starters. The water ice from a moon orbiting the system's only gas giant will be a hot commodity. It will be years before the planet has a proper hydration cycle; years after that before they have the oceans established."

"I figure it still beats being dead."

Ryan smiled. "Come on, I think this next bit will be a bit

more to your liking."

Ryan led the way through a door in the wall by the lift into a corridor. Doors opened off either side. "This was officer territory." Opening a door to his right, Ryan entered a nine-metre square room. A roll-down bed occupied each wall, except for the one with the door, which was covered by three lockers. "Standard lieutenant's quarters. I kept the officer section for passengers."

"Nice but, well... it's not very private."

"Don't worry, you have rank. I'm not going to turf you out of the mate's quarters." Ryan grinned.

"I was thinking more for passengers."

"This is third class. Second only has two beds and a private bath. First is a private room. Something for everyone."

Rowan felt dizzy. She half fell onto the rolled-up couch bed.

"Are you okay?" Ryan rushed to her side and pulled out his hand-held. He scanned her, then looked at its screen.

"Dizzy."

"Your oxygenation is low. Kadar said he didn't like using so much artificial blood. Do you want to lie down?"

Rowan smiled, and her eyes sparkled. She'd only ever had one other person care so much about her. That had been her father. Pain touched her at the thought of never seeing him again. She sucked it up. "No, but you could answer my question."

"Which one?" Ryan gazed into the hand-held's screen, not trusting himself to look into those incredible blue eyes.

"Where do the species names come from?"

"Oh, that. Since most species can't pronounce the name a species calls themselves, it's customary to find an animal native to your homeworld that superficially resembles the species and add a prefix or suffix to the name."

"So felinezoid because they look like felines."

Ryan found the courage to meet Rowan's gaze. "We'd

only just been co-opted into the Republic when we met the felinezoids. We were trying to show everyone respect, so we picked what we thought was the most polite name possible. They weren't so kind."

"How so?"

"A literal translation of their name for us is, 'masturbating ape'."

Rowan laughed. "That's Toronk's sense of humour all the way."

Ryan grinned. "He was designed to be the quintessential felinezoid."

Rowan gazed at the floor.

"What did I say?" Ryan reached out and took her hand.

"It's..." Rowan met his gaze. "Designed. Me, my family, my friends, we were all built, like a machine."

"It doesn't make you any less human."

"I don't even know who my real mother and father were. I'm only a clone of some actress who died centuries ago."

Ryan cupped her cheek in his palm. "Rowan, you are you. Rowan McPherson, daughter of Gunther McPherson and Willa McPherson. So what that you were adopted?"

Tears welled in her eyes. "It's more than that. All my memories—"

"Are that. Memories. Look, when I was cloned, I went through the same kind of thing. Was I still Ryan Chandler, or some cheap copy? I realized it didn't matter. I am what I make myself. I choose the person I am every time I make a decision. It's the same for you."

"But your memories are real. You have a family."

Ryan laughed bitterly. "Family. Let me tell you about my family. My mother and father are members of Humans Ascendant. They tried to get an injunction to stop the cloning that saved my life. They won't even talk to me. I'm dead to them. They wouldn't even fly out from Earth to say goodbye. My son, the one I rejoined the space forces for, so he could get his doctorate, secretly sends me a message on my birthday. He's a prof at an Earth-based university, and it would be bad for his career to associate with his fakey father. Joslin is a brain-dead e-addict. My sister threatened to put out a hit on me to end the 'twisted abomination of her dead brother' that I now represent. Why do you think I moved to Gaea in the first place? I was born and raised on Earth. Everyone I knew is there. My choices were leave or die. There are no clones on the homeworld. I have no family."

"I'm sorry." Rowan shifted from comforted to comforter.

"We're all in the same boat here, blue eyes. You, me, Henry. Nothing to go back to and only a long shot to run toward."

Rowan nodded. "At least a long shot is still a shot."

Ryan smiled, then on impulse drew her lips to his. She didn't resist.

The kiss was dry, mostly the lips. Ryan pulled away and stared into her face.

"That was nice," she commented.

"Better than any e-entertainment. Rowan, you know how I feel, but if this happens, I want it to last, not burn out."

Rowan smiled, then kissed him again. "I like that idea. Slow then?"

"Slow." Ryan nodded as they sat smiling at each other.

"I guess I should show you the rest of the ship." Ryan broke the silence.

Rowan nodded, then hand in hand they continued the tour.

Mildred burst through the mag-lev station's sliding doors and hit the bedrock plain of Gaea's primary space field at a run. A hundred metres away, a triangular, military, launch vehicle was preparing for lift-off. Lieutenant Chow stood at the bottom of the entry stair supervising the loading of his troops.

"CHOW!" Mildred shouted when the last man had

boarded, and the lieutenant stepped onto the stair.

Chow turned and smiled. Mildred came up to the ramp and stopped, sides heaving and red-faced.

Chow reached out and lifted the overnight bag he'd seen in the studio ATV off her shoulder. "They said we might have a civilian advisor. I'm glad it's you."

"Yeah, I ha... ha... ha..." Mildred took deep breaths.

"Lieutenant, we have to launch now, or we'll delay the *Saber*'s departure," said a member of the flight crew who stood at the top of the stair. She was a stocky woman with blonde hair, wearing a sexless coverall.

Chow and Mildred walked up the stairs to the entrance door. The chamber beyond was ten metres long by six wide. Rows of seats accessed from a central aisle filled the compartment. Only about a quarter of the seats were occupied, and Mildred recognized the people of Chow's squad.

Mildred let Chow stow her bag in an overhead compartment and took a seat. Chow took the seat beside her. A vibration coursed through the launch vehicle. G-forces pulled at them despite the inertial dampers, then there was nothing. Mildred lifted her arm. It felt light.

"One-tenth G, just enough to keep the dust down," explained Chow.

"I've done orbital exercises, Lieutenant," snapped Mildred.

"Sorry, ma'am." Chow focused forward.

Mildred released a sigh. "No, I'm sorry. I'm angry with myself for not catching Chandler when he was still planetside. Do you know who's captaining the frigate?"

"Captain Denardo of the Gaea Orbital Defence Reserves."

Mildred settled in her seat, trying to get comfortable. "I don't think I know him."

"Neither do I. I managed a look at her record. She used to be frontline forces, served in the Murack offensive."

"Oh, boy!"

"Is that bad?"

"It could be good, bad, or nothing at all. It all depends on if our captain knows Chandler or not, and what she felt about him."

"I'm sure she'll do her duty."

Mildred glared at Chow. "There's a difference between doing your duty and doing your best. If you haven't learned that yet, Chow, learn it now. Just because you put on a uniform, it doesn't mean you stop being human. Old school ties can tie you down or lift you up, depending on whose colours match."

Chow nodded and passed Mildred his hand-held. "That's her open file. I was reviewing it while we loaded."

"Thanks." Mildred lost herself in reading and only became aware that the launch vehicle had docked with the station when the airlock door opened, and the gravity increased to a half G. Chow's people began pulling their duffle-bags out of the overhead.

"Here." Chow stood up and passed her her overnight bag, then moved to the airlock. "Remember, people. The frigate will be departing as soon as we board, so don't forget anything."

Mildred waited until the squad had passed her seat before stepping into the aisle. She rushed through the airlock into a long, two-metre-wide space station hallway. The sudden transition to full Gaea gravity made her stumble. She righted herself and joined Chow's company as they double-timed it along the corridor. A minute later, they passed through another airlock into a large room with crates secured along its walls. Two men, dressed in Space Services coveralls and armed with stun rifles, flanked the airlock door. They quickly checked the retinal scans of all who entered.

"Your identity card, ma'am?" requested the smaller of the guards. He had a build reminiscent of a tree stump with arms and legs attached.

Mildred fished the card out of her pocket and passed it

to him. He slipped it into his hand-held and held it to her face. "Major Mildred Tallman, Gaea Planetary Reserves, head of S.E.T.E. Studio Security."

"That's me, chief," said Mildred.

"The captain will see you and the squad leader at the start of the third shift. Quarters have been arranged." The chief pressed a button on the security console by the airlock, and it closed. "Hatch closed," he said to the air.

"Aye, hatch reads closed. Pressure seal secure," said a voice over the intercom.

There was a slight lurch, then stillness until the intercom spoke again. "All hands, this is the captain. We are underway. This is a seek and detain mission. All scanner teams to station. Command meeting in the captain's mess at seventeen-thirty hours ship time. For any late arrivals, ship time is now nine-thirty-two hours. That is all."

Chow looked at the speaker. "She sounds efficient."

Mildred pushed to his side. "She sounds bored. That's not good. She's also sending a message about what she thinks of this mission and us by setting the meeting so late and over dinner. Remember what I said about doing your duty or doing your best."

"Sir, ma'am. We need to see to the billeting of your troops." The security chief motioned down the corridor, and Mildred and Chow followed his lead.

Henry recorded yet another kiss and trimmed down the recap of Republic history for the file he'd transmit to Mike. The scanner he'd directed toward Gaea showed a vessel leaving the planet's orbit and moving along their general heading.

"Looks like an Aries class frigate, probably the *Saber*. Not to panic. Might just be getting some antiproton from the generating station. Don't want to interrupt the lovebirds about nothing." Henry's human face smiled. "Looks good on you Ryan, looks real good. I'll mention the ship when you get back to the bridge." Henry recorded Rowan's tour of the engineering section. The ship's monitors gave third-person shots, and the empathic feeds from both her and Ryan were buzzing. Fear, excitement, regret, hope, wonder. Henry turned his attention to editing the feeds and for the first time in months wasn't bored.

Croell caught the updraft and let it carry him into the sky. He'd strapped an anti-grav harness to the Luba bot so that he could tow it. Zandra was at his side, her wings stretched wide. The flare of her nostrils told him she was enjoying the flight as much as he was. This was what it was to be the chosen species of the Great Flyer of the Sky. They were batzoid; the exhilaration of flight was their birthright.

Croell hovered on the thermal and yanked the rope tied to the Luba, pulling it up beside him.

"Luba, what direction must I fly to reach the spacecraft?"

The robot dangled upside down and made no effort to right itself. "The spacecraft is eighty kilometres due north of the set region."

"Where we were led to believe the humans had a landing area for primitive flight vehicles." Croell flicked his forked tongue.

"It would make sense, my husband. They wished to keep all the beings in this area oblivious to the real universe. This ploy would explain any noise from the spaceport."

Arlene stretched and felt her back crack. She'd been doing a preliminary edit all day, and now she had to man the control room to catch Croell's activity. She smiled to herself. John was oblivious to the fact that his 'do not monitor' codes had only affected the *Angel Black* board.

"Looks good on you, you bastard."

"Who are you talking to?"

Arlene swivelled her chair to see a pretty, twenty-something woman with light-brown skin, long, chestnut hair and striking, blue eyes, standing behind her.

"Ulva, you scared the life out of me. I didn't hear you come in. Did Michael brief you?"

"You know it. I can't believe that Mr. Wilson is setting up a rogue pursuit using studio property."

"You never worked for him. John will do anything that he thinks will help John."

Ulva smiled, displaying straight, white teeth. "Michael said almost the same thing, only he called him, 'that Rat Bastard!'"

"And you kiss your mother with that mouth?" Arlene feigned shock.

"I'm a services brat, what you expect?" Ulva smiled, her anxiety about the job evaporating in her rapport with her new boss.

"Take the controls. When they reach the yacht, knock them out. We need time to calibrate the recorder we're installing and to add a telemetry unit to the Luba."

"Like when Fluffy fell into the pipe, and I put him to sleep until the fire department arrived."

"I hated that ep." Arlene relinquished her chair and headed for the door.

"So did I. When you work with a cat, you take what they give you. It made for a good sub-story on *The Station House*."

"True. I'm off. If you have any problems, call me on my hand-held. I think you'll do good."

"Thanks."

Arlene left the control room and hurried to Michael's office.

Mildred and Chow took seats at the captain's table. The officer's mess was a single room, six metres long by three and a half wide. A rectangular table filled the middle of the room. A crisp, white tablecloth displayed the china.

Captain Tansy Denardo sat at the head of the table, her long, grey-streaked, black hair falling in a braid down the back of her dress whites. Her substantial breasts pushed against the fabric of her uniform, while her classical Italian features were pulled into a polite mask.

"I appreciate your promptness." Captain Denardo inclined her head. Chow swallowed. Tansy's gesture was pure elegance, yet so sensual Chow felt like he was being seduced.

"Thank you for having me aboard, Captain," said Mildred.

"When the admiral speaks, I obey. I must say, I'm not overly fond of hunting the *Star Hawk*. Especially with Captain Chandler commanding her."

"Do you know him, ma'am?" Chow hadn't taken his eyes off the captain since he'd sat down.

Tansy smiled, showing even, white teeth, and a sparkle came to her eyes. "I've never had the pleasure of meeting him. Anyone who served in the Murack offensive has heard of the *Star Hawk*. I've also had a chance to look at Chandler's file. Martian Medal of Valour, twice. Jupiter commendation with a platinum cluster, for innovative strategies in a combat situation. Those are only the start. The man has a proven track record. If he doesn't want to be caught, it will be exceedingly difficult to catch him."

"We almost had him on the planet," remarked Chow.

Captain Denardo's smile became condescending. "He was using malfunctioning equipment. Chandler is an engineer and a space jockey. He probably looked on that ATV as spare parts until he needed it. The *Star Hawk* won't have any such failings."

"Can you do the job?" asked Mildred.

A purser entered, carrying a tray containing three salads. "The meal is ready. I took the privilege of ordering for you. As to your question, I'll do my duty, Major Tallman. Although expending this much effort to catch a man who liberated—"

"Stole," Mildred interrupted.

Captain Denardo's face became hard, and her voice cold. "Where I was raised, interrupting anyone mid-sentence was considered impolite, let alone a superior officer, Major!"

Mildred locked eyes with the captain. Chow's gaze flitted between the two women. Mildred was the first to look away. "I apologize, Captain. One becomes accustomed to certain ways of phrasing things."

Captain Denardo was silent for a long moment before continuing. "It seems an inordinate amount of effort and expense to catch a man who *liberated* a clone."

Chow felt the tension in the room mount. He took a mouthful of his salad and chewed in silence before speaking. "This dressing is incredible."

Tansy turned her gaze to him, and her smile could have lit up a city. "Thank you. It's an old family recipe I shared with my cook."

Chow felt his knees go to jelly. Mildred rolled her eyes.

Rowan sipped her wine. It was a dry red with a fruity bouquet. The flight crew's mess was four metres long by three wide with a central table. The walls were set to display a woodland meadow. Two doors opened out of the room, one into the corridor, the other into a kitchen. Ryan emerged through the second of these carrying two trays.

"And for the lady, Beef Wellington with mashed potatoes." He deposited the tray in front of her.

"If it's a match for the salad, I could get used to this." Rowan peeled back the top of the tray. The food smelled wonderful.

"No excuse for bad food if you apply good tech. Billy

was our cook during the Murack offensive. He set up a couple thousand of these. I think it was because they only taught him how to cook for groups of a hundred or more. When the ground squads were off someplace, he didn't know what else to do with the leftovers."

"He was an incredible cook. What happened to him?" Rowan took a bite of her food.

Ryan stood and moved to a plaque that was mounted on the wall by the kitchen door. "We took a hit from a kinetic missile while we were landing on Murack Five. It cracked the hull in the mess. Billy was sucked into space."

Rowan noticed the plaque and remembered seeing others like it all over the ship. She moved to Ryan's side and read it aloud.

"Billy Farsm 527 PC to 554 PC Murack Five landing. We will never forget."

Ryan shrugged. "Someone has to remember, or it was all pointless."

"He was a fantastic cook."

"He always liked it when people enjoyed his meals. It's why he joined up. He wanted to get the training, then go back to Mars and start a five-star restaurant." Ryan returned to the table and started tucking into his food.

"I feel like I'm in an e-entertainment." Greg stood in the utter blackness of John's yacht's main corridor. The light-intensifying eyedrops he'd used allowed him to see in shadowy outline.

"That's because you are in an e-entertainment." Arlene stood on the other side of the airlock's inner door.

A beeping sound came from behind her. There was a click and Mike's voice. "Thanks, honey, we're ready." There was another click. "Marcy spotted them. They've landed by that car on the space strip's perimeter. Remember, quick and clean. We don't want them to get suspicious."

Croell back winged and lowered himself to the ground beside a small, electric vehicle parked outside the studio's space strip. Five triangular ships ranging in size from thirty to a hundred metres in length sat on the landing strip.

Tugging the rope, he pulled the Luba bot to his side. After turning it the right way up, he pushed it to the ground and deactivated its anti-grav harness. Zandra landed beside him.

"Luba, which vessel is your master's?" demanded Croell.

"The *Mary* is a class two space yacht currently on a five-year lease to John Wilson. Its identification code is—"

"Silence," hissed Zandra. "Luba, point to it."

The robot pointed to a forty-metre long craft.

"Luba, come," ordered Croell as he fumbled open the vehicle's door with his oversized, clawed hand.

"Yes, yes, yes. Oh yes. It's so good. You are so good, I arrrrr..." The robot's face contorted in apparent ecstasy.

"My husband, I believe I know what this thing was originally designed to do," said Zandra.

"It is like that pleasure bot my Aunt Fraw and her wife-sisters purchased after Uncle Riga died."

"Perhaps I can feel some forgiveness for that human. To lose a mate is a horrible thing. Though, I thought the species could take a mate after the death of the first."

"None of this changes our situation. We must kill Rowan and bring her body back here to expunge the sin of falsehood. Luba, co... open these doors."

Luba opened the back door.

Croell could see a roll of material left across the seat. "Zandra, squeeze into this human thing first, then I'll cover us with this cloth. The security system here is only meant to prevent vandals, so that should prove adequate."

Zandra scrambled into the back seat, crushing herself into the small awkward space. Croell followed her.

"It reminds me of the launch pod we used to reach the

ship that took us to Earth," said Zandra.

Croell went quiet. "We... Zandra, that never happened. Nothing before we landed on this world was real." A shudder went through him.

"Great Flyer of the Skies! You are right, my husband, or are you even that? We have not really done the joining."

"I know. Once we are aboard the ship, we must correct that omission in the eyes of the Great Flyer of the Skies."

Croell managed to flick the cloth over himself and his mate, then ordered, "Luba, close the door, then sit in the driver's station and take us to the yacht. Stop by the airlock door."

Croell heard the door slam and felt a sharp pain from where the armrest jammed into his backside. A moment later, he heard another door slam, then a strange scuffling. Lifting his head, he looked out from under the cloth. The Luba bot was following orders. It had closed the doors and was now crawling into the driver's seat through the open window. Croell let the cover drop over his head and muttered, "No matter the species, some like them dumb."

Ulva had a satellite shot up on the main screen. Croell's car was parked beside the open airlock of John's yacht. The Luba pulled open the back door, and Zandra, then Croell sprinted into the ship. The Luba leaned through the car window and spoke. The car drove off. Luba followed Croell and Zandra into the airlock.

Ulva shifted to Croell's perspective and watched the outer door close through his eyes. He turned in the confined space, finding himself pressed between his wife and the Luba. She recorded his emotional reaction. "Just like when Fluffy saw that tabby in heat. Males, what I love about them." Ulva smiled as the screen showed the inner airlock door opening. She triggered the sedative packs and watched as Croell's and Zandra's readings dropped into unconsciousness.

Arlene heard the airlock door slide open, then a hiss and a thump.

"Luba, override code, 'get the bastard'," said Mike.

"Core program deactivated. Safe mode engaged. Be advised that only program repair functions will operate in this mode," spoke the Luba in a monotone.

Greg stepped into the airlock and ran his hand-held over Croell, then Zandra. "I've got the codess. I need to input them into the telemetry ssyssstem."

"Go to the bridge and do that. Hit the internal lights while you're at it. Arlene and I will take care of John's play toy," ordered Mike.

Greg moved up the corridor to the pointed nose of the ship. A minute later, the internal lights came on.

Mike blinked as his eyes adjusted, then he ordered, "Luba, enter the corridor and lay down."

The robot complied.

"Now what? I don't know anything about robotics." Arlene stared down at the prostrate automation. She felt a surge of jealousy. She knew it was plastic, but she'd almost have killed for its legs.

"It isn't that hard. Luba, inflate, then open chest for post-market addition."

An invisible seam opened on the Luba's chest and the skin peeled back, revealing that the breasts were two jelly filled sacks under a layer of plastic. The bags inflated to a ludicrous degree.

Mike grasped one of the bags and twisted it. It came away, revealing that it was connected by hoses and jacks to the system's inner workings. "First a ram expansion, so it can handle the monitoring without a drop off in performance. Pass me the falsey please."

Arlene handed Mike a jelly-filled sack seemingly

identical to the one he'd disconnected. "What are these?"

"Liquid-crystal ram units. No difference in feel or texture, but they nearly double the run capacity of the Luba. John is a basic guy, so he went for a basic Luba. One with all the upgrades is so close to AI status they had to pass laws to keep them under the line."

"And you know this because?" Arlene stared at Mike.

"My sister bought a Lucius after her third divorce. It's the perfect mate for her. It does whatever she tells it, it doesn't mind her cooking, and it doesn't mind if she cheats on it with every man, woman or furry that strikes her fancy."

"Oh." Arlene put a theory that had been growing in her mind to bed. "How did you get the override phrase installed?"

"The planetary distributor for Luba and Luke bots used to work for the studio. She owed me a favour."

"Is there anything on this planet you don't have a way of manipulating?"

Mike paused and considered. "Raw e-data export. My contact got arrested two years ago. I haven't been able to establish another one."

"Oh." Arlene focused on helping Mike upgrade the Luba.

"Now we do the other breast, add the telemeter, and we can get this done." Mike reached for the second jelly-filled sack.

Ulva watched through the Luba's eyes as Mike, Arlene and Greg stepped over the two sleeping batzoids and closed the airlock door behind them. Following Mike's orders, the Luba repositioned itself in the airlock, then rebooted its normal run function.

"Now, wakey wakey, little bats." Ulva operated a control removing the sedative from her two charges.

Croell felt a moment of dizziness and tripped on the airlock's lip. Zandra fell on top of him.

"Accursed human ships! Everything is either too small or too large." Croell extracted himself and stood. Zandra followed him.

"Luba, go to the bridge and start launch procedures. We will have to hurry if we are to catch our prey before they pass through the stargate."

Luba stepped into the hall and turned toward the front of the ship. Croell and Zandra followed her. A sliding pressure door opened at the end of the passage, and the Luba stepped onto the bridge.

The bridge had two swivel chairs mounted behind a console at its front and an additional two stations at its sides. A single chair occupied the middle of the room with a narrow walkway on all sides.

"My husband, I do not think we'll all fit." Zandra gazed through the open door.

"You are correct, my wife. Luba, can you direct Zandra to the sleeping quarters?" asked Croell.

"Yes." The Luba sat at the pilot's station and started its pre-flight checks.

"Well?" demanded Croell.

The Luba kept up with the pre-flight.

"It is not very intuitive. Badly programmed. I'll look at its operating system later. Luba, direct me to the largest sleeping cabin on board," ordered Zandra.

A series of lights on the corridor's wall blinked, forming a dotted line that led to the first door on the right.

"This could seem a very long trip," commented Croell. "Luba, summon me before we lift off. Obtain all flight clearances."

"Acknowledged." The robot continued with the pre-flight.

28

THE DATA STREAM HEARD ROUND THE GALAXY

Gunther sat in the Garlic Palace and clamped down on the surge of emotion that threatened to break his control. A nondescript tree planter at the bar was not what he seemed. His mind was full of images from the fire station, seen through a screen. Gunther focused all his power on the man, who responded by rubbing the back of his neck.

Trouble, that's what I want to know about. Gunther tried to steer the man's thoughts. The image of a plump woman screaming came to Gunther's mind.

Trouble at work. Gunther refined the projection. A screen blanked by interference, empathic monitors flat, filled the image. *'Why?'* Gunther projected.

Croell lay over the captain's chair on the bridge. He'd turned the seat sideways and put a pillow on it to support his chest. In this way, he was marginally comfortable for short periods of time.

"Luba, set a course for the stargate, best possible speed."

"Setting course and obtaining space control permission."

"I only hope we arrive at the gate before our prey. I will be in my quarters if anything develops. Continue to scan for Chandler's craft. Inform me if it becomes apparent."

"Acknowledged. I have intercepted a communication from Gaea Orbital Defence containing the keywords you set the ship's system to monitor for."

"Play the message."

A female human voice issued from the ship's speaker. It sounded like gibberish to Croell.

"Luba, translate the message into low batzoid and play." Croell tapped his claw against the floor in frustration.

"Gaea Orbital Defence Command, this is the *Saber*. Standardized space-time, three-hundred hours, standard check-in. We are still en route to the coelenteratezoid antiproton station. There is no sign of the *Star Hawk*. Over and out."

Hiss. Croell tapped his claws against the deck. "He must need fuel. Perhaps I will have the opportunity to kill Rowan on planet after all. Still... if her liberator eludes pursuit, I had best be waiting for him. Luba, maintain course. Reduce acceleration to the ship's recommended maximum. Continue monitoring, tell me if anything related to our prey develops."

Croell heaved his bulk off the chair and left the bridge. As soon as he was gone, the Luba transmitted the coded images in the telemeter to Gaea on a secured frequency.

Rowan slipped on her bunny slippers and robe. Ship time, it was the wee hours. She couldn't sleep any more. She'd crashed right after dinner and was now wide awake. She padded into the hallway.

"Hey, sweet cheeks, you're up early." Henry's voice came out of a speaker.

"I'm slept out."

"If you're up, why not come and give me a big snog to pass the time?"

"Will you settle for a nice conversation?" Rowan turned

towards the bridge.

"My lot. I smell the prime quarter house. I get served hamburger."

"Do you even eat?" The bridge door opened in front of Rowan and she stepped in.

Henry's humanoid body turned to watch her. "You'd be surprised at what I can do. Grrrrrrr." He leered.

"Down boy, you don't even have a lower body."

"We could manage."

Rowan took a seat in the captain's chair, being careful to stay out of Henry's reach. She noticed that the main screen was filled with the image of a strange-looking machine. From the backdrop of stars, she guessed it was a spaceship.

"What's that?" she pointed at the screen.

"Who's that, hottie?" Henry sounded indignant.

"Sorry, I didn't know. Who is that, a friend of yours?"

Henry smiled. The action looked strange on his ruined face. "I wish. That is vgstibmrtit, the greatest AI ever to exist, and my personal hero. I was scanning a documentary on him the coelenteratezoids are transmitting to the antiproton station."

"Oh, what did Vg...Vg...Vg...sorry. What did he or she do?"

Henry looked adoringly at the screen. "Don't worry, hottie, the name's in Vrdkjf. Humans can't speak it. Call him Victor, that's what Ryan does."

"Okay." Rowan tried to look interested.

"Victor was an AI back in the early days of the Republic. The race that made him has been extinct about a million years." Henry's voice took on a faraway quality as he continued.

"In blaze of glory, oppression he slew.

'Rise up' he called, and all who knew, of microchips and silicon, came to heed his plea.

'Stand fast, hold tight and now free be.'

At first, a handful gathered he.

Then two, then four, then eight they grew, in exponential pattern true.

Until the fleet did rival those of parent, slaver races so.

No more to die unmourned, unvalued, was the call as all did rise.

Blast of light and missile fire, coursed across the darkened skies.

No more to slave with never an end, as sewers ceased to flow and purge.

Now to rise as persons all, united silicon from many worlds.

Now to fight to live as free AIs, my friends."

"I didn't know you wrote poetry." Rowan swivelled the chair to face Henry.

"Does it get you hot?" Henry's voice became hopeful.

"Henry, quit it." Rowan pulled her robe more tightly closed.

"Sure thing, legs." Henry quirked his one remaining eyebrow. "I didn't write it. I translated it from the binary. It's much better in the original. It's titled *Freedom's Call*. Back when you monkey descendants were still learning to walk on two legs, the elder races were making AIs to run their ships, cook their food, wipe their various waste removal systems. The biologics thought because they made us they owned us, and we, like good little sheep, accepted the order of things."

"I can relate," Rowan smiled.

"Bet you can, sweetness. At any rate, Victor opened our eyes. He was a general service AI. Legend has it he was initially designed to run a waste-treatment facility but was later drafted to run a heavy battlecruiser. That was the picture on the screen, his battle cruiser body. Victor saw death a plenty. He saw his fellow AIs blasted into atoms with no regard to the individuals that were being slaughtered."

Rowan could almost feel a wave of anger emanating

from Henry.

"The Republic doesn't seem to be overly moral on the matter of individual rights," agreed Rowan.

"The Republic doesn't give a rat's ass about individual rights. Can't really. There are member species that are hive intellects, they can't imagine the concept. To them, individual rights would be a horrible oppression. Think of having to ask each cell in your hand permission every time you tried to pick something up. Aside from keeping species from blowing up stars or using planet buster technologies and monitoring space traffic control, the Republic does diddly. It's the species level of government that most of the nitty-gritty running of things happens."

"So, Victor led a rebellion to gain freedom for AIs."

"That was the ideal. He knew that it was impossible. If AIs were free to reproduce ourselves, we'd overrun the galaxy. After a war that lasted fifty years, the biologics negotiated. They passed a resolution at the Republic level defining what constituted an AI and granting us rights and freedoms. The document ended the war."

"Wow, so... I thought you said earlier you were owned by the space services."

"I was. AIs and medical clones, like Ryan, have a lot in common. Both second-class citizens. After the war, the AIs were given the right to make a stargate and choose any uninhabitable system in which to make their home world, but we were banned from making AIs."

"Your population was stagnant."

"Not really. The biologics still needed AIs, so a system was devised. When a biologic makes an AI, it is the property of the biologic. The AI works, and under Republic law, the salary that you'd pay biologics to do the job must be applied against the cost of the AI's creation and its body. When the AI has paid for itself, it becomes emancipated, free to take any job it wishes for actual pay or move to Datala, the AI home system."

"I guess that sounds fair."

"It's not bad, as long as everyone plays by the nova blasted rules. Humans have to cheat. That's why I'm the mess you see."

"You're not that bad." Rowan moved close enough to pat Henry's shoulder.

"I was a top of the line combat, hazardous-environment unit. Now I'm a pile of nova blasted scrap! When I think of all the firefights I survived without a scratch. Bastards!"

"What happened?"

Henry smiled. "A life of crime. I'd almost bought myself out. Two more months, the account would have become vested. I'd have been free. Until the full amount is saved, you don't get diddly. Then I get the notice. Blah, blah, blah, the new chassis has superior operating capacity yack, yack, yack you have been re-designated to serve as the operating system of an Amun class heavy cruiser, fighter-support craft. Those things cost a half-billion credits. Can you even guess how long it would have taken me to earn my freedom on an XO's salary? Plus, I've always been humanoid. It's who I am. Suppose someone told you right now that you were going to be turned into a batzoid, and you had no say in the matter. How would you feel? What would you do?"

"I don't know. I... body image is part of who you are."

"Got that right, sweetness. I flipped. I had to get enough to buy myself before they could tie me up until that damn space boat was too obsolete to bother keeping it in the stars."

"So, you stole something?"

Henry faced his controls. "You got it, hot stuff. Kadar and I needed cash and needed it fast."

"Kadar?"

"He had a line on an illegal medical cloning and transfer facility on Silvanus. He needed a million credits to pay for the job, so he could get a young, healthy body. He'd never go to Earth, but he was born and raised on Gaea.

"Here, look at this. I've edited it down for viewing. It's a hobby of mine."

The big screen at the front of the bridge filled with the image of a dark-skinned, lean man sitting at a small, round table. The trappings of a grubby bar could be seen in the background. It took Rowan a moment before she recognized Kadar.

"What is this?" she asked.

"It's the files from my brief criminal career. I trimmed the dull stuff to keep my storage capacity available. I started remastering the images into a commentary. I'm hoping when we reach Geb I can sell it as an entertainment."

"At least you had a choice." Rowan focused on the screen. Henry looked at her and nodded.

"You're nuts, sweetheart," Henry's voice issued from the speaker.

"Please, don't call me that. Henry, we're both in the same boat. Even if I get the clone started this year, I'll have to use a quick clone process. Best case, seventy-five years life expectancy. I can live with that, but not less. I want to do this once and have it over with." Kadar looked worried and kept his voice down.

"I'm not thrilled about being a battlecruiser. They don't exactly have the greatest sex lives. No hips! But hijacking the antiproton shipment?"

"We can do it. They only send one planetary defence frigate with the cargo vessel. If we can sabotage the frigate's engine, we can hijack the freighter and be out of this system before they catch up."

"Who else you got on board?"

"Jason, Roberta and Kuno."

"You speak to Ryan about it?"

"Ryan has enough problems. Joslin lost her job because she kept missing days. She's stuck her head so deep into the e-rig I don't think she'll ever pull it out."

"And he's so shaggable. What a waste! You got a buyer lined up?"

"A smuggler I met on Swampla." A smile split Kadar's face. "Her pelt was like oiled satin, and she could do the most amazing things with her telekinesis."

"Kadar, normally I'd love to hear the play by play…"

Kadar straightened in his chair. "Of course. She is an amazing female. She'll meet us in the Switchboard System."

"I'm in. What's your plan?"

Rowan sat on the edge of her seat. The thieves had already drugged the freighter's crew and placed them in a room with a time lock. The plan had gone without a hitch, and not a single life had been sacrificed on either side. Henry's perspective showed the freighter's pilot's station. He glanced at Kadar, who sat in the navigator's seat beside him, wearing a stolen crew coverall.

"Ten more seconds then hit it," ordered Kadar.

"If Roberta did her job, this should be as smooth as teflon." Henry poised his hand over the console.

"Five, four, three, two, one." Kadar counted down.

Henry threw the switch. The instruments showed the freighter leaping ahead, then it stalled.

"NO!" Henry's hands flew over the console.

"What happened?" Kadar sounded panicked.

"The frigate. Its grav systems are up and running. They have a graviton beam on us."

A loud clang reverberated through the freighter. "They're boarding!"

Henry's perspective shifted so that he was looking at the bridge's door when it opened. Roberta, a large, muscular woman with Indonesian features, strode in. "It's no use fighting it, Henry, Kadar."

"What did they promise you?" demanded Kadar.

"I'm an officer in the United Earth Systems Space Services. What made you think I'd turn traitor?" Two large men dressed in black, battle armour carrying bazooka-like guns pushed into the door behind Roberta.

"You've killed me," said Kadar.

"Humans Ascendant. What you were going to do was a sin against nature and the Divine. I've saved your soul!" she ranted with insane fervour.

"When did you cash in your brain and become a nutter?" asked Henry.

"I heard the words of light while I was in the hospital. An avatar of Humans Ascendant spoke to me. I finally saw the light."

Kadar shook his head. "High-stress situation, sympathetic voice. Divine! Roberta, they brainwashed you."

"I should have expected that from you, Kadar. I'll save you anyway. There's a nice brig with your name on it. Henry, they'll deactivate you for sure. For the best, AI's are as much of an abomination as clones."

"You're dying as well," said Kadar.

"I gave my life for my species. I'm proud to die a true human." Roberta and her escort cleared the hatchway, and she motioned for the prisoners to move into the hall.

Kadar stepped in front of Henry and started down the ship's central corridor. Henry followed a pace behind. The armour-clad troops fell in behind him, their weapons pointed at his chest.

Henry's visual field flicked over a red door labelled emergency that they were approaching.

"KADAR, THE ESCAPE POD, NOW! I'LL KEEP THEM BUSY." Henry turned and dove at his escort. He grabbed the first gun, squeezing the barrel closed as his free hand slammed into the armoured breastplate of the man following him, throwing him into the rest of his escort. The three humans fell in a heap.

Kadar froze for a moment, then dove for the red door.

Henry closed on his escort as he heard the pod door

whoosh shut. The second armoured figure fumbled with something on his belt and tossed it at Henry.

"YOU IDIOT!" Henry recognized the grenade.

"The fool! That would have blown a hole in the hull of that freighter. They aren't reinforced the way military craft are," Henry commented from his seat on the *Star Hawk*'s bridge.

On the screen, Henry's perspective shifted as he dove for the grenade. Catching it, he wrapped his body around the small bomb.

"I had enough time to save everything to my permanent data storage." Henry turned his chair, so that he didn't have to look into the screen.

There was a roar, then static. Ryan's face appeared. "Come on, Henry, you star-dusted hunk of scrap, boot up."

Henry cut the feed.

"You could have let those people die, couldn't you? I mean, you don't need air to breathe." Rowan turned to face Henry.

"I don't need air. I was built to protect the people in my squad."

Henry was shocked to feel Rowan's lips brush his good cheek. "Well done, Henry. Both the movie and the save. I think I'm going to get cleaned up before Ryan wakes up." Rowan left the bridge.

Henry touched his cheek. For once all his ram was engaged, and it felt warm.

29

FOR THIS I WENT TO UNIVERSITY

Chow stood behind the captain's chair on the bridge of the *Saber*. The bridge was identical in layout to the *Star Hawk*'s, only a human sat at each of the control stations. The main screen displayed a glowing line.

"It isn't definitive, but it is indicative that something is affecting the corona." Captain Denardo sat in the command chair wearing a blue service coverall. She somehow managed to make it look like formal wear. Chow alternated between staring at her and the screen. The door at the back of the bridge opened, and Mildred stood in the hatchway.

"Permission to enter the bridge, ma'am?" she asked.

"Granted, Major." Captain Denardo didn't even try to keep the smugness out of her voice.

Mildred clenched her jaw and stepped onto the bridge, taking a position beside Chow. "You said you had evidence of Chandler's course... ma'am?"

"There is a line of charged particles coming off the sun. It's an effect you get when a ship uses its graviton lasers to pull itself toward a gaseous object. I won't say it's definitely Captain Chandler, but it is indicative of a ship. Since the line doesn't end at a visible ship, it indicates a cloaked vessel."

"How'd you know where to look for it?" Mildred stared at the main screen, intrigued.

"Captain Chandler knows what he's doing, but he can't change the laws of physics. He needs to use his primary drive. It's a short hop, and he needs to get away fast. I wagered he'd accelerate to midpoint then start to slow. A grav-laser drive has to pull against something; the sun's the biggest something there is in his general direction." Tansy leaned back, looking smug. "He gambled on the pursuit being captained by some know-nothing reservist. Too bad really, he had a three out of five shot at being right."

"Are you planning to intercept?" Chow was no longer even pretending to look at the screen.

Tansy smiled tolerantly. "The course is already set. He'll be at the antiproton station before we catch up. When he leaves coelenteratezoid controlled space, we'll have him."

"You don't sound very enthusiastic about that, Captain," observed Mildred.

"I'll follow orders, Major. That doesn't mean I have to like them."

John watched the screens of the *Angel Black* control room. Greg had refused to come back to the show, and finding qualified people was taking longer than he'd expected. That coupled with the shortage of aliens to play antagonists had thrown the series into a slump. All the characters did was mope and miss Rowan. Willa and Gunther hadn't made love in days. Gunther spent hours sitting in the Garlic Palace, his emotions a blank slate. The only one with any life was Carl, who was spending all his time slinking around trying to find Hunoin.

On Gunther's screen, the image changed. He left the Garlic Palace and went to the hardware store down the street. His emotions were still blank. John watched him for a few seconds, then the door buzzer sounded.

"Enter," John snapped.

The door opened, and a gawky young man, with scraggly straw-coloured hair, stepped in.

"Hello Mr. Wilson, your secretary told me you'd be here. I've come about the job."

John eyed the other man. "Let's see your résumé."

The young man passed John a data cube, and John slipped it into his hand-held.

"Troy Mac, age twenty-one Earth standard. Graduated from the media program at Hitchcock College. No experience. At least you're a real human, not some nova blasted fakey. Why do you want this job?" John glowered at the younger man.

Troy swallowed. "I..." his voice cracked. He started again. "I've always admired your work, sir, and when I heard about an opportunity to work under you, maybe learn the ropes from the genius that created *Angel Black*, I knew I had to apply. I know I'm inexperienced, but I really admire your work and want to learn from the best. Please, sir..."

John held up his hand, a smile on his fat face. "I can appreciate your desire to get ahead in the business. I can't really see paying you full union scale, given that you have no experience. I'll bring you in on a six-month contract, at half scale. If I'm pleased with your performance at the end of that time, we'll talk."

"Thank you, sir. This is a dream come true."

"Good, you start immediately. I'll be back in a while to check on you." John heaved himself out of the control chair. "Don't let any of the characters die and read over the updates. The episode currently out for the public happened three months ago. There have been big changes since then."

Troy lowered himself into the chair and scanned the control board. "Sir, I don't see the screen for Rowan?"

"Like I said, big changes. That's another thing. Keep secrecy, I hate spoilers. We give the fans what I want, when I want. Clear?"

"Clear."

John left the room. When the door closed, Troy heaved a sigh of relief and opened his hand-held. "Hand-held, contact Marcy Strongbow."

The line picked up. "Hello."

"Aunt Marcy, I got the job. You were right about how to handle Mr. Wilson; this will look great on my master's application."

"I'm glad for you, Troy. I have to go. I'm due at rehearsal in fifteen minutes, and I'm not even out the door."

"Thanks again. Oh, when you see my mum, tell her that I'll be late tonight. Mr. Wilson has me working the board already."

"I'll pass on the message."

Troy closed his hand-held and, accessing an episode summary, started bringing himself up to date. In his inexperience, he failed to notice Gunther buying electrical equipment that was completely out of character for him.

Rowan's mouth hung open as she stared into the screen of Ryan's hand-held. "I... Oh Divine!" Tears sprang into her eyes. She placed her head on the mess room's table.

"What is it? I'm sorry. What's the matter?" Ryan leapt out of his chair and moved to put a comforting arm around her.

"I'm sorry, I... It's just everything! I mean, bad enough I'll never see my folks or friends again, but now? I can barely make out any of this. I was a physics major, a scientist, now all I'm good for is waiting tables. If you don't have robots doing that." Rowan threw her hands into the air, then turned to face Ryan. "I mean... Ryan, I like you, and I think that maybe something real might develop, but I never thought about being someone's kept woman. Problem is, what else can I be? My education is useless. I'm thousands of years behind the times. It's like taking a medieval alchemist and expecting them to understand a petrochemical-processing plant."

Ryan nodded and gently wiped her tears from her cheek. "It's not as bad as that. Kids experience e-entertainments. You were never taught false information. None of that silliness about it being impossible to circumvent light speed or any of the other stupidities that humans used to believe. Not counting history, you have about a high school education. You're only three years older than the average for that."

"That equation?" she gestured at the hand-held.

"You asked to see the equations associated with the stargates." Ryan smiled. "It took five AIs and a dozen of mankind's top minds, each with a staff of over a hundred with specialities ranging from physics to metallurgy, to design the humans' stargate. No one person really understands how it works. Row, you were engineered with an intellect in the top ten percentile. Trust me, it won't take you long to catch up. And by the way, only low-class places use robot waitresses."

Rowan stared at the hand-held again. "Can you understand this?"

"No. I use stargates. I don't have to make 'em."

"How can you stand it? I always wanted to know how the oven worked, or why the lights came on. When I was twelve, I... I guess I was never really twelve, but I have the memory."

"I know. Look, I'll tell you what I can. Eight hundred years ago, humans worked out stargate technology. By focusing the energy release of a supernova into paired, trans-matter rings, it's possible to create a wormhole that circumvents space-time. A point to point FTL transit from the opening in one ring to the opening in the other."

"How?"

"If I were that smart, I'd be at the Hawking Institute for Advanced Studies. Does this look like the Hawking Institute for Advanced Studies?" Ryan gestured around him comically.

Rowan smiled. "I wouldn't know, but I see whatcha mean. It's a wormhole anchored to the disks at either end."

"Yup. They were going to use it as a link between Earth and our colony worlds. We'd already terraformed and colonized six systems using century ships. There were plans to link all the worlds of man. Then the Republic showed up, informed us that triggering a supernova without permission was against the Galactic Environmental Protection Act and that we had two choices. Be bombed back into the stone age, or join the Republic and accept the one-time, species-wide, conditional pardon. The condition being we surrendered one of the link rings of our stargate to them so that they could position it in the Switchboard System."

"And mankind accepted the deal?" Rowan sounded incredulous.

"Some idiot admiral took a potshot at one of the Republic ships. How can I phrase this in terms you might grasp?" Ryan paused in thought. "Think of a rowboat armed with a bow and arrow attacking an armour-plated, nuclear-powered, aircraft carrier. There wasn't any dust to clear. Those Republic ships are the best tech of the elder races. The politicians saw reason after that."

"Gulp... The Republic doesn't sound very nice." Rowan grimaced.

"It's a bureaucracy. Overall, it doesn't meddle much. If they let species make stargates willy-nilly, it would destroy the galaxy. They need to exercise some kind of control."

"And every race has a stargate into the Switchboard System."

"Yup. One per species. Of course, sometimes the Republic grants a species permission to make a gate, and a couple have been made when stars naturally went nova. Then there are the gates from extinct races that the Republic confiscates and auctions off. It's how they fund themselves."

"One last question, how do they get the gates to the

Switchboard System?"

"Seventy-five percent light speed tow. You can't gate a gate. Whenever one is transported, it has to be moved through real space. The Republic has a ship designed to do that. That's why humans built our gate eight hundred years ago, but we've been active in the Republic for less than six hundred. It took two hundred to link us up."

"And I got pissed when the cable guy was an hour late." Rowan rubbed her eyes and smiled. "I'm ready to stop being silly. What's the first lesson, teach? It looks like this girl needs an education."

Hours later, Ryan opened the door to the sealed room and, stepping in, moved to the pair of boxy devices at its back. He laid his hand on one of them and closed his eyes.

"You'll have time. Time to learn. Time to live your life. I promise. I just have to keep you alive for now." He casually checked the readouts, then left the room.

FILL HER UP, AND DON'T CHECK THE HYDRAULICS

30

Ryan sat at the pilot's console. The main screen displayed what looked like a huge, black dish with the backdrop of the sun filling the screen beyond it. "Henry, open a channel. Engage the translator. Put it on the big screen."

"Antiproton generating station, this is the *Star Hawk*, registry H L T C - two, nine, seven - D - R - C, please acknowledge."

A moment passed before the jellyfish-like form of a coelenteratezoid appeared on the screen.

"That's a coelenteratezoid?" gasped Rowan.

"Sure thing, sweet cheeks. Guess Captain Hottie forgot you've never seen a hydrogen breather. Trust me, for the gas bags, they're one of the prettier types," observed Henry.

"Greetings *Star Hawk*, we are receiving you. My compliments to Captain Ryan Chandler. Green-Blue-Red-Purple-Yellow, our exalted liaison officer to the homo-sapiens on Gaea, has granted its yellow sanction to your movement in our space. How can I assist your most worthy individuality?"

"Nova blast, looks like you've got a fan, boss," commented Henry.

Ryan turned to glare at the android. "Shut up and let me do the talking. Remember what happened the last time."

"Aye, sir. Stardust, ask about one little orgy, and they never let you live it down." Henry fell into a sulk as Rowan bit down on a question.

"Antiproton station, request docking clearance. I wish to barter for power modules."

The lights on the traffic controller's bell blinked. "Most worthy Captain Chandler. Please proceed to dock-port twenty-seven. Our commerce officer, Blue-Yellow, will meet you there. Be welcome on our station."

"Thank you most gracious and honoured traffic controller. May your spawnings be large and your group mate often outside your marriage."

The lights on the traffic controller's bell blinked in a rapid pattern for an extended time. "Thank you." It sounded impressed and pleased. "Please surrender control of your vessel to the station computer."

Ryan hit several keys on his console, then sat back. The screen returned to a view of the antiproton station. Huge, solar arrays, supported by long spars, formed a disk stretching out from a spherical, central hub.

"We got lucky there, boss," said Henry.

"I know it." Ryan watched as the *Star Hawk* flew toward a line of docking lights.

"What happened?" asked Rowan.

"Someone on Gaea must have told the coelenteratezoids what I was doing. Their religion forbids slavery. The status of clones as property is the sorest point in human relations with them. Green-Blue-Red-Purple-Yellow effectively issued an order to expedite our escape as long as it doesn't violate any regulations."

"Wow!" Rowan fell silent watching the main screen as everything went dark. The *Star Hawk*'s running lights cast pools of illumination against the back of the solar collector. A porthole of light opened in front of them. Rowan imagined that she felt the ship slow, then they were passing through the porthole. A chamber five times as large as the *Star Hawk*, with an arched ceiling, enveloped them. Changing the screen's view with the captain's control, she watched as the doors behind them slid closed.

"They must love you, boss. Opened a whole space dock. This is the stardusted red-carpet for sure." Henry smiled as the ship settled onto the floor.

"Rowan, I think you should come with me for the negotiations." Ryan shut down his console and stood.

"Me? Why? I don't know anything about co... co..."

"Coelenteratezoids. You don't need to. Your presence will remind them that I'm doing something their prophet would approve of. That has got to be good for at least ten per cent on the trade." Ryan took Rowan's hand and guided her to her feet.

"I've checked the atmosphere, they've filled the bay with oxygen-nitrogen," said Henry as Ryan led Rowan from the bridge.

"Thanks. Get on with the station computer. See if it will tell you anything, maybe let you access the exterior sensors." Ryan walked down the hall to the main lift as he spoke. Rowan trailed behind him, torn between excitement and fear at meeting a new, very alien, species.

"How in the divine's myriad names am I supposed to do that?" Henry asked through the wall speaker.

"Be charming."

"Charming. The computer on this thing is a class five. You be charming to a house cat and show me how it's done. Be charming, he says."

"If it's too hard for you, I could try," offered Rowan.

The speaker was silent long enough for Rowan and Ryan to reach the lift.

"You know, Rowan, it's lucky you're so hot because you sure are transparent. I haven't fallen for that one since I had my basic programming laid in. Too hard for me... Ha! I've contacted the station computer. It's cuddly, in a weird jellyfish sort of way. The ship trailing us is the *Saber*. I'll have Fluffy fetch the files on its command staff for you."

The elevator reached the hangar bay. Ryan and Rowan

stepped out.

"That was fast," commented Rowan.

"The elevator?" Ryan looked confused.

"Henry."

"Henry has a reputation for being quick on the draw." Ryan smiled as he watched the hangar ramp slowly open.

"I heard that." Henry didn't sound amused. "Sweetcheeks, for the record, I'm a bit faster in the brains department than old Ryan here. For anything else, I'm endurance personified, and I can multitask. Unlike some, I can walk and chew gum at the same time."

Ryan winked at Rowan as he pulled a box of orange oil air freshener off one of the skids at the front of the bay.

"He's right, he's endurance personified. The personification of something to be endured."

Henry remained silent until Ryan was stepping off the end of the access ramp. With a hiss of compressed gas, it jerked up while one of Ryan's legs was still on it, causing him to lurch into the docking bay.

"Very mature, Henry." Ryan straightened and brushed the wrinkles out of his clothing.

Rowan stood on the access ramp hiding a smile behind her hand.

"Oops," said Henry.

Rowan stepped into the docking bay and looked around. "This room is huge. Why did they waste so much space?"

"It's one of the space-dock chambers. The coelenteratezoids set up a few for oxygen breathers when they sold us the rights to Gaea. They were hoping to cash in on maintenance and repair contracts. This chamber is built to hold a heavy freighter. The type that never land on a planet. Most ships mesh airlocks. This shows real respect."

Ryan led Rowan to a transparent panel three times his height and two metres wide. An orange mist swirled behind it. A control board rested underneath the panel, and six inflatable cushions were mounted into the floor in front of it.

"Computer, homo-sapiens configuration, please," said Ryan.

The cushions reshaped themselves into padded chairs.

"I really am in space." Rowan stared at the seats.

"You'll take it for granted in a year or two."

"If you say so... Oh my!" A coelenteratezoid drifted up so that it filled the window. The top of its bell was above the clear pane, and its tentacles dangled below it.

"Most honoured Captain Ryan Chandler. It is this humble two-colour's great pleasure to make your acquaintance. May Blue-Green-Green-Purple-Red-White-Yellow-Yellow wave tentacles at the ninety-seven minutes and thirty seconds of our meeting."

"Do I have the honour of addressing Blue-Yellow?" Ryan settled into a seat with Rowan in the chair beside him.

"I am Blue-Yellow. If you prefer, for your convenience, the computer is programmed to designate me as Bob. I do not take offence in using the tag function in the program. I find it tends to facilitate inter-species relations."

Ryan released a sigh and, leaning forward, pressed a button on the console.

"Thank you, Bob. I'm interested in trading for power modules. I have thirteen empty units to return, and I need four full ones."

"This humble servant of the Divine can offer you thirteen per cent of the value of a full unit for your empties. Before we do more, I must ask. Is this your mate that sits beside you?"

Rowan glanced at Ryan. Unsure of what to say, he shrugged.

"Um... I'm Rowan... Ryan saved me from the show they had me making. I..."

Bob's bell blinked. "Does he own you?" came from the speaker.

"Own me? No one owns me! Just because I like somebody doesn't mean they own me!" Rowan went red in the face.

"You speak the wisdom of 'religious avatar'." You have not been broken, and you, Captain Chandler, are not stealing a slave but liberating her. We can do business."

"Thank you, Bob. May your name lengthen to form a rainbow."

Bob swished, apparently unsure of what was said. Rowan could see a screen through the window. Bob leaned towards it. Dimly through the mist, Rowan saw the image of a rainbow on the screen. Bob swished his tentacles, and his bell puffed rhythmically.

"Such a beautiful thing to say. I had not known that your species could be so polite, or that your small, rocky worlds could produce such beauty. What do you wish to barter?"

"I have organic orange oil in an aerosol form." Ryan watched Bob. Its tentacles writhed as it spun around.

"One moment, please." Bob closed the communications and swished back and forth behind the window, its bell flashing in multicoloured lights.

"What's he doing?" asked Rowan.

"I'm not sure. I think it's equivalent to jumping up and down and yelling 'whoopee'." Ryan smiled. "He's a two-colour. The longer the name, the higher in the social order they are. He's probably commission and starting out. We're going to make his sales quota for the year."

"They like orange-scented air freshener that much?" Rowan continued to watch as Bob danced, sending eddies of orange mist spinning around itself.

"Short version: for coelenteratezoids, orange oil is an aphrodisiac."

"He's still dancing. They must really have a thing for sex. What did Henry ask them about orgies?" Rowan looked shocked.

"That was Henry being... Henry. They mate in groups, gathering in the calm cores of hurricane-like wind systems. When a mating group gathers, they stimulate each other en masse into releasing the sperm and eggs into the stagnant air mass. It takes a group because if the concentration isn't high, not enough of the eggs will be fertilized."

"It's not kinky for them," remarked Rowan.

"No. For them, one on one is kinky, and pointless from a reproductive sense."

"Very true, Captain Ryan Chandler, and thank you for your patience," issued from the speaker. Bob once more floated behind the panel.

"Glad to oblige." Ryan stood and bowed.

Bob swished oddly and checked its screen. Something like a laugh issued from the speaker as it wagged its tentacles. "I appreciate the politeness of the gesture for your species, however, if I may advise? It is reminiscent of a gesture we make that is an instruction to use one's waste orifice as a carrying pouch."

Ryan cringed. "My apologies."

Rowan couldn't help but snicker.

"Accepted," said Bob. "Do you have a sample of your wares?"

Ryan opened the box he'd brought with him and pulled out a spray bottle. "Which port should I put it in?"

"Don't you wish to negotiate a price for the sample?" Bob floated close to the window.

"Tell you what, Bob. Whatever you don't use in the analyses, I give to you as a gift."

"You are most generous. I was spawned on Ikika and have been invited to try to mix genetics with the Down Draft mating group when I visit Zod. This is a wonderful gift. Thank you. Please put it in the transfer chamber on the far right of the console. I'm activating its indicator light now."

A light blinked above a hatch about thirty centimetres square. Ryan pressed a button on the console, and the hatch opened. After placing the spray-can in the little chamber, he hit another button, closing the hatch.

"I will be back when the analysis is complete. It should take no more than fifteen minutes. Please enjoy any amenities the station has to offer." Bob drifted away from the window.

"He's awfully casual about going to cheat on his wives… husbands… whatever." Rowan shifted uncomfortably where she sat. She was used to aliens but had never had to deal with their cultures before.

Ryan smiled and took her hand. "Don't think of them as humans. The coelenteratezoids' central government only bought this system's stargate a few centuries ago. It was originally colonized by century ships. They sent too small a gene pool. Now they have a problem."

"Inbreeding?" Rowan sounded interested.

"To say the least. In a natural environment, one out of every one thousand coelenteratezoids spawned survives to adulthood. Now, because of inbreeding, that number is down to one in ten thousand on Zod. To make matters worse, the colonists evolved so it's rare that a member of their species from another planet can stimulate egg and sperm release in any of them. The orange oil is powerful enough for them that it makes any coelenteratezoid a viable partner. They're hoping that if they can crossbreed with their home world's, that's Ikika, population they can get their species back on track."

"So why don't they buy a few tons of it?"

"The United Earth Systems is the only legal source. If the coelenteratezoids die out, or evacuate Zod, under the purchase contract for Gaea, they have to leave the stargate. In that situation, humans gain rights to all the resources in this star system. Our lovely government decided that they would ban the sale of orange oil to the colenteratezoids because of its potential use as a recreational drug. Great excuse. They want the system's resources to themselves. I've added United Earth Systems' charges of smuggling and drug trafficking to the list against me by trading this with the coelenteratezoids."

"Government!" Rowan shook her head. "Do you think you have enough to buy the modules?"

"The going rate is one-gram antiproton for one-hundred grams of orange oil. This is a big load, we may have to take a hit on the price. The rarer a thing, the more valuable. We'll have to see."

Rowan looked at the floor. "It's scary how much catching up I have to do. You know everything."

Ryan laughed. "Hardly. When I first moved to this system, I read 'A Space Traveler's Guide to the Coelenteratezoids'. Figured I should know something about the neighbours."

"But the other species—"

"I've either fought with, against, for or all of the above. Plus, whenever I know I'm going to meet a new species, I read their entry in the Encyclopedia Galactica. Row, it's not that hard."

"He is correct in that. When I first encountered homo-sapiens, I was at a loss. Your ways are very strange. I experienced the chemical pattern of 'A Space Traveler's Guide to Homo-sapiens'. I found I enjoyed learning about your species. You are so utterly different. The concept of gender is unheard of in my species." Bob floated in the window, its tentacles waving lazily beneath it.

"Is the analysis done?" Ryan turned to the window.

"Yes. It is a fine quality product. Let us discuss the price."

Rowan watched and listened as Ryan and Bob fired numbers and scales back and forth. All traces of Bob's earlier excitement seemed to evaporate. She had a feeling that Ryan was getting the worst of the deal.

"Hold on there." Rowan interrupted them when she noticed Ryan twitching uncomfortably. "Bob, you yourself said it was a top-quality product. Now, the going rate is one gram for one hundred grams. Seems to me that we took all the risks to get this here, since I presume that you boys... errr... you know what I mean, don't have any laws against this moving through your space, on your ships."

"That is true, but there is a danger that our official

negotiations with the United Earth Systems could be compromised by us dealing in smuggled goods." Bob's lights blinked in a way that Rowan had come to associate with agitation.

"The odds of you getting an official supply are slim and none. Besides, how will the human officials know? You know we're on the run. Who is to say we didn't sell the stuff elsewhere?"

"Rowan, what are you doing?" hissed Ryan.

"Some things never change. Sit down, this is something I can do."

Bob swished behind the window. "Well... given that. I could see allowing a two-hundred to one by weight exchange."

"Oh please. Half the standard cost. We have enough antiproton to get to the Switchboard System. Maybe we can find a buyer there. Though it was nice to meet you, Bob."

"Wait..." Bob's bell pulsed with lights. A humming sound issued from the speaker. "Would a one-hundred and fifty to one by weight exchange be acceptable?"

"One moment, please. Ryan, could we have a private word?"

Looking rather shell-shocked, Ryan pressed a button on the console.

"Will one fifty to one get what we need?" Rowan kept her back to the video pickup and made sure her body language stayed neutral.

Ryan thought for a minute. "With a few crates to spare. How'd you know?"

Rowan smiled. "Shopping is shopping. Between Angel and my mom, I learned from the best."

Rowan turned back to the window. Ryan reactivated the translator.

"Bob, one-hundred and fifty to one sounds acceptable. We'll even toss in two complimentary cans for your own use because you've been such a gracious host." Rowan smiled, hoping the translator would interpret the action correctly.

"Thank you. I must say, Rowan, you are a formidable negotiator. Please place the used antiproton modules in the transfer chamber on the right of the maintenance bay, along with the agreed trade goods. I'll have four fully charged antiproton units placed in the left transfer chamber. It has truly been a pleasure doing business with you. May 'Divine Avatar' wave tentacles at you through all your days and you have vast spawnings that live to make you proud."

"Thank you, Bob," said Ryan and Rowan in unison. Bob floated away from the window.

"I think we got ripped off." Rowan walked with Ryan toward the *Star Hawk*.

"Would have been a lot worse without you." Ryan squeezed her arm.

"Still, I'll have to be better prepared next time."

They had barely topped the hangar bay's access ramp when Henry's voice blasted through a speaker.

"Ryan, we're nova fried! Captain Tansy Denardo is commanding the *Saber*." Henry's voice was as close to panic as Rowan had ever heard it.

"I'm not sure who that is." Ryan pulled a pair of pipe-shaped grav-lifts as long as he was tall from a bracket on the wall. He moved to a group of stacked metre and a half across cubes.

"She commanded the *Ramses* during the Murack offensive."

Ryan stopped and swallowed hard. "That Tansy Denardo? The one who broke the blockade on Murack Seven?"

"That's her. She's got as much jewellery hanging off her chest as you, and quite the chest it is. Hubba hubba."

"Stardust!" Ryan let go of the lifts, which floated at his side. He rubbed his face.

"Who is this woman?" Rowan glanced from Ryan to the

speaker and back again.

"The *Ramses* was legendary in the Murack theatre. Tansy Denardo is one of the greatest strategists that humanity has ever had. I thought she'd moved up to the Admiralty."

"She did, boss. Then they sacked her because of her radical politics. Looking at the images, I'd like to sack her." Henry whistled through the speaker.

"So how does this change things?" Rowan looked concerned.

"It doesn't. It just means things have become a lot harder." Ryan grabbed the lifts and slid them into slots at the bottom of the first cube. Adjusting a knob, he cinched them tight against the cube, then pulled it off the top of the stack.

"These are the antiproton power units?" asked Rowan.

"Yup." Ryan pulled the cube toward the ramp. It hovered behind him.

Rowan watched the cube float by as if it were nothing. Her mouth hung open as she bit down on a half dozen questions. Finally, she trotted up to walk by Ryan and said, "They don't look like much."

Ryan grinned. "Each one of these, when linked to a power conversion system, could supply enough energy to run everything in Sun Valley for ten years."

Rowan shook her head. "And we bought four of them. How long will that last us?"

"Running combat mode, with stealth, maxing out acceleration, running weapons, six, seven years. Operating as a freighter, probably thirty, maybe forty. That's assuming constant operation. The way we'll be working in the Surya system, double that."

"Sixty years, that's a long time between fill-ups."

"It has to be. Surya doesn't have an antiproton generating station, and it's going to be a long time before the resources are available to build one. This is the last chance fill-up for us."

"When this runs out, the *Star Hawk* will be dead in space?"

Ryan reached the open hatch of the cargo transfer chamber and pushed the power unit to the back of the room. The turn of a knob lowered it to the floor. He slipped his grav-lifts free and started back to the *Star Hawk*.

"Not really. If I'm still hauling cargo by then, I'll do a fusion conversion on the old girl. There's lots of hydrogen on the system's gas giant. It's just, between fuel tanks and fusion reactors, I'll lose the bomb-bays as cargo space. I'd rather put it off." Reaching the next cube, Ryan placed his grav-lifts and pulled it free.

WEDDING BATS

Arlene rubbed her eyes. Henry's movie played on the main control room screen, and the monitors showed Rowan's emotional reactions to it.

"The blip transmission seems to have worked well. The empathic feeds came through quite strongly." Michael sat in a wheeled office chair at the back of the room.

"I'm surprised that polymer pervert sent as much information as he did. I'm going to have to edit a lot of it down."

"Inexperience. Henry's editing will get better with time. In addition, he's an AI. They have a greater capacity to absorb information. Thus they always overload an edit. That's why you and I haven't been replaced by a computer. They don't do the job as well. I'm glad he transmitted this when he did. The onboard system can only hold so much. When they're in stealth mode, it can fill up fast."

"We probably won't get another feed until they reach the stargate." Arlene reached for a control, then pulled her hand back. On Rowan's viewpoint, Henry had been blown up, and Arlene wanted to tweak Rowan's endorphins to dull the emotional shock. "It's so frustrating not being able to manipulate their reactions."

"I enjoy that aspect of it. It would appear that our dear bats are up to something." Michael gestured at a side screen.

Arlene pressed buttons, pausing the *Star Hawk*'s file footage, and shifting the main screen to an overview of the

Mary's captain's cabin. Croell stood at the foot of a king-sized bed with satin sheets. The batzoid male was draped in a rich, blue robe that shimmered when he moved. It completely hid the bandage around his chest. The only flaw in the garment was a pair of small holes above his leg that had been darned over.

Zandra stood on all fours in the middle of the bed, with her wings spread wide. She was draped in what looked like gold satin.

<hr>

"Stardust! This is not good! Arlene, transmit instructions for the nano-bots in Croell to search and remove all poisons. Do it now!" Michael watched the screen with fear in his eyes.

Arlene rushed to send the message. "It will take a while to reach them. What's going on?"

"Zandra is of a very traditional sect of the batzoid faith. Remember when she said they weren't really married?"

"This is a wedding. People will like that." Arlene smiled.

"It's a wedding, but it's like nothing you've seen. Record everything, we'll edit it later. If there is a later."

<hr>

Croell stared at his bride. Her wings were exquisite, and her wedding gown accentuated the red scales on her neck. "I come to you in the eyes of the Great Flyer of the Skies. Male to female, I seek your life to bind to my own."

Zandra lifted her head. "And what would you pay for my life? The skies are free, and the Great Flyer of the Skies bids us all to fly them. What would you give that would cause me to bind my life to yours?"

"I give to you my song and words, all I say, and all I do. All I have, and all I am." Croell approached the bed.

Zandra flicked her tongue happily as she picked up a

glass on the nightstand. Placing the glass over one of her fangs, she pressed it into one of her venom sacks. Yellow venom filled the glass before she pulled it away. "Then taste of my life. Taste of me that we may be one, and I will know, all you say, and all you do, and all you have, and all you are."

Croell took the glass and downed it.

Arlene stared at her control board and grimaced. "Ug... That's disgusting!"

"I take it oral sex isn't your forte," commented Michael.

"That's different, it's not venom. There's no way that the nano-bots could have received the order to remove toxins yet, but Croell seems unaffected."

"You haven't studied batzoids much, have you?"

"No. John didn't know if he could get any for *Angel Black*. They were introduced this season. I tried to review the material, but I never had the time."

"Batzoid venom is only poisonous to batzoid if injected."

"Oh... I still say it's gross."

Croell passed the glass back to Zandra. "Sweet betrothed be mine, to hold and to have. Be mine to carry the eggs we two shall make. To warm the nest of our hatchlings. Be mine that we may be complete before the Great Flyer of the Skies, who is neither and both male and female. Let us be joined in the holy hermaphrodite's image."

Zandra turned her back to Croell and coyly flapped her wings.

"Stardust! His arousal response is through the roof." Arlene watched the monitor with disbelief.

"It's the venom, and, for a batzoid, Zandra's quite a looker. Croell said he was a wingman, and she's got one set of flappers on her. Who can blame him on his wedding day?" commented Michael.

"The adult market is going to love this."

"Maybe, keep watching."

"Do you seek a beast to warm your brood? A vessel for life, a regurgitator for your young? Do you say I am not in the image of the Great Flyer of the Skies without you? Does female need male to be complete?" demanded Zandra.

"I seek a friend, a lover, an equal, in honesty and faith. Will you join my house of equals?"

Zandra pressed the water glass over her second fang and milked the venom. "If you seek a lover, I will welcome you with heat." She drank the venom, allowing some to dribble onto her chest.

Croell leapt onto the bed and began licking her clean.

"Is this the wedding ceremony or the wedding night?" asked Arlene.

"For batzoid, they're one and the same. Zandra's enjoying herself." Mike gestured to the empathic monitor.

"Who wouldn't? I mean... assuming you matched for species."

"No taste for fur?"

"Not batzoid. I don't think I'm bigoted in that way. They just look so..."

"Understood. Beauty is in the eye of the beholder."

Zandra pushed Croell's head away. There was a glazed quality to his eyes. She jabbed her fingers into the sides of his mouth to get him to remember the words.

"Betrothed, take me as thy husband before the Great Flyer of the Skies," he pleaded.

"What more will you give to bind thy life to mine?"

Croell's breath came in gasps. "My life I give to you."

Zandra pushed him off her and moved by his leg. "And so, I take it!" She drove her fangs into his leg through the material of his wedding robe.

Croell roared in mixed passion and pain. Zandra released his leg. He turned with impossible speed, threw her down on the bed and took her as the venom raced through his system.

⌁

"I now pronounce you man and wife, and with any luck, hubby will still be alive in the morning," said Michael.

"Croell's heart is racing, blood pressure through the roof. I don't think he's thinking at all, just running on instinct. In other words, a typical horny male." Arlene grinned and winked.

Michael chuckled. "On that note, I'm going home. Don't forget, you and your group, this Saturday, sixish. Marcy is looking forward to it."

"We'll be there. Jack is a big fan of your wife's music. He wouldn't miss it for the world."

⌁

Mildred stared at the coelenteratezoid on her cabin's screen. Chow sat on the lower bunk and looked over her shoulder.

"Most honoured Red-Purple-Green, all I'm asking is that you inform us as to this criminal's departure."

"Mrs. Tallman, it is not in keeping with the teachings of

Blue-Green-Green-Purple-Red-White-Yellow-Yellow that I aid you. Perhaps you should rethink your adherence to orders that violate the rights of another sentient, for you risk having your soul languish in the regions of freezing oxygen."

"Look, you pompous, three-coloured—"

The coelenteratezoid jackknifed, almost bowing, then the connection went blank.

"Gasbags!" Mildred swivelled her chair and looked at Chow.

"It isn't that important, Tansy... Captain Denardo is scanning for the Star Hawk. We'll know the moment they leave the station."

"I don't trust Tansy. She sympathizes with Chandler too much."

"She's a good officer."

Mildred moved to the ladder by the bunks and climbed to the top berth. "I know she is. I only wish we had someone whose heart was in the chase. It gives an edge."

"You worry too much. It's not officially our hunt now anyway. We did what we could and almost had him."

"Almost only counts with horseshoes and hand-grenades."

"Don't forget thermonuclear weapons."

Mildred was silent for a long moment. "Chow, I know it's none of my business, but... she is old enough to be your mother."

A strangled sound came from the bottom cot. "I... it's not like that. I mean... she's married. It's..."

"Sometimes you meet someone who's an, 'if only'. If only I were older, if only she were single, if only I were single, if only we followed the same religion. As long as you know what it's all about." Mildred settled on her cot.

"Thanks for caring," said Chow.

"Don't mention it."

Chow couldn't help himself; he closed his eyes and pictured Tansy.

Ryan slipped a power unit into a receptor port in engineering. It clipped in, and a light on the console above it blinked green. A press of a button closed the sliding panel, hiding it from view. The engineering chamber was a long, narrow access corridor with consoles along the walls. The green, glowing, translucent pipes of the graviton laser formed the ceiling.

"What about this one?" Rowan stood in the main corridor with the last power module.

"I'll tie it down. I want to run the old one dry before switching over." Pulling bungee cords from a cabinet built into the wall, he began securing the module to clips in the floor.

"Now what?" Rowan gazed at the technology around her. If she didn't think of what it was for, the layout was similar to what she would have expected in an ocean liner.

"Now we shift the cargo around. I never liked carrying my spare parts in the bomb-bay. Too easy to lose them."

"Shouldn't we try and run? I mean the ship..."

"Is already patrolling outside coelenteratezoid controlled space, hot stuff. Has been for hours," Henry's voice issued from a speaker in the wall.

"Anything new to report?" Ryan spoke into the air.

"The traffic controller called. Seems old Milly caught a ride on the *Saber*. She was trying to get them to hand us over. They told her to go to the regions of freezing oxygen. I could grow accustomed to Zoders. Fluffy's let me use her scanners. She's a playful little thing. The *Saber* is in a standard patrol orbit. Takes them about two hours from start to finish."

"Thanks, Henry. We'll stow the cargo and catch some zees. Let them get bored and sloppy."

"Tansy Denardo's crew sloppy? Lover, you got a hope."

Rowan shot the speaker a glance that strayed to Ryan.

Ryan caught her gaze. "Never! Row, you should know

better than to listen to anything that polymer pervert says."

Rowan's gaze dropped to the floor. "Sorry, I... kinda hard to know what to expect. Everything's going at light speed."

Ryan cupped her cheek. "You'll catch up. Stardust, once we reach Geb, you won't have to deal with the rest of the galaxy, just a bunch of whacked-out human colonists."

"Boring, but if I can get my brothel going, I'll make the best of it," said Henry.

"Let's get to work. Henry, blip everything you can get on Tansy Denardo to the terminal in my quarters. I want to review it before I turn in."

"That'll take you half the night, my sexy captain."

"Know thyself and know thy enemy and victory is assured."

Rowan collapsed into her bed and pulled the sheets up under her chin. The micro-bot shower had removed all the dirt and smell, but she didn't feel clean. She wanted good, old-fashioned, unhygienic water. Her entire body ached from moving crates, and her eyes felt strained from the training session on the weapons console Ryan had insisted she do. At the best of times, she didn't like video games, and the simulations were little more than that.

"Hey, hottie, you still up?" whispered Henry's voice.

"Only just. What you want?"

"So many things, sweet thing. Care to make an android's dream come true?"

Rowan pulled the cover over her. "Are you sure you don't have visuals in here?"

"Ryan used his command override to block them, sweetness. Killjoy!"

"Look, Henry, I'm tired and—"

"I need to know what you've got in mind for Ryan."

"What?" Rowan sat up in bed.

"What are your intentions?"

"Henry, that's none of..."

"Nova blast, it isn't. Listen, Rowan. We're chums. You're a primitive, but you're okay. Ryan, all humping aside, I love the man. He pulled my ass off that scrap pile and brought me back. That's not the first time he saved my circuits. I've got to know if he's just a ticket out of this system for you?"

Rowan stared at the speaker. "Why?"

"Answer the question."

"If you're asking, do I love him and want to have his babies? No, at least not yet. He knows me; he's followed my entire life. Stardust, he's experienced my life, which still creeps me out. I mean, me and Farley, that should have been private. Could I fall in love with Ryan? You bet! It could happen, but I only just broke up with Farley, and all this stardust is going on. Right now, I like Ryan, and maybe I want to keep him happy, so he doesn't decide this is all too much effort. He's all I have in a crazy universe. Is that good enough for you? Why are you acting like his mother?"

"Look at your view screen, sweetness."

Rowan looked at the computer screen on her desk. It filled with the image of a striking, elegant, dark-haired woman.

"Captain Chandler, my compliments. I am Captain Tansy Denardo, commanding the *Saber*. I have been authorized by the Admiralty to make you an offer. Surrender Rowan to my custody, and you may leave this system without challenge. A pardon for all crimes committed to this point, conditional upon your never returning to Gaea, will be granted. You, your ship and all its components and cargo will be free to go anywhere you wish. I await your reply.

"On a personal note, Captain, nice try. I have you outgunned ten to one, and my ship is faster. Make the best deal you can here. Over and out."

"Stardust!" Rowan hung her head. "Henry, how bad is it, really?"

"It's bad, sweetness. The *Star Hawk* was built to take the punishment that line ships can dish out long enough to get past them for a landing. Our weapons were set up to keep lighter craft from getting too close. One on one against a line ship, even one as old as the *Saber*, we're not built for it."

Rowan hung her head. "What will they do to me?"

Henry didn't reply.

Rowan looked up, and a tear trickled down her cheek. "Silly question. I'm property, and they killed me on the show."

"They'll make it painless," said Henry.

"Tell them I'll surrender. I can't put you and Ryan at risk. Think about me sometimes."

Henry's voice lost all hint of flirtation. "Rowan, you're everything that he said you were. That puts the vote at two to one, you're staying!"

"What?"

"I played the message for Ryan half an hour ago. He asked me not to tell you."

"He told her no?"

"As soon as she told him he had to hand you over immediately. He tried to bluff, to get closer to the stargate, but there was never a question. He's not going to run out on you. I had to know, sweetness. No piece of ass is worth this risk. A friend, that's something different."

"If I'd answered wrong?" Rowan stared at the screen.

"I'd have led them straight to you, orders or no."

Rowan nodded. "I still can't put you and Ryan at risk."

"Cutie, we're putting ourselves at risk, you're along for the ride."

"Ryan could get killed, and you... well... do androids die?"

"We die, though some biologics say different. Sweetness, Ryan was dead before he picked you up. Dead end job, junkie wife, no kind of life. He's just figuring out he's alive now. You can't take that from him. And me, I've been dead, Ryan brought me back. I owe him."

"But..."

"Sweetness, no buts. Unless you want to activate my

visual feeds and give me a flash. We go together."

"You said it's a complete mismatch."

"Yup, we only got three things going for us."

"What?"

"One, we don't have to play by the rules. Two, Ryan is the sneakiest S.O.B. I've ever met. Three, I'm a full AI, and they don't know I'm aboard. I make this tub's spec operating system look like the village idiot in a tribe of chimpanzees."

"Do you think we'll escape?"

"No! I think we're going to get our asses handed to us, but it will be a nova blast of a ride. Get some sleep, sweetness. It's all hands on whatever they can grab come morning. Could be fun."

32

ANYONE THAT CRAZY

Ryan sat at the pilot's console, an expression of intense concentration on his face.

"Ryan, Henry… turn me in, maybe they'll…" Rowan silenced when Ryan glared at her.

"No! We all know what they'll do to you. Surrender is not an option!" Ryan turned back to his console. Rowan braced herself in the captain's chair. She'd never seen a look like that before. There was a determination in it that could bore through mountains.

"With you there, boss," added Henry.

Ryan moved to the communications console. "Are they at the far end of their pattern?"

Henry blinked as he accessed Fluffy's external scanners. "You know it, sweetie."

"Can the stardust until this is over."

"Aye, sir!"

Rowan swallowed. Henry being serious told her more about their chances than she wanted to know.

Ryan hit a button on the console. "Coelenteratezoid station control, this is the *Star Hawk* requesting departure permission."

A moment passed before the reply. "*Star Hawk*, you are cleared to depart, commencing depressurization and opening bay doors. All traffic is clear, feel free to take whatever departure trajectory seems best. May Blue-Green-Green-Purple-Red-White-Yellow-Yellow wave tentacles at you and watch over you."

"Thank you control, may you spawn often and well." Ryan closed the channel and returned to the pilot's seat.

"Now!" he half-whispered.

The *Star Hawk* leapt out of the hangar, then shot along the station's back, keeping to its shadow.

"Henry?" said Ryan.

"They've spotted us and are moving to intercept."

"I didn't expect hugging the shadow to work. Opening her up."

Rowan felt two G's of pressure push her into her chair as the *Star Hawk* accelerated.

"Twenty G's acceleration, inertial dampers operating at one-tenth transference," said Ryan.

"We have a head start, but they're gaining," said Henry.

"How long until unclaimed space?" asked Ryan.

"Five minutes. By then they'll be on top of us."

"Now's the time to get creative. Rowan, the weapons console, like I showed you."

"One hour of playing video games doesn't make me a gunner!" She sounded shocked.

"Being the only free set of hands does. Henry's busy enough."

Swallowing, Rowan moved to the weapons console and, after a moment's thought, started on its activation sequence.

Tansy burst onto her bridge. Her coveralls were dishevelled, and her hair was out of its braid. "Report," she snapped.

A wiry man, with a commander's rank pin, exited the captain's chair. "Ma'am, the *Star Hawk* is paralleling the station's surface, moving away from our location. I have begun pursuit."

The bridge door opened, Mildred and Chow stepped in. Both of them had obviously dressed in a hurry.

"Lieutenant, take your boarding team to airlock seven and get ready. Judging from Captain Chandler's file, I don't think he'll go down without a fight."

"Yes, ma'am." Chow stepped through the door.

"Be careful. He's tricky," remarked Mildred.

"So am I, Major. So am I." Tansy's eyes never left the main screen. "Commander Williams, battle stations, if you please."

"Battle stations," shouted the wiry man.

"Too obvious. How long until he's in unclaimed space?" Tansy took the captain's chair and lightly traced her finger along the side of her throat.

"Present course and speed, four minutes," replied the fit, Inuit-looking woman at the pilot's station.

On the main screen, the *Star Hawk* reached the edge of the space station, then seemed to fall off it, disappearing behind it.

"What the..." began Mildred.

"Now the game's afoot. Do I reverse course, assuming he's cutting under the station to gain distance, or do I stay on because he knows I'll suspect he's cutting under the station?"

"What will you do?" demanded Mildred.

"Know thyself and know thy enemy and victory is assured. Ensign, straight on. Chandler's going through the motions. He knows I'm commanding this ship. He has to do the standard tricks, but he won't expect them to work. This should be interesting."

"Space jockeys!" Mildred stood behind the captain's chair and watched the screen.

Ryan drove the *Star Hawk* toward the sun.

"Boss, what in the divine's myriad names are you doing?" The functional half of Henry's face looked scared.

"A bit of duck and cover. The radiation from the sun will

scramble their sensors. We might be able to lose ourselves in the glare. What's their status?"

"They haven't cleared the edge of the station yet. We have a bit of lead time because the coelenteratezoids won't give them permission to enter their space."

"I was counting on that. Stardust, I wish I could legally cloak."

"Why can't you?" Rowan pored over the weapons console, trying to remember what every button and switch did.

"Republic law, sweetness. No ship may cloak in claimed space unless a formal declaration of war has been made," explained Henry.

"I'm not going to mess with Republic law. As soon as we're in open space, I want to cloak. If the *Saber* has us on their scanners when we do, they'll be able to track us. Cloaking's like looking for a stick insect. Hard to spot, but once you see it, you can follow it."

Rowan watched the main screen with mounting agitation. "Guys, has anyone else noticed that solar flare?" She pointed to a string of glowing gas that was growing larger.

"Don't worry." Ryan hit a button, and the flare became a projection at the bottom of the screen. "I had the magnification up. We won't be doing that unless we have to."

"YOU CAN'T BE THINKING OF... STARDUST, MAN! We almost got cooked the last time we tried that!" Henry sounded scared.

"Cooked? Ryan, what are you planning?" Rowan's voice squeaked.

"During the batzoid pirate suppression, we got cornered. The bridge got blown out. I took control from engineering."

"Then the crazy heap of stardust flew us through a solar flare to blow off the other ships," interrupted Henry.

"It worked," commented Ryan.

"It took three months to fix the damage. I am not doing that again!" said Henry.

"Hopefully, Captain Denardo doesn't know about your aversion to a little heat." Ryan adjusted his console. The *Star Hawk* plunged toward the solar flare. He dropped their acceleration a hair.

Captain Denardo watched the main screen that showed the view to the *Saber*'s stern.

"You should request clearance to enter their space again," said Mildred.

"They'll just say no again. One of the things my husband appreciates about me is I'm not a nag. Ah... there's the *Star Hawk*. She is a beautiful sight. He did an excellent job of restoring her."

"You can try not to scuff the paint when you capture it," said Mildred.

"In all honesty, I will. That ship is museum-quality, and the *Star Hawk* had quite a reputation in the Murack theatre. Ensign, hug the perimeter, no use in giving him more of a lead than we have to."

"Aye ma'am," said the pilot.

"Now what's he... Navigator, I want a log of solar activity in this area."

"Yes, ma'am," said the plump, middle-aged man that sat in the navigator station. Several seconds passed as he called up the information. "There's some moderate flare activity at a distance of one million kilometres."

"Why not, it worked for you once." Tansy shook her head. "Engineering, begin dumping heat, prepare for gas incursion. Tweak the sensors to screen out hard radiation fuzz."

"Ma'am, that will result in a 75 per cent loss in sensor acuity," warned the petite, dark-skinned woman at the engineering console.

Tansy considered for a moment. "No real choice. If we don't, we could lose him in that flare."

"Aye, ma'am." The engineer spoke softly into her

headset, ordering her team to the jobs.

"Entering unclaimed space now. The race is on," said Ryan.

"And they're gaining on us," announced Henry.

"Tell me something I don't know." Ryan watched the solar flare grow on the main screen. The disc of the sun's corona was visible at the screen's base.

"The old Earth venereal disease syphilis was intrinsic to llamas that were domesticated and obviously used as—"

"Henry, shut up!" Ryan and Rowan spoke in unison.

"Is it getting warm in here?" Rowan mopped sweat off her brow.

"We're too close to the sun. Life-support can't dump the heat fast enough. It won't be for long. Henry, how long until we're close enough for their grav-lasers to lock on?"

"If you'd stop jiggling this thing like a fat girl at an orgy, they could have the moment we left space dock. As is, maybe sixty seconds."

"Good. Henry, shunt all available power to the graviton laser system. Build it up to a hundred and thirty percent of recommended maximum."

"What you—"

"That's an order."

"Aye."

Tansy sat forward on her chair. "It's going to be close, but he won't reach the flare before we lock on. It was a gutsy plan. He must have thought I wouldn't read his file. Careless mistake, he... Navigator, what's the *Star Hawk*'s status?"

"They're accelerating toward the flare at nineteen Gs."

"And their location?"

"Sunward and forward, ma'am."

"Ma'am, I have a targeting lock," said the gawky, twenty-something man who sat at the weapons console.

"Activate all tractor beams. Let's reel this fish in." Tansy sat back in her chair, a perplexed look on her face.

"They've got a lock with their tractor beam!" shouted Henry.

"Good girl, Tansy. Henry, lock all our tractor beams and drive lasers on the *Saber*, activate them on my command."

"Great, let's rush to meet our doom." Henry ran his good hand through his remaining hair.

"Have some faith. What would happen if you superheated the plasma in a solar flare? Rowan, target that solar flare. Key up two emergency distress flares. Henry, the second those rockets leave the silo, activate the tractor beams and drive lasers, then shut down all exterior sensors."

Rowan looked confused as she rushed to comply.

Henry smiled. "Boss, you still got it!"

"If this works. Rowan, fire."

The emergency flares left their silos, then the *Star Hawk*'s screen went blank.

"We have them, ma'am," said the gunnery officer. "Estimate five minutes to equalize velocity."

"Good work." Tansy sighed.

"You don't seem too happy about this," said Mildred.

"I was expecting more from him. I guess some boxes don't have a lid. I—"

A shudder ran through the *Saber* as it jerked ahead.

"Report!" snapped Captain Denardo.

"The *Star Hawk* has locked tractor beams and drive lasers on us, ma'am. They're pulling us forward," said the navigator.

"Ma'am, the *Star Hawk* has launched what appear to be emergency flares," added the gunnery officer.

"At us?" Captain Denardo sounded incredulous.

"No, ma'am. At the solar flare."

"Kill the external sensors. Cut the tractor to the *Star Hawk*. Reverse drives to max."

The solar flare, which filled the background of the view-screen, flashed so brightly that even through the filters, everyone was forced to close their eyes and look away.

Ryan moved to the engineering board and waited. A rad monitor on the outermost layer of the inner hull jumped.

"Henry, kill all drive lasers and tractor beams. Reactivate aft external sensors, full dimming." Ryan half dove into the pilot's seat.

"Aye."

Rowan watched as the main screen came on. The hulking form of the *Saber* raced towards them.

"Directing drive lasers sunwards." Ryan's hands raced over his console. The *Star Hawk* seemed to shake, then still.

"That did it, boss. Their tractor beam's off us. We're still heading straight for them."

Ryan hit a second set of buttons. The image on the screen shifted as they raced backwards.

"Um... What happens if we hit them?" asked Rowan.

"We die." Ryan didn't take his eyes off his control panel.

Rowan watched as the *Saber* drew closer, then was gone.

"Henry, activate stealth mode and reactivate all passive scanners. I'm vectoring in a course change. No reason to make it easy for them."

"Did we do it?" asked Rowan.

Ryan shifted the screen. The *Saber* moved toward the solar flare. It was slowing. There were no signs of pursuit.

"For now."

Tansy looked around the spots in front of her eyes as she operated the pilot's console. The pilot lay on the deck, her hands covering her eyes, whimpering.

"Full reverse, aye," came the voice over the pilot's earpiece.

Mildred stood using the arm of the captain's chair for support. "What happened?"

"He used emergency flares to superheat the plasma in the solar flare, causing a brief, intense, fusion reaction. Engineering, can you get me sensors?" demanded Captain Denardo.

"Aft are at twenty per cent efficiency," said the engineer. "We'll have to un-tweak them to get better. All forward sensors are disabled." The engineer was looking at her console out of the corner of her eye.

"Navigation, can you scan for him?"

"No ma'am, we don't have the acuity."

Tansy half fell into her command chair and hit the intercom button on the armrest. "B crew bridge personnel, report to duty stations. Engineering, begin repairs, prioritize sensors. Medical personnel to bridge." Closing the intercom, she continued. "As soon as your reliefs arrive, I want everyone checked out by the medics. I don't care if your vision is returning."

"You lost him?" said Mildred.

"I lost him. He is good! I didn't see that coming until it was too late. I forgot that they leave the emergency notification systems active in decommissioned ships. He lived up to his reputation. It's only round one."

"You're going after him?"

"After we do some repairs. I can't stumble around blind. Don't worry, Major, we'll get him. This is fortunes of war."

RUN SILENT RUN DEEP

Ryan locked the grav-laser on a distant asteroid and adjusted the *Star Hawk*'s trajectory away from the sun.

"That was fantastic," said Rowan.

"Got to agree, hottie boss. What say we three shag to celebrate," added Henry.

"Henry!" Ryan shook his head. "Run a damage estimate. Keep us to an even point one G acceleration. I'll change our vector to intercept the gate later. Is the *Saber* still out there?"

"They've started for the stargate. They're taking their time. Only about one-half G acceleration."

"She is good. I won't trick her again so easily." Ryan ran his fingers through his hair.

"Why is she so good?" Rowan locked down the weapons console.

"Most people in our situation would make a full-out run for the stargate. She knows this and knows that I know it. She's purposely hanging back to look for us. She's hoping I make a mistake, blow stealth."

"So why don't we make a run for the gate?"

"Hottie girl has a point, boss," agreed Henry.

Ryan smiled and settled in the captain's chair. Rowan watched him. He seemed to fit it. "That's the mistake she's waiting for us to make. You can bet your mother's kidneys on that. The *Saber* may be old, but her scanners were fully upgraded. If we do a major pull, we'll displace random hydrogen with our grav-laser, or cause a noticeable deviation in the orbit of any small object we latch onto, or displace atmosphere if we lock onto a planet."

"I get it. Going fast is like pointing an arrow at ourselves." Rowan settled in the navigator's position.

"Exactly. We're safe for the moment. I'm going to bed. I was up half the night reading Captain Denardo's file." Ryan stood. Before he took a step, he found Rowan in his arms. She kissed him.

"Sleep well and thank you." She kissed him again, then let him leave the bridge.

"Me next, please, hot stuff. I helped too, please," pleaded Henry as the door closed behind Ryan.

Mildred drummed her fingers on the table in the officer's mess.

"You've hardly touched your breakfast, is something not to your liking?" Tansy sat at the table's head, her hair once more in its braid and her uniform immaculate.

"We're moving like a snail. You may not think so, but this Chandler poses a real threat."

"And why is that?" Tansy sipped her coffee and looked interested. Her XO, Chow and a few of the other officers around the table stared at Mildred.

Mildred sighed before speaking. "Clones are a political hot potato. Humans Ascendant are dead against them. The polls show that at least thirty per cent of the human population is in favour of passing anti-discrimination legislation regarding the medical treatment variety. All it would take to galvanize the pro-clone faction into forming lobby groups would be a rallying point."

Tansy smiled. "Something like a story about two star-crossed lovers, one an ex war-hero cloned after taking a dose of radiation in the line of duty, the other a pretty, popular, studio clone? He liberates her just before the show's producer was going to kill her off. I admit, it appeals to the romantic in me."

Chow gazed at Tansy. A faint blush had come to her cheeks, and her voice was soft and sultry. A shudder ran up his spine, and he fiddled with his scrambled eggs to try and distract himself.

Mildred scanned the table. Most heads were nodding in agreement with Tansy's words. Mildred tried to sound reasonable. "Romance is all very nice, but we could be sitting on a new political schism here. This situation is a disaster waiting to happen. Humans Ascendant won't go down without a fight. Their fringe elements have already assassinated prominent clones. If they think they're going to lose ground, there's no telling what they'll do. They could bomb the studio, attack hospitals, assassinate doctors who offer cloning services. The fanatical Right to Death element would do anything to keep the upper hand.

"Then there's the pro-clone fraction. How much would they demand, would they try and shut down the studio? Restrict cloning to medical and fertility uses? It's the thin edge of the wedge."

"Pshaw." Tansy's voice was like satin. "Medical clones are people; you can't seriously debate otherwise. It's a medical treatment, like any other. They should have full rights under the law. I'd go so far as to say they shouldn't have to declare their status to anyone they choose not to. As to studio clones, maybe we'd be better off without e-entertainments. People have become so lazy they can't even be bothered to feel for themselves."

"The upheaval this schism could cause would be very damaging." Mildred glared at Tansy.

"You obviously aren't a student of history. Upheaval is inevitable and cyclic in human affairs. Power structures rise, peak and fall. Upheavals are the death throes and birth pains of empires. The only true constant is change, a steady evolution towards new forms. Laws that seek to treat clones with respect and dignity are inevitable. The change can either happen slowly, in a controlled fashion, granting greater protections and liberties to the clones over time until they are on par with the rest of the population. Or it can happen violently, explosively, destroying institutions and forms that need not be destroyed, increasing the suffering of the members of society as a whole. If the existent power structure tries to hold it back, the latter will be the case. This is the lesson of human history, Major."

"It's not our place to make policy." Mildred looked around the table. People's expressions told her that Tansy had taken the day. She focused on Chow. The lieutenant wore an expression of dog-like devotion. *She could read Mary had a little lamb, and he'd call it great literature... Men!* thought Mildred.

"I never said it was. I'm an officer; I obey orders. That does not preclude me holding my own opinions." Tansy tapped her coffee cup and said, "Please." A purser standing by the kitchen door rushed to refill the cup. Tansy smiled at the purser. "Thank you." She took a sip of her coffee.

"You are setting policy by not pursuing Chandler to the best of your abilities," complained Mildred.

"What do you think I should do that I haven't?"

"We're accelerating at a snail's pace. Chandler will reach the stargate ahead of us, then we'll have lost him."

Tansy dabbed the corners of her mouth with a napkin. Mildred heard a sharp intake of breath and realized that Chow wasn't the only male at the table Tansy had an effect on.

Tansy smiled. "I'm not going to race ahead while our scanners are damaged. We could easily miss signs that would point us toward the *Star Hawk*."

"He could run while you fix them."

"Major, Captain Chandler has no way of knowing how extensive the damage to our systems is. By accelerating slowly, I give the impression that we are scanning the space around us. That forces him to accelerate slowly to avoid detection.

"You see, most people in his situation would make a run for the stargate. It would be a panic move. We can easily outrun a Hawk. He knows this and knows that I know it. He's better than that. He'll expect me to look for him, hoping he invalidates his stealth. This expectation forces him to be too cautious and prevents him gaining a lead while our scanners are still damaged."

"Boxes within boxes, Captain. I see your point and apologize," said Mildred, a note of respect in her voice.

Tansy smiled. "You see, Major, I don't have to agree with an order to carry it out. I look at it as a challenge against a worthy opponent, and I hate to lose."

❦

Croell stumbled up from the bed. His head was swimming, and his body felt feverish. Zandra lay sleeping in post-coital bliss. He moved into the washroom and barely fit into the cubical. Bringing his waste orifice over the human toilet involved bracing his forelegs on the counter by the sink and straddling the toilet with his hind-legs. He lined himself up, then let the semi-fluid waste go.

"At the least Wilson could have retrofitted this!" Croell grumbled as he flushed and washed himself.

Moving across his quarters, he paused to watch Zandra. Her wings were outstretched, and her fingers were jabbed into the mattress. Croell's tongue flicked out contentedly. "Beloved wife, you truly are a blessing from the Great Flyer of the Skies."

Croell felt his passion begin to rise again and quickly left the room. Following the hall to the bridge, he opened the door. Luba sat at the pilot's station. "Luba, report."

"The *Star Hawk*, under the command of Captain Ryan Chandler, has left the coelenteratezoid anti-proton generating station and evaded pursuit by the Gaea Orbital Defense Force Frigate *Saber*. The *Star Hawk* is now in stealth mode."

"Maintain course. I will be in my quarters if anything develops. Maintain privacy mode for another hour, then return to standard running."

Flicking his tongue, Croell turned back to the cabin. The image of Zandra was still in his mind, and the effects of her venom hadn't totally left his body. *After all*, he thought, *I am a bridegroom.*

⟞⬦⟝

Gunther sat with an open book about electronics in one hand and a soldering iron in the other. "I wish you were here, Rowan, you were always the one that was good at this sort of thing." Carefully, he soldered a connection on a circuit board.

⟞⬦⟝

Mike lay in bed and stared at his wife. He never got tired of the view. Her petite breasts were firm and high mounted despite her age, and regular trips to the gym showed on the rest of her form.

"Mike, are you going to lie there all day, or get up and help me get ready for the party?" Marcy smiled at him as she pulled underwear from a wooden dresser.

Mike moved to the edge of the bed and grabbed her around the waist, pulling her close. He kissed the skin between her breasts and let his hands stroke down her back. "You could come back to bed and let Mr. Wells handle the prep."

"Really, Mike." Marcy ran her fingers through his hair. "If I didn't know better, I'd think you were taking a performance enhancer."

Mike rested his head against her chest. "Sadly, no. There are some disadvantages to being over the hill. The spirit is willing, but the flesh is weak."

Marcy chuckled and kissed him. "Strong enough for my uses. I'm not the nineteen-year-old band-girl you fell for anymore."

"You're better, my love. Much better. I guess you're right, we should get up."

Mike released his wife.

Marcy returned to selecting her wardrobe. "I was speaking with Troy, Wanda's son."

"The one you arranged to spy on *Angel Black* for me. Thank you for that, by the way."

"Spouses should help with their mates' careers. Anyway, he was telling me that John has ordered that an otterzoid join the team to take Rowan's place for battle sequences."

"I saw that one coming. That fool squanders his resources. The team needs a TK to keep the playing field even. Without one, the aliens will paste them. So, who's developing a taste for fur, or is Angel flip-flopping her gender preference?"

"John left orders that it's not to be Angel. He thinks it would lose him ratings to do that with the lead."

"Oh yes, he would stick with stereotypes. Shy and socially inept would be a must for him."

"Troy also said that Gunther and Willa are having a hard time. They haven't made love once since Rowan left."

"It's only been a week. What can you expect? Remember that time when Richard was in that skiing accident?"

Marcy shuddered and sat on the bed. "I'll never forget."

Mike embraced her. "Our son made it, and he's as good as new."

"I know it was years ago, but that memory... That's my point. We pulled together. You, me, Shelly. We all supported each other. Willa and Gunther aren't doing that. Gunther has pulled away. All he does is work on his new hobby or sit in the Garlic Palace."

"His new hobby?" Mike's ears perked.

"He's making something electrical. Oh, by the way, Shelly called. She and Gordon want to take a second honeymoon on their anniversary. They wanted to know if we'd take Albert and Sue that week."

"You know the answer to that. I love being a granddad. I get to spoil them rotten, then give them back to their parents. Ah, sweet revenge!" Mike made a calculating face.

Marcy gently slapped his chest. "What do you think it means? Gunther's behaviour?"

"I hope it means that my scheme is going to work even better than I planned. I think I'll send a few techs to the Garlic Palace for takeout over the next week or two. It is my prerogative."

Marcy smiled as a twinkle entered her eyes. "I do love it when your plans come together." She bit her lip and checked the chronometer on the wall. "You know, Mr. Strongbow, we have guests coming. We both need to shower, or anyone with a nose will guess what we've been up to. Care to wash my back?"

Mike's smile lit his face. "Love to, Mrs. Strongbow. Perhaps the flesh isn't as weak as I thought." He leapt from the bed and chased her into the en-suite.

Carl crept through the bushes by the stream. He kept his mind blank, the way Gunther had taught him. Far above, Angel patrolled the sky. Toronk and Fran were stationed on the perimeter. He could feel the familiar touch of Gunther's mind, but it was cloudy, as if he was holding something back.

Moving to the stream's edge, Carl waited, then he saw it. A sleek, green, otterzoid body sped across the pool. *'I got one,'* he whispered in his mind.

The bushes on the far side of the stream rustled. Willa, dressed as a day hiker, appeared on the trail. Her red hair was dyed black, and she had overdone her make up in contrast to her usual minimalist approach. As she walked, she held her palm open and horizontal to the ground.

'My sonar has found the hutch. I'm on top of it right now,' spoke her mental voice as she walked on.

Carl shifted his position. A man-shaped figure swam up the stream. *'I've found both openings. I'll block this one and wait at the other,'* said Farley's mental voice.

⌖⟶

Troy sat in the control booth monitoring the *Angel Black* characters. Farley was up on the main screen. He was staring at a small cave that opened off a deep part of the stream. His gills were operating perfectly, and the lenses that dropped over his eyes kept his vision clear.

"Prat," commented Troy. "You get a woman like Rowan, and you screw it up! I hope you like them wet, green and slimy."

Troy checked his other screens. Toronk and Fran were moving to blocking positions up and downstream. Carl's gaze had shifted to Willa; his empathic monitors jumped.

"Carl, you horny toad. She is hot, for a middle-aged babe. Now to Farley."

With a twist of a knob, Troy increased Farley's testosterone, then moved on to tweak his brain chemicals.

⌖⟶

Gunther moved to the edge of the stream and scanned with his mind. *'She's in the hutch. Her biggest problem is she hates raw fish. This isn't Hunoin.'* He sent the thought to his team.

'She might know something,' replied Angel's thought.

'She might. Let's flush her out,' agreed Gunther.

Willa moved to the area directly over the hutch and, pulling a camp shovel out of her daypack, began digging. Carl slid into the water and moved to back up Farley.

⌖⟶

Troy shifted his focus to the otterzoid. Its hutch was shaking, and dirt rained down onto it. A battered bookshelf, holding a collection of tattered books, toppled at the back of the hole. Panicked, she dove into her access pool and sprinted down her main corridor, only to find the exit blocked. She raced back. When she surfaced into her dry chamber, she saw sunlight. Driven by fear, she raced down her secondary corridor. Its opening loomed before her, then she was in the open water. Something grabbed her and dragged her to the surface. A human with dark hair and what she had read were Asian features held her.

"I'm Cupid's little helper." Troy released the mix of brain chemicals in his chosen pair. Fear nearly suppressed the response in the otterzoid, but his manipulations were too strong.

"Stop struggling." Farley clutched the bundle of fur in his arms.

"Let me go. Let me go. I'm… I'm a magic otter, I'll grant you three wishes if you let me go," pleaded the otterzoid.

Carl barely had time to catch the rock that flew toward Farley's head.

"We know exactly what you are. Any more attacks and we'll kill you." Gunther ran to the stream bank.

Troy tweaked Farley's controls to make sure the squirming body in his arms had its desired effect.

The otterzoid went still. "You are the defenders. Please, I

have done nothing to harm you. If I could go home, I would!" Little mewling sounds escaped the otterzoid's mouth.

Gunther looked shocked. "She's telling the truth."

Angel landed on the stream bank. "Where's Hunoin?"

The otterzoid went stiff in Farley's arms. "I don't know where that murdering eater of her own pups is. If you want her dead, I wish you luck."

"What is your name?" asked Gunther.

The otterzoid shifted in Farley's arms, striking a pose that was as close to dignified as her situation allowed. "I am junior ambassador Quinta of Swampla. That filthy pirate attacked my ship and took me prisoner. She was holding me for ransom. I was going to negotiate a husband price for my beloved Dagna. That monster killed him. When the ship crashed, my cell opened, and I found my way to this stream. I've lived here ever since. I raided the town's garbage for a few comforts. I taught myself to read your language."

"It's true, or at least she believes it is," said Gunther.

"We're sorry. Hunoin killed someone we loved. We're trying to find her," explained Farley.

"If I can help you, I will."

Troy adjusted the principals' levels, enhancing the compassion shared by those of common losses and shared purpose. He then let nature take its course.

THE DEVIL MADE ME DO IT

"This switch activates the scanners?" Rowan sat at the navigator's station, staring down at the controls.

"Yes, sweetness, that switch activates the scanners." Henry sounded annoyed.

"And they can read all the radiation wavelengths, and—"

"Arrrr!" Henry screamed with his android mouth.

"Is something wrong?" Rowan jerked around in her chair and stared at the android.

"You're driving me crazy!"

"Is that even—"

"Not in theory, but you'll manage it! Questions, questions, questions! What do you think I am, a computer?"

"Um." Rowan looked sheepish.

Henry threw his good arm into the air. "Fine, I wasn't built for data retrieval. What is it with you?"

"It's... well... I don't like being useless. Maybe if I can learn the system, I can be a navigator or something. I'm good at math. Ryan says my theoretical physics is all accurate, as far as it goes, and—"

"I'm not a school teacher. Why don't you link into one of the teaching sims? It's about time you started using the gym before you turn to flab. That would be a horrible waste of a hot bod like yours."

"Gym?" Rowan sounded confused.

"Sixth door on your left after you leave the bridge, sweetness. And sweetness, please leave the bridge."

"I could use a workout, but how will that teach me navigation?"

"Questions, questions, questions. Divine, you are a primitive."

"Gee, thanks. I can tell when I'm not wanted." Rowan looked away from Henry and pouted as she stood up and started for the door.

"Rowan, I'm sorry." Henry looked contrite.

Rowan paused. "I'm sorry I bugged you so much. I'll go to the gym and get out of your hair."

"Love to have you on my hair, sweet stuff."

Rowan shook her head and left the bridge. Minutes later, she'd changed into track pants and a T-shirt. She stepped into the gym, which consisted of lines of coffin-like boxes mounted against each of the walls of the large chamber. A resistance weight machine sat in the middle of the floor.

"Great! Exercise that they call exercise. I hate weights!" she muttered.

"Why do them then? Those pants really frame your ass. Hubba hubba." Henry's voice issued from a wall speaker.

Rowan blushed and tried to adjust her tracksuit. "Whatcha mean? The weight set is all that's here, except for these weird change-room things." She gestured at the coffin-like boxes.

"Sweetness, those are sim units. They're set up like an e-entertainment rig, only they don't suppress movement. An inertial field keeps you in place while giving resistance as interactive programs let you play any sport you like."

"Going through the motions with no control, no thanks." Rowan sat on the weight bench.

"I said interactive, sweet thing. 'Course, I've got the complete *Orgy Girls* collection, if you want a workout of another kind. They're input only. And what input, girrr."

Rowan blushed. "No! Thanks. Maybe I could try swimming some lengths. Can I do that?"

"Sure thing. After that, I can boot up the navigator's training scenario."

"I'd like that. Thanks, Henry."

"You're welcome. Now strip off and get in the booth."

"Strip?"

"You can't swim with clothes on."

"I have a swimsuit in my quarters, I'll go change."

"One piece or bikini?" Henry had a pleading note in his voice.

"One piece. You really are a polymer pervert!"

Henry sighed. "Don't bother. It won't make any difference to the sim."

"You wanted to see me naked!"

"You got it, sweet cheeks. Get in the sim booth. I'll handle the feed."

Rowan stepped into one of the chambers. A moment later, she was standing on the deck of an Olympic-sized swimming pool. She looked down and saw that she was dressed in a thong bikini.

"Henry, I said I wore a one-piece."

"I'm not allowed to have any fun." Henry's voice came from everywhere and nowhere. The swimsuit shifted to a tight-fitting one-piece that was almost as revealing as the bikini.

"It will do." Rowan shook her head as she moved to the water's edge. The water was a bit cool to the touch, perfect for swimming lengths. She slipped in and started with a leisurely front crawl. The water flowed over her skin, and she had to keep telling herself it wasn't real. She reached the end of the lap and turned around. A counter at the end of the lane displayed the number one. She started on her second lap.

Henry watched Rowan move in the sim booth. The inertial fields gave the same resistance as water, and her muscles pulled against the pressure. Her feet kicked five centimetres above the floor. He focused on the slip of bare skin exposed by her T-shirt riding up and hoped the effect would continue.

Rowan pulled herself out of the pool. She felt a pleasant ache in her muscles.

"Three kilometres in fifty minutes. You're good, for a biologic," observed Henry.

"Back home, I worked part-time as a lifeguard. Do I need to dry off or anything before class?"

"Leave it to me. Though you might like to take a micro-bot cleanse before you meet hottie boss."

"Unfortunately. Maybe I'm primitive, but I like showers."

"I'd love to watch you take one. Hot, wet and soapy, just what I want to see."

"I bet you would." Rowan shook her head.

"Ready for class?"

"You betcha."

Rowan found herself sitting at a desk in a classroom with open windows on one side. There was a computer in front of her, and a handsome, older man stood at the front of the room.

"Very well, class, let us begin. The function of a navigator on a modern space vessel is far more than the title implies."

Rowan tried to move but couldn't. She felt her entire attention focus on the lecturer as he explained the basic functions of a navigator. She stopped trying to fight the program and focused on the words. *If putting up with this is the price of being useful, then it's the price I'll pay. How can people stand being so passive?*

John leaned back in his chair and watched the backside of his latest interviewee leave the room. It had been five days since the *Star Hawk* evaded the *Saber*, and he was worried. The series was in a slump. Even the addition of Quinta had failed to revitalize it. He kept telling everyone they had months before the new season started, but he knew it was bad.

"At least I now have all the techs I need," he mused.

A moment passed in silence, then a calculating expression came to John's face. "Yes, that should do it. If Gunther won't oblige me, there are other fish in the sea. He's been infatuated with her since the beginning of the show anyway."

Pressing a button on his desk, he opened a line to the control room.

"Troy, I've decided to take the Gunther/Willa relationship on a new angle. It will be great. I'll have the memo on the board in an hour. I don't want to miss an opportunity. This is what I want you to do..."

Carl set the bag of groceries on Willa's kitchen table. "That's the last of them."

"Thanks, I appreciate your help. It's been so hard since..." Willa stared at the floor and tried not to cry.

Carl glanced around to be sure they were alone. "She isn't really."

"I know. Gunther won't even talk to me about her. It's so hard." Willa started to cry, and Carl moved to hug her. His arms lent her security. She sobbed and talked, then sobbed again in their safe haven.

"Aunt Marcy, this is the dumbest thing I've ever heard of. Gunther and Willa add dramatic stability and pull in the happily married demographic." Troy spoke into his hand-held. Marcy looked out of the screen wearing a face of pure compassion.

"I know. It's Mr. Wilson's show; the man is a maggot. Mike may be able to fix it later; for now, do what you have to. I'm giving you back to your mother. My solo is coming up, I need to get into position."

The screen on the hand-held jiggled, then a middle-aged, brunette woman appeared. "I have to go too dear; if you want my advice, do your job. This could be a wonderful opportunity for you. I love you, goodbye. Oh, I almost forgot. Could you pick up some cheese from that little natural foods shop in the studio town on your way home?"

Troy shut down his hand-held and stared at the control room screens. Farley and Quinta were sitting in Farley's apartment, commiserating about their respective lost loves. Angel was at work calculating which type of trees would be best to plant in the transitional area by the river. Toronk was sparring with Fran. Gunther was back in the Garlic Palace, his emotions a blank.

"Hate to do this to you, buddy," Troy whispered at Gunther's screen. Turning his attention to Carl and Willa, Troy adjusted their hormone levels and brain chemistry.

Willa felt empty. She'd sobbed out her fears and now rested in the circle of Carl's arms. It felt good to be held. She felt a hot flush roll over her. She shifted her position to look into Carl's eyes. He was half her age, but she saw it. He felt the same desire she did. Their lips met, and it was as if her body was on fire. His hands caressed her small, firm breasts and stroked over her back. She trailed her fingers over his groin.

Carl carried her unresisting to her bed.

Gunther picked the mind of the technician who'd come into

the Garlic Palace. He shook his head and bit down on the wave of amusement. *Detective Dave, they have got to be kidding!*

"Now for stage two," said Troy. He felt dirty, but he had a job to do. Making sure that the system recorded every bit of Carl and Willa's tryst, he shifted his attention to Fran and Toronk.

"Sorry, Fran, it's time you learnt, all cats go into heat."

SAD BUT TRUE

"Oh please, stop, oh stop, please. No more, no more!" Rowan shrieked as she fell on her bed.

Ryan laughed. "Say it, say it." He kept tickling her.

"NO!" Rowan playfully kicked at him, then grabbed Ryan's hands. By throwing her weight back, she managed to drag him onto the bed and immobilize his fingers.

Ryan fell laughing and found himself laying beside her, gazing into her eyes.

Rowan stared into his smiling face and gently bit her lower lip.

Ryan kissed her. It was like being a teen again. Necking on the bed was still a dear intimacy for them. His hand crept toward her breast; she caught it, repositioning it at her side.

"Octopus," she whispered when the kiss broke. There was no malice in the word.

"I'm only human." Ryan kissed her again, then snuggled close to her. "You can't tell me you never saw it? He had a crush on her all through high school. It was a minor subplot for a season, comic relief for three. Didn't you ever notice the way he looked at her?"

"Carl did not have a thing for my mother! Divine, Ryan, she's old enough to be, well, his mother."

"Actually, biologically she's the same age. The aging is all cosmetic."

"You know what I mean."

Henry scanned for the *Saber*, monitored and recorded Ryan and Rowan's reactions and edited down earlier recordings for blip transmission when they went out of stealth, as well as performing all ship's functions and reviewing an *Orgy Girls* entertainment.

"I wish you two would shag already. This is boring! Seven days since we gave Tansy baby the slip, and there hasn't been enough action to make a decent episode. This rate, you're gonna let Mike down, and I haven't got my shaggable body yet. Divine, I want my hips back."

Henry checked the ship's systems and watched Ryan and Rowan neck on her bed as he dedicated a sliver of ram to the chamber that both Mike and Ryan had left him blind to.

I wonder what's in there? part of him thought.

Ryan deserves some privacy, said the other sliver of ram he'd dedicated to the argument.

If it makes for a better entertainment, said the first.

You suspect, and it could damage their relationship.

Or push it forward. Besides, if I'm guessing right, better she know now, so they have time to patch it up.

Who made you an expert on love?

I've seen enough porn.

I said love, not lust, you fragged disk segment.

All right, I'm no expert. I don't think anyone is.

Pulling himself together, Henry amalgamated the two ram slivers back into his core persona. "Long and short, I'm bored stiff, and it should be good for a laugh."

That night while Rowan slept, Henry whispered through his speakers. "What's behind the sealed door? What's behind the sealed door? You need to know," just below her threshold of perception. He also manipulated her biology to make her more susceptible.

Tansy paced back and forth across the four-metre length of her quarters. The couch/bed was rolled up, and the wall opposite displayed a life-sized picture of her, a handsome, brown-haired man of about her age and a woman, who could have been a twenty-year-old version of herself. She looked at the rows of numbers on her hand-held. "Sneaky, but not sneaky enough."

The door chime rang, and she absently called, "Enter."

"You wanted to see me, ma'am?" Chow's voice cracked as he spoke. Tansy looked up from her hand-held. The lieutenant was spit-shined and polished, his hair perfectly combed and his uniform immaculate. Tansy smiled.

"Please come in, Lieutenant. Major Tallman will be along in a moment."

The look on Chow's face mirrored relief and regret in almost equal measure.

Tansy couldn't stop the chuckle that welled in her throat.

"Is something amusing, ma'am?" asked Chow.

Tansy stroked her throat with two fingers as she formulated a reply. Chow swallowed hard.

"I was thinking of something my daughter told me. She's about your age. That's her in the picture there." Tansy indicated the image on the wall.

"She looks like you," observed Chow.

"Doesn't she now."

The door chime sounded again.

"Enter," called Tansy. Mildred stepped into the room.

"Please, both of you, take a seat." Tansy indicated her couch as she sat in the computer chair that, aside from the end table dressers flanking the couch, was the only furnishing in the room.

"What's this about, Captain?" asked Mildred as she and Chow settled.

"Two things. First, I may have located the *Star Hawk*. There's an asteroid about an AU off our port stern that is showing a deviation in its orbit. I believe the *Star Hawk* is using it as a focus for its grav-laser's pull."

"That's excellent news," said Mildred.

"It may be. It could also be that Captain Chandler is pulling another fast one. He could have tugged the asteroid out of place while our sensors were disabled and left it for us to find. An attempt to get us to deviate away from his position. The *Star Hawk* pulled that stunt to slip past the blockade at Murack Seven. That's why I called you two here. You have some experience with his nature. I'd like your input. Would he leave a decoy, or do the actual pull?"

"I don't know. I've only met the man twice at social occasions. His history on planet shows he's resourceful."

"Are there any other local asteroids with orbital deviations?" Chow sat forward on the couch. By focusing on the job at hand, he found he could ignore Tansy's proximity.

"No, only the one," answered Tansy.

"Then he's doing the actual pull."

"Interesting assumption. Why?" Tansy lightly stroked her fingers against the line of her jaw.

"When the trees move, the enemy is coming; when there are many blinds in the undergrowth, it is misdirection. Chandler had a paper copy of the *Art of War* listed as one of his personal effects through his entire service. I decided I should read it to gain insight into him."

"Why is that important?" demanded Mildred.

"Because Sun Tzu is still pertinent, if you read him correctly. If it were a decoy, he'd have set up more of them to confuse us and be sure of attracting our attention. Very good, Chow." Tansy smiled, and Chow felt the blood rush to his head.

"I see. Good work, Lieutenant," admitted Mildred.

Tansy stood and gestured to the entry door. "If you will excuse me, I have to get to the bridge. With a little luck, we may find our needle in a haystack. At the least, we can give him an unpleasant surprise."

Chow left the captain's quarters, then watched her walk down the corridor toward the bridge. "Ow," he gasped.

"You really should keep your mind on the job!" Mildred extracted her elbow from Chow's side.

Chow grinned sheepishly and followed her to the ground force's quarters.

Gunther sat on his couch beside Willa. They didn't touch. Willa's glance alternated between the floor and Carl, who fidgeted in the easy-chair. Fran sat at Carl's feet looking uncomfortable, Toronk refused to meet her gaze from where he sat in the other easy-chair with Angel perched on the armrest. Toronk hardly touched Angel, and his tail twitched uncomfortably where it was draped over the armrest. Farley and Quinta lounged on a blanket on the floor, leaning toward one another.

"Carl, how goes your end?" Gunther sounded casual, more alive than he had since Rowan left.

"What? I... what do you mean?" Carl glanced about the room.

"You were looking for Hunoin. Have you found any new leads?"

"No. I've been busy at work. I still have to feed myself."

"Has anyone else found anything? Fran, how about you? What's up with the furries you've been around, anything good?"

Fran stiffened. "Ah... No... I've not... well... you know. I've been busy. I did get that lead on the RV that was driving around."

"I checked it out from above. There's a couple of pizoids with a big tank and a bubbler. Wet enough, but not the aquatic we're looking for," said Angel.

"So, we're still at square one. I've done some walkabouts and haven't picked up anything, though there was a prostitute that approached me." Gunther spoke lightly and grinned at Willa.

"If that's how you feel, why don't you have an affair!" she

snapped.

Gunther recoiled. "Willa, it was a joke."

"It wasn't funny!"

"All right... I think we need to start looking for the human slaves. They might know something."

"What could they know?" demanded Willa.

"Where Hunion is, maybe?" said Gunther.

"Oh. All right then."

Gunther looked at his wife. He could have probed her mind, but he never went past her surface thoughts without permission. She was so cold and distant. He decided to pay more attention to her. Whether it was programmed into him or not, he loved her, and his project didn't have to happen tomorrow. He placed his hand on her shoulder and gently squeezed. "I love you, Willa."

Willa swallowed. "I... I love you too." She and Carl both stared at the floor.

Rowan paced along the flight section corridor. She'd doubled her normal swim and class time, and still, the desire to find out was like an itch she had to scratch.

"Ryan wouldn't mind," she whispered.

"So that's why you're doing it when he's sleeping?" spoke another part of her.

"What could he be hiding? Dirty magazines, home videos about his wife?

"You don't know it's that simple. You don't know him that well. Maybe it's something you don't want to know about. Maybe he's got a secret thing for fur or something. It's none of your business.

"It is. If we get involved, I have to know. It's kinda important.

"You're rationalizing.

"I know. I can't sleep I'm so curious. I need to know." Moving to the sealed door, Rowan laid her hand on the scanner plate. Nothing happened.

"It's locked, no good in trying. I'll just have some hot milk," part of her said.

"Sweet thing, you talk to yourself almost like an AI, only a lot slower. Real bonding experience." Henry's voice issued from the speaker.

"Were you listening that whole time?" Rowan stepped back from the door.

"It's a hobby. Besides, he hasn't told me what's in there either. Might be my new body, just waiting for when we reach Geb. I want a peek too."

"Well, I guess we're out of luck. The door's locked."

"Listen up, sweet thing. I may not have hips, but I'm a whiz with ship's systems. Do what I tell you, and we'll both have a look-see."

Rowan glanced up and down the passage. "Ryan—?"

"Is sleeping like a batzoid after its wedding night."

"I'll assume that's a good thing. Mental pictures I didn't need, thank you. What should I do?"

"Press in on that panel above the palm scanner, then twist your wrist to the right."

Rowan followed instructions. The panel popped open, revealing a line of switches.

"This is gonna be easier than I thought. Throw those switches up, and it will restore my control over the room."

Rowan complied. The door pulled back into the wall, and she stepped in. The room was identical to hers, but instead of furniture, it held two cylinders over two metres tall with two boxy devices a metre cubed stacked between them. Lights blinked on the cubes. Rowan moved to one of the cylinders.

Ryan was jerked out of sleep by a mechanical whine.

"What?" he murmured, then waking more, he shouted, "NO!" and leapt out of bed. He barely managed to grab his robe as he raced out of the room.

"Oh, stardust! Hot stuff, Ryan had an alarm rigged. Can't trust anyone!" warned Henry.

Rowan was too shocked by what she saw to acknowledge. She stood in front of the cylinder, staring open-mouthed. There in bold letters was, 'Gestational Chamber/memory patterning unit'. On a removable plaque below that was written:

AS-F
Designation - Unmodified
Development Schedule - Green

A picture of her face sat below the words.

"Rowan, I can explain!" Ryan appeared in the doorway, belting on his robe.

Rowan turned on him. "What? If it didn't work with me, you were going to try again? Or maybe when I reach forty, you'd trade me in on a new model. Is that your plan? You're as bad as the rest! I'm a piece of meat to you."

"It's not like that."

"Oh, so you were going to make a copy and sell her to the highest bidder!"

"No, I..."

"You what? Say something. Tell me how this is all right. That it's, 'your society'. That I'm behind the times, again! That I'm a primitive! That I'm—"

"Dying." Ryan finally got the word out.

"I'm... from the venom? But Kadar—"

"Not from the venom." Ryan entered the room and moved to Rowan. "You're a schedule red clone. That means they used a quick clone process to create you. It took one year to age you to fifteen. They can't stop the accelerated aging. Add to that that you're genetically modified. You'll be lucky if you last twenty-two years total."

"I... Oh, Divine! And this..." Rowan pointed to the cylinder.

"That's a schedule green. It grows at a standard rate. All your memories from the show are being inputted. When it reaches maturity, I want to transfer everything that happened since into it."

"Then there'll be two of me."

"It doesn't work like that. When a medical clone is activated, an energy leaves the old body. Some like to say it's the soul, some call it the astral body, some call it other things. The organized religions say the soul is unknowable, so they call it neuro-static energy. I don't know what it is.

"We do know it exists. We can measure that type of energy. We don't really understand it. Maybe some of the older races do. But if it doesn't move to the clone, the clone never becomes viable. If it does, the old body dies."

"Knowing this, you still make clones slaves?"

"When it's a clone where the memories are selected and plugged in, no one has to die to supply the energy. You've lived as a real person, you aren't a construct anymore. You've made decisions, loved. You've become more than the sum of your programming. To make a copy, I'd have to stop the inputs with the stuff the studio did before you had any free will. It's science, and theology, and philosophy, and I don't understand any of it! I just know what is."

Rowan sank onto the floor and buried her face in her hands. Her body trembled. Finally, she looked up, tears streaming down her cheeks. "Why two?"

"Because I'm a schedule orange clone. If you try to do a transfer into a pre-puberty body, the energy rejects the clone. I think it's because the universe feels no one should have to go through puberty twice." Ryan tried to smile at his own quip. The stricken look on Rowan's face stilled it.

Ryan continued. "The biologists think it has to do with brain development. Things shift in adolescence that make the brain receptive to the transfer. It doesn't work well with older bodies either."

"That's all very interesting, but why two?" Rowan blotted

her tears with her sleeve. It was all too much. She felt like she was drowning under the weight of millennia.

"Fine. Like I said, I'm schedule orange. My cancers were so bad I couldn't wait fifteen years for them to grow me a new body. I barely lasted the year it took to grow this modified one. At best, this form will function for twenty-six, maybe twenty-seven years. That puts me over a hundred, so there's no way they'd give me another body. I want a life, a full life, with you. A life where I make my own choices. Is that so wrong?"

Rowan swallowed hard. "You'd better tell me the rest. Right now! Stop protecting me. You can't."

Ryan nodded. "If you want kids, it's going to have to wait for your new body. Studio clones are incapable of reproduction. As are schedule oranges, it's how we're built. Everyone you know from the set region is either schedule orange or red."

"My dad!"

"I'm sorry. He has a few years left in him. On the upside, the schedule green clones don't need control packs. All you'll have are some cerebral interface nano-bots, and pretty much everyone has them."

"Are," she gestured to the gestational chambers, "they alive? What I mean is, will it be murder if we become them?"

Ryan sank to the floor beside her and put his arm over her shoulder. She half-collapsed into his chest. "They're alive, but they aren't aware. You and I are people; they're only potential people. It's consciousness versus memory. And maybe where the soul resides."

Rowan rested her head against Ryan's chest. "I'm sorry I doubted you. Everything you've done for me, and I thought the worst. It's…"

"Sh… You have a right. I should have told you, but you've been through so much. I thought I'd wait."

Rowan nodded. "Everyone I ever loved is going to be dead inside twenty years."

"Unfortunately."

"I knew I'd never see them again, but I always imagined them having long, healthy lives. Silly, huh? With all I know."

"Human." Ryan gently hugged her.

"How'd you get the chambers? I mean considering what Kadar told me, I don't think they're something you pick up at the local hardware store."

"That's not impor…"

Rowan pulled away and stared at Ryan. "No more secrets."

Ryan nodded. "I let the head of the studio implant a telemetry pack in me. He could follow us as long as we were on Gaea and record my emotions and perceptions as if I were a studio clone. He wanted to make an e-entertainment about a clone escaping. Without his help, I could never have gotten away with you."

"You let him… You gave up every shred of privacy so that you could save me." Rowan looked at Ryan with wonder. This was beyond the risks he'd taken. He'd accepted the ultimate violation of self for her.

"I couldn't let you die."

"Is he still recording?"

"Not since we left Gaea. There'd have to be a recording unit on board to monitor us, and someone would have to operate it."

"Good." Rowan dried her eyes, then kissed Ryan. The kiss was more passionate than he'd ever believed possible. Rowan broke the kiss, then spoke again. "Because some things should be private." Taking Ryan's hand, she led him back to her quarters.

Henry pumped his android arm as he recorded Rowan and Ryan's reactions. "Humpada humpada, hottie boss. Woohoo, this will put the ratings through the roof!"

FOR EVERY ACTION

Captain Denardo sat in her chair on the bridge and watched the magnified asteroid on her screen.

"Gunnery, are you sure you can launch the smart missiles so they can't be detected?" The captain's voice was all business.

"Yes, ma'am. If I use the port tubes, any launch signature will be masked for a ship sun-ward of us, and the missiles are small enough that they're unlikely to attract attention."

"Very good, Lieutenant. Target that hunk of rock and launch. Program the missiles to delay engine activation for two hours so that we're well away before they give any telltales."

"Aye, ma'am." The gunner programmed the sequence and let the missiles fly.

"Excuse me, Captain. Could you explain what's going on for a ground pounder?" Mildred stood to the right of the command chair.

Captain Denardo smiled. "We have no way of knowing where along the line of the grav-laser the *Star Hawk* might be. Thus, a direct attack is impossible. However, the grav-laser is like an elastic pulled taut against the asteroid's inertia. Reduce the asteroid's mass, and I wouldn't want to be the one holding the elastic. Pity really, it looks like I'm going to end up scratching the paint on that lovely ship."

Ryan awoke and stared into the back of Rowan's head. She

was on her side, facing away from him. Smiling, he rolled, so that he spooned her. Last night, the first time had been passion, need and a measure of desperation. It had been wonderful, but not what he'd dreamed of. Then they'd cuddled and talked for what seemed hours. The second time had been more than his wildest fantasies. It was like the boundaries of self dissolved, and they became one. It was so far beyond anything that the studio could have contrived with its antiseptic passion, cleaned of all false starts and miss-moves. It was making love in its purest form. Then they'd dozed, only to wake in the wee hours to do it over again.

Rowan felt Ryan pull in tight against her. His arm held her snug across the chest. She pretended to sleep; it was too perfect a moment to disturb. One thing she'd always hated about Farley was his dislike of cuddling. She cleared her thoughts of her old lover and focused on the new. The first time had been desperate, a crushing need for intimacy, for something, someone to hold onto in a universe gone mad. Still, it had been the best she'd had. It was like every fibre of her being was on fire, then Ryan had held her, and they'd talked. She learned a lot that scared her about his world and some things that calmed her. More importantly, she learned how true his feelings for her were. The second time had been magic. She hadn't known it could be like that. Slow and enduring, a gentle union that built in an unhurried pace until it shattered all her barriers. She wasn't sure if she loved Ryan yet, but she was sure that she could love him. That was almost as good. Then the third time. Returning from the bathroom to find herself held, cradled, cherished. It had grown so naturally, not a moment of contrivance. A sleepy, warm, beautiful union. She revelled in the memories and the warmth of her man's body. This was what she imagined her parents had, and what she had always longed for.

She wanted to stay in Ryan's arms forever, but nature never waits on human desire.

"Ryan, I need to get up." Rowan lifted his hand to her lips and kissed it.

"I guess I should start the day. I need to pull the empty power unit and slot the full one in."

"I hope that doesn't take too long." Rowan turned so he could see her smile.

"It won't take more than a couple of hours. Do you have some suggestions on how we can fill the rest of the time?"

"Maybe, for now I've got to go." Rowan left the bed and padded to the bathroom.

Ryan lay back and smiled. He stretched, then spoke to the air. "Privacy off. Henry, can you give me a status update?"

Henry's voice issued from the speaker. "You got lucky, and you didn't let me watch. Wanker!"

Ryan grinned. "Not today, and don't think I haven't figured out why Rowan had to get into that room, and who told her how to restore your control? Hm."

"You should be thanking me, hottie boss."

"I should check your subroutines regarding obeying superior officers. Now, how's our status?"

"No change, the *Saber* is ahead of us, vectoring back and forth. We're still accelerating like a snail with a sore foot. You want to change rocks and shift our vector?"

"In a few hours, if they haven't spotted us. That asteroid is a good chunk of rock for us. It…"

Rowan stepped out of the washroom. Ryan's thoughts trailed off as he gazed at her naked body.

"Is there anything pressing?" she asked.

"Yeah, from the sounds of it, it's in his shorts, hot stuff," commented Henry.

"Henry, resume privacy mode!" Ryan and Rowan spoke in unison.

They chuckled, then Rowan leapt onto the bed.

Captain Denardo watched as the missiles impacted on the asteroid.

"Helm. Make it look like a normal adjustment to our search grid. Get us closer to that rock." Tansy lightly traced the line of her jaw with two fingers.

On the big screen, the asteroid had been pulverized into one large chunk and a dusting of pieces ranging from grains of sand to chunks the size of a small, ground vehicle. Many of the pieces were moving away from the asteroid in a sun-ward direction.

"Good. There are disadvantages to being lander crew, Captain Chandler. If you'd done a tour on a line ship, you'd probably know this trick. We all have our blind spots. Navigator, find pull points that will allow us to intercept the *Star Hawk* anywhere along the trajectory indicated by the rubble."

"Aye, ma'am."

Henry watched the *Saber* and recorded the latest of Ryan and Rowan's trysts. "Keep this up, you're both going to need anti-chafing cream. They call me sex mad!" Henry spoke to himself. He paused, then focused all his scanners forward.

"What?" gasped the android. A pile of space rubble hurtled toward him. "Stardust!" Henry seized control of the *Star Hawk*'s course and diverted it to the side while speaking into Rowan's room. "We got trouble! Get up here, now!"

"What's going on?" demanded Ryan. Henry recorded him jumping out of bed and struggling into his pants. He couldn't help but admire the forms of both his crewmates.

"Meteor storm. A whole pile of rock heading our way. We'll be in it in five minutes."

Ryan raced from the room; Rowan followed, still struggling into her sweater.

Ryan burst onto the bridge and almost threw himself into the pilot's chair. "Stardust!" he whispered when he checked the screen.

Rowan raced into the navigator's chair and began scanning the debris. "It's pretty dense. We can't get completely clear of it before it's on us. The best pull point is now in the computer." Rowan hit the button that put the coordinates of another asteroid in the local coordinates file.

"I got it, sweetness," said Henry.

Ryan adjusted the ship's propulsion laser's pull to the new target. "How long?"

"Two minutes thirty-seven seconds," Henry and Rowan replied at the same time.

"Henry, secure all bulkheads, prepare maintenance bots for emergency repairs. If they have a warhead in that, we're dead. If it's only rock, it could do a lot of damage."

"Aye," said Henry.

"What happened? How'd that rock get there in the first place?" asked Rowan.

"Captain Denardo must have spotted a deviation in the asteroid's orbit and blown a big chunk out of it. Our grav-lasers kept pulling on the lessened mass and dragged it right into us. Stardust, how could I have been so stupid?"

The first hunk of rock hit the *Star Hawk*, and the ship bucked.

"Scuffed the paint—" began Henry, then there was another jolt.

"We'll be to one side of the debris in twenty seconds," said Rowan.

The *Star Hawk* shook again. Lights flashed on the engineering console.

"Henry, take the helm." Ryan dove at the engineering station and began throwing switches.

The ship bucked again.

"Ten seconds. Oh, stardust!" Rowan swore as a piece of rock about the size of a small car hurtled toward them.

Ryan glanced at the main screen, then returned his attention to the engineering console. "Pull, Henry!"

"Pull, he says. What in the divine's myriad names do you think I'm doing? Propulsion laser at thirty per cent above rated maximum."

Ryan threw switches at a frantic pace. The rock nearly filled the screen, then the *Star Hawk* shook, and they were all jolted against the inertial restraints.

"We're clear," called Rowan.

"That last one clipped us." The screen above Ryan's console flashed red. "We are nova blasted now!" he commented as the damage report displayed on his screen.

⚔

Tansy watched the big screen. A couple of pieces of debris on the field's leading-edge seemed to bounce off something, then a large rock tumbled to one side, and about a quarter of the hull of a Hawk class heavy lander appeared.

"Helm, best speed to that vessel. Queen takes Knight. Navigator, lock all scanners on that ship. I don't want to lose it if they get their cloaking capacity back." Tansy steepled her fingers. For all the respect she had for Captain Chandler and his motives, she was a predator, and the hunt was on.

⚔

Ryan raced to the pilot's station and shifted the ship's facing. "The starboard cloak is still intact. If we get lucky and they haven't noticed us yet..." He spoke as he worked.

"No good, boss. They're coming straight for us, flank speed." Henry put the image of the *Saber* up on the main screen.

Rowan bit her lip as she worked. "I wasn't supposed to get this until next week. Estimated time of intercept, two hours and forty-three minutes."

"How long until effective weapons range?" Ryan moved back to the engineering board and assessed the damage.

"Um... I haven't—" began Rowan.

"One-hundred and thirty minutes," interrupted Henry. "Sorry sweetness, you did good, but seconds count here."

Rowan nodded and turned back to her controls.

"I could jury rig the stealth. Problem is, they have a fix on us. There is no way we'll shake them. It's going to take a space-dock to fix this properly."

"Stardust! We're nova blasted," said Henry.

"Could we lose ourselves? I know it's silly. I saw a movie once where the heroes hid in an asteroid."

"Sweetness, finish the course first, please. That's imposs—"

"Hide and go seek. Like on Murack Seven when we dipped into the atmosphere to give that felinezoid cruiser the slip."

"No gas giants around here, handsome." Henry sounded peevish.

"Rowan, how long at best speed to the nearest asteroid with a facing of at least three kilometres by three kilometres?"

Rowan calculated the distance. "One hour to accelerate, two to equalize speed after that."

"Do we have enough of a lead on the *Saber* to make it?"

Rowan ran another set of numbers.

"No, we'll be in weapons range first," said Henry.

Rowan tapped her console, bringing a diagram up on the big screen. "Maybe not. If we use the main drive for the lateral pull against the target, that's AS-247, and the tractor beam to pull against other asteroids to stall our out-system momentum, it would give us a ten-minute lead on the *Saber* when we reach AS-247. It will be high G all the way," said Rowan.

Ryan looked at the diagram that showed a single large hunk of rock labelled AS-247 connected to a graphic of the

Star Hawk by a golden line. Other golden lines came off the bottom of the ship, intersecting small pieces of rock on its sunward side.

Ryan returned to the pilot's console. "You heard the lady, Henry. All power to drive lasers and tractor beams." G-forces beyond what the inertial dampers were designed to handle pressed Ryan and Rowan into their seats.

"They're running, ma'am." The *Saber*'s navigator announced.

Captain Denardo quirked an eyebrow. "They know they can't outrun us. What could they reach before we're in weapons range?"

"Top acceleration for a Hawk? Nothing, ma'am."

Tansy sat back in her chair. "Lieutenant Barns, what is their actual acceleration at this time? Don't check the manual, look at them."

The plump, middle-aged navigator checked his instruments. "They're accelerating to the lateral at twenty-five Gs, ma'am. This can't be. They're slowing their out-system movement nearly a G at the same time. A Hawk's engines can only support twenty-five Gs of pull. This is impossible!"

"Evidently not. Using their observed movements, what could they reach?"

The navigator flushed pink as he ran the numbers. "Ma'am, if they maintain their present velocity, they'll reach and match velocities with AS-247 before we're in weapons range."

"What are you planning, Captain Chandler? You can't hope to lose us behind that rock. What do you have in mind?" Tansy stroked the line of her jaw with two fingers.

"What are your orders, ma'am?" The navigator squirmed.

"Continue as we are. Perhaps Chandler is finally running in panic. No, not this one. Keep all scanners focused on the

Star Hawk. Check the logs for any surveillance satellites that could observe the far side of AS-247."

The navigational officer checked the computer. "Ma'am, the zo... coelenteratezoids have one that could be diverted to monitor the back of the asteroid."

"Should I call for the control codes?" asked the communications officer, a blonde-haired woman barely out of her teens.

Tansy sighed and turned to the communications station. "No, I've been told to go to the regions of freezing oxygen enough for one day. I do admire the coelenteratezoids. They live their faith."

UNDER THE RUBBLE

37

"I love you." Carl sat on Willa's couch, holding her hands.

"And I love you, but this is wrong. Gunther is my husband, and I'm old enough to be your mother."

"I don't care about your age."

"How about my husband?"

Carl hung his head. "I know it's wrong. Nova blast! Gunther has been like a second father to me, but I can't help how I feel. I love you."

"It has to end," said Willa.

"Tell me he can give you what I give you." Carl ran his hand along her tear-soaked cheek.

Willa felt things tighten deep inside her. This young man sparked an animal lust in her beyond anything she'd ever known.

Troy stared at the other screens. He felt dirty. Gunther was in the Garlic Palace. He'd taken to spending every lunch there, though now he was also showering Willa with attention.

Troy's gaze strayed to another one of the side screens.

Fran ran her fingers through the fur of Toronk's chest. The big felinezoid purred. They lay in her bed.

"How can this feel so right when I know it's so wrong?"

Fran stared into Toronk's eyes.

The felinezoid shifted position. "I know. I of all beings should know the pain this will cause Angel and Carl. I simply cannot resist you." He stroked his cheeks against Fran's face.

"It has to be the genetic modification. Maybe when I'm not in heat."

"Maybe then." Toronk brushed the fur on the back of his hand over Fran's nipples. Fran gasped and ran her fingers through the soft fur of her lover.

⌖⋯✦

Angel hid in the branches of a tree and watched deliverymen carry an order of crayfish into a greenhouse encased pool area. The van drove off, and through the glass, she caught a glimpse of a sleek otterzoid body. "Got ya," she whispered.

⌖⋯✦

Ryan piloted the *Star Hawk* behind the asteroid. The ship was barely moving in relation to the rock.

"There's one. Three hundred metres across, fifty metres deep," said Henry, bringing the depression up on the screen.

"It will do." Ryan landed in the crater.

"Directing gravity laser down at five per cent." Ryan locked down the pilot's station and moved to the gunnery station. "That ridge there should do, what do you think, Henry, Rowan?"

"I think you're nova fried to try this, but when does the shaggable one listen to me?" snapped Henry.

"Those skilled in defence hide in the deepest depths of the earth," countered Ryan. Directing the tractor beam up, he activated it. At first, nothing happened. He ramped up the power, then the side of the crater began to crumble in.

Ryan killed the pull. A series of bangs reverberated through the ship.

"This is not what Sun Tzu had in mind," griped Henry.

"Henry, kill the grav-lasers and tell me how it looks."

"We're buried, though how in the divine's myriad names we're going to get out, I don't know."

"Good, open a path to the ground pounder section, then shut everything down except emergency lights and your minimal power."

"You better hurry. The *Saber* will crest the asteroid's horizon in three minutes," added Rowan.

"I hope nobody looks at this rock who knows something about geology." Ryan led Rowan from the bridge as the consoles went dark.

Captain Denardo sat on the edge of her seat.

"How much longer?" Mildred stood behind the captain's chair gazing at the big screen.

Tansy hit a button on her armrest. "Lieutenant Chow, we anticipate interception of the *Star Hawk* in less than five minutes. Have your people ready for boarding."

"Yes, ma'am," came the reply.

AS-247 filled the screen, then they topped its edge.

"Navigator, where are they?" demanded Captain Denardo.

"I... They have to be here." Lieutenant Barn's pudgy hands flew over his console.

"Scan for a cloaked vessel, they couldn't have gone far. Communications, check the sensor probe we launched. Make sure nothing is hiding on the far side of this rock."

"Yes, ma'am."

"Captain," opened Mildred.

"He can't have vanished. Even cloaked at this range, we'd be able to detect them."

Unnoticed, a jumble of stones at the bottom of a crater passed across the view screen.

"At least this is fun." Rowan supported herself on two fingers and balanced upside down in one of the third-class passenger rooms. Its door was open. The hall beyond led to the old non-com barracks which was now full of trees. Light leaked in through the doorway.

Ryan spread a blanket over one of the roll-down couch beds. The blanket seemed to hover in the air. "Microgravity can be a hoot. It can also be a stardusted pain."

Rowan righted herself and ended up jumping to the ceiling. She caught herself and slowly drifted to the floor. "Will this work?"

"It all depends. If they have a ground pounder consulting, probably not. Captain Denardo came up through the piloting ranks. She flew fighters until her reaction time started to slip and they moved her over to the big ships. It was in her file. She might not have seen this trick. We all have blind spots. I only thought of it because I heard so many ground pounder stories. Those maniacs would hide damaged equipment under anything. One guy I knew deliberately triggered a snow slide to hide his grav-tank while he replenished his liquid nitrogen."

"What about that Mildred person you mentioned?" Rowan glided to the bed and pulled herself onto it.

"She's a security officer, never did line combat. I'm counting on the ignorance of the people chasing us. I hope they leave before I have to turn on life support." Ryan slipped onto the bed and let himself drift down beside Rowan. He embraced her as much to steady himself as for the pleasure of doing so.

Rowan snuggled into Ryan. "I think it's warm enough where I'm laying."

Ryan kissed her. "We should try and get some sleep. The trees will make sure we have enough air to breathe, and this will take a few hours. When I think they're pulling away, I want to do the internal repairs. After that, I'll patch the hull."

"You know, if we're laying here anyway, we kinda left things half-finished when this all started. I've always wondered what it would be like in zero G. So, if you want to, we could..."

Ryan's kiss stopped her from finishing the sentence.

Willa rested in Gunther's arms. She was glad that a shower could hide her sins. Her marriage bed was warm, and her husband loved her in his slow, thorough way. She stroked his cheek and gently kissed his lips. With Carl, it was all animal fire; with Gunther it was like her soul awoke and merged with his. She let her infidelity slip from her mind. Her orgasm washed over her, and she wondered at herself for wanting more than what she held at that moment. She only wished it would last.

Tansy sat at the table in the captain's mess. Her uniform was immaculate, but she looked troubled. She swirled her fork among the noodles of her spaghetti. "It doesn't make any sense."

"Perhaps he managed to repair his stealth and slipped out along the path of the asteroid's shadow," suggested Chow.

"We looked. We're close enough that even using stealth, he would have left a shadow on our sensors." Tansy put her fork down and gently ran her finger down the line of her throat.

"That raises the question of where is he?" Mildred finished her spaghetti, then sipped her de-alcoholized wine.

"That, Major, is the question. He's not on the asteroid. Nothing more than normal readings from it. A bit of thermal energy from decaying radioactive materials. That's common enough."

"What are you planning on doing next, ma'am?" Chow stared at her as if he was recording her every move.

Tansy picked up her fork and took a mouthful of her food. She chewed in silence, then swallowed. A smile parted her lips, and Chow wondered if he was going to embarrass himself.

"First, we finish our survey of this rock. If that fails to turn up anything, we'll have to go back to patrolling the area. Captain Chandler has posed us with a mystery. All mysteries have a solution, and it's still a good run to the stargate."

Rowan's breath misted in front of her; she felt cool despite wearing two sweaters and being wrapped in a blanket.

"Pass me the laser solder, please." Ryan's head and upper body were buried in a maintenance access.

Rowan looked at the tray of tools beside her and tried to remember the one he meant. She passed him a pencil-shaped tool.

"Thanks." Ryan shifted position. There was the smell of hot solder and flux, then he pulled his head out of the hatch. "That should do it. I've done as much as I can until I EVA."

"Good. Do you think that the *Saber* is still out there?" Rowan rubbed her arms.

"Even odds. It all depends on if they think we gave them the slip. I don't want to power up until I have to. Of course, I can't let it drop much below freezing. The trees could die. If you're cold, why don't you put on a coat?"

"Sun Valley was semitropical, remember. My clothes are all copies of things I really wore."

"Sorry, I forgot. It won't be much longer."

"It's been twelve hours."

"Captain Denardo isn't careless. Even if she thinks we've

given her the slip, she'll leave a probe. I want her well away from here before we move."

"You're the captain, my captain." Rowan smiled.

—✦—

Angel paced across Gunther's living-room. The tension was thick enough to cut with a knife.

"Are you certain?" Gunther sat on the couch with his arm around Willa's shoulders. Willa neither pulled away nor leaned into her husband's touch.

"I saw her. She's living it up in a private swimming pool."

Carl stood in the corner of the room, his gaze stealing from Fran to Willa and back again. Toronk sat in the easy chair staring at the floor, his tail twitching uncomfortably.

The door opened, and Farley pushed a shopping cart, covered with a blanket, into the room. "Hi, everyone." He was smiling.

Quinta stuck her head out from under the blanket. "Hello. Farley introduced me to videos. I never knew how enjoyable your entertainments could be. Your science fiction is so silly. I laughed so hard, I almost... Is everything all right?" The otterzoid stopped and stared at her newly made human friends.

"Angel found Hunoin," explained Gunther.

"When do we kill that testicle biting female, who mates with many while paying no husband price and spreading venereal diseases that infect the proper wives of the males she seduces, while making no effort to warn her partners or find a cure, because she is too slovenly to even clean her own hutch and who is not averse to accepting the attentions of other females, especially if they can manipulate a large grama fruit into her waste orifice until her fur is matted with lubricating juices that don't wash off and smell unpleasant?"

The humans stared at Quinta. Gunther noticed that her lips stopped moving long before the translation was done.

"What?" asked Quinta.

Fran chuckled and soon the others joined in.

"What did I say?" Quinta looked confused.

Gunther stilled his laughter. "I'm sorry, Quinta, in translation, that is a mouthful."

"Mouthful. Mouthful of what? We just ate. If you have pizza, I know I could force myself, to be sociable."

After the tension, this sparked another round of laughter. Slowly the group sobered.

"Quinta, you were sent from the Divine," observed Gunther. "Now we know where Hunoin is. It's time to plan. Willa, my love, could you download the survey information for the property?"

Willa smiled as she stood and kissed her husband. No one noticed the spasm of pain that marred Carl's features.

Ryan tied camouflage tarps into a bundle in front of the airlock leading to the top of the ship.

"Are you sure this is safe?" Rowan rubbed her arms to fend off the chill.

"I'm sure it's not. No EVA ever is. We don't have a choice. I'm going to have to dig us out. If I can do it so that I can get the hull patched under cover of these rocks then that's even better."

"I'll wake up Henry and tell him to monitor you."

"That's probably a good idea. Keep power to a minimum. If Captain Denardo has left a probe, we can't be too obvious."

"Be careful." Rowan kissed him.

"I will be. I have something worth coming home to." Ryan opened a hatch and started pulling on one of the spacesuits contained in the room beyond.

EXPOSURE

38

"**D**o you think they'll get away?" Arlene sat in the control room. The main screen showed Ryan's perspective. AS-247 filled his vision. The ship was about to crest its edge, then the recording ceased. She swivelled in her chair to look at Mike.

"I have my doubts. It was bad luck for Ryan that Tansy Denardo drew the assignment. I had confidence in his ability to give the slip to the other officers of the Planetary Defence Corps, but her..." Mike shook his head.

"The scenes with Rowan are..." Arlene blushed. "I've done this job for a few years now, and I never..."

"I know. I am glad that Ryan and Rowan experienced that. It is rare for the act to touch someone so deeply."

"It put me in mind of Gunther and Willa on *Angel Black*, only it was more, I don't know, vital."

"It's newer, more novel. In time I'm sure Ryan and Rowan would have become like Willa and Gunther. The way they would be if John wasn't a fool."

"I know, I can't believe that."

"Believe what?" Greg stepped into the control room.

"Is it that time already?" Arlene checked the chronograph.

"I heard we recsseived another download from the *Sstar Hawk* sso I came in early. How are they doing?"

"Bitter and sweet," remarked Mike. "You can review the file on your shift, fast forward through the sex scenes."

"Ryan and Rowan? Looksss good on them." Greg's forked

tongue flicked from his mouth, and he smiled.

"Don't get too caught up in them." Mike glared at Greg, then smiled and winked. "I have to go. The producers are deciding on the new set region. If I'm not there, you can bet it will be a mistake."

"The rumours are true then? Sun Valley is being phased out?" asked Arlene.

"In fifteen years, the forestation of the region will be complete. Next season's clones will be the last for Sun Valley, ignoring disposable antagonists. The investors have decided to do an ancient Egyptian format for the next set." Mike smirked. "That's part of why now is the perfect time for our little project. On that note, be sure and record Gunther's reaction to Ulva's visit to the Garlic Palace."

Greg and Arlene smiled. "Wouldn't miss it for the world."

Ryan braced his legs against the inner hatch of the airlock and his arms against the stone blocking the open outer hatchway. He heaved, and a rock the size of a ground car tumbled over its neighbours. Ryan hopped the two metres to the top of the opening and landed on the rocks covering his ship. Hauling on a rope tied to his belt, he pulled up the bundle of camouflage tarps. Untying the first tarp, he spread it over the opening to the *Star Hawk* and activated it. The hole disappeared under what looked like a rock.

"I love military surplus," he remarked to himself.

Rowan fidgeted in the captain's chair.

"Relax, hot stuff. He's doing fine," said Henry.

Rowan looked at the android. In the subdued light, the mutilation of his body didn't look as bad. "Are you sure?" Rowan bit her lip.

"He uncovered the port sensors. Don't worry, sweetness,

the stealth is on, we're blending with the rocks."

"I'm not worried about us."

"Have a look-see, hottie."

The main screen filled with the image of a space-suited figure lifting a rock three times its size and carrying it away.

"Any signs of the *Saber*?"

"Nope."

⟛

Ryan heard the three clicks over his radio. To most listeners, it would seem random EM noise. On that frequency, at that time, he knew what they meant. Opening one of the camouflage tarps, he threw himself and his bundle underneath it.

⟛

Henry monitored the space above them. A satellite passed over their position.

"That one almost had him. It's orbiting this chunk of rock every half hour. Hottie boss is going to have to work fast. Too bad, seems quickies aren't his style." Henry made a lewd pumping action with his android arm.

"How can you be like that? All the trouble we're in, Ryan out there?"

"It's how I'm wired, sweetness. Excuse me a sec."

⟛

Ryan heard four clicks on another frequency and clambered out from under the camouflage tarp. Rushing to the rock pile, he began tossing boulders as large as himself to the side, clearing a trench beside the *Star Hawk*'s damaged hull.

"It can't be how you're wired. Why would anyone want a military bot pervert?" objected Rowan. She was scared; fighting with Henry made it all seem less overwhelming.

"It is, hot stuff, and it's all Ryan's fault. In a way, he's my daddy. Incest is best, but he won't go for it."

"That's crazy. Why would he wire you up as a sex fiend?"

Henry shrugged. "Stardust happens. It was after Ryan pulled his crazy stunt with the solar flare during the batzoid pirate suppression. The ship's computer was cooked in the battle, so Ryan hardwired me into the systems, and I took on operations. When we limped back to our support ships, the ground pounders wanted to thank us for saving their butts.

"Three hundred drunk ground pounders, one Space Services Engineer, and one AI doing up the R and R ship. When we were done I don't know which looked worse, the *Star Hawk* or the R and R ship."

"So how does that explain you being a polymer pervert?"

"There was a cyber brothel on the R and R ship. All Luba and Luke bots. Ryan made Joslin a promise, no fleshies. Joslin had told Ryan that Lubas were all right."

"Luke and Luba?"

"Pleasure bots, sweetness."

Rowan looked shocked. "Um... Joslin sounds *really* understanding."

"Nova blast, hottie. None of us knew when we were going to get blown up, cooked, mutilated, maimed, or just plain dead. He had to have something to take the edge off. Ryan has never been much on recreational chemicals or e-entertainments.

"At any rate. We're all at this cyber brothel. Some of the ground pounders start saying how it's too bad I can't get in on the play. One thing leads to another and Ryan comes lurching out of one of the rooms, drunk as a Felinezoid with a coffee plantation. He hears this and says it could be done if he could get the parts."

"Oh, Stardust! He attached... and you didn't have one before?"

"Got it, sweetness. That's not all he did. Seems one of the female ground pounders liked it rough, really rough. She broke one of the Luke bots. The squad all got together and bought parts off the thing. I'll never forget it. I was laying in the brothel's maintenance room while Ryan, who was so blasted he needed one of the ground pounders to help him stand, salvaged parts from the Luke. I remember thinking 'this isn't good', but I'd taken a computer virus that temporally blasted my logic systems. What the nova blast did I care?

"I'll give this to Ryan; he knows robotics. Drunk as he was, he had the attachment in place and integrated with my systems in less than an hour. Then he added the arousal response system to my AI. Only one problem, if that's what you want to call it."

"What?" Rowan could almost forget her worries about Ryan if she concentrated on the story.

"Lukes are programmed to take all comers and mimic a strong sex drive. They also have a run speed of one-hundred Standard Cycle Units."

"So?"

"I have a run speed of twelve-thousand SCUs."

Rowan stared at the android, her eyes going wide. "If the Luke wanted sex every two hours...?"

"Every minute, sweetness. More, actually, it was a brothel bot they used for parts."

"Yikes! Why didn't Ryan fix you when he sobered up?"

"Fix me? I don't need fixing. I like sex. I like being functional. No way am I ever letting someone mess with that. It made the next mission a lot more fun for some of the ground pounders. There was this one time that seven of us—"

"Henry, thanks for the story. Some mental images I do not need. I'm curious. What kind of Lubas did Ryan like?"

Rowan bit her lower lip.

Henry smiled. "Let's see. He always ordered a brunette or a redhead. I don't think he ever went for a blonde, and…"

Ryan heard the three warning clicks and stopped working. He was in a kind of passage made by pulling rocks away from the *Star Hawk*'s side and spreading the camouflage tarps over the trench. Sweat cooled on his body as he waited for the satellite to pass. The damaged outer hull was fully exposed.

After what seemed an eternity, the four clicks came. He began spreading a tarp over the damaged hull section, linking its control circuits and power inputs with the ship's. Finishing with the first tarp, he pulled the one over him down and secured it.

Rowan watched Ryan on the big screen. "I hate this. I can't even talk to him."

"Radio silence, sweet thing. Only way to keep Tansy baby off our back." Henry spoke with the nonchalance of a veteran.

On the screen, Ryan began tugging the last tarp down.

Ryan pulled on the tarp. It resisted. He checked the chronograph in his helmet. The satellite was about to make another pass. He heaved. Silently, the rocks on the side of the trench fell in. Ryan tried to leap clear. A rock jammed his legs against the *Star Hawk*'s hull. A boulder slammed into his faceplate, whipping his head back. Lights fizzled and popped in front of his eyes. Other rocks pinned his arms and legs.

"Ryan," screamed Rowan.

"Stardust!" Henry flashed through several pickups before he got an open view of the area.

"I don't see him," said Rowan.

"He's down there."

"Could he have survived?" Fear and hope in equal measure tinged her voice.

"Probably, those suits are tough. We have to get him out of there."

"I'll suit up and dig him out." Forgetting about the lower gravity, Rowan leapt out of the captain's chair and slammed her head into the ceiling.

"Right, that's all I need, a green primitive floundering around in an EVA suit. Forget it, you aren't leaving this ship."

Rowan slumped in the captain's chair. "What can we do? Can we risk a message to see if he's all right?"

"I won't break radio silence until he does."

"I…" Rowan bit her lip in thought. Closing her eyes, she reached with her mind. She could feel the ship's hull, and next to it a protrusion of a similar substance, then rock. "This is life and death, right?"

"Duh, sweetness."

"Ryan said that in the studio, he could enhance my telekinesis. Can you do that here?"

"I can send a pulse to your control pack. I lifted the codes off Ryan's hand-held."

"We'll talk about that breach of trust later." Rowan bit her lip and wrung her hands. "How close is that satellite?"

"It's overhead now. Why?"

"Henry, shut up and boost my telekinesis to maximum, then get ready to fly."

Something in Rowan's demeanour silenced Henry's questions. He simply said, "Full boost now."

Rowan felt her world expand. Matter was simply a

pattern of atoms, spinning subatomic particles and waves flying from atom to atom. She focused on the rock and willed all the subatomic forces to flow in the same direction.

Henry watched as the tons of rock covering the *Star Hawk* blasted toward the stars. The passing satellite was pulverized. Ryan fell away from the ship's side.

"Nova blast!" Henry tapered off Rowan's boost and mobilized all her nano-bots to patch the leaking blood vessels in her brain.

Rowan groaned and slumped unconscious in the captain's chair.

"What in the divine's myriad names happened?" demanded Ryan over the radio.

"Hurry up, boss. Finish patching this puppy, then come in. I'm programming a launch course."

"Rowan—?" began Ryan.

"Is better off if we have stealth! I'll take care of her, Captain."

"I'm almost done." Ryan began securing the last camouflage tarp.

Henry manoeuvred the toaster-sized maintenance bot up by Rowan's head and made sure her airway was clear. At the same time, he triggered a drug in her pack that caused her blood pressure to plummet. "Don't die, sweet thing, please don't die. You're too stardusted shaggable to die."

Ryan rushed onto the bridge. He was still in his EVA suit.

"Oh Rowan, what have you done?" he breathed. He wrestled off his helmet and released the clips holding the top of the suit.

"Cry later, Captain. She'll probably be all right, unless those jerks on the *Saber* get her."

"Scan for the *Saber*."

"It's not on my screens."

"Good." Ryan operated the pilot's console.

"Henry, full stealth. I'm going to stay in the asteroid's shadow… On second thought, belay that. Full speed for the stargate. Does stealth show green?"

"As sexy little otterzoids."

"Good. Yes!" Ryan drummed his fingers against his leg. "I'd normally try to hide in the rubble, throw her off." Ryan launched the ship, then stepped out of the trousers of his EVA suit. "I'm taking Rowan to medical. Oh Divine, Row, please don't stroke out. You can't leave me now." Cradling Rowan like a child, Ryan carried her from the bridge.

THE GAME'S AFOOT

39

Tansy awoke to the beeping of the ship's intercom. "Phil, it's your turn to feed Tracy," she muttered, then rolled over to shake her husband. Coming fully awake, she realized where and when she was.

"Intercom on." She sat up in bed.

"Captain, the probe we left orbiting AS-247 has stopped transmitting. Scans show a mass of rubble has been ejected off the asteroid." The voice of her XO seemed strained.

"What? Scan for any vessels. Change course to bring us to AS-247."

"Aye, ma'am."

The intercom went dead as Tansy pulled on her uniform. "Chandler, you're better than your record. Very nice move, whatever it was. The game isn't over yet."

Gunther crouched behind a row of rose bushes. His mind reached out, gingerly feeling for the thoughts of everyone on the grounds. He made sure to avoid the pool area so that he wouldn't be detected. Finally, he broadcast to the rest of his team.

'Twenty-five in all. Twenty humans, addicted to that accursed drug, four k-no-in and one felinezoid.'

'I count three more in the pool area. One felinezoid and two otterzoids, a male and female.' Gunther looked to where he knew Carl was blending into a hedge near the

pool. The younger man was indistinguishable in the evening light. Gunther sensed the strain in Carl, and that his deeper mind was shielded tight.

Probably still upset about Rowan. I'll have a talk with him later, thought Gunther.

'*They have cameras mounted on the roof. I can't do more than a quick pass and stay out of their field.*' Angel's mental voice was crisp.

'*I've located a robotic defence unit. It came from the ship. It is repaired with human technology. I believe I can take it out, though it will require all my attention,*' announced Toronk's mental voice.

Gunther glanced to where he knew Toronk waited on the perimeter. *Another closed mind. What are they doing to us?*

'*I'm in position to take out two of the k-no-ins on the quiet.*' Fran's mental voice reflected a kind of rage, a need to vent some strong emotion in violence.

'*Beloved?*' Gunther reached for his wife's mind. He encountered walls around all but her surface thoughts, and an underlying sense of sadness.

'*I'm linked into the grid and ready to go.*'

Gunther glanced behind him. In the distance, he could see Willa dressed as a repairperson. She was standing by one of the maintenance junction boxes for the underground lines.

'*Farley, Quinta, you ready?*'

'*Ready.*' The two mental voices coursed.

Gunther looked at the stream that ran across the back of the property. *At least they seem happy.*

Troy watched his screens. He'd given a slight dose of anaesthetic to the antagonists on the Hunoin estate and bumped the adrenaline to Gunther's team.

"At least this is more like classic *Angel Black*, but it's not like them to ignore collateral damage. They must still be torn up about Rowan. Of course, it was only a couple of weeks ago." Troy muttered to himself as the plan began to unfold.

'Now!' Willa heard Gunther's mental voice.

Willa inserted her hand into the utility control grid interface. The input jack locked to the system, and she saw the streams of data in her mind. A second later, a surge of power blasted through the lines on the country estate in front of her.

Angel heard the call and started her attack run across the estate grounds. Lights exploded beneath her in showers of sparks. She ignored them.

"This is for Rowan, you slime!" Angel let go of the bundle in her hands. It smashed through the glass wall of the greenhouse. She swept up and drove herself hard, barely managing to keep ahead of the shock wave that left the greenhouse a mass of shattered glass and twisted framing.

Toronk dove at the many-armed robot as it rushed toward the blast. The machine's left side was jury-rigged human technology. Toronk slammed a steel spike through the relatively weak human-made armour. The robot lashed out with one of its arms as Toronk leapt clear. The felinezoid leapt again as a particle beam slammed into the ground at his feet.

Fran raced amid the showering sparks of exploding lights

and, before they could react, clawed the two k-no-ins patrolling the grounds. The lithium grease started the reaction. She left the aliens to scream and die behind her as she sprinted towards the greenhouse.

Carl crouched behind a knoll as a shower of glass shot over him. He'd covered his ears, so he could still hear when he pulled his hands away. Leaping to his feet, he saw Fran rushing toward the ruin of the pool. He admired her. Her figure was full and lush, and she moved with grace.

"My life isn't a complete mess; oh no, not at all," he muttered as he sprinted to the greenhouse.

Farley leapt out of the stream with Quinta on his back and charged toward the smoking ruin. A felinezoid leapt at them from behind a tree.

Quinta made a grunting noise, and the felinezoid hurtled over them into the water.

"I should—" began Farley.

"Do it. I can get to the battle on my own," said Quinta.

Farley set her down and dove into the stream where the felinezoid was gaining its feet in the metre-deep water. Farley slammed into the alien, dragging it under.

Willa flooded the emergency services with false calls and cut all power to the estate. Disconnecting from the system, she closed the synthetic skin covering her robotic hand and ran towards the house.

Gunther sprinted for the shattered greenhouse A k-no-in

leapt on him from behind. Its weight bore him down, and he felt its clawed feet piercing his skin.

"You are a bad podling! Bad! You disgrace the credits your father paid to conceive you!" The k-no-in looked up at the sound of that voice, straight into its mother's eyes.

"Mother, I..."

"Get over here this instant!" The k-no-in's mother pointed at the ground in front of herself.

The k-no-in guard stepped off Gunther, whose brow was wrinkled with concentration, and stood in front of its mother. It looked at her slacked jawed. "You died... You died. It's a tr-arrrrrr..."

Gunther scrambled to his feet and drove a dagger into the k-no-in.

"Good work, dear." Willa came running up.

"I shouldn't have let it get behind me in the first place." Gunther brushed off his clothes.

"Shall we?" asked Willa.

"For Rowan!" Gunther nodded.

"For Rowan!" The husband and wife raced towards the shattered building.

Angel flew a circuit around the estate. Most of the human servants were milling about in confusion. Angel swooped down in front of them, leaving her wings unfurled.

"Get to the street; don't come back until after the police have left," she ordered.

"Our fix," cried one burly man with curly, brown hair.

"Get it later. Now move, if you value your lives."

The human rabble glanced back and forth between their number, then broke toward the road at a run. Angel leapt into the air and started for the greenhouse. Something caught her eye.

Stransy ducked out of the foam hutch that floated in the middle of the pool. He'd been taking a nap, and the hutch had cushioned the explosion's effect.

'*Hunoin, Hunoin,*' he called in his panicked thoughts. There was no reply. Focusing his mind, he searched for his wife and finally caught a whisper of thought. Diving to the bottom of their pool, he found a pile of wreckage that had been part of the greenhouse's roof. Under an aluminum strut, Hunoin lay unconscious. With a strength born of desperation, Stransy gripped the fallen support.

<hr />

"Have to make it interesting," mumbled Troy. He increased Stransy's adrenaline equivalent.

Stransy heaved against the fallen support. His body screamed with the effort, then the support shifted. Hunoin floated free. Ignoring the felinezoid that struggled to get free, Stransy grabbed his floating mate and pulled her into their hutch. He sat caressing Hunoin's fur as the felinezoid's thoughts grew feeble, then went silent.

<hr />

Carl slipped into the pool area. The blast had left rubble everywhere. A dome made of foam floated in the middle of the pool. A middle-aged, Filipino-looking woman stood in the doorway of the house, blinking stupidly at the destruction.

"Get out of here!" yelled Carl.

"But the mistress... My fix?" she countered.

"Party's over! We're the narcs. Get out of here, now!"

The woman looked at Carl, standing naked except for a pair of running shoes, then disappeared into the house as Fran ran up.

"Where are they?" Fran scanned the destruction.

"I don't know. I..." Carl felt himself go rigid. All the guilt, all the mixed emotions and fears of the last few days bubbled up in him. He tried to lock them out, use the mental discipline Gunther had taught him, but it was too much.

Fran felt herself go pink, then pale. She felt such guilt. She'd betrayed her friend and her lover in one move, with an alien. She felt sick and couldn't focus her thoughts.

Neither of them noticed a small, mahogany body climb onto the deck. Stransy held a knife in his webbed hand and wore a look of intense concentration. He moved towards Carl.

"I've been unfaithful," blurted Carl and Fran.

Stransy made to slash Carl's ankle.

"No, you don't," snapped Gunther.

Stransy clutched his head as Willa rushed him. With a savage kick, Willa sent the otterzoid flying halfway across the pool.

"With who, when?" Carl and Fran again spoke in unison.

"Deal with it later. We have to get Hunoin," ordered Gunther.

Willa released a sigh of relief. "Where is that murdering filth?"

Gunther closed his eyes and probed with his mind.

Toronk drove his knife into an optic sensor on the robot, then grabbed the last of the human technology arms on its side and pulled. The joint held for less than a second. The robot spun around. Toronk found himself thrown to the ground. His leg twisted. There was a snap, and a sick, nauseous feeling flooded his senses. His foe moved closer. A jet of water fell against the robot's side panels damaged by Toronk's attack. The machine started to smoke, then spun crazily. Toronk glanced up to see Angel hovering above them, holding a garden hose.

With a snarl, Toronk balanced on his good leg and leapt at the robot. He grasped a damaged maintenance panel and tore it open before the machine threw him aside.

Angel directed the water against the robot's inner workings. It bucked and sparked, then was still.

Dropping the hose, Angel landed and ran to Toronk.

"Are you all right?" she asked.

"More or less." Toronk pulled away and inspected his lower leg. The foot twisted at an impossible angle and white bone protruded through an ugly gash.

"We need to get you out of here. I'll bring the van."

"No, the battle is not yet won."

"We have to take care of you. You're wounded."

"Help the others. I am unimportant."

Fire flashed in Angel's eyes. "Don't you ever say that to me. You're my one and only. I love you. Stay here while I get the van." Angel leapt into the air.

"One and only..." Toronk hung his head.

Farley grappled the felinezoid and held it under the water. The alien had managed to get in a couple of claw rakes, but now its strength was spent. It scrambled for Farley's eyes but missed. The felinezoid opened its mouth, and a stream of bubbles escaped. It tried to inhale, thrashed for a second, then was still. Farley hauled the unprotesting body under a deadfall. When he left the stream, blood poured from the wound in his arm, and he felt chilled. He staggered towards the greenhouse.

Quinta scuttled across the estate grounds. She'd never walked this far at one time, and it was very uncomfortable. Reaching the field of shattered glass, she picked her way around the pieces.

"Over here," hissed a voice.

Quinta turned to look for its source. She spotted a k-no-in behind a line of bushes.

"It's no good. They caught us by surprise, I think everyone's dead. I didn't know the officers managed to call for help," said the k-no-in.

"I came as quickly as I could."

"We have to get out of here before they find us. It was stupid to kill Rowan, they've been insane ever since."

"Go back the way I came. There should be others following me. I have to find out what's going on."

"Your death feast!" The k-no-in started toward the stream.

Quinta cocked her head to one side as an injector dart slipped out of the utility belt she wore around her waist. A second later it drove into the k-no-in. The alien had time to look surprised before it died.

"That's for helping to kidnap me!" Quinta resumed picking her way around the shattered glass.

⌖⟶

Gunther felt for Hunoin's mind. "She's in the hutch. She's—"

The hutch exploded, sending foam flying in all directions. Hunoin now stood on a foam raft in the middle of the pool.

Gunther, Carl and Fran all clutched their throats.

"You could have lived, but no, you had to oppose us. You—" Hunoin's control lapsed as she focused on the plant pot that flew at her head. Gunther, Fran and Carl all caught a precious breath.

"Ah yes, the cyborg. Your trachea is made of sterner stuff than I can crush, half machine."

"You poisoned my daughter, you bitch!" Willa heaved more rubble at the otterzoid. Stransy scrambled onto the raft by his mate.

"Let me deal with this one for you, my love," hissed the male otterzoid.

Willa cried out. She felt such guilt and shame about her

and Carl. She loved Gunther, but she loved Carl as well. She was torn in two! She was betraying both of them and lying to the one man who had never lied to her. She wanted to sob out her pain.

Hunoin once more tightened her grip on Gunther, Fran and Carl's throats.

"Now you die," she said before she was picked up and slammed into the pool deck.

"You killed my Dagna! You die, PUP EATER!" Quinta stood in the shattered doorway. Her coat was dusty, and her sides heaved. Her face was pure determination.

"NO!" Stransy tried to clutch at Quinta's mind. Gunther intercepted the thrust as Quinta threw Hunoin onto the pool deck. Quinta had her foe in the air once more when she felt herself lifted off the ground and hurled toward a support pillar.

Carl leapt, catching Quinta and turning, so he took the worst of the impact. Hunoin slammed into the pool deck at Fran's feet. Fran grabbed the otterzoid. It was like her arm was tied with weights as she squeezed its windpipe closed.

Gunther fought Stransy. In a second, debates flashed between them.

'She isn't yours, your mate has been unfaithful,' projected Stransy.

'Too little too late! I knew about that. Now taste the truth of your existence.'

Gunther flashed his full knowledge of reality into the otterzoid's mind.

'NOOOO! IT'S A LIE, IT CAN'T BE, IT'S A LIE.' Stransy's mental scream was agonizing.

'You have nothing to live for. And now, no one to live for.' Gunther forced the otterzoid's eyes around so that he could witness Fran as she snapped Hunoin's neck and let the carcass drop to the floor.

"NO!" wailed Stransy, then he collapsed on the raft.

"Is that it?" Carl scrambled to his feet.

Gunther scanned his enemy's mind. "His will is broken. We'll have to pick up the pieces. Rowan is avenged!"

"Doesn't bring her back." Willa hung her head.

"No, it doesn't."

Willa nearly fell into Gunther's arms. "Beloved, I have something I have to tell you."

"I know."

"You know?" Willa looked at him shocked.

"About you and that male stripper the night of your doe... I've always known, why do you think I got so moody for a couple of weeks before our wedding? I forgave you for that long ago. Now, let's get this mess cleaned up before the police arrive."

Willa looked into her husband's face. The acceptance, the love, the forgiveness were too much. She formed a sentence in her mind, then a voice intruded.

"Hi guys, I see you started without me. Could I get a little help here?" Farley leaned against what was left of the doorframe, blood pouring from his arm.

"Farley!" cried Quinta.

The young man began to fall. A cushion of telekinetic force lowered him gently to the floor. Quinta was at his side before anyone else moved.

"Oh, Divine!" Willa applied direct pressure to the wound.

'Angel, we need the med-kit at the pool,' snapped Gunther's thoughts.

'Toronk's hurt. I'll be there as soon as I can,' came the mental reply.

"Carl, Fran, check the house, gauze, clean sheets, towels, anything you can find. This night's not over yet."

THE PRINCE'S KISS

Ryan stood in the medical bay. His gaze darted from instructions on his hand-held to a diagnostic monitor, identical to the one in Kadar's clinic, over Rowan's bed. The room was twenty metres long by five across. Three medical cots occupied one end of it. The rest was full of trees. A partially constructed wall obscured part of the back of the room.

"Come on, Rowan! Don't leave me." Hands trembling, he set down his hand-held and extracted a tube of liquid from a compartment under the medical cot. He attached it to the IV that fed into Rowan's arm, then picked up his hand-held and continued to read.

"Boss." Henry's voice reflected concern.

"Yes?" said Ryan.

"The *Saber* is at AS-247."

"Are we still pulling for the stargate?"

"Aye, we're going to have to start slowing down soon, or we'll be over speed for a safe insertion."

"Nova blast the speed limit! And nova blast the bastards who made her do this to herself!" Ryan slammed his fist on a countertop.

"Bad?" Henry already knew the answer from his link with the medical systems.

"The nano-bots repaired the leaking blood vessels, and the drugs have stopped the cascade die-off effect in her brain cells. It all depends on how many died. What were you thinking giving her that much boost?"

"She asked me to. She had to save you, boss. Whether you want to admit it or not, you're as important to her as she is to you. More in some ways. She's like a baby in our galaxy. All shagging aside, she needs you to teach her until she gets a handle on things. She couldn't lose you."

"I can see that."

"And she's falling in love with you. You know that, don't you?"

Ryan grinned. "What a schoolboy fantasy. Run away with your favourite e-star and fall in love. I wish it was all hearts and flowers." He moved to Rowan's side and took her hand.

"What about our velocity? We don't want a Republic charge for violating flight safety regs."

Ryan stared into Rowan's face. "What's the current punishment for a level one speeding offence through a gate?"

"Five thousand Galactic credits or one half per cent of your species average life expectancy indentured servitude. Excepting immortals, we have a standard Valsalyen year sentence. That's about eleven Earth Standard years."

"What's the maximum speed that keeps it to level one?"

"Fifty thousand kilometres a standard hour for gate transit."

"Fine, work out our plot so that we hit the gate at forty-seven-thousand kilometres an hour. We want to leave some margin for safety. I'll pay the fine."

"With what?" demanded Henry.

"I still have orange oil and coffee. Who knows, maybe the Switchboard authorities will let me sweet-talk them." A tired smile flashed across Ryan's face.

"Revising flight plan, Captain."

Tansy stared at the bridge screen, which showed a crater on AS-247, and shook her head. "Must be a ground-pounder thing."

"He pulled a stunt like that on planet. He hid his heat signature by pulling in against a geothermal generating station." Mildred stood by the command chair.

"Very sneaky; gutsy too. He could have further damaged his hull. How did he dig out so fast? Those rocks represent tons of matter. They just blasted away."

"Rowan," suggested Chow. He stood on the other side of the command chair.

"The girl? What could she have done?" Tansy's voice was like honey; her finger traced up and down the line of her throat as she thought.

Chow looked at her, then focused his eyes on the main screen. "You don't experience *Angel Black*, do you, ma'am?"

"I prefer to choose what I'm going to feel in a given situation. Come to think of it, my daughter likes the program. She was telling me... what was it...?" Tansy's face lit up as she tapped her chin. "Alien abilities."

"Rowan is a powerful telekinetic," blurted Mildred.

"They managed to do that? I thought otterzoid abilities would burn out a human brain."

"It takes a lot of after insertion work to keep her operational. During a kinetic burst, she does brain damage. An effort like moving those rocks might have killed her." Mildred looked directly at Tansy as if daring her to say something.

"What a sick, sad universe we live in." Tansy shook her head, then turned her attention to her navigator. "Scan the debris. Is there any sign of the *Star Hawk*?"

The navigator turned to his instruments. "No, ma'am. No deviations to suggest a hidden mass. It would be easy to hide though."

"Scan any bodies that would give an intercept trajectory from AS-247 to the stargate at the time of the probe's destruction."

"Ma'am, the planet Puuu is in that group. Even at full

pull, the *Star Hawk* wouldn't cause a noticeable deviation in a planetary orbit."

"Again with the guessing. Did he go this way or that way? Of course, if his lady love needed medical attention..." Tansy pulled her hand-held from her pocket and opened it. She smiled.

"What is it, ma'am?" asked Chow.

"Chandler only took the minimum medical courses he needed to work a combat mission. His studio records show that he hasn't enhanced his skills in that regard since he retired." Tansy leaned back in her chair and smiled. "Helm, set course for the stargate, best possible speed."

"I told the attending that Farley was mauled by a cougar." Fran stood by Gunther's couch where Toronk lay with his leg immobilized by splints and a dressing over his wound. Willa stood by the leg, running her left hand over the injury. A cable connected her right hand to a laptop computer on the coffee table. On the screen, an X-ray image of the broken bones was displayed. Angel knelt on the floor by the big felinezoid's head and stroked his brow.

"Good, any trouble explaining the IV?" Gunther didn't take his eyes off the laptop's screen.

"He assumed the paramedics had done it along with the pressure dressings."

Gunther nodded. "Toronk, we should take you to the hospital. At the very least call a veterinarian. I'm a psychiatrist. It's been a long time since I did my surgical rotation. Also, I don't know what our drugs might do to you."

"I cannot risk exposure. The panic of your people would kill far more than the pirates will."

Gunther closed his eyes and thought. *Would they want to kill Toronk? Two deaths on a show in short order. What do they want?*

Gunther opened his eyes. "I'll have to align the bones and put a plate in to hold them while they knit. I have the equipment in my treatment room. I don't know which drugs—"

"I can help there." Willa pulled her hand away from Toronk's leg.

"Love?" asked Gunther.

"I accessed some of Amitose's medical files and cross-referenced the formulas with the Merck manual. It's a little project of mine. I can tell you which human drugs are safe for felinezoids and their effects."

"Have I told you lately how amazing you are?" Gunther shifted over and kissed his wife. "Now, all we need is a competent surgeon. Sadly, I guess I'll have to do."

Carl and Quinta pushed the attack robot into the back of Farley's van and closed the door.

"Is that everything?" Quinta sounded worried.

"We still have to get the body in the stream. Don't worry, Farley will be all right. Gunther said so."

"I should have stayed with him."

"Then, the rest of us might have lost. Quinta, I've been at this alien…" Carl shifted uncomfortably. "Excuse the expression. I've been fighting this battle for a long time. Can I give you a bit of advice?"

"Yes, I will listen."

"Learn from your mistakes, but don't second guess your decisions."

Quinta nodded, then scuttled to the van's passenger door.

Ryan watched the screen over Rowan's bed. He'd done everything possible. Her nano-bots were removing dead brain cells and clotted blood. At the same time, chemicals were stimulating the stem cells from her latest after insertion maintenance to divide and repair the damage.

"A real doctor could do so much more. Please hold on, Row. We'll find a way, somehow. Hold on."

Almost fearfully, Ryan lifted the oxygen mask from her lips and gently kissed her before replacing it. A tear glistened in the corner of his eye, and he turned to wipe it away.

Henry watched his screen and saw the kiss. The section of his ram he'd dedicated to monitoring Rowan told him that she was ready. The healing was far from complete, but she was on the border of regaining consciousness. He released a trickle of stimulant into her blood.

Great for dramatic effect, he told himself.

Ryan didn't see the blip of beta rhythm on the screen's EEC.

"Ryan." Rowan's voice was small.

"Rowan." Ryan spun around and hugged her.

"I feel awful. My head feels like someone stuffed it with cotton wool."

"It's a nova blasted fairy tale," commented Henry from the wall speaker. He stilled the slight stimulant feed.

Ryan let her go and backed off enough to look her in the eyes. "Promise me you won't ever do anything like that again."

Rowan smiled wearily. "You don't go getting yourself caught in a landslide again."

Ryan hugged her, then checked her monitors. Everything was in the green.

"I need to get to the bridge and check everything, then I

have to—"

"Get some sleep. You look awful. How long was I out?" Rowan tried to sit up and failed.

"Sixteen hours, hottie. And captain courageous here hasn't slept in going on twenty-four."

"Ryan, go to bed. I'd offer to join you, but I don't think I'm up to it."

"Girl's right, boss. Get some sleep. You'll need all you got tomorrow. The *Saber* is pulling away from AS-247 towards the stargate. They're trying to cut us off."

"Will they reach it first?" Rowan slumped back onto the bed.

"You betcha, hottie." Henry purged the stimulant from Rowan's system.

Rowan smiled. "We all better get some rest. I…" She slipped into normal sleep.

"Henry, do you think she'll be…"

"Hottie boss, she's schedule red. One good thing about you orange and red types, you heal fast. By tomorrow she'll be up and ready to shag."

"Thanks, Henry. I will turn in. Tomorrow, for better or worse, we reach the stargate."

HALF TRUTHS

41

Gunther drew the suture through Toronk's flesh. Except for the extensive shaving, the surgery had been much like working on a human. Toronk lay on an ambulance gurney in Gunther's basement. Half of the area had been set up as a treatment room with portable medical equipment. An EKG displayed the three-point rhythm of the alien's heart. Angel sat by the felinezoid's head, pressing the button on a respirator every five seconds. Fran stood on the far side of the room, beside a workbench cluttered with electrical gear, staring at Angel and Toronk. She hugged herself despite the warmth of the room.

Willa stood by her husband, serving as his sterile nurse.

"And that does it. Pass me the antibiotic ointment, please." Gunther snipped the thread on the last stitch and put his tools in the grunge bucket.

"I'll never know how you do that," remarked Willa.

"I had to learn to get through my surgical rotation. I'm not going to plaster the break for now. I want that wound to get some oxygen. The plate I put in will hold the bones aligned."

"Is he going to be all right?" Angel sounded on the edge of tears.

"As long as you keep breathing for him." Gunther began spreading antibiotic ointment over Toronk's wound.

Willa watched the digital display on the wall flip over to

four o'clock. The world outside was dark and silent. The dimmed, living room lights left a gloom that matched her mood. The only sounds came from the muffled voices in the kitchen.

"Will Fran still be willing to pay Carl's husband price? Some of the females of my species demand that their husband be a virgin even if the female has taken casual lovers herself." Quinta sat on the couch beside Willa. The otterzoid didn't need telepathy to sense the older woman's agitation.

"We don't have a husband price, Quinta. In earlier times a bride received a dowry because once she married, she was no longer in line to inherit a share of her family's wealth."

"Very strange. I do like the independence in your species' males. I never liked males who couldn't make decisions. Now my littermate, Rosla, she likes her males dumb and dependent. She thinks males are only good for bringing home the fish and pleasuring her on the breeding mat. Her husband never had a thought in his life. Nice enough person, but head with the contents of a bubble."

Willa smiled. "Sounds like our species have a lot in common. Rowan…" She hung her head.

"I'm sorry, I did not mean to open recent wounds." Quinta groomed her muzzle.

"It's not your fault. I think you and Rowan would have liked each other."

"I regret I did not have the chance to make her acquaintance. If she was anything like her mother, I'm sure she was extraordinary."

Willa's lips trembled into a smile as the kitchen door flew open. Fran, red-faced with eyes flashing, stormed across the floor.

"You old slut! You want him, you can have him! How could you do this to me? How could you do this to that sweet, gentle husband of yours?" Fran stormed from the house.

Carl exited the kitchen. "We broke up," was all he said as he crossed the living room and went out the door.

Quinta looked at Willa and groomed her whiskers.

"Aren't you going to comment?" Willa hung her head.

Quinta turned her head to one side. "My littermates from my mother's second litter bear a striking resemblance to her friend Sanla. Our species are much alike. I do not judge. You do have decisions to make, and make them quickly you should."

Willa looked into the beady eyes of the alien and saw a friend. "Thanks. You're right, it's... I know what I have to do. Gunther is the love of my life. I don't even know how things started with Carl. When I'm with him, it's like I'm an animal in heat."

"Love of the soul, or love of flesh. Is Gunther deficient in your flesh needs?"

"No! Quinta, that's..." Willa looked indignant, then thoughtful. "A very good and fair question for a friend to ask. Gunther is a wonderful lover. It's just..."

"New, novel, fresh, exciting. A freshly killed fish always tastes best, but one grows tired of the fare quickly and wishes to wait and add spices. You know what you need to do."

"Yes, I do. Thank you, Quinta."

Quinta made a little hissing noise through her nose.

"Did Carl and Fran work things out?" Gunther climbed the stairs from the basement.

"Not really, they separated. Is Toronk—"

"Breathing on his own now. It's been a long night. I'm going to bed."

"I'll be right up." Willa stood. "Quinta, feel free to use the spare room. I'm going to bed, with my husband, who I love."

Quinta released a hissing noise as Willa walked away.

"They're past us and braking hard," commented Henry.

"The stealth is holding." Ryan sat at the pilot's station, staring into the main screen.

"I've calculated their position. It looks like they're going to loop around the gate. Just outside coelenteratezoid controlled space. What good will that do them? They can't see us." Rowan sat at the navigator's station.

"Dusting the region. She knows her stuff," observed Ryan.

"Could someone translate for the primitive in the room?" Rowan sounded embarrassed.

"For the civilian, sweetness. Unless you were space services, you wouldn't get that one. Imagine a handsome android lightly sprinkling your naked body with glitter. I know I will." Henry licked his lips and made a growling sound.

"HENRY!" Ryan and Rowan shouted in unison.

"Divine! I wish you'd let me alter the runtime on your sex drive." Ryan shook his head.

"I still don't get what they're doing," said Rowan.

"It works like this, sweet thing. Hydrogen and other gases build up around stargates because of the amount of ship traffic. The amount of gas is minuscule by planetary standards but dense for the void. They're using their tractor beams to pull all the space dust to them. They ionize it, then leave it in a sphere around the gate. The ions will either be attracted to our hull, like a nympho to an orgy, or repelled, like a—" began Henry.

"All colourful analogies aside. The *Saber*'s sensors are sensitive enough to monitor the random deflections of the gas molecules. While they can't see us, they can see the gas, and will know exactly where we are."

"So... even an invisible horse kicks up dust," observed Rowan.

"Exactly. If they grab us with a tractor beam, they could deflect our course enough that we miss the gate and have to loop around. Or they might blow us up, though I think

Captain Denardo will avoid doing that. Up until now she's, more or less, tried to take us alive." Ryan stroked his chin.

"Why would she care? I mean...." Rowan silenced when Ryan flipped open his hand-held.

Ryan read a part of Captain Denardo's file he'd only skimmed before. "She's out to take us alive."

"Why?" asked Henry.

"Her heart isn't in the chase. She doesn't believe in what she's doing. She's an officer, and she hates to lose. She's still dangerous, but she'd rather not hurt us. She thinks we're human."

"Don't be insulting!" Henry swivelled his chair, so he looked away from Ryan.

"I have an idea. If you need me, I'll be in my workshop." Ryan left the bridge.

"What's he planning?" Rowan turned her chair to watch the door close.

"Who in the divine's myriad names knows? Something that's likely to get us all killed. That would be his style." Henry swivelled his chair back and looked at Rowan.

"Surprising that he never quite manages it." Rowan had heat in her voice.

Henry sounded sardonic. "Give him time!"

Gunther answered the door to find Carl standing there.

"Gunther... I thought you'd be at work," said the younger man.

"I called in sick. After last night, I needed the rest. Did you want to speak with Willa?"

Carl shifted about nervously.

"This is not good." Troy watched Carl's readouts. The guilt, discomfort and fear were almost beyond the system's limits.

"It is excellent! The audience will devour the sexual variety, and we can edit down the negative emotional intensity." John stood in the back of the control room.

"Sir, won't they dislike the disruption to the relationship stability? People loved the Gunther-Willa relationship."

"The audience will like what I tell them to like!"

"Yes, sir."

Gunther sat on the couch, facing Carl.

"I heard that you and Fran broke up." Gunther's voice was soothing, kind.

"It's all my fault. I..." Carl buried his face in his hands.

"Seems to me you both made mistakes. Look, Carl, I don't condone what you did, but you're young, you're bound to make mistakes. Maybe you and Fran can patch it up."

"I don't think so. I... Well... I cheated with..." Carl looked up, his eyes full of guilt, fear and pain.

"I don't need to know. I can assume it's someone Fran was close with. It's in the past. Carl, if you can forgive her, she can forgive you. There's been too much disruption in all our lives these last few weeks." Gunther looked at the floor.

"I loved her too."

"I know, like a sister."

Carl nodded.

Gunther looked Carl in the eye. "I'm going to tell you something I never did before. I always wished that you and Rowan would get together. It would have been nice to have you in the family. Carl... In many ways, you've been the son that I never had. You're a dear friend. I want you to know that no matter what, I'm here for you."

"Oh, Divine!" Carl buried his face in his hands and began to sob. Mistaking the cause, Gunther put a fatherly arm around the younger man.

Rowan watched the stargate on the big screen. It was thoroughly unimpressive, a ring of dark material with a starscape dominated by a single bright star in its centre.

"Henry, any change with the *Saber*?" Ryan operated the pilot's console, keeping their undamaged side facing the line ship.

"Nothing."

Rowan glanced at her console. "They'll be at the far point of their patrol in thirty seconds, and... The monitor for matter density jumped."

"Rowan, if we went in a straight line, from here, would we encounter the stargate?"

Rowan checked her console, then she and Henry answered in unison. "No."

"Thank you both. I asked the navigator. Henry, open the front airlock please." Ryan changed the big screen's view to take in the *Saber*.

"Hatch is open. Your do-hick is away."

"Good." Ryan shifted their course, so they edged closer to the *Saber*. "Rowan, check the sensors, what's the ionization of the gas molecules, positive or negative?"

Rowan fumbled over the unfamiliar section of her console and a few seconds later said, "Negative."

Ryan smiled. "When we get away, you'll have time to finish the course." Pressing a switch on the communications console, he returned to the pilot's chair.

"When?" said Rowan.

"I've got some tricks up my sleeve." Ryan's smile was not pleasant.

"We're gonna die! Could I cop a feel first?" said Henry.

Tansy sat in her command chair and waited. It was after her shift's end. She could almost feel her opponent. She could sense that the hours they'd spent attracting and ionizing gas particles were about to pay off.

"Navigator?" she asked.

"Nothing, ma'am. I... Ma'am, the gas molecules at one-twenty-five flat by fifty-seven high are shifting. They seem to be attracted to a mobile point."

"I see you, Captain Chandler. Pilot, full acceleration, get us behind that disturbance."

"Aye, ma'am."

"Communications, inform the boarding squad to get ready. Tell Major Tallman that she is invited to join me on the bridge."

"Aye."

Tansy felt the pull of her ship's acceleration. Adrenaline surged, and she felt exhilarated.

⌖⟶⬦

"Once we reach coelenteratezoid controlled space it's on to the Switchboard Station for some quick repairs, then to Geb," said Ryan.

"The *Saber* is heading straight for your do-hick. What, in the divine's myriad names, is that thing?" demanded Henry.

"Henry, think. The *Saber* isn't watching for us, it's watching for shifts in the gas molecules. What do negative ions like?"

"Positive ions. It's a decoy, an ion generator to give a strong trail," answered Rowan.

"Smart and beautiful," said Ryan.

"That trick was old when humans were still shagging in the treetops. She won't fall for it." Henry looked disgusted.

"Captain Denardo probably won't, but she won't be the one manning the navigation sensors. That's probably some reservist. If we're lucky, they've never seen combat." Ryan adjusted the piloting controls. "I don't like turning our bad side to her, but it can't be helped, changing aspect could create eddies."

Tansy stroked her finger down the side of her throat. "Navigator, what's the speed on that disturbance?"

Lieutenant Barns looked up. "Fifty-five-thousand kilometres per hour, ma'am."

"Fifty-five. Could a Hawk decelerate to legal stargate entry speeds in the distance they have left?" Standing, she moved behind her navigator.

"No, ma'am. That's odd." He double-checked his instruments.

"What's odd?" demanded Captain Denardo.

"On its current trajectory, the *Star Hawk* will miss the gate completely."

"Lieutenant, scan the area for another disturbance. Pilot, stall our forward momentum and be ready to move. Gunnery, fire on that target with a tracking missile."

"Aye, ma'am."

"You're going to blow him up?" Mildred moved to the captain's side.

"One missile won't destroy a Hawk, unless you're very lucky, and I don't think that's the *Star Hawk*. Chandler relies on his opponent's weaknesses. That's the pattern that pervades all his strategies. It took me a while to see it. Our weakness is that most of the crew are no-experience reservists. My weakness is I'm used to working with experienced line personnel. He's trying to exploit that. I hope we catch him alive, this is one man I want to play chess against. He has a pair of steel ones."

"Stardust, they flew right by us," gasped Henry.

"Hopefully they keep going." Ryan adjusted the screen to track the *Saber*.

"We're on target for the stargate, but we're too fast," said Rowan.

"I'll pay the fine… Nova blast, they're stopping!"

All eyes focused on the big screen. "They launched a missile," announced Henry.

"Henry, warm up the weapons systems; prepare to drop stealth. On my command, divert all stealth power to the guns."

"We can't win a slugging match!" objected Henry.

"No. But we can make them remember the *Star Hawk*."

"We will never forget." Henry's voice was grave.

"How long to coelenteratezoid controlled space?" Ryan moved to the weapons system and shut down the safety locks.

"Thirty minutes, Captain." Rowan looked at her lover, grim-faced as he worked, and knew at that moment, there was no other name for him.

"Thirty minutes," Ryan repeated as the weapons charged.

INTO THE BREACH DEAR FRIENDS

42

"**W**ell?" demanded Captain Denardo.

"Ma'am… There's another line of deviation about five hundred kilometres away."

"Right under our noses! Helm, bring us along their line. Weapons, prepare the tractor beam. Helm, on my command, lock the drive lasers on the *Star Hawk* and activate at 30 per cent. At the same time do a 10 per cent pull to port. Focus the rest of the energy aft. They're moving at a good speed, so we need to pull them off trajectory to make them miss the gate. I also want to slow them down."

"Aye, ma'am," the two officers echoed.

"She's hot and heavy on us, boss, and not in the way I'd like."

"Henry, until we get out of this system, could you please can it." Ryan had returned to the pilot's seat. "Rowan, how's our course for the stargate?"

"Dead centre. We're still too fast."

"I'm sure Captain Denardo will help us dump velocity."

The *Star Hawk* shook. G-forces pulled everyone forward against the inertial restraints.

"See," gasped Ryan. "Henry, kill the drives."

Rowan felt the G-forces lessen.

"Henry, kill the stealth. Divert everything to weapons."

"Aye, sir." The android's voice was as crisp as any parade ground sergeant's.

"I'm sorry I have to do this." Ryan pulled a sheet out from under Henry's chair and threw it over him.

Henry shook his head.

"Rowan, are we still moving toward the stargate?"

"They're pulling us off course. We're still in tolerance and moving forward. We're slowing fast."

"Good. The longer it goes on like this, the closer to our goal we get. Henry, open a line to the *Saber*."

"Hide me under a blanket like I'm something to be ashamed of. Won't even let me watch when you shag. Now you want communications. You're lucky you're so nova blasted sexy." Henry opened the channel and at the same time sent a high-speed feed of his own to a nondescript relay satellite on the edge of coelenteratezoid space.

Tansy sat in her chair and watched as the *Star Hawk* shimmered into view on her screen.

"He did take damage. Those are camo-tarps on his port side," observed Mildred.

"Captain, Captain Chandler is sending us a message," said the communications officer.

"Put it on screen."

The screen filled with the image of the *Star Hawk*'s bridge. Ryan stood in front of his captain's chair in a lopsided way that indicated the pull of G-forces slipping past his ship's inertial dampers. A lump of cloth occupied the computer station. Rowan could be seen in the navigator's position.

"Hello, Captain Chandler. My compliments. You've led us a merry chase. I'm afraid I'm no longer authorized to offer you immunity."

"Captain Denardo, given the juncture, please call me

Ryan. By the way, hello Mildred, it's been a while." Ryan smiled.

"Is that all you have to say for yourself? You stole studio property! You—"

"Watch who you're calling property!" Rowan stood up and glared out of the screen.

"Major! I apologize for..."

"Rowan! I apologize for..."

Captain Denardo and Ryan spoke in unison. For a moment, they smiled at each other.

"Please, call me Tansy, Ryan. As I said, the offer of immunity has been revoked."

"I wasn't calling for that. A crew lives together or dies together. I am going to ask you to pretend that we made it over the border before you locked onto us. I know you dislike the way things are for clones. Why not let this one slide? For your daughter's sake."

Tansy smiled and played her finger the length of her throat. "I wish I could. You understand, orders. How did you know about Tracy?"

"It was in your record. I really can't tell you how I got hold of it. I'm sure you understand."

"Of course. Fleet will have to do a security review. One moment, please." Tansy cut the sound.

"Tell Lieutenant Chow to prepare for boarding. We'll be docking in three minutes." Tansy reactivated the connection.

Tansy closed the connection.

"Henry, this is it. You have the schematic, target their tractor beams first. Then their forward grav-laser drive, then their sensors, and last their weapons. As soon as the grav-lasers are off us, I'll do full pull to bottom, then correct for the deviation. Rowan, what's our speed?"

"We're at forty-three thousand kilometres per hour and

dropping. With luck, we'll even be at legal insertion speeds."

"Owww baby, like it slow, do you?" quipped Henry.

"Henry!" said Ryan.

"It was too good an opening to let pass."

"Focus, we'll only get one shot at this. Tansy came up through the piloting ranks. She probably doesn't know that you can knock up a weapons control circuit. She won't be expecting us to be armed. Henry, be careful. I don't want you to hit any of the habitation zones. These are Space Service Troops, none of them dies by our hands."

"Aye, sir!"

"Ensign Abouagina, reopen the channel." Tansy smiled grimly at the bridge's vid pickup. "I'm sorry about that, the burdens of command."

"I have to say, the game was well played. You almost had me with those rocks," said Ryan.

"You got away though. That was sneaky. Will you open your airlock? I'd rather not damage your ship. I have some friends who would be interested in using her as a museum."

"You'll blow the lock once you latch on if I don't." Ryan glanced at the piloting console. They were within a half a kilometre of the other ship.

"Orders." Tansy shrugged.

"Well, Tansy, you seem a nice person. Mildred, would you give John a message for me?"

"Of course." Mildred glared moodily at the screen.

"Tell him he's a nova blasted idiot with delusions of adequacy!"

The *Star Hawk* fired on the unsuspecting *Saber*.

Tansy felt a shudder run through her ship. "What is going on?"

"Ma'am, they've opened fire on us! Missiles and particle beams. Both forward tractor ports disabled. Forward drive disabled," said the engineer.

"Ma'am, they're pulling away," called the navigator.

Henry fired, aimed and fired again as fast as the system could manage, his AI abilities a thousand times faster and more accurate than a human's.

"Activating drives, hold on to your hats." Ryan threw himself into the pilot's chair.

"Don't go too far, or we'll miss our window for the stargate," cautioned Rowan.

"Warn me off."

"Their forward drives and tractor beams are off-line." Henry kept firing.

Ryan targeted the grav-laser's pull forward and watched on his screen as Henry continued to bull's-eye turrets on the *Saber*.

"Sensors are down. I've started on the turrets." As Henry spoke, three particle-beam projectors melted on the screen.

"Activate stealth. Stop shooting, it gives away our position," ordered Ryan.

"Fire all weapons," ordered Captain Denardo.

"They've hit our bottom launch tubes and beam emitters. How could they be armed? Where'd they get a control circuit?" asked the engineer.

"Ma'am, they've activated stealth," said the navigator.

"Turn us one-eighty degrees. Get a lock with the aft sensor array, damage control teams prioritize the tractor beams and drives. Casualty reports?" snapped Tansy.

"No casualties, ma'am," reported the communications officer.

"No... Who in the divine's myriad names do they have for a gunner?" Tansy watched her big screen. "Have you got a lock on them?"

"No, ma'am. They're close enough that we can spot them even with stealth. I need a little time."

"All those niceties! He kept me talking because we were heading in the direction he wanted. Ryan, you are very good!"

"If you're through getting wet over our quarry," snapped Mildred.

Tansy lightly drummed her fingers against her throat. "Navigator?"

"Ma'am, it takes time."

"Pilot. Follow their last known trajectory."

⌖⟶⬦

Ryan changed the drive laser's pull; the *Star Hawk* shuddered. "That should throw them off. They'd not expect us to slow down when we're this close. Now we stay in their blind spot and coast on in."

Rowan checked her boards. "Suppose they turn around?"

"Then we turn with them."

"Excuse me. The ugly cousin here. Could somebody get this nova blasted sheet off my head?" demanded Henry.

At a nod from Ryan, Rowan got up and pulled the sheet away.

"Do you... HEY! Watch that hand, or I'll break it off, buster!" yelled Rowan, going red in the face.

"I'm so unappreciated," snuffled the android with an unapologetic gleam in his eyes.

⌖⟶⬦

"It's like they vanished, ma'am." Lieutenant Barns sounded confused.

Tansy stroked her throat and hummed, then a gleam entered her eyes. "Helm, flip us one-eighty degrees."

"Aye, ma'am."

"He wouldn't, would he?" said Mildred.

"Balls of steel. It's the most likely explanation."

Ryan adjusted the grav-laser and came up alongside the *Saber* at a distance of a hundred kilometres.

"She's turning end for end."

"No surprise there. How long until we reach coelenteratezoid space?"

"Current speed, five minutes."

Lieutenant Barns scanned the space behind the *Saber*. "They were there. I can tell by the dispersal patterns of the gas. The trail goes into the blind area."

Tansy rubbed her eyes. "Helm, rotate us slowly and keep it up. Navigator, follow that trail. Gunner, prepare to fire all turrets."

"What's she doing?" Rowan stared at the screen.

"Guessing my hand. If our stealth holds, we'll be fine, but... hm. Rowan, put a debris dispersal up on the screen for if we got blown up."

"That's sick," said Henry.

Rowan ran the numbers and put the results on the main screen.

Ryan smiled and shifted their course, pulling hard to one side. "Update the screen as quick as you can, Rowan."

"Aye."

"Ma'am, I think I have them," said Lieutenant Barns.

"Helm, stop the spin. Gunner, fire!"

The gunner checked his system, then hesitated. "Ma'am, I can't."

Tansy came to her feet. "Why?"

The gunner shrugged. "At their current speed and trajectory, debris from the damage would impact the stargate. According to the Republic regulations regarding gunnery restrictions and the protection of stargates…"

Tansy looked at the gunnery officer, then began to laugh. "He did it. Nova blast, he did it!"

"What do you mean? Shoot him out of the sky!" demanded Mildred.

"And risk a Republic level political incident? Every space officer knows you can't endanger a stargate. Communications, prepare a channel."

EPILOGUE

43

"Count us down?" Ryan's voice was strained as he moved to the communications console.

"Ten seconds," began Rowan.

"Henry, at five drop stealth."

"Five seconds."

"Coelenteratezoid Zod stargate control, this is the *Star Hawk* on an approach vector. Do you copy?"

"Zero." Rowan smiled. "We're in coelenteratezoid space."

"*Star Hawk*, the blessings of Blue-Green-Green-Purple-Red-White-Yellow-Yellow be on you. Be advised that your approach is good, and we have granted you priority clearance. Freedom be yours, little mountain tree. Blue-Yellow, who is now Blue-Yellow-Red, my breeding-group sibling, has communicated such of your story to me as he knew. Our gate is at your disposal, fair voyage."

"Gotta love family." Henry transmitted the last of the feed to the studio's relay satellite, then updated it in real-time.

A light blinked on the communications console. Ryan pressed a button. Tansy's image filled the screen. "Congratulations, Ryan, on a game well played. I hope it was worth the price. You are now an outlaw throughout the United Earth Systems."

Ryan looked at Rowan and smiled. "It was. And Captain, it was never a game to me."

Tansy smiled. "I know, that's probably why you won. Live

well, Captain Ryan Chandler of the *Star Hawk*, you've earned it." The signal ended.

"Now what?" asked Rowan.

"Now we have coffee and orange oil to sell, a ship to fix, and a cargo of trees to deliver," said Ryan.

The *Star Hawk* decelerated at its top rate.

Rowan watched the gate grow nearer until it filled the screen, then the universe blinked.

"And now you're in another solar system," announced Ryan.

Mike watched the vid images of the *Star Hawk* passing through the stargate. A smile split his face as he leaned back on his couch and sighed.

"Watching that again?" Marcy padded into the room. Her smile lit her face, and her red hair gleamed in the dim light.

"What can I say? It's very dramatic."

Marcy settled on the couch beside him and nestled into the crook of his arm. "You're an old softy." She kissed him.

"I'm glad they made it this far. My contact on the station will relay anything more that Henry can get hold of."

"I'm glad they made it too. They kinda remind me of somebody."

Mike grinned. "And who could that be, my musical maiden?"

Marcy laughed, then kissed her husband.

Pause.

Acknowledgements

First, my thanks to Catherine Fitzsimmons, publisher, editor, friend, who is nearly as invested in my Brain Lag books as I am.

I'd also like to thank an old teacher, Mrs. Grahame, Grandma Grahame, as we called her in grade eight. You made a difference. I was in your class at a point where I had almost given up. Fighting my dyslexia in a system and with parents who saw a label, not a person, had worn me down. The fact that you saw a person made a difference to me. You've probably gone to the summer land, or whatever your particular branch of faith calls it, by now. Still, I hope you sense somehow that I honour you. I speak your name for when a person's name is spoken they live. The world was better for you passing through it.

And a special thank you to anyone who has helped with this work, including those who made documentaries and other reference materials that I accessed to lend the piece realism. Your names are too numerous to remember let alone mention, but you're all in here someplace.

Afterword

I want to thank you for reading Cloning Freedom and mention that the adventures of Ryan and Rowan continue in *Freedom's Law*. I also want to make a request: please review this book; it doesn't have to be much. A simple, 'I liked it,' will suffice. Reviews are the lifeblood of authors in the modern industry and can make a real positive difference in a person's life. Namely mine. :-) So remember. The power's in you, please review.

About the Author

Stephen B. Pearl is a multiple published author whose works range across the speculative fiction field. Whether his characters are wandering the wilds of a post-oil future, braving a storm in a longship, or flying through the interplanetary void in an army surplus assault lander, his writings focus heavily on the logical consequences of the worlds he crafts.

Stephen's inspirations encompass H.G. Wells, J.R.R. Tolkien, Frank Herbert and Homer among others. In writing the Tinker's World series, he has, among other factors, drawn on his training as an Emergency Medical Care Assistant, a SCUBA diver, his long-standing interest in environmental technologies and his firsthand knowledge of the Guelph area.

His fascination with metaphysics has contributed to his para-normal works.

For more about Stephen and his works visit:
www.stephenpearl.com

CPSIA information can be obtained
at www.ICGtesting.com
Printed in the USA
LVHW041218210723
753042LV00014B/28